A MEMORY OF HELL

Suddenly, unwillingly, Sean was there again, stumbling out of Merrywood Hall into the colorless dark of the new moon, punching through the crumbling surface of the melting snow, his shoes filling with beads of ice as he ran through the deep wet snow to the body. *Her body!*

He dropped to his knees, his head and shoulders slumping down. Shallow breaths collected around his head in the heavy night air as the cardboard-thick wool of his pants began sucking cold muddy water up out of the ground. Her arms, twisted and broken, were folded over her chest, which was ripped open like a freshly dug grave, and just as empty. Her long cinnamon-brown hair was splayed out from her skull as if pulled by vermin, tugging and chewing on the knotted ends. The earth had begun to reclaim her.

Sean reached down, his hands, his whole body shaking, and lifted the mask of ice off of her battered face. It crumbled through his fingers. Dust. He brushed away the white powder left behind. Snow had melted in the sunken sockets and frozen into frameless lenses. He pried them out to find her eyes, once as bright and warm as a summer sunrise, now dark and dead, and blindly staring past him into the black heaven. He bent down as if to kiss her cracked and swollen lips....

THE TAKING

DONALD BEMAN

LEISURE BOOKS **NEW YORK CITY**

*For Lynn Susan, my beautiful and brilliant wife,
whose love and support kept me afloat during my
stormy voyage to freedom, even when she feared I
was sailing away from her.*

A LEISURE BOOK®

March 1997

Published by

Dorchester Publishing Co., Inc.
276 Fifth Avenue
New York, NY 10001

Printed in the United States of America.

Acknowledgments

For their invaluable assistance and encouragement, I would like to thank: Greig Farms, Red Hook, NY, and particularly Norman and Michele Robinson Greig; the friendly and helpful librarians at Bard College, Anonville-On-Hudson, NY; Fort Orange Travel, Albany, NY, and my dear friends Gerry and Mary Ann Marmillo, for their loving generosity; Eleanor Grace Miller, a truly gifted painter, and my first editor; my brother Richard for his endless help; Brett Munson; Dave Conner; Charles Garton, Professor Emeritus, Classics, University of Buffalo; Dr. Justin Uku, Chief Medical Examiner, Erie County, and especially Lynn Biondo Miller for her guidance; and finally, my wonderful children, Christopher and Tracy, whose lives changed greatly when I chose another path in life—one with far less gold but greater riches—yet whose faith and love and support never once wavered.

THE TAKING

Saturday, December 1, 1990

In the dark just before dawn the huge second-floor kitchen of the aging country Victorian was painted over in thinning shades of gray and black and leftover midnight blue. Sean MacDonald sat alone, staring out the window, watching the thin pink line of the horizon slowly etching itself into the frozen night sky. The ship's clock mounted on the wall behind him clicked, breaking the cathedral quiet of the enormous room. Shutting his deep-set hazel eyes, he began nodding his head methodically in perfect time with each metered chime, rhythmically counting the crystal-clear strikes of the tiny brass bell.

Sean leaned forward and cracked the window open, testing the December air with his hand; it was bitterly cold and bone dry, but breathless. He threw the sash up and sat back, burying his bearded face in the ghostly swirls of steam rising up from his coffee, sipping slowly, waiting for the sun to show its round orange face. A pair of crows hiding somewhere in the barren cornfields surrounding the house began arguing. A third one joined in as if taking sides. Then another. And three or four more, until nothing but the raucous and rowdy caw and cackle of crows could be heard echoing across the fields.

Sean smiled, wrinkling his face awake, and spun out of the rigid hardwood chair, taking aim at the pot of coffee sitting on top of the oversized cast-iron stove. With its short fat legs, double-width lower oven bulging out, matching pair of upper ovens squeezed together, and vanilla cream porcelain skin, the century-old stove created the shadowy image of a sumo wrestler, squatting on his hulking haunches, about to charge across the room. But the curious illusion fit in with everything else left behind from yesterday in the old kitchen. The linoleum floor with its deep, embossed seams of make-believe mortar that crackled to life when it was walked on. The old oak cabinets, painted over with layer after layer of white enamel skin, hiding the elegant wood grain. The tarnished brass lamp suspended from the ceiling, a miniature glass lantern dangling from the end of a frayed cotton pull string. Or the tin ceiling, once ivory white, but now stained with age and cooking grease to a soft honey gold.

A sharp metallic click broke the silence again. There was a pause, a seemingly endless wait for one small invisible gear inside the brass belly of the clock to turn a fraction of an inch in time, before the hammer struck six times, slowly. "Six bells. Seven o'clock!" Sean announced to no one but himself. He then tipped his head back and ceremoniously drained the heavy ceramic mug of its last few drops of lukewarm coffee.

The narrow band of color rising above the sepia-brown hills had grown brighter, burning away what was left of the night, melting the full moon. Without looking, Sean reached back and blindly patted the table with his hand, searching for the book he'd tossed there when it was still too dark to read. He never turned on the lights in the kitchen at this time of day, his time of day, that precious, quiet time of day few claim as theirs and most never want to see, except in the passing lines of a poem, or painted on a canvas.

With a gentle sweep of his hand, Sean scooped the book around, held it up to the newborn light, and started flipping through the wafer-thin newsprint pages, looking for *December, The Twelfth Month.*

He pressed the pocketbook-sized almanac flat on the wide wooden windowsill in front of him, cracking the binding with the heel of his broad hand, and began reading the small italicized print at the top of the left-hand page, ignoring the biting cold shriveling up the skin on his hands.

The Taking

Two full Moons this month, giving us a rare, and some say, unlucky 13th Moon. The first (on December 2nd) causes very high tides . . .

He laughed. It was a conceited laugh, a laugh that said that he knew something no one else did. Then, with a hurried, almost frightened slap of his hand, Sean turned the page over to *January*.

"January fifth," he muttered. "Twelfth Night. Then the Feast of the Epiphany." A note of contempt rang in his voice. With soft woodpecker taps of his finger, he checked off the next two days, reading the cryptic entries.

13 1st Sunday after Epiphany
14 Propitious day for birth of women.

The notation for the fourteenth of the month elicited another uncomfortable laugh from him. The entry for January 15, the date of the new moon, snagged him with the jagged edges of memories that still refused to be sanded smooth by time.

Just then the air outside stirred. The harsh wind rattled the leafless branches of the frozen trees, startling the thieving band of crows. They exploded into the air, flapping and cawing and scattering every which way. Before he could reach up and shut the window, the frigid air slithered into the kitchen, wrapping itself around him and chilling him into an unwanted all-over shiver. Suddenly, unwillingly, Sean was there again. . . .

. . . stumbling out of Merrywood Hall into the colorless dark of the new moon, punching through the crumbling surface of the melting snow, his shoes filling up with prickly beads of ice as he ran through the deep wet snow to the body. *Her body!*

He dropped to his knees, his head and shoulders slumping down. Shallow breaths began collecting around his head in the heavy night air, a halo of white, as the cardboard-thick wool of his pants began sucking cold muddy water up out of the ground. Her arms, twisted and broken, were folded over her chest, which was ripped open like a freshly dug grave, and just as empty. Her

11

long cinnamon-brown hair was splayed out from her skull as if pulled by vermin, tugging and chewing on the knotted ends. The earth had begun to reclaim her.

Sean reached down—his hands, his whole body shaking—and lifted the mask of ice off of her battered face. It crumbled through his fingers. Dust. He brushed away the powdery white left behind. Snow had melted in the sunken sockets and frozen into frameless lenses. He pried them out to find her eyes, once as bright and warm as a summer sunrise, now dark and dead, and blindly staring past him into the black of heaven. He bent down to kiss her cracked and swollen lips, but suddenly, violently started jamming his hands into her icy grave, again and again and again, until his fingers were red and raw and bleeding.

Hands were reaching out behind him, touching him, tugging gently, trying to lift him away. His jacket caught on her splintered fingernails, pulling him back down. He turned his head and shut his eyes, as if trying to hear something she was saying. But the beating of his own heart was the only sound that broke the silence of winter's clear night. Gently, he brushed his hand over hers, freeing himself. A crumpled-up wad of paper tumbled out of her clenched fist onto the blood-stained snow. He picked it up and held it to his chest, crushing it to nothing as he stood up and walked away, deaf to the voices calling out to him. . . .

Sean slammed the almanac down onto the windowsill. The defiant wind opened it back up and started turning the pages, one at a time, as if looking for something, then faster and faster, fanning them into a leafy blur. Something blew out. With a quick snap of his hand, Sean snatched it out of mid-air. It was thin and brittle and translucent, with rough, fibrous edges. There was writing on one side. The graceful letters, curling up thick and thin, were scrolled out in faded indigo ink.

> Here Faith died, poisoned by this charnel air.
> I ceased to follow, for the knot of doubt
> Was severed sharply with a cruel knife:
> He circled thus, for ever tracing out

The Taking

The series of the fraction left of Life;
Perpetual recurrence in the scope
Of but three terms . . . dead Faith, dead Love, dead Hope.

Life divided by that persistent three,
LXX divided by 333 =
.210210210210210210 . . . three, ad infinitum.

"You goddamn bitches!" His agonized cry ricocheting off the walls, rattling the brittle sheets of crystal in the tall Victorian windows. "It's me you want, you fucking whores! Why did you take her and not me? And my son! He was so young, so innocent. Why! Answer me, Goddamn you!"

1

On the rolling estate-turned-campus of Hart College in upstate New York stands Merrywood Library, facing west across the Hudson, the epitome of an English country manor house in the New World a century ago. Its mountainous roof of peaks and valleys and vaulted gables is encased in copper, eave to eave and soffit to soffit, no doubt looking as bright and shiny as a new penny when it was first coined. But it's green and crusty now. And the rugged limestone face is stained with a poisonous gangrene dripping from the mortared seams and weathered sores of its quarried skin.

Behind the library, perched high above the river's rocky shores, is an aging Victorian garden. The withered fingers of the scrawny green ivy, clinging desperately to the six-foot-high, powder-red brick walls, have succeeded in scratching the mortar loose that holds the old Kingston brick together, leaving seams a thumb deep. The hand-hewn cedar beams resting peacefully atop rows of wannabe Greek columns for the last hundred years are now split and cracked and bent with age. The sturdy soldier bricks proudly guarding shifting borders of grass and pebbled stone for decades have finally lost their battle with the legions of clumsy gardeners. The only remnant from yesterday seemingly untouched by the hands of time is the smooth weathered body of a naked woman, standing silent and alone in her sun-parched basin of granite, tears from a century of neglect staining her white marble cheeks.

Directly across the grassy common from Merrywood Library
stands its stately Georgian cousin, Merrywood Hall, a mirror image in stone and stain. But unlike the library, a pair of larger-
than-life-sized lions guard the entrance to Merrywood Hall.
They're bronze, not stone, with signatures that were scratched into
their thick metal skins just before they were basted with a black-
green goo and fired to a rich, dark brown patina. But time,
weather, and ten thousand hands rubbing their hard alloyed bodies
have burnished them to a soft polished gold.

The faculty offices in Merrywood Hall are all the same size,
small. A few on the ground floor, like Dr. Sean MacDonald's,
are double offices, complete with kindergarten-sized bathrooms
hidden behind narrow, out-of-square doors fitted with painted-
over brass locks that never work when they should. Sean's office
also has a pair of towering leaded-glass windows that drop from
the ceiling to hip height, or what Sean calls "sitting height" because of the deep stone windowsills. Whenever the late afternoon
sun slips through the stained-glass panels, scattering into a kalei-
doscope of colors, invisible specks of silver and black imbedded
in the rough-cut stone walls sparkle to life like diamonds and
coal.

Embracing each of the elegant windows are heavy, smoke-blue
drapes, hanging from solid brass rods and falling in perfectly
pleated folds to within a breath of the oak-stained hardwood floor.
In one corner of the office, pushed safely away from the sunlight,
is a tattered silk tapestry mounted to a rickety old easel. The
tapestry is French, late eighteenth century, obligating Sean to describe the colors in terms such as burgundy and claret, not simply
dark red or light red.

Warming the medieval dark of the room are copper-green mal-
achite bases set beneath each of Sean's French animalier bronzes.
The largest depicts a lion locked in a deadly embrace with a
monstrous snake curling about its head and body. Another's a
hawk, its wings spread wide, its eyes on fire, its hooked beak
open and ready to rip the flesh off the bones of the struggling
hare locked in the deadly grasp of its powerful talons. And there's
a majestic wild stallion, rearing up, valiantly fighting off a pack

of hungry wolves. Then there's Sean's favorite, barely twelve inches high. It's a pair of monkeys, standing erect, bespeckled, with quills and papers and books in hand—gesturing pompously—aping man.

"It's not locked," Sean called out in response to the soft but determined knock on his office door. "Just let yourself in." Sean didn't look up; he was too busy trying to keep the unruly pile of papers on his lap from spilling back onto the floor.

Sean MacDonald's once-sharp angular features had been sanded smooth and ruggedly handsome by time. The meticulous beard he'd taken twenty years to get just right was now brushed with gray. His body refused to give testimony, in appearance or performance, to his forty-seven years. However, his face had begun to speak up. It wasn't anything like the loud cracks that can be heard on the windblown faces of Kansas farmers, just thin, delicate creases, whispering quietly around his eyes and back across his temples, before disappearing into the quiet graying of his sandy brown hair, which time was yet to touch.

The heavy oak-and-brass-hinged door moved open a foot, seemingly by itself. A deep baritone voice sang out, "Good morning!" as a bushy red beard pushed through the narrow opening, followed by the rest of Oliver Shore, barrel chest and all. Holding the knob tightly in his hand, Oliver closed the door, taking care not to let the latch click. He then leaned up against the door and folded his hands behind his back, as if standing guard, all without making a sound.

Oliver Shore was Professor of Ancient and Modern Religion. He was short and stout, an overgrown bear cub, with a beard that appeared to be held in place by the gold wire-rimmed glasses hooked over his ears, ears so large that not even his long and curly Irish-red hair could hide them. His eyes twinkled with curiosity. His hands were large enough for a man easily a foot taller than he, and they appeared to have been hammered into shape by hard labor, not scholarship, yet his touch was as gentle as a child's. With his blue oxford blazer, brown high-topped shoes, and plaid wool tie cinching the collar of his wrinkled white shirt to his tree-trunk thick neck with a full Windsor knot, Oliver Shore looked like he'd just walked off the stage of a Victorian play. Adding to this endearing Shavian illusion was a pair of red suspenders, loudly bracketing his portly midsection.

Oliver stood perfectly still, watching Sean fight with the uncooperative papers, turning down the crumpled-up corners, tamping the wrinkled edges, then patting everything flat, all in a losing effort to put them into a neat, orderly pile. After a minute of this, Oliver cocked his head, squinted one eye half-closed, and asked cautiously, "Busy?" This was his way of clearing the decks so that he could have someone's undivided attention. But it could also be a warning that he was about to say something he knew you didn't want to hear. Sean was the only one who didn't stand-to when Oliver did this, which always earned him one of Oliver's rare approving smiles, as it did now.

Sean ended his hopeless struggle with a furious shuffling of his hands, sending the papers fluttering onto the floor all around his chair. Then, acting as if nothing had happened, he motioned for Oliver to have a seat. Oliver pushed himself off the door and walked over to the large Victorian leather sofa in the center of the office. He glanced to his right, his left, took a quick quarter-step to his right as if centering himself, then tipped up onto his toes and settled down onto the middle cushion, which promptly gave up an unwilling sigh of air. He then locked one foot behind the other and began sweeping his feet back and forth above the oriental carpet, the heels and toes of his heavy oxfords brushing the tattered cotton fringe into untied knots. "Still grading third-year essays?" he asked, staring at the mess on the floor. Oliver was the only faculty member who called the senior theses third-year essays. But it was an improvement over his referring to them as amusing little anecdotes, which is what he called his students' hasty and poorly written efforts in his first year at Hart College after arriving from Oxford.

"Yes, I am." Sean glanced up to find Oliver staring down at the papers on the floor, his eyes crossing playfully. Sean clapped his hands. "Ollie?"

Oliver broke free of the papers with a blink of his eyes. "Awfully late, isn't it?" he asked. It sounded like he was asking

Sean for an explanation, as if he were the headmaster and Sean a student in jeopardy of being sent down.

Sean nodded, knowing that he had little choice but to wait for Oliver to work through this ritual of his before he got to the real reason he was there, and why it was so important for him to have dragged himself out of bed and onto campus long before noon, something that was simply unheard of for Oliver Shore. The afternoons were his mornings. At the end of the day he ate his lunch. And after everyone else had gone home, save for Bruce Fanning, and sometimes Dean Potter, his day began. It ended at sunrise. Or when the janitor arrived to open Merrywood Hall. Or when Sean showed up. Whichever occurred first.

"About done?" Oliver's question had the feel of a friendly pat on the behind trying to nudge Sean along.

Sean's affection for Oliver and his curious gnomelike ways tickled his face into a relaxed smile. "Almost. And after I'm done here, which I hope will be sometime around noon with a little bit of luck,"—Sean tossed a made-up frown in Oliver's direction—"and no interruptions! I'm going straight home and open my last bottle of Chassagne Montrachet, which I let stand overnight so the crust would settle. Care to join me?"

Oliver gave up his tenuous toehold on the carpet's fringe and began clicking his leather heels together as he curled his hands into an oversized ball of knuckles and flesh, one far too big to hide even in his generous lap. "If you have another appointment, I'll come back later." Oliver tried sitting up straight on the sinking leather cushion, but started listing to one side, looking like he might keel over.

Sean's amused smile broadened. "Other than commencement this Sunday, which I dread knowing Sarah Potter and her penchant for sappy soliloquy, I don't have one single appointment for the rest of my life." Sean wanted to add, *Come on, spit it out my friend. Why are you here?* But instead, he just folded his hands in his lap, mimicking Oliver, and waited.

Oliver raised his hand. "And one other appointment." His deep voice turned his words into a reprimand. "The meeting Dean Potter wants you to have with your successor, who, I understand, was confirmed by the trustees last evening in executive session. Hasn't Potter told you?" Oliver began casting his eyes around the office as if trying to avoid Sean. He settled on the tapestry in the corner. His nervous schoolboy fidgeting was replaced with an absentminded tapping of his finger on his chunky thigh. "It's exquisite."—he was obviously trying to change the subject— "I've always liked it." Leaning to one side, he sat up straight again and peered over Sean's shoulder, trying to get a better look.

Sean ignored Oliver's postscript about Dean Potter, since only twenty minutes earlier he had told Sarah Potter in no uncertain terms that he would not meet with Dr. Jennings. "Period! And you know why." Sarah had stormed out of his office, speechless with anger, but not before taking a swipe at him, something she was known to do now and then, but only with Sean for some reason. In her pique, Sarah missed him and knocked the pile of term papers, which were neatly stacked on the corner of his desk, onto the floor.

"Would you like it?" Sean asked.

"You can't be serious!" Oliver began examining the tapestry in a whole new light. "Do you have any idea what it's worth?" His question told Sean that he just might know what it was worth. And he probably did, knowing Oliver.

"Nope!" Sean said with a popping of his lips. "And I don't want to know either. It was given to me out of friendship by my philosophy instructor at Buffalo, Father Bollman, a house of a man! Bob showed up at my apartment the night before he was scheduled to board a train to join some off-the-wall ecumenical enclave in a monastery somewhere out in Missouri, never to be heard from again." Sean zeroed in on the center of Oliver's prodigious chest with a rigid point of his finger. "I'm giving it to you in the same spirit of friendship. Partly because I know you really don't give a damn what something like this costs, and partly because I have no place for it in my apartment and don't want to stick it up in the attic. Besides, you love things like this simply for their beauty and history." Spinning around in his chair, Sean joined Oliver in admiring the tapestry. "Take it the second I'm out of here. But you better make sure you get it before Bruce lays

20

claim to this office, or you'll never get near it." Sean tried laughing diabolically, but it came out as a nervous wheeze, followed by a cough. It was the kind of cough dissipated characters in somber nineteenth-century novels have and ominously referred to as consumption.

Oliver was shaking his head, still unable to believe what Sean was doing. "May I at least pay you something for it?"

Sean replied through a sinister smile as he turned back to face Oliver, "Yes."

Oliver perked up and pushed his ear in Sean's direction, but kept his eyes on the tapestry, tracing with subtle movements of his head the faded outlines of the mythical images woven into the old silk. A rearing white horse and caped rider, a dense forest, and the black clouds stitched into a faded cobalt-blue sky beneath a cold, yellow sun, all carefully laid down on a wine-stained bed of wool, and framed with imaginary leaves of green and tied neatly together with a brown curlicue vine.

"Your payment will be that you must agree to pass it along in the same way in which you got it." Oliver turned to face Sean, this time with his whole body, including his large round eyes. Sean and Oliver's mirrored look at each other, followed by a serious nodding of their heads, was that of two ten-year-old boys making a silent pact, one that would damn them both forever if it was broken.

Sean sat back, looking pleased with himself, until Oliver got stiff all over. "About your research, Sean," Oliver asked solicitously, "I would like—" Oliver stopped in mid-sentence and swallowed hard, looking suddenly unsure of himself.

Perplexed, and suspicious at hearing mention made of his research, Sean waited behind a tolerant smile for Oliver to finish what he'd started to say.

Oliver squared his lapels. "I know you filed it all away and told me that you didn't *ever* want to have anything to do with it anymore. And I know you said you didn't believe in any of it anymore,"—he took a tiny sip of air—"but I would like to continue with it, that's if you don't mind, of course, and merge it with my own work." Oliver pitched back against the deflated leather cushions, as if to brace himself for Sean's reply.

"Why?" Sean asked, a half-pained, half-confused expression etching itself onto his face. It was the kind of look you get from students in the front row of a lecture when you call on them and they suddenly wish they'd hidden themselves in the back of the room. "Why," he said again. However, this time there wasn't the slightest hint of a question hooked onto the end of his sentence; he was demanding to know why.

Oliver's adolescent fidgeting returned. "I think your extensive effort can help me with my work, that's all."

Sean suddenly became serious. "You want twenty years of my life and all you can say is 'That's all'! You're going to have to do a little better than that, my friend." Sean tilted his head to one side and sat waiting for an explanation.

Oliver became equally serious. "When I was at Oxford, I met a young Anglican priest assigned to the Archbishops's staff at Canterbury. We kept bumping into each other in the rare books room and soon became good friends." Oliver was growing more uncomfortable with each word, which, for some reason, he appeared reluctant to turn over. "He told me in confidence that he was working on a project involving a ritual that he loosely referred to as 'The Taking.' When he told me that he was having difficulty finding anything about this ancient religious ritual, other than what he already had, I offered to help. After all, that's my field. I immediately got hooked when he showed me photocopies of untranslated text from some sort of scroll, which was in Sanskrit. He wouldn't say where he'd gotten the material from, or what the scroll was, and I never pushed him on it. Perhaps I should have in light of what happened later."

Oliver sighed, his shoulders slumped. "I found indirect references to the ritual in most of the ancient cultures surrounding the Mediterranean. But nothing concrete, just oblique entries alluding to the devil, or a devil, and orgiastic, almost violent, but deviant sex. This all changed when I found a few pages from a diary, which were written much like an illuminated manuscript. It was in Latin, although a strange, almost encrypted form of it, integrating ancient Greek and various dialects of early Hebrew. The text was intertwined with numbers, many of which were used as letters to make words and build cryptic sentences.'' Oliver lowered his head and stopped talking and moving, as if his batteries had run down. He sat motionless. Not even his feet or hands were fidgeting.

Sean's first thought was heart attack. He started to get up, but saw Oliver's eyes blink. He leaned back, waiting for him to continue. ''Ollie?'' Oliver took another breath, but one much deeper than before. ''You OK?'' Sean asked.

Oliver nodded and went on. ''When I finally succeeded in translating the half-dozen pages, I learned that they were from the personal diary of another Anglican priest who, coincidentally, was, like my friend, assigned to Canterbury. When my friend checked the church records, he learned that the priest's name was Reeves Knight, and that he was the recording secretary to the Archbishop of Canterbury for most of the last quarter of the nineteenth century, until he was found dead on his sixty-sixth birthday, brutally murdered.''

Oliver looked up and took on Sean's expectant gaze. ''He was killed the same way your wife was. And mine.'' Oliver's eyes glazed over. ''And very much the same way my priest friend was found, not a week after we'd pieced things together. I didn't know it at the time, but he had reported back to his superiors, telling them everything, which is something we had agreed shouldn't be done until we'd found the rest of Father Knight's diary, or diaries, since I found a reference to a second journal which, according to my reading of the entry, was a complete summary of the names, birth and death dates, and all intervening milestone events and dates for every priest ordained by the Church of England during the nineteenth century. To this day, I don't know why Father Knight had done this, but I can only guess.'' Oliver looked deep into Sean's eyes. ''As I'm sure you can.''

Sean rejected Oliver's penetrating stare with a cavalier sweep of his arm and said loudly, ''Take the files, have a ball with them. I hope they give you what you want.'' Surprised but pleased with Sean's sudden change of heart, Oliver started beaming. But it went unseen by Sean. ''That oak cabinet behind you, the one against the wall between the windows, contains all of my notes. There are also a dozen or so old books in Latin and ancient Greek, with notations tagged to certain entries, which I collected on my journey to nowhere. The only things not there are my journals, which are in the attic at home.'' Sean hesitated. Oliver leaned forward with a worried look on his face, as if he thought Sean was about to change his mind. ''I'll dig them out and bring them in sometime next week. I'll leave them on top of the cabinet, since it's already full.'' Sean turned around, opened his top desk drawer, and fished out a small key not much larger than a guitar pic. He tossed it into the air underhanded like a pop-up fly. ''You can even take the cabinet, since I no longer have a need for it.''

Oliver fielded the shiny chrome key with a clap of his hands, then hopped off the sofa. It was more of a kick and a slide than a hop. He landed with a heavy-footed thump. ''This means a great deal to me, my friend. I don't know how to . . .'' He paused. Sean eased back in his chair, waiting to hear what Ollie was going to say. But instead, Oliver just nodded once, smartly, and turned to leave.

But before he could make it to the door, Sean hooked him back. ''You're not telling me everything, are you?''

Oliver stopped and looked down, staring into his hands as if his answer was cribbed on his palms. He spoke deliberately, without looking back at Sean. ''No,'' he said firmly, ''I'm not.''

''Well?''

Oliver took an unnecessary breath and turned around. ''Sean, I want to know who, or what, killed our wives as much as you do.'' The tune of self-confidence that rang through his words only minutes ago suddenly went sour. He said softly, ''And in your case, what caused the death of your son.''

Sean knew Oliver too well to accept what he'd just said at face value. However, he let it go at that. After all, Oliver's wife of only a year had been murdered in almost the same brutal way that his own wife had been killed. Moire Shore was found in a small country churchyard outside London, impaled on a massive wrought-iron gate, her arms spread wide, her palms pierced by the rusting spikes of the gate. Crucified. Her heart had been ripped from her chest just as Janet MacDonald's had. But unlike Sean, who found his wife's body pushing up through the melting snow of a January thaw not fifty yards from his office window in Merrywood Hall, Oliver wasn't the one who found Moire.

Oliver reached for the door. Sean raised his voice. "What about *why*?" he asked. Oliver turned the knob. "Oliver! Answer me, damn it!" Sean's angry outburst startled Oliver into letting go of the doorknob as if it was hot-wired.

"Yes and no," Oliver shot back with conviction on both sides of his terse reply, and with an equal measure of anger.

Sean got up and started pacing about. He stopped just as suddenly and shook his head impatiently. "And the number six?"

"I thought you didn't believe any of this anymore," Oliver said as he turned to face Sean. "So why the sudden interest?"

Sean bristled. "Just answer my question, damn it."

Raising his hands, Oliver patted the air in a calming gesture. "Have a seat." Oliver returned to the sofa, scrunching himself into one corner. He looked silly when the cushions made a funny squealing noise. "Now." He peered over the top of his glasses. "Before we get into this, refresh my memory about a few things." He pointed at Sean menacingly. "And without your flowery, anecdotal literary comments, OK?"

Sean flopped down into his chair and draped one leg over the arm. "I'll try."

Oliver folded his burly arms over his chest. "If I remember correctly, you said that the autopsy report placed your wife's death on January 8, 1974. Correct?"

Sean sighed again, only this time it was more a sigh of disappointment than impatience. "Correct."

Oliver was unfazed by Sean's petulance. "Wasn't it also the same date as the full moon for that month?" Sean shut and opened his eyes in time with a lazy nod of his head. He made it look like he was bothered by Oliver's question. "Do you see any significance in that?" Oliver asked, still unaffected by Sean's attitude.

"It was the full *Wolf* moon to be exact. And yes, I thought it was significant, even if no one else did. Like that idiot Assistant

District Attorney, Arnold Kratz. I realized too late that I never should have told that repugnant little man what I thought, since he tried his damnedest to make a fool of me. And that son-of-a-bitch did everything he possibly could to convince the grand jury I'd murdered my own wife. Asshole!'' Oliver sat listening patiently. Sean appeared to calm down. ''But I can't say with certainty exactly what the coincidence of the full moon could have meant, simply because there are too many possible explanations, as you well know yourself.'' Sean leaned back in his chair. ''Next question?'' he asked, and shut his eyes.

Oliver slid his glasses back up to the bridge of his nose. ''Tell me about your new moon and full moon theory, the one which has something to do with—''

''Why?'' Sean asked sarcastically. ''So you can ridicule me again?'' Seeing that Oliver was startled and perhaps hurt by his biting response, Sean dealt out a smile of reconciliation as he lifted his other leg over the arm of the chair and folded his hands behind his head. ''In a nutshell, part of my theory was predicated upon the ancient belief that evil was conceived under the dark of a new moon.''

''Are you speaking figuratively or literally?''

''Both,'' Sean replied almost indifferently. ''The literal aspect is the dark of night, and man's ages-old fear of it.'' Sean waited to see what Oliver's reaction was going to be to what he'd just said. But Oliver just sat there, waiting for him to continue. ''But the figurative—some say real aspect—rests with the symbolic presence of the devil and the rape of a mortal under the dark of the new moon, which results in the perpetuation of evil by the offspring of this unholy union.''

There was a glimmer of doubt in Oliver's eyes as he asked, ''Like the story in Genesis about Enoch, the father of Methuselah? Or the one in the Book of Enoch, which tells of fallen angels lying with mortal females and fathering malformed giants who roamed the earth, signaling the increase in wickedness and the coming of Satan's reign?''

Sean smiled ever so subtly. ''That's *two* versions. However, there are many others, and in many other cultures. And all tell of

26

similar events evolving from the belief in angels, the bright, shining stars of heaven, secretly fathering children of darkness with mortal women, then falling from grace when exposed for their lust and their infidelity to God—or whichever god was in favor at that point.''

Frowning, Oliver looked serious enough for the both of them. ''But why under the dark of a new moon, discounting man's childish fear of the dark?''

Sean's reply was as clinical as he could possibly make it, and delivered in a controlled and soft-spoken monotone. ''Under a new moon the night sky is lighted only by the stars, and the brightest star in the heavens is Venus, which is both the morning and the evening star. As you know it was given two names by the ancient Greeks, Phosphorus and Hesperus, for morning and evening respectively. The morning star is referred to in Isaiah, Luke, Corinthians, and Revelations as Lucifer, which comes from the Latin for light bearer. Venus is also the third-brightest object in the heavens, next to the sun and the moon, thereby creating the first heavenly trinity for primitive and ancient man. The sun ruled the light of day, and the moon held sway over the night, while Venus ruled the morning and the evening, and those nights when the moon was swallowed up by the universe. Venus was the gatekeeper to heaven and earth, so to speak. And to many Venus was, and still is, symbolic of the Holy Spirit.'' Sean was now smiling. ''Given these facts, Satan, the brightest and most promising of God's angels, takes a mortal. Rapes her. Unless of course she consents, which I find unlikely, and which is not supported in any Christian or pre-Christian writings. Then, six months later, one-hundred-ninety-two days, and beneath the light of the last full moon of the year, the illegitimate offspring is born. But only in those years with a thirteenth moon. I found it curious that nowhere in the original scriptures were these offspring, regardless of what they're called, specifically referred to as men, or male. Their gender appears to be at the translator's discretion, no doubt a function of syntax and the translator's own particular religious or social perspective.

''If the child is conceived a male, for some reason it usually dies in the womb, turning to stone and producing what for centuries has been known as a calcified fetus. If a male somehow survives to full term, in this case six months, it's born a mooncalf, a hideously deformed creature forever dependent upon its host. However, what seems unclear is the birthing of the stronger fetuses, the females. From what little evidence there is, which was pieced together from shattered figurines found in various archeological ruins, it appears that they may not be delivered vaginally, but abdominally. This belief is based upon the striated markings found on the shards of the pieced-together figurines, which appear to represent scars. In light of the fact that a caesarian birth is a relatively modern practice, one must conclude that they deliver themselves, leaving their host horribly scarred, or dead. Their will to live must be fierce.''

An incredulous look settled over Oliver's face. After what seemed like minutes, his expression slowly dissolved into an inquisitive frown. "Illegitimate?" he asked. "As in bastard?"

Sean answered quickly and without reservation. "Yes. If history can have its bastard kings and bastard sons, why not bastard queens and bastard daughters? God knows there have been enough of them throughout recorded history."

Sean saw Oliver wince at hearing this, but maybe it was just his imagination. He could then see Oliver's next question forming on his lips. "And why is there a gestation period of one-hundred-ninety-two days?" Oliver erased his question with a hasty wave of his hand. "Of course," he mumbled to himself, "the sum of the digits of one-hundred-ninety-two equals twelve, which is a pair of sixes, or six twos, thereby creating a powerful dualistic force." He peeked at Sean over his glasses, this time looking like a student waiting for his grade. "Am I right?"

"Yes, but that's only part of it." Sean was exhibiting an increased confidence in Oliver's seriousness, but he was still wary, and rightly so, based upon Oliver's persistent criticism of Sean's work. "The gestation period for the devil's offspring can also be found in the numerology of the events in Genesis, arising from the conception, then the birth of the world, all of which took place governed by the numbers two and six. This also included the creation of Adam and Eve, an event that, from the very beginning of biblical time, produced a monumental conflict that survives to this day. And not because of the theological questions raised by their actions in the Garden of Eden, or even the means through which Eve, woman, was created. It was a joining doomed from the very start since the name Adam equaled one and the name Eve equaled five, numerologically speaking, resulting in the number six when they were joined.''

"But why a thirteenth moon?"

Sean kicked his chair around, grabbed three large books off the shelf above his desk, and turned back. "Here," he said, holding the books out for Oliver to take. "I think you'll find many of the dates that I've circled in these to be quite fascinating when you compare them with corresponding events in world history, especially evil or violent events, which all reveal the darker side of mankind."

Taking the books, their bindings cracked and split from use, Oliver read off the titles. "*Moon Tables. Phases of the Moon for Times Past, Present, and Future. New and Full Moons. 1001 B.C. to A.D 1651. Astronomical Tables of the Sun, Moon, and Planets.*" He set the books down beside him, stacking them in order of size, then patted the top of his pyramid. "What in the world are you doing with these?"

"Giving them to you. I won't be needing them anymore." Sean flopped back down into his chair like a tired old ragdoll. "As for what I'm driving at now, today? Absolutely nothing. But when I was infected with all of this, when I still believed, as you seem to, I was convinced that evil was incarnate on the earth in the form of woman, not man as we've all been led to believe." Sean couldn't help laughing at himself because of what he'd just admitted. "I saw the number six in virtually every violent act in history, specifically in the image and likeness, literally and figuratively, of woman. In many instances the presence was so subtle one had to look deep into the events of the day to find her symbolic presence, but she was always there. To my surprise, I found the same pattern in nineteenth-century American fiction, which gave me a renewed perspective on everything I was teaching, which I now sorely regret.''

Oliver's expression abruptly turned from doubtful to curious. "Are you trying to tell me that Satan is a woman?"

"Yes," Sean retorted brazenly, responding more to the look on Oliver's face than to what Oliver had asked. "It's documented fact that female sacred images are associated with the oldest archaeological evidence for religious expression, predating the Bible and its male gods by forty thousand years. The artifacts include cave paintings and various forms of sculpture, which are commonly, and erroneously, referred to by scholars as Venuses. These sacred female images appear in literally hundreds of Upper Paleolithic sites throughout Europe and northern Asia. Some have been discovered in Aurignacian deposits as old as forty thousand years; however, they appear more frequently about twenty-five thousand BCE. These very same goddess figurines have also been unearthed from sites as late as the Early Neolithic period, around eight thousand BCE. They're spread throughout Europe, northern Asia, and even into the Ukraine and Siberia. Goddess images and female figurines outnumber male forms ten to one in hard archaeological evidence.''

Oliver had been nodding all along at everything Sean was saying. "You're right," he said in a patronizing tone of voice. "But the interpretation of those artifacts remains controversial. You've got to accept the fact that we cannot be certain how to interpret these figurines. They might be no more than part of an elaborate cult associated with later discoveries of a similar type.''

Sean kicked back in his chair. "Oh, I see. For you and your male god, it's automatically a religion. But for anything else, especially if it's female dominated, it's no more than a cult. The facts clearly show that the worship of goddesses dominated early man's life. It wasn't until the early Semitic peoples that religion evolved into a male-dominated order, with goddesses subservient to men and their newly discovered male gods.'' Sean was now up and pacing about his office, forcing Oliver to twist around in order to follow him. "Men are afraid of women," Sean said out of nowhere. "They're terrified, because they unconsciously sense that women are more powerful than they are, and not just sexually either. Women are the true givers and takers of life here on earth." He snorted. "When you think about it, our role in the evolution of life is insignificant in the whole scheme of creation."

Sean saw Oliver smile and braced himself. Oliver asked drolly, confirming Sean's suspicion, "And how does the Virgin Mary fit into this goddess theory of yours, Dr. MacDonald?"

Sean pressed his hands together in mock prayer. "Ah yes, the ultimate goddess, unpolluted by a male consort. I find it curious how church scholars and theologians refuse to acknowledge Astarte, the ancient prototype of the Virgin Mary. In Syria and Egypt, her sacred dramas celebrated the rebirth of the solar god from the celestial virgin every December 25. Sound familiar?"

Oliver gave in with a broad, toothy grin. "Do you have any idea what you're saying with all of this?"

"Yes, of course I do," Sean replied emphatically. Then he appeared to wilt. There was a bitter grating to his words. "No, quite honestly, I don't know what the hell I'm saying, at least not anymore."

With a determined, almost victorious pat of his hands on his legs—which didn't go unnoticed by Sean—Oliver stood up and dutifully collected the books off the sofa. "It's time for me to leave you to finish what you were doing before I interrupted."

"Wait," Sean said. He walked over to his desk and slid open the bottom drawer, stopping just short of letting it fall out onto the floor. He fingered an envelope out of the last folder, way in the back. "Here,"—he handed it to Oliver ceremoniously—"maybe you can make heads or tails out of this." Sean's voice was now thin and hollow. "I sure as hell couldn't, but then maybe I was too close to what happened." Sean pushed the drawer closed with his foot, and wandered over to the window, looking suddenly very tired.

The envelope was old and gray. The words *For Sean* were penciled where an address would have been. And there was a date written in faded blue ink in the upper-left-hand corner. Oliver opened it, withdrew the paper inside, and read what was on it.

Donald Beman

Take this kiss upon the brow!
And, in parting from you now,
This much let me avow—
You are not wrong, who deem
That my days have been a dream;
Yet if Hope has flown away
In a night, or in a day,
In a vision, or in none,
Is it therefore the less *gone*?
All that we see or seem
Is but a dream within a dream.

I stand amid the roar
Of a surf-tormented shore,
And I hold within my hand,
Grains of the golden sand—
How few! yet how they creep
Through my fingers to the deep,
While I weep—while I weep! . . .

O God! can I not save
One from the pitiless wave?
Is all that we see or seem
But a dream within a dream?

"Sean?" Oliver asked quietly, then reread the poem as he drifted toward the window. He didn't look where he was going, and bumped into the oak file cabinet. "What is this?"

Sean's reply came from a far-off distant place. "A poem, or more accurately part of a poem. The opening stanzas are missing. Why, I don't know."

"I see that," Oliver said curtly, but respectfully.

"Is this sheet of paper from a book?"

"I think so. At least it looks like one to me."

"What's the title? And who wrote it?" Oliver was reading it again.

" 'A Dream Within a Dream,' " Sean replied quietly, almost

32

capriciously, which seemed to pique Oliver's interest. "As for who wrote it, it's by Edgar Allan Poe."

Oliver studied the poem again with a newfound respect. "Where's it from? What does this date on the envelope mean? And why are you giving it to me?" Oliver was now standing in front of the other window, looking outside, as if trying to find what it was that had stolen Sean's attention from him. "Sean?"

"One of the nurses in the hospital gave it to me after my mother died. She told me she found it on the nightstand beside the bed when she went back to clean out the room. She said that she hadn't seen it there when they took my mother into the operating room. But she said she couldn't be certain, since Mother was screaming at everyone to leave her alone and let them die."

"Leave her alone?" Oliver asked. "Let *them* die?"

"I'm only repeating what the nurse told me."

"And did you say 'operating room'?"

"Yes," Sean replied solemnly. "From what I understand, there were complications of some sort, and when my mother's condition changed for the worse, her doctor decided to take her into the operating room."

Oliver turned the envelope over and checked the date again. "How old were you in December of 1950?"

"Seven."

A shadow filled Oliver's scarlet red eyes. "What exactly did your mother die from?"

"I really don't know." Sean added a sloppy shrug of his shoulders. "Childbirth, I suppose. I was never told exactly what it was that she died from. But then, I was just a kid."

"And the child?" When Oliver looked at Sean for an answer, he saw tears bleeding through his eyelids, which were shut so tight that the skin on his temples had wrinkled into wiry folds.

"The doctor told me that she died, too. Or was already dead. I'm not sure which it was." Sean's words floated around the room, refusing to fade away. "That's all I know, Ollie, other than my father was never the same after she died. I often think his stroke six years later was a blessing in disguise for him."

2

Sean took the sharp left turn onto Molly Lane far too fast. The rear tires on his Austin Healy roadster squealed in protest, then broke free. He started drifting sideways, heading for the barbed-wire fence guarding the pasture, daring him to test its razor-sharp resolve. He downshifted and floored it, spinning out and spitting gravel everywhere as he rocketed down the narrow country lane, turning everything around him into a blur of grays and greens and streaks of shiny wire. He could feel the tires nibbling over the pebbly black macadam, sending the wood-rimmed steering wheel into nervous flutters every time they gobbled up another bump or dip or hollow in the road. He held the accelerator to the floor, pushing the little engine to an excited scream as he raced headlong through the tunnel of leafy maple trees blocking out the sunlight.

The wind began slapping at him, as if telling him to slow down. When he saw he was doing seventy, he let off the gas and pumped the brakes, slowing to a crawl, then pulled off the road onto the grassy shoulder. Leaning back and looking up into the ceiling of green, smiling at having the rag top down for the first time this year, Sean withdrew a folded-up letter from his shirt pocket and settled down to read it for the umpteenth time.

Dear Dr. MacDonald:

When I learned of your resignation, I went to see you. But every time I stopped by your office in Merrywood Hall, you were either with someone or not there. So I've decided to write. In so doing, I hope you will not find me forward, or this note impersonal.

I would like you to be my guest here at the farm, perhaps for lunch, or even dinner. It's Greene Farms—remember?—in Red Hook. You can't miss it, we're on both sides of Molly Lane, from end to end.

The strawberries will be ready before Memorial Day this year, which is early. And we're expecting a bumper crop. But please don't wait for that to visit. And there's no need to call ahead of time; at this time of year I'm virtually a prisoner here. Besides, my housekeeper can prepare something on short notice.

You can usually find me at the farm market. But if it's really busy you'll probably find me helping out at the entrance to the fields. You'll know it's busy if you see a long line of cars pulled over to the side of the road, waiting to get into the fields to pick strawberries, or whatever else is ready.

I'm looking forward to seeing you again after all these years. And soon, I hope.

Sincerely,
Cathy Greene

With a blink of his eyes, Sean had Catherine Greene in front of him; long, strawberry blond hair, always wind-blown; cerulean blue eyes; thin, and tall, taller than all of the other girls. Save for one, Patricia Hawley, who was a few years ahead of Cathy, and who left in the middle of her senior year without notice. And there was that warm, easy smile of Cathy's, a smile that came to life whenever she spoke to him. At first he thought it was because of him, but he had quickly put that thought aside, along with others. He remembered liking her, a lot. After Janet's death, he often found himself wishing that Cathy wasn't a student. She was so alive. And she had made him feel that way too whenever she was around him. Smiling, Sean reached back for those feelings again, but came up empty-handed.

Like most of his students, Sean didn't keep up with what Cathy Greene did after graduation. Not because he didn't want to, but because he couldn't, since two weeks after commencement she joined the service, the Marines, rising to the rank of captain before returning home to Red Hook and taking over the management of the family business. There had been something in the paper about the "unusual circumstances" surrounding her discharge, but the paper wasn't very clear on exactly what had happened. So except for her graduation photograph, which was in the paper with the short notice of her joining the Marines, Sean had no idea what Cathy Greene looked like now, other than that she was tall, with blue eyes, maybe blond hair, maybe still thin, as she had been fifteen years ago.

Folding the letter back up, Sean tucked it into his shirt pocket. There was another letter there, which he slipped out to read.

Dear Dr. MacDonald:

Thank you for your kind letter. It's funny, but I wasn't sure that you would remember me, let alone answer my letter. I also didn't know if you would think me odd, or forward.

I'll expect you around one o'clock on Friday, just as you suggested. In case you haven't been out to Greene Farms, the following directions may . . .

Sean stopped without finishing the letter. He knew it by heart now anyway. It was a letter that he was surprised to receive, since he thought her first note to have been nothing more than a lark, and his own reply no more than a courtesy. But he wasn't so sure now if that's all they were, at least as far as his reply was concerned. Stuffing the letter back into his pocket, Sean began inching his car along the side of the road, listening to the crisp crackle and crunch of the gravel beneath his tires. The sounds, and the unusually warm May afternoon, brought back childhood memories—like the fat balloon tires on his repainted, candy-apple-red, secondhand bicycle, and the hot, gooey patches of tar, bubbling up from the road into shiny black blisters, asking to be stomped on, or the red, white, and blue plastic streamers left over from the Fourth of July, and the stolen clothespins he clipped to his fender braces, loading and reloading rejected baseball cards or rookies with no future, rookies like Roger Maris.

Out of the corner of his eye, Sean spotted a farmhouse on the left. Slowing down again, sitting up as tall as he could, he peered over the forsythia bushes lining the front yard, mentally checking off what he recalled of Cathy Greene's house from the description in her letter, "white clapboard siding . . . large wraparound porch, painted gray . . . kelly green shutters, and matching trim." Sean smiled and whispered, "Except for the front door, which you painted hunter-green 'to go with the brass door knocker.' " Sean slipped his car out of gear and coasted along in neutral, locating everything else Cathy Greene had taken the time—why, he didn't know—to describe in her chatty note. Clay pots "filled with red and white and pink impatiens." A wicker porch swing, "just big enough for two." And a pair of rocking chairs, painted white, "with red gingham seat cushions."

Something caught his eye, and Sean squeaked to stop. It was a huge old barn, standing alone, back from the others, which were plain everyday working barns, stained brown or left untouched to weather into a splintery gray. They were dry and stiff and uninviting compared to the soft, washed-out red lead of this tired old barn. Its curving mansard roof was drooping down over the eaves. The loft door was swung open and dripping with hay. Sean sat looking at it for the longest time, fighting the urge to sneak across the empty paddock, hop the fence, slip inside, and climb the ladder to the loft so he could hide from everything, and everyone, like he did when he was a kid. The faded red barn was one of six frame buildings lining the north side of Molly Lane for over half a mile, all stitched together by a sturdy, split-rail fence. At the end of the long wooden chain was a galvanized steel silo, towering over a huge dairy barn, and a farm stand surrounded by a recently paved parking lot, waiting for its white stripes.

Sean took his place in the line of cars jerking their way along the side of the road to the cut in the fence. When he turned in and pulled to a stop, a young girl leaned out of the small, make-shift gatehouse. "Good morning." She was bright-eyed and perky. "May I help you?" she asked, merrily drumming her fingers on the wooden shelf serving as a counter.

The little gatehouse was put together with two-by-fours, odd lengths of weathered barn siding, leftover splits of cedar shakes, and topped with a sheet of wavy galvanized metal roofing, folded at the ridge and bent over both sides, looking like a steel party hat, and more like a clubhouse than a gatehouse.

"I'm going to pick strawberries," Sean said officiously, trying his best to sound like he knew what he was doing. "And string beans, but I don't know how much."

The frizzy-haired teenager smiled. "String beans aren't in season, sir." She leaned out over the counter, ogling his car.

You should know that, MacDonald, you idiot! he thought. He looked into the young girl's blank face. "How about peas?" he asked bashfully.

A stack of four green plastic baskets, nesting one inside the other and still wet with fleshy chunks of strawberries, was slid off the shelf to him. She then held up a clear plastic bag with a pinch of her fingers, and let it go. It started floating down like a deflated hot-air balloon, until the wind caught it. Sean jumped up and grabbed it, fumbling the baskets off his lap and onto the floor when he did. "Shit!" he mumbled to himself.

"I beg your pardon, sir?"

Sean blushed, shook his head, and sat waiting for the car ahead of him to pull away, a long black Cadillac with New Jersey plates and tinted windows all rolled up so no one could see in. But before he could move, a woman, working the opposite side of the stand, stepped around and held out the bottom of a cut-down cardboard box. "Here," she instructed, tossing the box past him and onto the passenger seat. "Use this for the baskets when they're full."

Sean spun around at the sound of the distinctive voice and found himself staring into faded, pattern-worn jeans. They were so close to the car that he had to tilt his head back and look up in order to find her face. "Hi!" was all he could think to say as he fought to keep from glancing back down and following the welted seam of her skin-tight jeans as it dove between her shapely thighs.

"I wasn't sure you'd come," Cathy Greene said, then leaned down to hear Sean's reply over the clatter of plastic baskets and idling engines.

"I almost didn't," Sean admitted, trying his very best not to stare at Cathy's breasts, which were straining against the sun-bleached blue of her worn denim shirt. But the large round shadows pushing through the fabric, nipples nearly the thickness of his thumb, broke his resolve. Before he could look closer, the car behind him beeped loudly. Others joined in, adding their two cents' worth of impatience.

"You better move," Cathy suggested with a gentle pat on his shoulder. When she stepped away from the car, her fingers brushed up his neck, grazing his ear. Goose bumps jumped off his skin and raced down inside his shirt, making him shiver all over. With Cathy's attention diverted, Sean was able to look more closely, and to his surprise and delight, he found a full-figured woman, not the gangly girl etched into his memory, bringing to mind the image of an Olympic swimmer, until he got to her hips, which spread into womanhood before melting down into her strong, powerful thighs. Her dirty blond hair was pulled back and cinched into a long ponytail, which made him smile at the contrast of young and old.

They're blue, baby blue, he thought, trying to find her eyes. But she'd already turned away. When Cathy raised her hand, waving the line of cars down to a quiet idle, her arms and shoulders pressed against the thin fabric of her shirt, revealing even more of the athlete inside. Sean felt a confusing mix of feelings, but they didn't stop him from peeling her clothes off with his vivid imagination.

"I'll find you in the fields a little later, Sean," Cathy called back, then motioned for him to go ahead.

Sean? he thought, reluctantly blinking her shirt back on, and answered with a short rev of the engine and quick wave of his hand as he pulled away, turning his attention back to the reality of the rough dirt road in front of him, which rudely began bumping and jostling him out into the fields.

After a few hundred feet, a homemade wooden sign with bold, stenciled-on white letters proudly announced STRAWBERRIES in bright, fire-engine-red paint, and pointed right with a paper arrow nailed to the wood as an afterthought. He turned as ordered to find another sign shouting PEAS, only this one was carefully lettered in soup green, which made him smile. He continued on, passing row after mounded row until he found that made-to-order patch of ground that let him park well away from the tire-worn dirt road and upwind of the dust blowing across the open fields.

With a knowing glance, Sean stepped over the first few dozen rows, moving farther out into the fields. Stopping, looking up and down one row, he dropped the baskets onto the ground, knelt down, and started fanning through the leaves of the strawberry plants. After a few passes, he found what he wanted and picked the fattest, roundest, and reddest strawberry he could find.

Pinching the stem, he pushed the juicy strawberry into his mouth and sucked on it, then spit a mouthful of gooey brown liquid onto the ground, watching his saliva roll up into a floury ball. "Dust snot," he giggled boyishly to himself, and swallowed what was left in his mouth. Ours were sweeter, he thought. But that's probably because we raised sheep and didn't have to buy fertilizer. Just the thought of that made him smile. Then, with a flick of his wrist, Sean popped the strawberry into his mouth, and squashed it flat with his tongue. "At least *that* hasn't changed." He laughed, lying back on the ground. He shut his eyes, turning his head into the sun, letting it dance on his face while the damp earth pushed up through its dusty skin and seeped into his shirt, cooling him asleep as the warm May wind wrapped him in a fluffy blanket filled with forgotten dreams.

. . . it's all right, son, I'm right here with you. Now, are you sure that it wasn't just the shadows from the moonlight?

Yes.

Are you certain that it was your mother, and not someone else?

The Taking

Yes!

Calm down, son, it's all right. Now, tell me exactly what you saw. And remember, you're safe here with me. . . .

"Did you pass out from the shock of manual labor?" Cathy teased as she stepped out of the white, flatbed truck, which was dented and spotted all over with rust. It had no doors or fenders, and the knobby rear tires were half-again as big as the front ones.

Sean sat up like a windup toy and wiped the sweat off his brow with his shirt sleeve. Cathy was standing beside the truck, resting her arm on one of the splintered planks bolted to the frame, slowly combing the knot out of her long hair with her fingers. As she shook it free with a twist of her head, a warm inviting smile found its way onto her face. Her eyes were blue, just as he remembered, a soft blue, like a steady gas flame. But cool, not hot. Climbing to his feet, Sean started dusting himself off, slowly and methodically, first one leg, then the other. He ended with playful slaps of his backside and started for the truck, grinning sheepishly. Cathy braced her hands on the heavy wooden planks behind her and hopped up onto the bed with amazing ease, and equal grace, and started thumping the heels of her work boots against the rear tire.

Sean came to a stop directly in front of her. "Room for two up there?" He clapped the dust off his hands. Before he could join her, Cathy braced her hands on his shoulders and vaulted off the truck with a sudden, split-legged kick, knocking him off balance. Sean started falling backward and reached out to catch himself, grabbing hold of Cathy's shirt and tugging it open. Sean landed flat on his back and got the wind knocked out of him, but he didn't for one second take his eyes off Cathy as she followed him down, landing on top of him, straddling him on her knees, then falling forward onto his face, flooding his lungs with the sweaty smell of hard work. He could taste the salt and oil on his lips, and something else, something sweet, like honey, but not as thick. Cathy pushed herself up and came to rest with her hands braced on Sean's chest, looking down at him, smiling, waiting for him to say something.

Donald Beman

"Miss Greene. Catherine!" He gasped for air. "What if some-one sees us?"

"What is there to see?" Cathy asked, an angelic smile lighting up her face. "And please, call me Cathy. I'm only 'Miss Greene' to my suppliers." Seeing Sean glancing down, up, then back down, Cathy asked, "What are you staring at?" Sean's eyes told her where to look.

"Oh!" She laughed awkwardly and buttoned herself closed, but not before the smooth white skin covering her full breasts blushed pink. Tucking her shirt into her jeans, squirming into Sean as she did, Cathy stood up. Her worn denim shirt was now drawn tightly over her breasts, confirming everything that Sean thought he'd seen earlier, and more. Cathy stepped back, then up onto the running board on the driver's side of the cab. "When we didn't see you moving about anywhere out here, I decided to drive out to make sure you were all right." Cathy was stifling a private laugh. "But I guess I should have remembered those corny stories you told us in class about growing up on a farm, and known better." Her laugh was delicious, and it infected Sean, just as it had fifteen years ago. "Only a farm boy could lie down in the fields in the middle of the day and fall sound asleep. It comes from years of practice," she told him.

"Practice?" he asked, feeling silly. "For what?"

"For hiding from work!" Cathy slipped behind the wheel.

"Do you have to leave?" Sean's question came out sounding more like an anxious plea, which he quickly buried in his chest when he asked in a steady, and much deeper voice, "Are you sure have to go . . . Cathy?" There, you said it! he thought.

"You know," Cathy said with a lilt in her voice, "it's a lot nicer out here in the morning, just before sunrise, when the dew is still on the ground, holding the dust down, and the air is cool from the night." Without looking back, Cathy spun the tires in the dirt, kicking up dust as she circled around, and came to stop no more than a foot from his toes. Holding the steering wheel with both hands, she leaned out of the door-less cab and kissed Sean on his cheek, surprising him. He tried stepping away, but his feet didn't, or wouldn't, work for him. "It's really nice to see

42

you again, Sean,'' Cathy said with the calm self-assurance of a woman, not the young girl that Sean once knew as one of his students. She reached out and set her hand on his shoulder. ''I don't know why it's taken me so long to invite you out here.''

Unaware that Cathy was using him for balance, Sean shifted his weight, causing her to pitch out of the cab and into his arms. The truck lurched forward and chugged to a stall. A man's voice came out of nowhere. ''Are you all right, Catherine?''

The word husband detonated inside Sean's head. He stiffened and pushed Cathy away. She frowned at him and looked hurt as she answered without looking up. ''Yes, Daddy, I'm fine.'' Suddenly she sounded very different; the grown-up woman was a little girl for those four quick words. Sean gingerly nudged her back into the truck and glanced around.

''He's over by the fence,'' Cathy whispered. ''Behind you.''

Sean waved and smiled when he found the man, who was bent over and twisted with age. But it couldn't hide the fact that he was tall, like Cathy. His faded blue eyes were buried deep inside his face, which was weathered by the wind and bronzed by the sun. Roger Greene returned the wave with his large, arthritic hand, looking like it was a chore to raise his arm. He then turned and walked away, leaving Sean wondering just how long he'd been standing there.

''How about dinner tonight?'' Sean asked, surprising himself. He felt his face and ears warming up, and hoped it didn't show. What are you doing? someone somewhere inside his head asked.

''I can't.'' Cathy added a disappointed shrug of her shoulders. ''I wish I could, I really do, but we're busy earlier than usual this year. Good busy, thank goodness. What about after the weekend, say Monday or Tuesday?'' Her eyes were even bluer than before.

''I can't,'' Sean replied with a discouraged shake of his head. ''Graduation.'' Just the thought of it made him sigh.

Cathy sat back, eyeing him. Sean lowered his head, as if looking around on the ground for something that shouldn't be there. Cathy raised her voice over the groaning of the engine turning over. ''I guess it's not meant to be. Perhaps some other time.''

She curled her mouth into a pout and pulled away, this time without kicking up any dust.

Sean waved and called out to her. He wanted to change his mind. He didn't know why, he just did. But Cathy didn't hear him. He brought his hand to his face, cupping it over his mouth and nose, exhaling gently, warming the air trapped inside. She was still there—he could smell her on his beard, sweet and sour and salty, all in one delicious breath.

3

Wednesday, June 12, 1991

The walls of Sean's office were stripped bare. His heavy oak desk was cloaked in a quilted blanket and rope-tied, waiting to be moved into storage. The drapes were gone, leaving the stately stained-glass windows looking common without their mantle of royal blue. All but one of his bronzes—his favorite, the bears—had been wrapped in a white cotton sheet, tied loosely with twine, and laid to rest in sturdy wooden crates filled with straw. The silk tapestry had been secreted away, but the file cabinet, now weighted down with twelve threadbare, linen-backed journals, was still to be claimed. Boxes cluttered the floor, bulging at the seams, threatening to burst open with only the slightest provocation. Each one was labeled with black felt-tip marker, listing its contents. In front of the empty bookshelves were dozens of small corrugated cartons neatly stacked into columns seven and eight high, and lined up in a row, the words "Books" and "Heavy" printed on the sides and tops in fat red letters, then overstruck, making them look even heavier.

The Taking

It was almost dark. She knocked, then waited. There was no answer. She pushed the door open. It swung wide and eased to a stop just short of hitting the wall. She looked in, her eyes raking the room, stopping, checking, then moving on to something else until she'd touched every object in the office, as if making sure that it was dead. She walked in and closed the door, hesitated, then locked it behind her. She was graceful and quiet as she moved about the room. The hem of her coarse-weave linen skirt brushed against the rough skin and jagged corners of the corrugated cartons, brushing away the evening silence. Dropping her hand, she let her fingers glide over the tops of the boxes, tracing the seams, then pushing and testing them.

Her eyes lit up when she saw a note taped to the wall over the file cabinet standing between the undraped leaded-glass windows. She was there in two steps, reading it.

Oliver,

  The journals from my attic are here as promised. Let me know when you have finished copying what you want so we can arrange a time for you to return everything. Perhaps we can have lunch?

  Since you're taking the cabinet, would you mind putting everything into storage boxes for me? And tape them shut, since I don't plan on opening them ever again!

  Good luck, my friend. But maybe not.

Sean

She took a journal off the top of the pile, one marked with the Roman numeral II, and dated 1975. She stepped close to the window for better light, then sat down on the deep stone sill and started flipping through Sean's notes. The entries were printed, not written in cursive, and in pencil not pen, except where he'd gone back and retraced, or rewritten his thoughts in red ink. She brushed her fingers back and forth over the numbers and letters printed at the top of one page, reciting them under her breath, as a wry smile carved itself into her face.

$\underline{1}$ $\underline{2}$ $\underline{3}$ $\underline{4}$ $\underline{5}$ $\underline{6}$ $\underline{7}$ $\underline{8}$ $\underline{9}$

A B C D E F G H I

J K L M N O P Q R

S T U V W X Y Z

```
S E A N   M A C D O N A L D
1 5 1 5   4 1 3 4 6 5 1 3   4=43=4+3=7
J A N E T   P E T E R S (MACDONALD)
1 1 5 4 2   7 5 2 5 9   1=42=4+2=6
```

The marriage, the joining of 7 and 6, resulted in the number 13. To some, the number 13 is seen as misfortune, since it is considered bad luck to tamper with the number 12, the number of perfection as believed by Pythagoras. 12 was also the great cosmic number for the ancient Chinese and Sumerians, representing the 12 signs of the heavenly Zodiac. And there were 12 tribes of Israel (a fact refuted, however), with their 12 heavenly gates into Jerusalem. Other uses of the number included: 12-hour days and nights; 12 gods—6 male and 6 female—of Olympus; 12 apostles; and medieval Christian exegetes saw 12 as symbolizing faith in the Trinity, diffused to each of the 4 corners of the earth. The contemporary notion that 13 is unlucky is drawn from the story of The Last Supper, and the 13th apostle, Judas, who betrayed Christ for 30 pieces of silver.

NOTE 1: 30 pieces of silver $(3+0 = 3)$ can also symbolize the Trinity. Other examples of the occupance of the number 3 surrounding the life and death of Christ include: the trinity; the 3 wise men; the 3 gifts; the sacred, thrice-bent man in early Christian burials; Christ buried for 3 days; resurrection on the 3rd day; hung on cross for 3 hours; the use of 3 spikes to nail him to the cross; number of blows struck as extracted from the

The Taking

(implied) narrative in the gospels; and Saint Peter's denial of Christ 3 times before the cock crowed twice.

NOTE 2: Christ was also believed to have lived 33 years, which means that he was crucified in his 33rd year on earth. On the surface this appears to fit in with the New Testament writers' repeated use of the number 3 when writing about the life of Jesus Christ.

But there are many non sequiturs to the dominance of the number 3, which clearly symbolizes the presence of the Trinity throughout Christ's life. He was crucified on the 6th day. And hung on the cross from the 6th to the 9th hour. These values are a multiple of 3, as is their sum [15], which breaks down to 6. The other is Christ's age at his death, 33 [3+3 = 6]. The numeral 6—the sign of Satan—appears at the time of Christ's death. Curious! Or is it?

As for the number 13, the 13th apostle was seen as the Angel of Death (to some he was one of the avenging angels from the Old Testament), which only further solidified the superstitious belief that the appearance or occurrence of the number 13 foretold the coming of evil.

But, as noted above, 13 is also the sum of two diametrically opposed numbers (6 and 7). 6 is even, and unlucky. And female. It also symbolizes all that is unfinished, therefore evil. 1This idea is partially rooted in the numerology of the Book of Genesis, which calls for a 7th day in the story of creation. 7 is odd and lucky and male. It symbolizes ultimate completeness, and all that is "good" in the universe. It is also the sum of 3 and 4, which is the sum of heaven and earth. [3 = Trinity or god, and 4 = mortal world or man.]

And the number 7 is found, coincidentally (or not) in the numerology of the name given to the man-god, Jesus Christ.

Donald Beman

```
JESUS  CHRIST or JESUS  CHRISTI
15131  389912 or 15131  3899129

sum=43=4+3=7    or    sum=52=5+2=7
```

Can all of this be just a coincidence?

"And have you answered that question yet, Dr. MacDonald?"
she wondered aloud. "Or have you given up, like all the others?"

Placing the journal on the sill beside her, she reached around,
slowly, almost painfully, and took another. She set it in her lap.
It was marked with the number I, and dated 1974. She didn't
seem to be in any particular hurry as she paged through Sean's
research notes from the year following his wife's murder. It was
as if she already knew what was written, and was simply checking
off this or that entry with a tap of her finger and approving nod
of her head. Or, as was the case with some of what she read, a
quick, disapproving shake of her head.

2: The number signifying duality. Contrast. And tension. The
tension between the positive and the negative. Inhaling and
exhaling. Male and female! It stands for the very push and the
pull that generates the continuous ebb and flow of life. The
Chinese yin and yang is a perfect example. The yin is the
female or cosmic element. The moon. Femininity. The recep-
tor. While the yang is male. The sun. The projector. The yin
and yang symbolize the eternal strife between darkness and
light. Black and White. The struggle between the organic and
the inorganic from the very beginning of time. Or the battle
between spiritual good and material evil. Or the constant battle
between male and female.

3: Is two plus one. It is an odd number. It heals that which
two has split apart, ending the conflict and duality and tension.
As the first number that has a beginning, a middle, and an end,
3 is viewed as the first "real" number. It's also seen as the

second number for God, after the number 1. And not only in the eyes of Christians, since there were numerous trinities thousands of years before they came up with theirs. 3 is also the number of the brightest lights in the heavens, the first real trinity; the Sun, Moon, and the morning star, Venus.

4: Brings order to chaos. 4 symbolizes the created, or mortal world (preformed in the name Adam). Other symbolic representations are: the 4 cardinal points of the earth—N, S, E, and W; the 4 winds; the 4 seasons; the 4 phases of the moon; 4 "authoritative" Gospels; the Christian cross, with its 4 points and 4 right angles, is seen as the "rightest figure of all"; and Jewish tradition emphasizes to the faithful the mystery of the tetragrammaton, YHVH.

The Pythagoreans saw the number 4 as the number of justice. Their geometry discovered 4 perfect solids. And the term square points to that which is right, orderly, and an ordering structure.

5: Is the number of natural man. It is also the first number mixed of even and odd (a numberless conflict in the struggle between good and evil?). It is the number of fingers on a man and woman's hand, forming the basis for one of the first counting systems.

In antiquity the number 5 was the number for Venus and Ishtar, and is therefore connected with sexual life and marriage (see Matthew 25, the parable of the 5 foolish virgins and the 5 wise virgins). The pentagram, which can be derived from the zodiacal stations of Venus, is endowed with apotropaic and magic powers. While in alchemy the "quinta essentia" contains the rejuvenating forces of life.

6: Is 7 minus 1. It is, therefore, seen as the number of incompleteness. 6 is even, and female. 6 is also the joining of three

Donald Beman

2s or two 3s, therefore it generates more conflict and tension—
metaphysically speaking—than any of the other root numbers
from one to nine.

And 6 stands uniquely alone as an ominous number in mankind's psyche. This perhaps stems from the centuries-old use
of 666 in Western civilization to denote the presence of the
Devil. This belief was derived from a passage in Revelation
13—where John the Divine wrote about a beast rising up out
of the earth. The second of two, the first having risen out of
the sea. The beast was identified, or "named," with the number "six-hundred, three-score, and six." Many lay scholars
interpret this as a metaphor for Nero. While traditional religious theologians, and many lay scholars, too, believe it was
intended to symbolize all that is evil on earth, therefore the
Devil; hence the basis for the number 666 becoming a symbol
for Satan.

The association with Nero resulted from converting the
numbers St. John used in his original text (in ancient Greek)
using the 22 letter Hebrew alphabet, since each letter, or pho-
netic value, had a specific corresponding numeric value assigned to it. Therefore, "six-hundred, three-score, and six"—
or 666—translated to QSR NRWN, which in (ancient) Greek
spelled KAISER NERON for the beast rising up out of the
center of the earth. The association with the Emperor Nero and
evil (Satan) quickly became interchangeable. Note: Q = 100;
S = 60; R = 200; N = 50; R = 200; W [V] = 6; N = 50

Twilight was falling into night, painting the tall stained-glass
window beside her into an opaque sheet of fractured color. She
opened it, inviting the moon inside to light the pages of Sean's
journal. She now appeared to read more with her fingers than her
eyes, brushing her fingertips over the cryptic entries, line by line.
When she stopped, it was only long enough to inhale with a silent
breath something Sean had written. She read the rest of the journals, finishing the last one just as the moon was giving way to

50

the light of day.

Closing the final threadbare journal, its pages tattered and finger stained, she looked outside, to the east, and into the rising light of the morning star ascending above the distant horizon to take its rightful place in the heavens. Watching it grow brighter, the radiant glow of the false star reflected in her eyes, she smiled and nodded just before the light of day erased it. Then she was gone.

4

Friday, June 14, 1991

"Absolutely not," Sean said in response to Dr. Lucien's question. He arched his back, pulling himself away from the bite of the unforgiving Windsor chair. Sharon Lucien made a quick entry in her notes. Sean just shook his head. "For the umpteenth time, Sharon, I do not feel guilty about my wife's death. And I don't even know why you brought it up now, after all these years." With a bewildered shrug of his shoulders, Sean pushed himself up out of the chair and walked around to the window behind him. Reaching through the drapes, he tried to open the window, but it was painted shut. Disappointed, he threw the drapes open with a decisive sweep of his hands. Sunlight burst into the office, burning itself into Sharon Lucien's coal-black eyes before she could look away. Pleased with himself, Sean started across the office.

Sharon sat watching him, tipping back in her padded rocker, which never made a sound no matter how hard she kicked the floor. Her feet were propped up on the edge of the oversized ottoman between her chair and his, her iodine-red ankle-length skirt tucked loosely between her legs, which were parted just enough to make Sean look out of the corner of his eye to see if he was missing something. Her snug tie-dyed blouse was stained with patches of teal and burnt orange and tiny swirls of licorice. There wasn't a spot of white on her, except when she twisted to one side or the other, or leaned forward to make a point. Then her blouse would scallop open between the mismatched buttons to reveal her pillow-soft skin, linen white and untouched by the sun. It made Sean want to touch her all over, but with his face, not his hands.

Sharon spoke up when Sean grabbed hold of the doorknob. "Please, don't open it," she said, wrapping one hand around the other.

Thinking to himself, Thanks, but no thanks, Sean pulled the door open, then began pushing it closed and open, repeatedly, forcing a breeze to snake through the stuffy office in hopes that it would chase away the stale smell lingering in the air.

When Sharon Lucien's office was warm and closed like this, they weren't alone; her other patients were with them, or what was left of them. The smell of curdled milk spilled by the young married couples, when they fought with each other to see which one of them wouldn't have to grow up. Or the ammoniated stench of fear from the overweight middle-aged businessman, recently fired and trying to cope with his newfound impotence. Then there was rage, which hung in the air like an invisible fume, waiting to be breathed in so it could infect someone else. But today it was anger, and from a woman, not a man, and Sean knew the difference only too well after so many years. When men are angry they give off a rank, sweaty, unwashed smell that pushes you back. But you can swallow it away, even though it burns your throat going down. Women, on the other hand, drip with a thick oily smell that's sort of sweet, like melted butter. It pulls you close to them before you realize what it is, and then it's too late— it's already stuck itself to the back of your throat.

"Do you think I had something to do with Janet's death?"

Sean asked, fanning the door, driving the air a little harder. There was a thin edge of resentment cutting through the veneer of Sean's relaxed demeanor. "Like that district attorney did? And still does, if what I hear is true."

The persistent breeze found the loose strands of her almost-black hair on Sharon's forehead, playing with them until she tucked them out of reach with an experienced poke of her fingers. "You weren't listening to me, Sean." The muscles in her jaw began tying themselves into sinewy knots. "I wasn't *accusing* you of anything."

Bullshit! he thought, leaning back against the door, feeling his shirt soaking up the sweat that had been squeezed out of his pores by the suffocating heat, which was unusual for early June.

"Look, Sharon, as I told you when I called, all I want are copies of those transcripts. I've resigned from the college and just want to put everything behind me, tie up loose ends, you might say. I even turned over my research to someone who wanted it, a colleague of mine. For me, the transcripts are unfinished business, one of those loose ends. I simply want to read them, then file them away with everything else I'm not taking with me. What did you call it, 'baggage'?" Sean sighed, deliberately loud enough for Sharon to hear. "And I don't really want to get drawn into rehashing what I consider to be things that I've dealt with, and buried." He immediately regretted his choice of words when he saw the expression on Sharon's face, then watched her jot something down. "It's all over, for me at least." He was trying to be reasonable even though he no longer felt that way, and that bothered him. "Let's just be friends, if that's possible, OK?"

"What are you running away from?"

Sean shut his eyes. "You're amazing!" He slapped the air. "You just won't give up, will you." He walked over and sat down.

As a therapist, Sharon Lucien had all the right words when she needed them, each with its own special meaning and special purpose. Verbs misused as adjectives, or turned inside-out and neutered into nouns. Adjectives tied into long, thin chains of small, tight, hard, beaded knots, until they were no longer recognizable.

And wonderfully lyrical adverbs, stripped of their musically pleasing sounds.

Sean waited until he had Sharon's attention. "Could it be that when you make these outlandish statements now, and I don't bite anymore, that it pisses you off?" He folded his arms and waited, as if challenging Sharon to say something.

After scribbling a long note to herself, Sharon glanced over at Sean with a look of clinical curiosity. "Do you think it's possible that you could be refusing to face reality?" She leaned back and took a deep breath, straining the small tortoiseshell buttons on her blouse.

Fuck you, suddenly flashed inside Sean's head, unearthing feelings he'd just said he buried. Damn! Just forget it, he told himself, and shook off the thought. "Now, getting back to why I asked to see you today. May I please have a copy of the transcripts from my hypnosis sessions?" Kicking his shoes off, Sean put his feet up on the padded ottoman. His leg came to rest against Sharon's. "You know"—he smiled awkwardly—"I felt like I was drawn through a wringer after each of those sessions." This sounded like a boast, but in a painful sort of way. "After waking up, I could have sworn that Dr. Kaplan's office smelled like someone had been sick in it."

"You were fighting the process." The relaxed tone of Sharon's voice matched her steady, uninterrupted writing on the pad buried in her lap. "It was all in your mind."

Fuck the "process," he thought. "Well," he said, rubbing his hands together briskly. "May I?" he asked again, only without the veil of self-control.

Sharon smiled graciously. Sean braced himself. "I never told you that I would give you copies of the actual transcripts."

Sean sat up, blocking the sunlight seeping in through the window over his shoulder, casting Sharon's face in a shadow. Then, leaning forward, resting his elbows on his thighs and propping his chin on top of his folded-over hands, he just sat there, watching her, saying nothing.

"I think you've created a fantasy about this," Sharon said in a practiced professional monotone. Sharon patted her lap, then glanced over at the file cabinet beside her desk. "My notes are perfectly clear on what I told you and what we agreed to."

This is silly, Sean thought, and wanted to tell her just that. But her rapidly cooling eyes made it clear that nothing would be accomplished by it. He started to say something, but stopped. Sharon leaned forward and turned her head to one side, as if trying to hear what he was saying. The sharp movements pulled a button loose on her blouse. She turned back to face him. "Did you want to say something?" she asked. Sean shook his head. Sharon shrugged her shoulders, pinching the top of her breasts into a crevice of flesh, then stood up and turned away. The orange sunlight slipped inside her blouse unnoticed, warming her muslin-white skin, melting her nipple into a wrinkled patch of delicious milk chocolate. Sean let his eyes follow the sun, but kept his distance. Turning back, Sharon traced his electrified gaze. "I think we should end here," she said with an abrupt tug of her blouse without looking down. Even though it had been five years, the images were still there for Sean, just like the stains on the carpet in front of her chair.

You love this, don't you? he thought, feeling her chewing on him with her eyes. Janet loved it, too. She would keep after me, trying to get me to fight with her. She loved to fight. And when I wouldn't, she'd sink her teeth into me and shake me until I finally fought back. A shiver ran down his back. He thought he saw Sharon smile, but it was his imagination. How stupid we are, he thought. Little boys playing at being men, thinking you needed to be protected, when all along you were just waiting for us to grow up so you would have someone you could really fight with, someone you could hit, and hit hard.

"As you wish," Sean finally said as if talking to himself, then threw his arms up in mock defeat. "Yes, I do feel guilty in a peculiar sort of way about what happened to my wife. Not that I was responsible in any way, just that it was her, and not me, who was murdered. But there's more pain than guilt." Sean wasn't sure if he was giving up, or giving in, but he was certain of one thing. He didn't care anymore what she thought. "And there's anger," he added hesitantly. "And no doubt far more than I realize, or am willing to admit to." Sharon nodded. "But it's not at myself."

Sharon was waiting for him. "And what about your son?" Sean sat up as if something had been stuck into him, something sharp and hot. "Do you feel the same way about his death, too?" Without warning, something burst open inside his chest, taking his breath away, then flooding his eyes closed. When he tried blinking himself to the surface, he saw Sharon through the watery blur, watching him, indifferently, as if he was some*thing,* not some*one.* "And just what do you think those feelings are?" she asked wryly.

Sean cleared his throat. "I don't know. Sorrow, I guess."

"Just let go," Sharon whispered softly. "It's all right." She waited, patiently, which was uncommon for her. But not even the unfamiliar tenderness in her voice could unlock the feelings Sharon wanted Sean to show her, to give her, not after what had happened the last time he was here, the last time he saw her.

Sean pushed the ottoman to one side with a kick of his foot. He wanted to make sure the stains were there, that he hadn't made it up, fantasized it, as she wanted him to believe. Someone had tried removing them, and had done a pretty good job, but blood is hard to get out. Though faded, the outlines were still visible, but not nearly as clear as the memories of what happened that afternoon.

Sean pulled the door to Sharon's office closed, and paused in the hallway outside. "Why did you came back?" he asked himself out loud, not caring if Sharon heard him. "Just walk away and put it all behind you," he told himself, racing down the two flights of stairs, then darting outside, finding the warm afternoon air cool after Sharon's stuffy office. Or is it really me? he wondered, stepping over the door of his Healy, and sliding down into the leather seat, still hot from the sun. "Fuck it."

5

The howling wind and driving rain roared in just after midnight, blowing away the moon and flooding the skies. There was thunder and lightning, too, odd for this time of year. It all stopped just before dawn and became whisper quiet, leaving the early-morning air filled with that bittersweet smell of burnt sugar, the cracked gingerbread on the old house swollen shut, and the cedar shingles on the roof leaking into the clogged gutters, and spilling over, playing lazy, drip-drop tunes on the porch roof below. When it's like this, hot and muggy and close, you're almost afraid to breathe, afraid that you're really under water and might drown if you do. And your clothes cling to your skin like plastic wrap.

Dear Sarah,

All of my lesson plans for the summer courses accompany this letter. Sorry they're late, but I wasn't into it last semester. Dr. Jennings should have no problem whatsoever when classes start in July.

No doubt you've guessed that I had my phone disconnected. I decided it was the only way I would get some peace and quiet. But not from you, of course, my dear, Dean Potter.

Well, Sarah, have a nice summer. And take care of yourself. And please don't be so hard on me because of what I did. It's really best for everyone; it was no longer working for me;

57

Donald Beman

therefore it couldn't work for the students. I know you really do understand. Don't you?

And don't you dare take it out on poor Bruce—you know that he can't stand up you.

I'll be in touch. And be sure to write if you need me.

Sean

Before printing out the letter, Sean read it one more time to make certain that he'd said exactly what he wanted, nothing more and nothing less, and nothing that could be construed by Sarah as an invitation for her to visit him, unannounced. That's when Bruce Fanning's words came tumbling out of his head, and Sean found himself repeating them, verbatim, like he was reciting a childhood prayer. "If you're going to write, write well that is, you must to be totally honest with yourself. Then, and only then, can you hope to tell fiction's fanciful lies with conviction." As if Bruce was standing there beside him, Sean snapped, "Fuck you and your fanciful fictional lies, Fanning." He smiled to himself at the rhythmic sound of the words and immediately began playing with the alliteration between slurpy sips of cold coffee. "Fuck Fanning and his fanciful fictional lies. Fanning's fanciful fucking fictional lies. Fanciful fucking fiction." Laughing, Sean hit his computer keyboard with two haphazard pokes of his finger, and growled, "Fictional, fanciful fucking!" over the irritating scratching and screeching of the old printer he'd come to hate.

Compared with his office in Merrywood Hall, the study in Sean's apartment was spartan to the point of looking abandoned. There were no curtains on the windows. The walls were painted bone white and left bare, except for a solitary nineteenth-century pencil drawing hanging over his desk. It was of a peasant woman, tall and sturdy and ruggedly handsome, standing in the fields of Brittany, with a secret sketched onto her finely drawn face. Her arms were at her sides, her large hands clutching unruly heads of cabbage, her eyes clear as ice—but warm, not cold—and focused on something off in the distance, perhaps her future. Or maybe she was looking back into the past, which could be why Sean liked the drawing so much. The drawing was bordered with a wide silk mat that had faded to a soft comforting gray, and was framed in a narrow strip of bird's-eye maple.

The clunky desk from his office, which he decided at the last minute not to put into storage, looked like a wooden boulder that had tumbled into the room and come to rest up against the wall. To the left was a matching credenza, crowned with a row of books stretching from one end to the other. On the left was his set of the *OED*, all ten volumes. On the right were his falling-apart dictionaries, including the ones in French, German, and, of course, Greek and Latin. Serving as one bookend was the only bronze he didn't pack away. On the other end were twenty-four tattered copies of *The Old Farmer's Almanac,* beginning with 1967, stacked flat to keep them from curling open.

After slipping his note to Sarah Potter into an envelope, Sean reached for the unopened letter that he'd saved for last, as if it was dessert. And maybe it was, since the return address was Greene Farms. But there was no name, not that one was needed, not now. He opened Cathy's note.

Dear Sean,

Shall we try again for dinner? I tried calling, but learned that you had your phone disconnected. Is someone chasing you? Only kidding. How does Tuesday, the 18th sound?

If this heat holds up, and since I don't have air conditioning in this old farmhouse of mine, I'll have my housekeeper set up a table out on the back porch. At least we won't have to worry about bugs. It's too early for them.

Call and let me know. Or stop by and talk. And no excuses this time, OK?

Cathy

Sean replied, "Don't worry, Catherine, there won't be any." There was a hunger to his words that he hadn't felt in years, or at least hadn't let himself feel. "Be careful," he warned, then wondered why he'd said it. The thought of dinner brought up the thought of breakfast, which he hadn't had yet, followed by images of steaming hot scones buried under melted butter. *I wonder if Julian's is open yet?* He was down the hall, through the kitchen, and standing on the landing before any other thought could elbow its way into his head.

The stairs rising from the porch to the landing outside the kitchen in his second-floor apartment were extra wide and further apart than modern ones. There wasn't a handrail either. And it was dark, since the light over the landing, a white porcelain fixture with a draw string and no shade, didn't work anymore. So the only light in the stairway was what leaked out through the four wavy-glass panels in the kitchen door, or what crept up the stairs during the day when the downstairs porch door was left open, which was most of the time since Sean never bothered closing it during the day, unless it was cold out. At night, when the kitchen lights were out, the stairwell was pitch black.

The slap of a screen door shutting made him look up from unzipping the leather tonneau covering his Healy, then back over to the porch. "Dr. MacDonald!" Jean Murphy called out as she stepped to the edge of the porch, wiping her hands on her apron. "What in the world are you doing up at this ungodly hour?" She let go of her tattered white cotton apron and braced her hands on her hips, staring at Sean, waiting for an answer.

Jean Murphy's skin was smooth and hard, like fired clay. What few wrinkles there were appeared to have been drawn there with great care, not pressed into her flesh by time, or scratched into it by worry. She wasn't fat or thin. And she had that sturdy look of hard work about her, years of hard work, at least seventy years by Sean's reckoning, but he hadn't asked. Her hair was solid gray, like the bark of a tree in winter. And she stood just as straight. Her eyes were tired and faded, and wrinkled, but still Irish green. When she spoke, it was clear and in your face. She listened the same way.

"Jean, please," Sean said, carefully tucking the driver's-side half of the leather tonneau behind the bucket seat. "Will you please call me Sean."

The Taking

Jean turned one foot out, stopping just short of tapping her toe. "And just where are you off to?" she demanded, but nicely.

"Woodstock." Sean jumped into his car and screwed himself down behind the lacquered wooden steering wheel. "I want to get some scones for breakfast, and Julian's Bakery over in Woodstock has the best damn scones in the Hudson Valley."

Jean's face lit up like a ten-cent sparkler. "Wait!" She disappeared into the house, then scurried back out, waving a bill in the air as she ran across the lawn, showing no signs of her age. "Bring some back for this old lady," she said, tucking the bill into Sean's shirt pocket. She then pressed it flat with an affectionate pat of her hand.

The Healy purred to life. "I don't expect to be back for at least two hours," Sean said over the smooth, steady idle of the engine. "I've got one special stop to make."

Dear Bruce,

I didn't see your car in front of the house yesterday morning on my way back from Woodstock with a bag of fresh scones, so I didn't stop. My landlady and I ate them. Another time, my friend!

I had dinner last night with Catherine Greene. You may remember her, she's a former student—blond hair, a bit over six feet, with piercing blue eyes. She's quite a woman now, intelligent, beautiful, and with a figure that would turn most women green with envy. And she's still single. However, she could be divorced. I never asked. I think I'll be seeing her often in the coming weeks. At least I hope so.

It's funny, but the girl I once knew—or thought I did—no longer exists; she's a grown-up woman. And more. I wonder if I can keep up with her? And no smart remarks from the tenured debaucher of underage women!

I am, however, going back for breakfast; she tells me that there's something about the farm early in the morning, which she says is almost poetic. My recollection is hard work, so I'm looking forward to finding out what she's talking about.

I'm bringing the scones, Cathy's supplying the coffee and fresh strawberries. I don't know what she sees in me. After all, I've led the life of a priest for the last seventeen years— save for one month of indiscretion, reckless passion, which we won't talk about. I'll keep you posted.

Lunch soon? Or how about getting together for the party Sarah throws before the start of the summer session in Merrywood Garden? I think she'll let me attend, even though I'm no longer a member of the faculty. Besides, there are a few things I left with Oliver, which he should be finished with by now—one way or the other! I can kill two birds with one stone; you, the vulture, and Oliver, the owl.

See you soon, my dear friend.

Sean

Pressing his hands against the walls in the stairwell for balance, Sean double-jumped down the flight of stairs like a rowdy teenager. The screen door was stuck. He pushed it. It didn't move. He tried again, only a little harder. His hand slipped off the frame and punched through the crumbly black screening. "Shit!" He started fumbling with the frayed ends, trying to fit them back into the seam of the door frame.

"Shame on you!" came flying at him through the screening. He looked out. It was Jean Murphy, sitting in one of the oversized wicker rockers, watching the sweat drip off the glass of iced tea in her hand. The puddle on the porch was already the size of a silver dollar.

Sean slipped outside with a contrite look on his face. "I'll fix it later. I'll get what I need at the hardware store on my way back from mailing this letter." He raised the envelope he was holding to offer proof, then felt silly for having done it.

Jean raised her glass and tossed a mock toast at him in a lazy sort of way, which made Sean wonder if there might be something more than just sugar and lemon in her tea. "Don't worry about it, son." Jean started a long slow sip, cupping one hand under the dripping glass.

The Taking

Sean thought to himself, You're a queer duck, Jean Murphy, nodded his acceptance, and leapt off the porch. "You've got to change your date with Catherine," he whispered to himself as he sprinted across the lawn to his car. But the thought couldn't, wouldn't, be left alone. "Date?" Sean laughed. "Yes! Date," he argued with himself, and let his mind go refreshingly blank.

6

Saturday, June 22, 1991

Sean was standing in the portico at the far end of Merrywood Garden, leaning against one of the marble columns and listening to the rising chatter of the evening wind, his thoughts buried deep in the darkening shadows of the Catskills beyond the Hudson. At the sound of footsteps in distance behind him, muffled by the soggy, rain-soaked lawn in the aging Victorian garden, Sean began counting under his breath, mentally measuring the rapidly shrinking distance. The pace quickened, then stumbled, kicking up the gravel surrounding the fountain in the center of the garden and covering the narrow paths shooting out like spokes in a wheel. There was a quiet laugh, then a winded cough. Smiling affectionately, Sean pushed himself off the fluted column and pinned his arms to his sides, bracing himself.

With a fiendish but playful laugh, his long arms spread out for balance, Bruce Fanning leapt over the muddy puddle drowning the white pebbled path in front of the portico, and immediately slipped on the rain-slick terrazzo floor. He reached out for Sean's arm, his fingernails scrapping over the coarse weave of the Harris tweed of Sean's jacket, but slipping free just as he pitched pre-

63

cariously over the knee-high stone railing. Sean grabbed a fistful of Bruce's sweater, pulling him back to safety.

With an appreciative pat, and equally caring rub of Sean's arm, smoothing away wrinkles on the coat sleeve that weren't there, Bruce spun around and peered back into the twilight rapidly filling the walled-in garden.

He turned back to Sean, who had given up on him and returned to staring out across the river, chasing shadows again. "A penny for your thoughts?" Bruce asked. There was an impish smile even Puck would have been proud of spreading effortlessly across Bruce's boyish face, his bright, sapphire-blue eyes alive and asking to play. "Well, Mac?" he prodded.

Bruce Fanning hadn't aged a day since joining the faculty of Hart College, except perhaps for the steady thinning of his silky blond hair. But that somehow made him look even younger. And he was still thin as a rail. Thin, not trim. And he was yet to have to shave more than twice a week. He and Sean had joined the faculty at the same time, coincidentally arriving on the very same day late one afternoon in August just as the towering pin oaks lining the ridge above the river were carving up the light of the setting sun into perfect parallel rows. The two men couldn't have been any more different in personality and appearance if they had been cast opposite one another in a play. Bruce was rarely seen without a winning smile, a playful wink of his clear blue eyes, followed by a wave and a friendly "Hi" for everyone he met. Sean was more reserved, almost shy in his manner, simply nodding and almost smiling when he passed. Unlike Bruce, Sean took everyone on with his piercing, gray-green eyes, something that Bruce never did with anyone.

But in spite of their differences, or perhaps because of them, Sean MacDonald and Bruce Fanning became fast friends on that lazy summer evening twenty years ago, tossing a flurry of acerbic but playful barbs back and forth at each other, then flinching and ducking and laughing like little boys playing cowboys and Indians with plastic bullets and wicker arrows tipped with rubber suction cups.

Not having gotten the response he wanted, Bruce tried another tack. "Well then," he said, stomping the grassy slime off the bottom of his penny loafers while discreetly slipping his hand into his pants pocket, making the coins jingle, "if a penny won't buy you out of your morose silence, how about that antique silver dollar you gave me for my birthday a few years ago?" Bruce pulled the heavily rubbed coin out of his pocket and waved it in front of Sean's face. He didn't see, or perhaps didn't care about, the subtle, irritated tic of Sean's head, pulling himself away from Bruce's taunting gesture. "I keep it with me all the time for good luck. You never know when you might have to pay the ferryman!" Bruce delivered one of his fun-loving laughs. "Isn't that what you told me when you gave it to me?" Then, with an amused smile, Bruce tapped the end of Sean's nose with the silver dollar.

Sean slapped his hand away, sending the coin flying against one of the marble columns surrounding the portico, then careening down onto the face of the colorful mosaic under their feet.

"I see we're a little testy tonight," Bruce said, clucking his tongue and shaking his head, yet all the while still smiling. Bruce's affection for Sean was imprinted on his face; it was part of him, just as his hand or arm was part of him. "Are we feeling sorry for ourself for having resigned, Dr. MacDonald?" Bruce chuckled to himself. "Or is it that dear Patricia Jennings is replacing you?" Sean shivered at hearing this. Pleased with the rise that he'd gotten out of him, Bruce laughed again and kicked the coin with the toe of his shoe, sending it skittering over the cracks in the fractured floor and tumbling to a stop at Sean's feet. Sean bent over, but quickly stood back up. Bruce clutched his chest with his hands. "Oh, no, it must be tails! Do I dare touch it? After all, I wouldn't want my hair to fall out, not any more than it already has! Or be struck by lightning. Or face seven years of bad luck. Or, God forbid, be rendered impotent."

Sean gave in to Bruce's needling. "You? Impotent? The campus pedophile? Fat chance!" Sean laughed. But Bruce didn't. "Anyway, it's not antique." Sean snatched up the dollar with a looping swipe of his hand and began flipping it nonchalantly, intentionally close to the railing, and out of Bruce's reach. Bruce couldn't take his eyes off the coin. "It was minted the same year you were born. It's simply for good luck." Sean tossed the silver dollar high into the air with a jerk of his wrist and flick of his thumb. Bruce grabbed at it, lost it in the dark for a few precious seconds, then caught it against his chest with a slap of his hands. He slid his reclaimed prize down his sweater and back into the safety of his pants pocket.

Sean and Bruce were now standing side by side, facing west across the Hudson, watching the golden crown of the setting sun melt down into the earth. Sean started to put his arm around Bruce's shoulder, but stopped with an awkward twitch, and instead began fingering the blotches of red and orange and cobalt blue swirling around overhead, as if repainting the upside-down canvas hanging in the evening sky. He then spoke in a whisper, forcing Bruce to lean closer. "There. It's over. Just like that!" He snapped his fingers close to Bruce's face, forcing Bruce to blink away. "For centuries, painters have tried capturing that instant of fleeting color, and the fragile feelings that go with it, but few of them ever succeeded."

"What are you talking about?" Bruce's voice crackled with feigned indignation. "There were hundreds. *Hundreds!*" Then, looking over at Sean suspiciously, seeing the amused expression on his face, Bruce realized that he'd taken the bait. Again.

Sean stood staring at the amber light dissolving into the yellow cracks in the horizon. "I don't agree." He waved his hand, brushing away Bruce's silent protest. "Most of the members of that little band of self-taught artists you art historians have put on a pedestal couldn't have painted a decent sunset if their lives had depended on it." Sean drew his hands behind his back and leaned at Bruce, taunting him with a crooked smile, waiting for the rebuttal he could tell was being mounted by the way Bruce's eyes were flashing side to side inside his face.

There was an irritated but confident snap to Bruce's words. "What about Thomas Cole?" He stuck his jaw out, daring Sean to hit him with his reply, certain that it couldn't hurt him.

"Cole painted by numbers," Sean ruled with an authoritative swipe of his hand. "And his large paintings make me wonder if

66

he didn't lie them down on the floor of his Catskill studio and dribble melted crayons all over the canvases. And don't try telling me that just because a handful of modern-day Horatio Algers are naive enough to be duped into paying ridiculous prices for his work, that it means the man could paint. His paintings are historically important, not great art. End of discussion."

"You're in rare form tonight, MacDonald. You've got to realize that I'm an art historian, not a critic. I don't analyze an artist and his paintings the way you literary types conduct a postmortem on some wretched writer, carving up the poor bastard's artistic psyche—and his novels—trying to find his pain. For me, painters just paint. After they've been dead long enough for most everyone to forget about them, I resurrect them and their work, and put it all into historical perspective. Think of me as a file clerk with a Ph.D. It's that simple!" Swinging around and facing the lost horizon, Bruce declared a unilateral truce with his renewed silence.

Sean wanted to disagree, to take Bruce to task as they always did with one another, but he didn't want to push too hard and risk losing him, not tonight. So he held his tongue, which was unlike him, and waited, looking around, watching the tiny leaves on the very tops of the branches flicker blue and gray, like dying flames on ashen coals, before being snuffed out by the night. He could feel the summer air turning cool from the steady breeze slipping down out of the mountains and across the river. "Any news on the book?" Sean finally asked, trying to jump-start their conversation by changing the subject.

Bruce snorted quietly. "Yes, unfortunately there is."

"Well?" When Bruce didn't respond right away, Sean started to nudge him with a playful poke but thought the better of it and asked, "Have they made many changes?"

Bruce unfolded his arms. "Many? I'll say! To begin with, University Press is only printing thirty-five-hundred copies, not the seventy-five-hundred called for in my contract. And not ten minutes after they called to tell me that today, I received the galleys by Express Mail, only to learn that the final text I gave them had been cut in half, then ground up into coffee-table talk. And what's worse, that pimply-faced editor they assigned to me

added a bunch of meaningless halftones without my permission!''
Bruce abruptly stopped speaking. But his hands and lips were still
moving, making it look like an argument had broken out between
them. ''My book is going to become nothing more than an excuse
for all of those gypsies, beggars, and thieves camping out on
Madison Avenue to raise their prices. They do it every time one
of their precious paintings is illustrated in a legitimate book, and
not one of their Mickey-Mouse gallery exhibition catalogues, the
ones with more pictures than words in them.''

Bruce's rising anger finally found the top of his balding head,
making it shine. It was all Sean could do to keep from saying
something about it, since he knew that it would only inflame him
more. ''I really don't see what your problem is,'' Sean said with
an even keel to his words. ''You're getting published. And paid.
And paid pretty damn well, too, when you consider all you're
doing is turning your art-in-the-dark lectures into a book.''

Bruce opened his blue eyes as wide as he possibly could in
response to Sean's silent, beady-eyed challenge. ''How would
you like it if some smart-mouthed kid just out of college cut one
of your stories in half, changed those silly, superstitious numbers
of yours from odd to even, switched new moons with full moons,
and turned your little devils into gods?''—he took a much needed
breath—''simply so everything would fit into some dumb-assed,
fucking format that his marketing department told him will sell?''

''No one will publish my work, and you know it,'' Sean said
in a quiet, disconsolate voice.

''What do you expect!'' Bruce shot back.

''And just what do you mean by that?'' Sean added the poke
that he'd held back earlier.

''You and your dumb numbers, that's what. And your crazy
off-the-wall belief that our lives are no more than a series of odd-
or even-numbered events that we have no control over. And your
truly weird notion that our names and the dates and events in our
lives are a complex web of interlocking numbers. Jesus!''

It was like a switch had been flipped, turning the light out in
Sean's eyes. He and Bruce parted and stood at arm's length in
silence, looking around at nothing in particular, before settling on

the silhouettes of their colleagues moving in and around the heavy oak tables on the other side of Merrywood Garden. Hand-painted Wedgwood, heavy-handled Sheffield, and silver-plated trays covered with tea sandwiches were set out on antique lace tablecloths, tattered and graying with age. The wildflowers on the Wedgwood had worn thin, the china was no longer bone white, and the plated silver refused to give up its tarnished Victorian charm. Endless rows of turquoise napkins, carefully folded one over the other, rippled over the tables like linen waves on oak-stained beaches. A seventh table, holding up a huge cut-crystal punch bowl, three feet wide and holding twenty quarts, stood near the rarely used south-facing entrance to the garden, which was blocked by a rusting wrought-iron gate that opened with a horrible screech to an abandoned path leading to nowhere.

Without warning, Bruce jammed Sean with his hip, forcing him to skip sideways and grab hold of one of the columns to keep from pitching over the railing. "Not bad for a man your age!" Bruce teased, then started walking backward off the portico, trying to pull Sean with him. "Come on, let's go get something to drink, I think we both need it."

Sean shook him off. "No." He patted the air reassuringly. "You go ahead without me; I'm not quite ready for people yet."

"Are you ever ready for people anymore?" Sean shrugged his shoulders and started to turn away. But before he could, Bruce stepped forward and put his arms around him, startling him. "I'm going to miss you. Take care of yourself, Sean. And please, don't be a stranger." Bruce then spun away. He was a half-dozen steps down the path before Sean composed himself and whispered quietly under his breath, "I'm going to miss you, too."

June's Strawberry Moon grew brighter with each unseen step into the night sky. The soft light from its penetrating lunar gaze was staining the delicate greens of the sweet summer grass to flaxen yellow and melting down the bisque whites of the marble statues into the gray of potter's clay. The bronzes had turned into cast iron in the dark. Not even the old brick could escape its touch as moonbeams turned them to rust. Sean wanted more, to touch with his eyes and see with his heart. The night wind suddenly picked up, blowing his jacket open, chilling him with its uninvited breath. His skin drew tight, his eyes started watering from the invisible slap on his face. Straightening, Sean stepped off the portico and started after Bruce, but he suddenly turned and began walking around the perimeter of the garden, close to the wall, whimsically dragging his fingers over the rough surface of the old brick like it was a picket fence, feeling every mortared seam on its jagged face.

A skirted figure, mirroring his every move, caught his eye. He stopped. There was a flash of light, like a shining star, an earring perhaps—a diamond—telling him that she'd turned to look at him before disappearing through the archway up ahead. Curious, he followed, quickening his pace to match hers, which was fast and sure. The muted sound of leather scuffing over stone told him that she was escaping up the hollowed-out sandstone steps notched into the terraced hillside rising to the library. There was silence. Then the slow, painful creaking of a heavy door, and a burst of light, as she slipped into the warm, incandescent belly of the library.

From where Sean stood, she was no more than a shifting silhouette of black velvet. She removed her floppy, wide-brimmed hat. Long hair fell down around her neck and onto her shoulders in curling clusters. A shiny satin ribbon dangling from her hat began swaying to the tune of the wind whistling through the open doorway, coiling and uncoiling, searching for something to wrap itself around. Another woman, short and stocky, approached her with a hand held out. She accepted it, shook it briskly, then pulled her hand back and raised her hat in hooded defense as the massive door sighed shut with a dull clunk.

Intrigued, Sean started up the steps after her. But the familiar voices of his colleagues, loud and boisterous and challenging, offered him a much-needed taste of reality.

Reluctantly, he turned back.

7

Sean sat down on the porch steps and leaned up against the railing, holding the note from Oliver in his hand. It was handwritten on the front of a manila file folder taken from one of the four cartons sitting on the porch, crammed full of Sean's research notes and journals.

Sean—

I tried calling, but learned that your number had been disconnected, so I was not able to make certain you would be home when I came by to return your files. After making copies of everything, including every page from your journals, I put them into folders, in date order, then into these storage boxes just as you suggested. Be careful, they're heavy.

While I'm sorry to have missed you, perhaps it's best, since I have so very many questions to ask you, yet I know that it's too early to start asking you to explain this or that entry. Perhaps when I've read through it all, most of my questions will have been answered. At least I hope so, and I'm sure you do, too.

I do have one small request however; Would you mind terribly preparing a summary for me of all important or milestone events and dates in your life? I would also appreciate knowing your thoughts on a meaning behind the poem.

I probably will not get to see you before leaving for England—yes, I'm going back to continue with my own research there—so please send this schedule to me at the address below.

Oliver

Sean leaned back and slipped the folder into the carton Oliver had left open. "All important or milestone events and dates, you say?" Sean shook his head. "Why don't you just ask me to write a book, for Christ's sake!"

"Sean MacDonald!" Jean Murphy called out. "You watch your language, young man." Sean jumped and turned around. Jean was standing on the porch in front of the entrance to her apartment, which was the entire lower half of her house. Sean hadn't heard her come out, but that wasn't unusual, since he never seemed to hear her until she was already there and had startled him by saying something, like now. "The man who left those cartons said he couldn't wait for you, something about having to meet a young lady, but the way he talked, I wasn't sure. Strange man. Sounded English to me. Dressed that way, too, almost sloppy, but not. He wanted to take them upstairs, but I said he couldn't." Jean stood beaming, her face looking even younger than it already did, obviously pleased with herself.

Sean thought, Young lady?

Jean pointed to the file boxes. "Want some help carrying those upstairs?" She started rolling her sleeves up.

Sean started laughing to himself at the thought of a seventy-year-old woman helping him carry boxes that had to be at least fifty or sixty pounds each up two flights of stairs to the attic. "Sure," he said, rolling his sleeves up, too, masking his embarrassment behind a smile of appreciation.

8

Blocking the entrance to the fields was a galvanized steel chain with a red-and-white DO NOT ENTER sign hanging down in the center, touching the ground. The heavy chain was held up at either end by a pair of square wooden posts set in overflowing puddles of hardened concrete. When he didn't see Cathy anywhere, Sean guessed that he was early and picked a spot along the side of the road, well out of the reach of the sap-dripping trees, then stretched into a lazy yawn, shutting his eyes, listening to the lazy, schook-click, schook-click of the automatic sprinklers watering the fields. The thought of seeing Cathy again began replaying the clip of their first meeting, frame by frame—falling backward, reaching out, shirt popping open, hitting the ground, breathless, bare breasts smothering him, smelling her, tasting her, wanting her—it had become a regular replay for him.

Sean grabbed hold of that precarious edge of sleep he loved so much, floating between light and dark, between hearing and not hearing, knowing and not knowing. It was the only time he could remember his dreams, and not just wake up and feel what they'd done to him, feel the wet and the cold. It was delicious when he got it right. He pulled Cathy with him, spreading his arms, catching a stiff breeze, rising, soaring higher and higher, beyond the clouds, beyond the reach of reality. But the angry growl of a passing tractor yanked him rudely back to earth before he could get away.

Sean looked at his watch. Seven-thirty? This doesn't make any

73

sense, he thought. She has to have been up for hours by now. Sitting up, he looked up and down Molly Lane. There was no sign of her. Squinting his eyes half-shut to block out the glare from the morning sun, he scanned the fields. The only thing he found was the rusting flatbed truck, clear on the other side of the field, casting a long gray shadow from the raking light of the rising sun. Sean shook his head when he saw someone sitting on the bed, leaning against the door-less cab, arms folded, head bowed, as if asleep. "You should get your eyes checked, MacDonald!" he chided himself, and climbed out of his car, feeling dumb at the thought of Cathy having been out there all this time, and him sitting in his car, daydreaming.

Sean stepped sideways over the sagging chain, then hesitated, trying to decide which row he wanted to follow out to the truck. With a decisive nod of his head, he started walking, head bowed, hands slipped into his back pockets, kicking at the ground. The soles of his shoes began collecting clumps of wet dirt, while the hand-sewn uppers of his cordovan loafers were buried under a layer of damp dust that hid the old pennies, each one dated 1943, one heads up, the other heads down. When he stomped and scuffed his feet, the clumps fell off the bottom, and some, but not all, of the dust flew off. But only a few steps later it was all back, prompting him to laugh and turn it into a little-boy's marching game.

Twenty yards from the truck he waved, took a second look, then laughed out loud and skipped into a lazy jog, shaking his head. Hopping up onto the bed of the truck, jumping from the prick of the splintered edges of the rough planks, Sean snatched the crisp sheet of white paper out of the finger-less hand of the straw-stuffed scarecrow, and started reading it through a muffled laugh.

Dear Sean,

If you're reading this note, you've met my stand-in for breakfast—you can call her Kate! But don't get too affectionate, I understand she can be rather prickly when pressed!

74

The Taking

You'll find a thermos of hot coffee and a container of sliced strawberries on the front seat. They should go nicely with the scones you said you were bringing.

The reason I can't be with you now is that we got a call late yesterday afternoon from a caterer in the city, who was looking for 10,000 strawberries for an exclusive private party. When she told me that it was being held in the American Wing at the Met, I thought she was some kook. Then she asked that they be handpicked and sorted so they would all the "exact same size." That's right, 10,000! Over 500 quarts.

Before I could say anything, she requested that someone from the farm personally deliver them. And prepare them, too, but under her supervision. She also asked if we grew mint, since she needed 12,000 mint leaves. And all the same size, of course.

I thought the woman was crazy and half-seriously told her it would cost a dollar a strawberry, plus delivery, and that we'd have to be paid COD. And that the mint would be a nickel a leaf since that had to be sized, too.

To my surprise, she said, "I'll see you at seven AM sharp, tomorrow morning, young lady." She then switched me over to someone in her office to make the business arrangements.

Since I knew that I couldn't reach you by phone at your apartment, I called your number at the college, thinking you might be there, or least somewhere in Merrywood Hall. Who is that woman who answered the phone in your old office? She's was not very nice to me.

When I get back, I'll tell you all about my day in the Big Apple. I expect to be back late tomorrow afternoon or early Thursday morning, depending upon what this woman meant by our helping to prepare the strawberries. I have to be back by then anyway, since the south fields are waiting to be planted with late corn.

I'll make this up to you. Promise.

Cathy

Looking around, Sean found a smooth spot on one of the weathered boards of the truck bed and carefully folded Cathy's note into a sleek paper airplane. He then stood up and turned in a circle, searching for the light breeze that was swirling over the field. Finding it, feeling it push against his face, he tossed the paper plane into the air as he leapt off the truck, tripping and stumbling after his makeshift glider, his arms outstretched, his hands open, waiting to snatch it back. But a surly gust of wind caught it and took it tumbling with it, higher and higher. Watching it, wishing he could go, too, Sean gave up with a parting wave of his hand and started back to his waiting car, wondering what to do with the day—and the bag of scones in his car.

The double doors of the main entrance to Merrywood Hall were propped wide open. The bronze lions lying on either side of the steps appeared to be sleeping in the hazy heat of the day. The large brass hinges strapping the oak planks of the doors together looked soft to the touch. Sean found himself sniffing for the familiar smells of paste wax and pine cleaner and stale smoke from hidden cigarettes as he moved down the main corridor. The only sounds cutting through the cloistered quiet of the marble hallway were the whirling fans in some of the offices.

He started with Sarah Potter's office, probably out of respect. It was empty and dark and smelled of licorice, real licorice, which she kept in a Waterford crystal dish on her conference table, something Bruce Fanning was addicted to, but would never tell Sarah. Although she was gone, Sean knew that she wouldn't be for long. And she wasn't very far away, not Sarah Potter. Frank Stearns's office was next. Frank was Professor of European History. He was German, born and raised there, and he was shaped like a bass fiddle, a very tall one, with a deep, plunky voice to match. His office was neat as a pin, just as he was. Nothing was left out, everything was locked up tight. If he had a place to put it, Frank probably would have locked his blotter up, too. As it was, he taped it down to his desk. Frank's office smelled like him, too, a little sour, because he never used deodorant. Around the corner, and down the hall, in the opposite direction from his old office, Sean slipped into Ruth Stein's overstuffed office. Ruth was Professor of Philosophy. She was also Frank Stearns's lover, but no one was supposed to know that. Everyone did, of course; they just acted like they didn't. Ruthie, which is what Sean called her—but no one else could—had been at Hart College two years longer than both Sean and Bruce, and five more than Frank Stearns. Open and shut books were lying about everywhere, even on the floor. Papers were scattered over the top of her desk, making it look like a wind had just blown through. Some had fallen off onto the floor and were curling up from her heavy handwriting. The lamp on the desk was still on. Sean whispered, "And who turns your light off for you now, Ruthie?" and switched the lamp off.

He tiptoed past Carol Mathews's office without even looking in, which is exactly what he'd done every day for the last five years, ever since Carol had joined the faculty. Carol had been a visiting lecturer from Berkeley who made her stay on the East Coast permanent by getting appointed Associate Professor of Sociology. Carol Mathews was quiet and rarely spoke whenever the faculty got together, which was a perplexing contrast to her athletic six-foot-two height. She also kept to herself, saving her energy for the lecture hall, and her students. She was known to become animated with enthusiastic, almost evangelical dissertations on the plight of women in twentieth-century America at the ruthless hand of men.

Sean paused and knocked softly on Zoe Bernstein's closed door, hoping, but not expecting her to be inside. There was no answer. Zoe was Professor of Anthropology, and as much as she tried not to, she was the spitting image of Margaret Mead, right down to her wire-rimmed glasses, loose-fitting, calf-length dresses, and laced oxfords. But Zoe was trimmer at the waist, and larger breasted. Higher and firmer, too, unlike Margaret's more matronly appearance, even when she was young. Zoe was also very sexual, but in an intellectual sort of way. She possessed an appetite for men, of any age, but not too old, swallowing them up when she wanted one, then spitting them out when she was done and moving on without bothering, or caring, to look back.

With a disappointed sigh, blinking Zoe's beautiful breasts away, Sean ran up the stairs at the end of the corridor to the second floor. Racing down the hallway, he slid to a stop in front of Bruce Fanning's office. "Shit!" He sighed out loud and looked around, startled at the sound of his own voice. He then took a poke at the padlock Bruce always put on his door when he went out of town. "I bet you're wandering through the galleries in Manhattan right now, hoping to find the owners on vacation, and some unsuspecting, nubile young assistant left in charge." Sean slapped the lock again, smiling proudly when it stuck upside-down.

Turning away, he walked to the opposite end of the hall and hesitated, toying with the thought of going up to the third floor to see if Susan Grace was in her studio. Susan was Professor of Fine Arts, and a highly successful painter. Her frail face, waiflike frame, and birdlike hands were so unlike her, and the young children she was famous for painting in traditional, late-nineteenth-century manner. Words had long ago become unnecessary for Sean and Susan, but more so for her than him. It was as if she could read his thoughts, much the same way she read a blank canvas and knew what it wanted her to paint over its white linen face. There was something in her soft blue-gray eyes that said "Hold me," while her reedlike body whispered "But not too hard." There had been times when he almost did—he even found himself reaching out for her, but had always caught himself and quickly left her studio without saying another word. Sean was convinced Susan knew why he left, because she would tell him so with a smile and twinkle of her eye when they next saw one another in the halls on their way to somewhere, or something, something that kept them from stopping and talking.

Sean bolted downstairs, chasing after the invisible echoes bouncing off the walls ahead of him. The sight of sunlight falling out of Oliver's doorway made him smile as he shuffled his way down the hall and peeked in. The walls were covered with books, floor to ceiling and corner to corner, old books and fat books, and books with cracked and peeling backs. Small brass lamps were set out like flowerpots on a pair of tiny end tables, the credenza, and the massive rolltop desk—anything that was wood was old and rubbed smooth. The fabric covering the lone wing chair, buried under a two-week-old Sunday edition of the London *Times*, was worn through on the arms. The oblong crocheted antimacassars on each of the armrests, and the large oval one behind his head, were stained dark with oil and sweat. And the smell of stale tea hung in the air.

Disappointed that Oliver wasn't there, Sean turned to leave. But then he spied a thin blade of light knifing into the hall, offering a sliver of hope that the door to his old office was open. He walked on the soles of his shoes, making barely a sound, and came to a stop facing the door, holding his breath, listening. A shiver come over him, but he chased it away with a brisk rub of his arms and reached out, easing the door open.

The sofa, his sofa, the oversized Victorian leather sofa, its skin dried and cracked, was piled high with books, squashing the fragile leather cushions flat, making him want to throw the books on the floor that very instant. There was spindly old furniture perched all around the room, looking frail against the powerful stone walls. Stepping inside, he stopped beside a quarter-round table tucked into the corner behind the door and ran his fingers over the dark, wavy surface.

There were paintings everywhere. Some were on the floor, leaning against the walls, waiting to be hung. One caught his eye, in the corner, where his tapestry once stood. Walking over, he picked it up and took it to the window. The overcast sky was soft and blond, with rouge brushed across the horizon and bleeding up into the clouds. A hundred shades of brown and green and yellow had been scumbled over the canvas, creating the illusion of fields, trees, a stone wall, and soft rolling hills covered with hay, waiting to be harvested. There was a solitary figure, a woman, gathering twigs. Off in the distance was a river, wet, moving, and alive.

Sean turned to the others, enjoying them. Over the desk was a painting filled with the serenity of early morning, a soft, diffused light radiating from inside and far away. It was a harbor scene, with sailing ships asleep at anchor, and one solitary vessel underway, sailing, drifting into the morning mist as if manned by a ghostly crew. He closed his eyes, trying to imagine the cool ocean breezes spilling out into the stale heat of the office.

Hung on the wall between the windows and the new pink and white drapes, which were soft and sheer, looking fragile against the rough-cut stone, was a clear, never-ending winter scene. Sean could feel the cold and the wind on his eyes as he moved closer. "That's mine!" he squeaked, and snatched up the small bronze sculpture sitting on the stone sill. It was no more than five inches tall, depicting a fox, a spindly-legged stork, and a raven gathered around an empty well, eyeing a tiny cluster of grapes hanging from a vine wrapped around a dying tree. The inside of the well was threaded like the socket of a lamp to take a glass reservoir that was no longer there.

"Recognize it?" The sound of another voice startled Sean into almost dropping the inkwell. He spun around, clutching the small bronze to his chest. She was standing in the doorway, her arms folded, leaning against the jamb, smiling, but not really. She was taller than he remembered. He couldn't help staring, which only made her face glow that much brighter when she found the light in his eyes, fanning the fire in hers. Her white silk dress pressed against her taut body, revealing that she'd added a few pounds, which looked good on her, very good. Her body was still soft and cool on his eyes, making him feel just the opposite. She stepped into the office, into the breeze suddenly pushing its way through the open windows. Sean smiled to himself at seeing the strands of tarnished silver hidden inside her raven-black hair, freed by the gentle breeze to play with the diamond-bright sparkle in her blue eyes.

"You left it at my apartment, remember?" She stopped no more than a foot from him, waiting, then placed her hand on his arm ever so gently. "I'm sorry," she said in a soothing voice that matched her touch. "I didn't mean to frighten you."

Sean could feel the heat of her body pushing him back. "I shouldn't have let myself in," he said nervously, looking around, avoiding her gaze. "Especially with everything that's here." He continued surveying the room while working the bronze with his hands, trying his best not to look at her.

Patricia Jennings didn't move her hand, even after Sean glanced down at it. "I hope you'll always consider this your office, too," she said with a possessive curl to her words. "As for the things that are here, they're some of my favorites." She smiled, knowing that she'd answered the question on his face, the one wanting to know how long she'd been watching him. "But most of my paintings are too big for this little office."

"Little?" Sean let slip out.

Patricia patted his wrist affectionately. "You know what I meant." She tried brushing the side of his face with her long fingers.

Sean slipped her touch, not knowing why. Then he did, and remembered hearing her say to him, six years ago, "They're not wrinkles, Dr. MacDonald. They make your eyes smile when you won't." She had reached out, cupping his face in her hands. He hadn't rejected her touch that evening, as she began toying with the lines around his temples, smoothing away time with the tips of her fingers, pushing his eyes shut. He felt the strength in her hands and didn't want her to stop, ever. He had smiled when a rich bouquet of fragrances evaporated into his senses from her warm, moist palms, pulling him deeper and deeper into her touch. Inhaling, he had invaded her secrets and instantly wanted to taste where he knew her hands had been. "Sean! You're blushing!" he remembered her saying. His face had betrayed him. He jerked his head back, wincing at the pinprick tugs on his face when her nails scratched through his beard. He immediately drew the protective curtain of teacher down over himself and walked away to join his colleagues without saying anything more. She left, too, walking through the garden, ducking under the archway, then up the three flights of sandstone steps. Her stride was slow, purposeful, and determined. It didn't look like she was running away from what had just happened, but more like she simply had somewhere else to go. She returned an hour later, just before dark, having changed into a casual, ankle-length dress. It was white, and cotton soft, with nothing between it and her dark olive skin.

Her coal-black hair was untied and slithering down her back, curling up at her waist. She'd showered, leaving only the sweet smell of her damp body for him to find this time. He would never forget that night, nor the others that followed.

"Have you been avoiding me?" Patricia Jennings asked, walking to the chair in front of her desk and sitting down. Sean waited, watching her, then followed when she gestured for him to have a seat. He found a space on the sofa, which he widened by moving books to either side, all the while suppressing the urge to throw them off of the aging cushions.

"Avoiding you?" Sean repeated. "No, of course not," he lied, and watched Patricia frown discreetly. "Perhaps," he recanted, which turned her frown into a smile.

"Sean?" she asked, folding her hands together and letting them settle into her lap. "Can't you ever forgive me?" Patricia laced her fingers together, squeezing them into a knot.

Sean replied cautiously, "I think I can," then wondered if he really believed what he'd said. Patricia eased back into the overstuffed armchair, letting it wrap itself around her, testing Sean with her eyes. "I was frightened," he said, the hint of a frail edge attached to his words. "No, terrified would be more accurate. And afterward, I was mad as hell at you." He looked away. "Let's just put it all in the past, shall we?" Sean could hear the faint sound of air being drawn over Patricia's delicious lips. Looking into her eyes, not thinking what he was saying, he told her, "I wish that it never—" Sean froze into silence. But it was evident from the look in Patricia's eyes, eyes that were never closed to him, that nothing more needed to be said.

In the quiet of the office, they began talking, first about nothing, then slowly, cautiously, about old things—and old feelings. Feelings that were still tender for the both of them, even after five years, and the end of their brief affair, which had taken place the year Patricia had returned to complete her degree. She had returned after having been away for twelve years following her unexplained departure during the winter of her senior year. When she came back she was no longer the shy young girl Sean had remembered, but a self-confident and recently divorced woman, a woman determined to resurrect the feelings she believed Sean had for her years earlier but had hidden behind a new marriage, and the recently acquired mask of academic reserve. The reserve, however, proved to be anything but the case during that sensuous, tension filled semester in the spring of 1986, when their passion, his passion, and his unsatisfied needs, erupted following Patricia's return to the graduation reception being held in Merrywood Garden.

But their affair had cooled just as suddenly a month later, on a hot and sultry night in June. However, for Patricia Jennings it never really ended, convinced as she was that Sean still wanted her, in spite of what she had done. It was only this past winter that her letters finally stopped, letters that read like entries from a personal diary as she recounted her life to him without inhibition, in page after page of intimate, handwritten vignettes that left nothing to the imagination. Patricia had been determined not to let Sean forget her, not that he ever would, or could. If nothing else, the scars on his side, thick enough to feel through his clothes, were a sobering reminder.

Sean had read her letters with the same visceral hunger that had originally drawn him to her, like a moth attracted to the flickering flame of a candle, circling ever closer, unaware of its deadly touch. Bruce Fanning was the only one who knew of the letters and something of the reason behind the sudden end of their affair. But he only knew what Sean had chosen to tell him. Bruce never once asked Sean about the letters he saw on his desk, week after week, open and set out carefully, as if the words on the scented pages were expensive chocolates to be eaten, slowly.

Patricia stood up. "Care to have dinner with me this evening?" she asked, smoothing her dress with her hands.

There was no question in Sean's mind what he wanted, right that second, but dinner would have to do. "I'd love to," he said casually.

Patricia offered Sean her hand. He took it, but she didn't move when he stood up, forcing him to press into her to keep from falling backward. He hesitated for a split second. She did, too. He then put his arms around her. She held her breath. Sean buried his face in her hair. She kissed his neck, tenderly, like she wasn't even hungry. He felt her eyelashes sweeping over his skin, long and soft, then wet. Turning her to face him, Sean kissed away her tears, caressed her lips with his, feeling her mouth relax, then open wide with a suddenness that aroused him even more. This shouldn't be, he told himself. Patricia kissed him again. His hips found hers. She wasn't cold anymore, and he wasn't soft. *No! You can't do this,* he told himself, but knew he could, and would, if he didn't leave. He tried, but she held fast, without even touching him. He fell into her, wanting to be held, needing it more than he could bear. Patricia's arms slipped around him, pulling him closer. Sean fingered the back of her blouse, scratching gently, pulling it out of her skirt, then slipping his hands down inside, filling them with her warm flesh. She dropped her head, teasing his neck with her lips and hot tongue and bringing him to her with a pounding he knew she could feel through their unwanted clothing.

"Anyone still in the building?" a man called out. Patricia stiffened. Sean withdrew. She tucked her blouse into her skirt and buttoned it up, all in one graceful move. The footsteps came closer. Smiling, nodding, Sean and Patricia turned away and paced off the proper distance between them. "Well, hello, Dr. Jennings. Still moving in?"

Sean turned and stepped forward, finally able to. "Hello, Andy," he said with a lazy wave of his hand.

"Oh! That's you, Dr. MacDonald. Good to see you, sir." Andy drew back and stood just outside the doorway. "Miss your old office?"

"I suppose."

"We miss you, too. Especially Dean Potter. You're all she talks about." Andy sensed he shouldn't be there. "Well." His eyes were searching for something to land on, other than Sean or Patricia. "The front door will be locked in ten minutes, so unless you two want to spend the night here, you better be on your way." Andy turned and walked down the hall, chuckling to himself over the thump of closing doors and jangling keys.

Patricia pulled the stained-glass windows shut and latched them with a soft slap of her open hand. Sean watched as she walked around the office—her office now, not his—as if mentally taking inventory. Slipping her key in the door, Patricia looked back at him. "Dinner?" she offered again, and smiled when he scurried past her out into the hall. He watched her lock the door. He felt uneasy, and wondered why. "Well," Patricia asked, striding briskly down the corridor, "coming?"

Sean caught up and playfully kissed Patricia's ear, then wondered if he should have when she thread her arm around his waist and pulled him to her. "Just dinner, right?" he asked.

Patricia Jennings's custom-built contemporary house was covered with a rough-sawn mahogany skin, trimmed with clear redwood, and surrounded by decks. There was even a deck on the second floor outside the master bedroom, which faced west. The house sat on a bluff above the river across from Kingston Bay, and a few miles north of the centuries-old riverfront community of Rhinecliff. It was a twenty-minute drive due south from Hart College, on River Road, along the rising escarpment bordering the eastern shore of the Hudson. The view, looking west into the foothills of the Catskills and beyond, was unobstructed.

The interior was simple, yet elegant. There were four rooms, three down and one up, occupying three thousand square feet. Upstairs and downstairs were joined by a sweeping circular stairway, rising from the living room to the balcony of the master bedroom on the second floor. The eighteen-foot-high cathedral ceilings were unstained walnut. There was an open and airy California-style kitchen, which opened onto a deck that ran the width of the house, matching the second-floor deck above. During the day, the butcher-block countertops were flooded with sunlight pouring down through the overhead skylights. At night, hidden lights warmed the room. The living room, its massive fieldstone fireplace rising up to find its slightly smaller mate in the master bedroom above, stood between the kitchen and the study, which was the only room without windows. And paintings filled every square inch of the walls, except for the west-facing wall, which was solid glass, floor to ceiling, upstairs and down, from one end of the house to the other. Everything—the towering wall of glass, the antique mission furniture, the stone fireplace, the out-of-reach ceilings, and the breathtaking paintings in their gilded period frames—was oversized. Yet it was perfectly balanced, perhaps because everything inside was in keeping with everything outside, such as the mammoth trees girdling the house and reaching to the sky, as if trying to snuff out the sun. Or the fingers of recently exposed granite, yet to be weathered smooth. Or perhaps it was Patricia Jennings, tall, statuesque, and elegant, who drew everything into perspective as she walked up the slow, curving stairway, a glass of champagne in her hand, her eyes fixed on Sean, who was a few steps ahead of her, draining the last few drops of amber from his long-stemmed crystal goblet.

9

Wednesday, June 26, 1991

There were no cars lined up along the side of Molly Lane, and the fields were almost empty, save for a handful of straw hats bobbing up and down under the watchful eye of the sun. Pulling off the road, Sean eased up to the gatehouse, slipped into neutral, and sat back, waiting for Sally Curtis to finish with another customer on the other side of the gate house. Sally was patient and pleasant, as were all of the women, young and old, working for Cathy on the "customer side" of the business, as she called it. Sally's light brown hair was dry and powdery, like corn silk. She was hard-working thin, with long wiry arms that moved with a slow, mechanical grace, unwinding, lowering her hand, snapping her fingers shut, plucking money from outstretched hands, then depositing change into their palms, while nodding and saying "Thank you, come again."

"Hi, Dr. MacDonald!" Sally added a perky wink of her eye, wrinkling her face when she did, confirming Sean's belief that she was older than she looked at a distance. "Cathy's not back from the city yet. When she called early this morning, and I mean early, she told me that the reception at the museum ran well past midnight and that she was staying with someone named Martha MacGregor, the woman who catered the party. She's the one who ordered the truckload of strawberries we all worked through the night picking and sorting. Cathy said she didn't expect to be back until early tomorrow morning, since she and this Martha person are going to another reception, but as guests. Some rich art dealer, I think she said his name was Jensen or Janson, is having an opening at his gallery on Madison Avenue. She left a number for you to call in case you wanted to drive into the city and join her." Sally added another wink, this time revealing the weathered face of a farm hand. "I wrote the number on a piece of paper towel, since I was in the kitchen making coffee when she called." Sally pulled a folded-over paper towel out of her jeans and handed it to Sean. "I couldn't find a pencil either, so I wrote the number with a piece of burned toast." Her smile spilled over into an embarrassed giggle. "I hope you can read it." Resting her arms on the planking that served double duty as a counter and a windowsill, Sally leaned out and peered down into Sean's lap as he carefully unfolded the crumpled-up paper towel, only to find charcoal smudges that no longer resembled anything close to numbers.

Sean shook out the blackened crumbs and handed the useless note back to Sally. They smiled at each other, but for different reasons. Without saying anything more, Sean pulled away slowly, heeding the warnings of DRY FIELDS, BLOWING DUST, and DRIVE SLOW hastily nailed to stakes that had been hammered into the hard ground until the tops of their wooden heads had been splintered open. He kept it in second gear, groaning along and rocking back and forth between first and reverse whenever he dropped down into one of the rock-hard ruts.

Donald Beman

Halfway out into the open strawberry fields, Sean spied two oddly dressed old women on bicycles, riding side by side and approaching head on and showing no sign of yielding one inch of the narrow dirt road bordering the side of the field. The dust hanging in air scattered the late-afternoon sunlight into a veil of sepia brown, creating the illusion that they were peddling out of the past. Each of them was wearing a long white linen dress, dusty and dirty from the hem up to the knees, with leather sandals strapped to their bare feet. Floppy straw hats were tied to their heads with thin strands of finger-soiled lace, snugged under their chins with carefully tied bows, keeping their snow-white hair from falling out and melting in the hot sun. They were sitting upright, perfectly straight, their arms outstretched and their bony fingers locked around the fat rubber grips of the wide handlebars. Sean smiled when he saw the old balloon tires, fat and round and soft. Hanging from the handlebars of each bicycle was a deep wire basket, one stacked with four quarts of strawberries, the other stuffed with plastic bags crammed full of snap peas. Not knowing whether to turn right or left, he stopped and waited, trying to stare them down with a playful frown. With a synchronized twist of their shiny chrome handlebars, the women parted, passing one on either side of him. One kept her eyes fixed straight ahead. The other, the one on his side, turned and smiled, and for an instant she was a generation younger than her equally mischievous twin.

Sean resisted the temptation to look back and see if they were real, and started moving from one planted section to the next until he reached the very last one, at the farthest end of the field, easily a quarter-mile from Molly Lane. He turned right, into the wind, and shut his eyes against the sudden burst of blowing dust, but he didn't stop. When he opened them, he saw a small white car up ahead, parked nose in and well off the road separating the strawberry fields on his right from a meadow blanketed with soon-to-be hay on his left. Squinting through the dust-covered windshield, Sean turned left and rolled to a stop beside the brand-new Dodge Shadow. Eyeing the dings on the door, he backed up and pulled in again, giving himself more room.

After snapping the tonneau in place, Sean slapped it smartly and stepped back, listening to the whupping of the leather. The wind abruptly changed again, painting his car with dust, turning the leather brown. Sean felt himself getting angry, but caught it and laughed it off as he turned and crossed the dirt road into the field, stepping from one tractor rut to the next.

Shit!''—he started back to his car—''you forgot baskets, Mac-Donald!''

A woman's voice, deep and sure, called his self-imposed retreat to a halt. ''I've got a few extras. Would you like them?'' Sean spun around in the dirt, kicking up a small cloud of dust. ''Here,'' she offered, and stood up, startling him. She slipped the large straw hat off her head, letting her cinnabar red hair, the color of an ancient Chinese vase, fall down onto her sun tanned neck and shoulders. She was barefoot, which looked curiously out of place with her white silk blouse and straight, navy blue skirt, which was decorated with dusty brown fingerprints. Her skin, damp with summer sweat, had dissolved her sheer blouse, allowing the lace pattern of her bra to etch itself into the transparent fabric. Her face was untouched by time, except for a few delicate lines, shooting back from her liquid green eyes. In one breath she looked years younger than Sean, then older, much older, if that was possible, leaving him sure of only one thing—his sudden, and uncontrollable attraction to her.

Sean pointed to her bare feet. ''That's a great idea,'' he said, then instantly covered her body with his eyes when she glanced down.

''It feels good,'' she said with a girlish lilt to her words, erasing the voice he'd heard only a minute ago. ''Why don't you take yours off, too. It's nice and cool just below the surface.'' Sean accepted her dare, kicking his loafers off and burying his feet beneath the dusty soil. He then snatched his shoes up and tossed them, underhanded and without looking, back to his car. Her eyes widened. ''You're lucky,'' she said, shaking her head, which served to unravel more of her hair. ''They could have put quite a dent in the thin skin of that little Healy of yours.''

Sean leaned back ever so slightly. ''How do you know what it is?'' he asked, his voice cracking from having spoken before clearing his throat, making him feel silly. "Not many—"

She raised her hand. "Let me guess," she said. "Not many women know about cars." Her line sounded rehearsed. She stuck her hands on her hips, as if challenging him. His eyes followed her moves. He liked what he saw.

"Well, they don't," Sean said in his own defense. "At least not when it comes to classic sports cars like this one."

"California women do." Her defiant announcement invited him to look even closer. He did. She smiled and gestured over his shoulder behind him. "It's a 1960, isn't it?" She really wasn't asking him to answer her. "It sounds like you keep it tuned perfectly. And it's almost original." She refocused her point. "Except for that right front wing, which looks like it was replaced in the last few years." Sean was fighting back a smile. "Is the leather Connolly," she asked, "or just a domestic cowhide?"

Sean threw his hands up in the air. "OK." He'd lost his battle with his smile. "You proved your point." He stepped closer. "I suppose now you want a ride in it, right?"

"Wrong again," she replied, looking at him, then through him. "I want to drive it." She opened her hands and held them out like she was making a peace offering. "But with you in it, of course." This was said in a patronizing tone of voice.

That's all Sean needed to hear. "There's no need to have me along," he said with a nonchalant toss of his head and hands. He then gestured, first to her, then back to his car. "I'm sure a California girl can handle it." Her smirk told him she didn't appreciate his sarcasm, but she didn't say anything. She just watched him, and waited. "But before I give my car to a stranger, shouldn't I know who it is that wants to drive it?"

Slapping her hands on her full hips to get the field dust off, adding a few handprints to the collage on her skirt, she marched straight up to him. "I'm Karen." She offered him her hand. He could feel experience in her grip, and much more. He held onto her hand, waiting for her to tell him the rest of her name. But it was evident that "Karen" was all she thought he needed to know. Sean withdrew the ignition key from the coin pocket of his jeans and held it out to her. To his surprise, which he knew had to show, she plucked the key out of his hand, and turned sideways to step around him and not bump into him on her way to the car.

What are you doing? he thought. You've never let anyone drive it, not even Fanning! Now you're letting a complete stranger—a woman—take it out! And you don't even know her name. Have you lost it, MacDonald?

As if reading his thoughts, Karen called back over her shoulder, "Are you sure you don't want to come?" But she didn't skip a beat in her determined advance to his pride and joy.

Sean tried discarding his fears. "No, you have fun," he said, trying to mask his anxiety with a casual, almost flippant indifference. But it sounded more like bravado, and he knew that she knew it by the way she tipped her head to one side and slowed her pace ever so slightly, giving him one last chance to change his mind. But he was damned if he was going to.

Karen unsnapped the tonneau, but only for the driver's seat, taking special care to pinch the grommets between her thumb and fingers so that she didn't have to use two hands. Watching her, Sean thought, You do know what you're doing, don't you. She then carefully folded the tonneau behind the seat, just the way it should be done, the way Sean did it, before getting in. She started the engine without so much as a flutter, as if it were her own. Backing around, she slipped it into first, waved without looking, and was on her way. Sean stuck his hands into his pockets and watched her drive slowly, yet confidently, around the field, turn right onto Molly Lane, then disappear behind the row of forsythia bushes bordering the road. He held his breath, listening. She was smooth and quick, taking the car through the gears without incident as the exhaust rose to a throaty growl, then faded into the distance like an old mahogany speedboat, skimming across a glassy lake on a lazy summer afternoon.

With an anxious sigh, Sean sat down and rolled back onto the ground, folding his arms over his face to block out the sun. "You've got to be out of your fucking mind, MacDonald!" When he tried worrying, Sean found that he wasn't worried after all. Somehow, he felt comfortable with this woman, whoever she was, and let his thoughts drift back to early this morning.

Donald Beman

There had been a note for him on the counter in Patricia's kitchen, lying beside a freshly brewed, untouched pot of coffee. The words that Patricia had left for him were those she had been unable to say in the dark. He had to read them more than once to know why, perhaps because there were two different women talking, and the handwriting changed from thought to thought, as feelings turned dark then light, cold then warm, shifting without warning between yesterday and tomorrow, between apologies and promises.

Sean could feel Patricia's hurt becoming his, and he didn't want it to be that way, especially not now. Grabbing hold of the familiar long-ago smells swirling in the air, he pushed Patricia Jennings out of his head and pulled the distant memories down over him like an old blanket, letting the lazy afternoon sun warm him to sleep. Not his half-sleep, real sleep, deep, but not silent.

. . . That's funny. All of the lights in the house are out. I guess she's gone to bed. No problem, I'll see her in the morning. After Mass. And tell her then why I didn't go to the retreat this weekend. I'll just tell her the truth, even though she makes it so damn hard to. Let's see, front or back door? Back, it's never locked. Besides, the back porch doesn't make a racket like the front porch does. Except for two of the steps.

Jesus! I can't believe these stars. Especially that bright one, just above the horizon. It's like a flashlight shining in my eyes. I never noticed how bright some of them get. I can even see my shadow on the lawn! Now, don't forget, the first step groans like hell. The middle three don't make a sound. And the top one creaks and moans like a bitch, but only if you put your foot in the center. And don't grab the railing,'cause when it's been hot during the day, then cools down real fast like it does in June, the old dried wood hee-haws like a dumb-assed donkey.

There. Not a peep. Now, let's hope she didn't lock the kitchen door. Boy! I can't believe how bright it is without a moon. I can see my reflection in the glass, clear as day. Hey! Look at the light in the kitchen. Say, where's the table? Wait! what's that? Who's there? I can't see with this damn reflection in the glass. Oh, Christ! No! . . .

Using the fleshy part of her palm, Karen muffled the sharp snap of the grommets as she secured the tonneau, all the while keeping one eye on Sean, who was lying on the ground, his arms over his face, sound asleep. She picked her steps carefully, trying not to wake him as she walked over and knelt down and started tickling his bare feet. He didn't budge. She ran the tip of the ignition key up and down his arch. His leg jerked, then flopped back down onto the ground. "You must really be enjoying that dream!" She dropped the key into the dirt and scratched the soles of his feet with her fingernails. That did it. Sean threw his arms open and raised his head, looking down at his feet with an angry scowl. But his face softened when he saw Karen smiling back at him. "You're soaking wet!" she said, reaching out, plucking at his shirt. "Was she good?"

Sean propped himself up onto his elbows. "How long have you been gone?"

"A little over an hour." Karen motioned behind her. "Your baby now has a full tank of gas, and I topped up the oil." Karen stood up and waited patiently for Sean's eyes to work their way up her body to her own.

"You've got grease stains on your blouse," Sean noted, squinting through the glare of the setting sun peeking around and over her shoulder. Karen declined to look; she just stood there, smiling. Sean felt awkward. "I take it that *Karen* liked my little Healy?"

"She loved it!" Karen said, rocking back onto her heels.

Sean climbed to his feet and started dusting himself off. Karen stepped forward, picking up the car key and tucking it into Sean's back pocket. She began wiping off the dirt covering his back. Sean unbuttoned his shirt and leaned over, shaking the dust out. He straightened up and unbuckled his pants. "Oops!" he said with a chuckle, "I wasn't thinking. Sorry."

Sean couldn't see the amused smile on Karen's face; he could only feel her fingers gently brushing the dust off his back, which, in spots, had caked into half-dry mud from the heavy sweat that had bled through his shirt. "Are you all right?" Karen asked, pressing her hand on his neck, holding it there.

"Yes, why do you ask?"

"Because you're soaking wet, like you're fighting a fever. Or wrestling with a nightmare!" she teased. "What were you dreaming about?"

Sean arched away from her touch. "I have no idea," he said brusquely. "I don't remember what I dream."

Hurt by his sudden move, Karen clapped the dirt off her hands. "Really? Has that always been?"

"No, it started—" Sean suddenly found himself at a loss for words. He began buttoning his shirt closed, looking down as if he was searching for something on the ground. Karen looked down, too as she stepped away and bent over, stiff-legged, to pick up the empty plastic baskets. Her skirt tightened around her hips and thighs, forcing the seams of her bikini panties to welt up through the summer-weight fabric of the dark blue skirt. Sean followed the converging lines, but before his imagination could take the delicious image any further, Karen knelt down, stealing herself back from him, and began picking strawberries. Moving beside her, Sean took one of the baskets and began to mirror her movements. But he quickly found himself watching her more than picking strawberries himself. Nothing was said as they moved down the long row, going from plant to plant. With a sudden jerk of her body, Karen pulled her skirt above her knees and folded up the hem to keep from kneeling on it. But it quickly slid back down again. Getting up, she walked to her car and reached into the back seat, pulled out what looked like a pair of jeans, and hopped into the front seat. Sean suddenly realized what she was doing, and it aroused him instantly. She was quick, leaning back, bracing herself, rising up, pausing for a second, then dropping down and tipping forward out of sight. Then she was up again, arching over the seat back, hesitating, then climbing out of the car, her blouse hanging out over her jeans. Turning away, she eased her jeans down, exposing a patch of shiny black silk for a fraction of a second before tucking her shirttails in and standing on her tiptoes, then wiggling her hips the way women do.

Turning around and walking back, Karen mused, as if talking to herself, not Sean, "You know, I've always thought that men should be the ones wearing skirts, not women. It makes so much more sense. Don't you agree, Dr. MacDonald?"

The sound of his name made Sean blink and sit back on his heels. "I beg your pardon?"

Seeing his startled expression, Karen asked, "Did I say something wrong?"

Sean was unable to shake off the look he felt carving itself into his face. "You know who I am?"

"Of course," Karen replied offhandedly. Sean's expression was infecting his whole body. "But I'm being unfair," she said, as if trying to console him. "What do you want to know?" Karen tossed her head back, untying the remaining knots in her red hair with a shake of her head, sending it tumbling down her back.

"You can start by telling me how you know who I am," Sean said, refusing to heed a voice somewhere in the distance telling him to leave, now. "I think that's only fair."

Karen stepped back, squaring herself to him. "My daughters attended Hart College," she said firmly. "Years ago, mind you. They often wrote about you in their letters. They also—"

"Who are they?" Sean asked bluntly, cutting Karen off.

Karen looked hurt. "They also spoke of you whenever I saw them, which is ironic when you think about it, since neither one of them knew the other was—"

"You're not answering my question," Sean snapped with an angry sweep of his hand, as if trying to knock Karen's words out of the way.

Karen measured Sean more closely than before, and her words were forced. "I was on campus last week, Saturday, during Sarah Potter's annual party for the faculty. I'd been in New York on business for one of my clients the day before, and when the contracts couldn't be ready until Monday, I took a train out of the city and spent the weekend up here."

Sean wasn't going to give her one inch of slack. "You *still* didn't answer my question," he said, locking onto Karen's evasive gaze, reeling her in with the slowly repeated words, "Now, how did you know who I am?"

Karen drew her hands out of sight behind her back. Her blouse tightened around her breasts. Sean wanted to look, but he couldn't, not now. "I asked Dean Potter to point you out to me," she said casually, almost indifferently. "Sarah and I go back a long way, long before she joined Hart College. But you left before I could speak with you. Are you satisfied now?" Karen asked, turning and walking away.

Wishing that he hadn't been so harsh—so stupid—Sean jumped up and followed her. Karen abruptly knelt down and began picking strawberries again, this time without speaking or looking at him. The silence was deafening. Sean tried to get her to talk to him, but she wouldn't answer. When she did finally say something, it was in fractured sentences, the way kids talk. Sometimes only a single word was passed back and forth, and they only talked about places and things, not people, and not about themselves or each other. Karen's eyes slowly, cautiously turned from ice to water, and her lips softened around her words. Little by little, she revealed more and more about herself, far more than Sean dared tell of himself. But the warm smile in his deep-set hazel eyes must have said everything Karen needed to hear, since she grew steadily more comfortable with him. It took them an hour to fill their baskets, or maybe they just made it take that long. Sean was aware of feeling younger and younger as they spoke, which slowed his answers, but not his questions.

When Karen bent down close to the ground, Sean followed, stopping inches from her and easing his face close to her hair, breathing in quietly, secretly, filling his lungs, his head, and playing with the warm, sweet fragrances drifting up from her body, trying to sort them out before getting caught. "You smell the apples from my shampoo." Karen laughed. "And me, of course, from this wonderfully delicious heat." Lifting her head slowly, testing to see where Sean's face was, she sat up straight. She was wet with sweat. Her silky blouse had melted the rest of the way into her bra, pulling her nipples to the surface. She tugged at the fabric but gave up when it wouldn't release its sticky hold, letting it fall back onto her, into her.

"It's different," Sean said with an upbeat snap to his words. "I like it. But I like the smell of you better. You smell like your red hair and green eyes and brown skin." His gaze reluctantly left the swell of her body to look at her face.

Karen's eyes were waiting for him. "And just what does that mean?" she asked, returning her hands to her broad hips.

Karen's question caught Sean off guard, and for the second time that afternoon, he didn't know what to say as he stumbled with an explanation. "It's fresh, alive, sensuous." He glanced around nervously, gesturing to the strawberries. Karen started to follow the movement of his hand, but snapped back as if there was a trick to what he was doing. "And timeless for a woman—"

Karen cut in. "For a woman my age?" she asked, reaching her hand into the top of Sean's open shirt. "Do these gray hairs of yours go all the way down?" Karen let her finger chase after her question, causing Sean's embarrassment to deepen. "And just how old do you think I am?"

Sean replied instantly. "Mid-thirties, but I'm older."

Karen tossed her head back, distracting Sean with the sensuous flair of her hair. "And what if I'm older than you, *Doctor* Mac-Donald?" Karen scooped up two handfuls of dirt and tossed them playfully into Sean's lap.

At that instant Sean wanted to touch her, hold her to him, and to feel the heat from her body that his eyes could see. He offered his hand, but she wouldn't take it. Don't be a fool, he told himself. He moved closer, raising his hand as if searching for something before letting it settle safely, but reluctantly, onto her shoulder. Leaning forward, he gave her a quick kiss, surprising himself. Karen pulled away. Sean motioned for her not to leave. Withdrawing a small pocket knife, he knelt down, poking through one of the baskets until he found what he wanted. Pulling the stem off of a fat juicy strawberry, he rested the heart-shaped fruit in his hand, halved it from top to bottom with a practiced slice of the knife, let it fall open in his palm, then cupped his hand to keep the juice from leaking through his fingers. Karen leaned forward, snatching the fruit away with her lips and tongue, leaving behind the heat of her mouth in trade on his skin. Smiling, Sean licked the tiny pool of juice clean, then pulled Karen to him, kissing her, tasting what each of them had stolen from the palm of his hand. He could feel the sweat beneath his shirt soaking through, making them both wetter. He felt her nipples pressing into him, and thought he would explode. Sean pulled back. Karen followed him like a magnet. "I can't," he muttered with an embarrassed shake of his head.

"Good!" Karen growled, pulling him back to her. He tried standing, but couldn't, not easily, and blushed. Karen picked the baskets up, jumped to her feet, and started walking back to the cars with a bounce in her step. Sean was at her side before she was halfway there. "Everything under control now?" she asked, a playful tease hidden in her words.

Accepting Karen's reprimand with a nod of his head, Sean led her to the far edge of the field, where they sat beneath a solitary old oak tree that quietly offered shade from the fading afternoon sun with its wide girth and broad umbrella of pointed leaves. This time when they talked, it was about each other, not things, and about feelings. No questions were asked, but answers were freely given. The burning each of them had felt for the other out in the open field under the hot sun cooled, but it could be brought back with the slightest touch or whispered breath.

Sean gestured to the sun falling into the trees off in the distance. "There's a full moon tonight." He sounded almost timid. "It's the full Strawberry Moon."

Karen leaned back against the broad tree trunk, lazily rubbing up against the bark, scratching her back, pulling her blouse tight. "And?" she asked, raising one eyebrow.

Sean braced his hands on the ground beside him, as if for support. "The Strawberry Moon is thought to be the most erotic moon of the year." He looked straight into Karen's eyes. "Folklore has it that you cannot keep from making love with anyone you're with when the light of that moon falls on your face and into your heart." Karen reached out and brushed the hair out of Sean's eyes, but said nothing. "Let's come back tonight, after the moon is up, and have a picnic. Right here," he suggested with a slap of the ground. "I'll bring the champagne—I've got a bottle or two left from a party years ago, when I was still social." Hearing himself say this, actually admitting to it, made him think of Bruce. "And I'll bring something special for the strawberries, something I doubt you've ever had." Sean held his breath, expecting to hear Karen tell him she couldn't, or worse, that she didn't want to.

But her throaty laugh told him he couldn't have been more wrong. "Why don't we meet over there," she said, turning Sean's head when she brushed her arm past his face to point. "See that large rock near the road, the one that looks like a giant box turtle?" Sean nodded as he continued searching for what Karen was referring to. "There's a narrow path cut into the field there, but you have to go slow or you'll miss it. Pull all the way down until you come to a small clearing, which is where I'll meet you. And be sure to turn your lights off well before you get to the path, so that no one will see you pull off the road." Karen stood up and started for her car. "What time will your moon want us here, Dr. MacDonald?" she asked in a routine way.

"Karen, please, don't call me that. I like Sean."

"So do I," Karen said with a warm glow in her voice, "Sean."

Sean scrambled to his feet. "Well, for it to be bright enough, we should meet no later than midnight."

"Midnight it is." Karen laughed. "Now, I've got some business to take care of," she said, and climbed into her car.

Sean watched her drive away. A part of him couldn't help wondering, *Do you really think she'll come? Of course she will,* another part replied. *Are you sure? Yes!* But he wasn't.

Stepping into the hot shower, Sean covered his chest with his hands, gently caressing his nipples with the very tips of his fingers. They were alive to his touch, igniting his whole body. Leaving one hand behind, his thumb pressing small circles over and around his erect nipple, he slid the other hand down his body, wrapping his fingers around himself, feeling what was left from the afternoon. The water was steaming hot and felt good, even in the muggy heat of the early summer's night. He stood motionless, water pouring over him, letting it run warm, cool, then well-water cold. He hopped out with a delicious shiver and ambled down the hallway, dripping wet, the unused towel hanging lazily from his fingers, dragging on the floor behind him. He climbed into bed naked and still soaking wet. The sheets instantly dissolved around him like sugared lace. He played with sleep, but couldn't catch it, so he got up and went into the kitchen.

Dear Bruce,

I hope you can read my handwriting. I'm writing in the moonlight pouring in through the kitchen windows. No, I haven't gone mad. At least not yet!

I drove onto campus the day before yesterday with the hope of finding you there. Merrywood Hall was like a tomb. Why didn't you tell me Potter had given my office to Patricia Jennings, and not you? She scared the hell out of me when she caught me poking around her office.

We talked for a while, then went back to her house in Rhinecliff for dinner. I think I now have a much better understanding of the woman than I did in '86. She's far more sensitive and complex than I ever gave her credit for. However, I'm not sure she's able to control her emotions—her anger—quite yet.

I'm writing to tell you that I'm on my way out to spend the evening with a beautiful lady, a redhead with emerald-green eyes and a voice that can melt stone. We're going to have a picnic of sorts. You can relax, though, she's not your type. She's all grown up. And she's not skinny and flat-chested like the girls you seem to like. Sorry—couldn't resist. She wants me to think she's older than I am, but I don't believe her. She looks at least twenty years younger, and makes me feel the same way. But there's also something about her that feels much older. Not a few years older, either, but centuries older! Make any sense to you?

Her name is Karen, which is all she would tell me. She did say she had a daughter—or was it daughters?—who attended

Hart while I was there. I couldn't get her to tell me who they were. Do you remember any beautiful, redheaded students that were sisters?

Say hi to Betty for me. See you soon.

Sean

Immediately after turning onto Molly Lane, Sean pushed off the headlights and slipped into neutral, letting the car coast almost to a stop before nudging it into second and creeping along the side of the road, listening to the engine flutter between a growl and a purr as he peered into the dark, searching for the cut in the road Karen had told him about. His thoughts were moving faster than he was. When he pulled off the road and down into the tunnel of trees, the ground crackled to life under the weight of his car. Moonlight was slicing through the leaves, cutting up the long, narrow path into chunks of yellow and gray and olive-green. There was a hint of pine in the air from an unseen evergreen, which he breathed deep down into his lungs, as if trying to soothe his heat and slow its hurried pace. At the end of the path, he pulled to a stop and killed the engine. A hand fell on his shoulder, giving him a start.

"I was afraid you wouldn't come," Karen said in an unnecessary whisper, tousling his hair, then combing it to one side with her fingers. "Follow me." She wrapped her arms around the rolled-up blanket she was carrying and started back down the path. Sean snatched the canvas tote bag off the passenger seat with a scoop of his hand and hopped out. He closed the door with a jaunty swing of his hip. Karen had melted into the night, forcing him to run after her and catch up just as she pushed her way through the bushes, out into the tractor path circling the field. Sean followed closely, then slowed, letting her get ahead of him.

"Come on, slowpoke," Karen teased, and without warning, she darted down between the planted rows rising up out of the earth like mounds created by giant moles holding subterranean races. Sean sprinted after her, kicking up dust as he ran past, and slipped into the huge shadow of the waiting oak tree. Karen raised her

101

hand to shield her eyes from the bright glow of the moon. "I can't see your face," she said in a secret whisper, and walked slowly up to him.

"I know. But I can see yours, and you're beautiful. You seem to look younger with each step you take in the moonlight."

"Maybe I am!" Karen sounded serious. She then stepped inside the jagged edge of the tree's leafy shadow and shook out the bundle she was carrying. A pillow popped free. Sean caught it in midflight. Karen snapped the blanket into a billowing wave that hung in the air for a split second, frozen by the moonlight, before floating down onto the ground.

Kicking his loafers off, Sean stepped onto the blanket. Karen followed his lead with a playful hop, which is when Sean saw that she was barefoot. It made him smile. Off came his shirt, as if he were at the beach. He tossed into the air, not caring where it landed. A gentle breeze was splashing over the ground and lapping at their feet. "You relax," Sean said, running his fingers through Karen's long hair and combing it straight with gentle tugs of his hand. He stepped close and kissed her, tenderly, on her temple. She leaned into the touch of his warm lips, pressing her whole body against him. "I'll pick us some strawberries," he told her, pulling away.

"Wait!" Karen slipped the pillow out of its case with a snap of her hand and tossed to him, making him jump for it. "Use this to hold them."

The strawberries were buried under the leaves in the midnight shadows, forcing Sean to crawl from one plant to the next and pick by feel, until he had filled his cotton basket. Ambling back, he held up his prize, as if making an offering to the gods. Taking it, Karen cradled his harvest in her arms and knelt down. Sean dropped to his knees across from her. "I'll get the glasses." He reached into his tattered canvas tote bag. "Damn!" He slapped his thighs. "I left them sitting on the kitchen table when I sat down to write Bruce."

Karen asked in a whisper, "Does he—" but quickly silenced her thought and reached out, covering Sean's mouth with her hand. "There's no one here but us," she said in a soothing voice.

"Don't worry about how things look." Karen sealed her instructions with a lingering kiss. But her kiss couldn't stop Sean from asking her in his head, *Do you know Bruce?* Then she kissed him again, clearing his head of any thoughts but of her.

Sean began fingering the wire cage holding the cork prisoner in the bottle, and he started laughing to himself at not being able to work it loose with the savoir faire that he was accustomed to. Next came the cork, which he twisted back and forth ever so gently while pulling it out slowly, trying his best to keep it from announcing their presence. But it echoed across the open field like a shot from a popgun. Karen's unguarded giggle chased after it. Sean's followed, as he offered the bottle to Karen. She took it willingly, raising it to her lips, taking a long, slow sip, then gasping for air. "This is heavenly!" She took another. "What is it?"

"Like it?" Sean asked proudly.

"Love it. What is it?"

"Is that really important?"

With a girlish pout, Karen lifted the bottle into the air, turning it slowly in the light of the moon, examining it closely. "I can't read the label," she complained, bringing it close to her face, then pushing the bottle out to arm's length. "And I don't recognize the shape either." A smile tickled onto her face, warming her suntanned skin to a chestnut brown in the moonlight. "Come on," she purred. "What is it?"

Sean gave in after a throat-clearing protest, and said in a single stern breath, "Piper Heidsick, Flouren Louis, 1945," as he gathered up a handful of strawberries and started halving each one, this time with a paring knife extracted from his tote bag. They began dripping all over, forcing him to stick his hand out beyond the shiny ribboned edge of the yellow blanket to keep from getting it all wet and sticky.

"Don't worry about that." Karen blindly patted the air near his hand, then grabbed it and pulled it back. "It'll only make everything that much sweeter."

Don't get started, Sean told himself, not yet. You could barely control yourself this afternoon. He switched his train of thought.

"They're still unbelievably warm inside." Sean held his hand out to Karen.

Karen took Sean's hand in hers, bringing it to her lips, eating each of the strawberry halves. She then licked every last drop of nectar off his palm until there was nothing left but the memory of the touch from her hot tongue on his skin. Realizing what was happening to him, Sean slipped out of Karen's grasp, nervously halved more strawberries, then fumbled with the lid on the plastic bowl, peeling it off with an impatient snap of his wrist and sprinkling sugar all over the blanket. Dropping the halves in, he rolled them around as if he were panning for gold.

"Here, try this," Sean suggested. "It's superfine sugar laced with crystalline vanilla." With a curious smile, she did, running her tongue over her lips to get every stray granule of sugar. Then she lifted the bottle of champagne with a made-up groan and took a shallow sip, smiling at Sean. The moonlight dripping down out of the midnight-blue sky suddenly spun her red hair into gold, burning away the gray, and melting her eyes down to molten bronze. With a mischievous smile that lit up her face, she stood up, stretching lazily, the thin fabric of her white linen caftan evaporating into the ebony black of the night, inviting the moon to slip through the misty weave and caress the graceful swell of her full breasts before wrapping its heavenly arms around her hips and burying its face in the shadows of her thighs. Sean watched, turning everything into slow motion. Then, grabbing fistfuls of fabric, Karen lifted her dress up over her head and nonchalantly dropped it onto the blanket. Taking his cue, Sean rose up, looked around as if someone might be watching in the dark, then stepped out of his unwanted pants, but awkwardly, the way a man does when he's aroused. Karen slipped her panties off and sat down, drawing her knees to her chest, holding them to her with her own embrace, watching streaks of moonlight trickle down over Sean's naked body.

Before he could sit down beside her, Karen reached up with both hands, touching him, teasing him—he thought he would explode—then coaxing him down to her. When she kissed him, spreading his lips with her tongue, finding his, she inhaled, leaving him breathless.

Easing Karen down onto her back, Sean slowly, tenderly, halved her swollen flesh with his hot tongue, listening to her cry out as she threaded her fingers through his hair and pulled him up to her. "Come in me," she whispered. "Now." There was a painful sense of urgency thinning her words.

"So soon?" he asked, bewildered at her request.

"Yes." She tightened her grip on him, wrapping her legs around his waist. He was cautious. She wasn't, pulling him down, taking him inside her with a single, experienced thrust of her hips and kick of her legs. He tried moving. She held him fast. "Be still," she told him. "I want to feel your heart beating inside me." She guided him to where she wanted him. "There!" she cried, and opened wide, making him feel inadequate, until she tightened around him, again and again, until she was all alone and far away. Sean's heart started pounding louder and louder, until it exploded. Karen covered his mouth with hers, silencing his cries, swallowing his pleasure.

The second time was slow and sweet. Sean brought himself back up, little by little. Karen didn't have to; she was already there, waiting for him. Rolling him over with a graceful push of her arm, Karen moved on top. Finding him not quite ready, she paused, waiting for him, helping with experienced strokes of her hand. He reached up, cupping her breasts. She bent over, giving herself to him, then rose up and jammed herself down hard, making their bodies shake. Karen was now facing the moon, her eyes wide open, her hips moving in small tight circles, lifting herself up, then down, floating, weightless in the thin night air.

Sean found the ends of her breasts with his moistened fingertips and squeezed, freezing her around him with each tender pinch. Shutting his eyes, Sean answered with gentle thrusts of his hips. "No!" Karen suddenly cried out, startling him. There was a furious flutter of wind. Sean's eyes blinked open to shadows moving about, the moon gone, the night pitch black. "I won't," Karen whispered through her teeth, and suddenly turned ice cold inside, chilling him all over. The dark was now lighted. Sean looked up to find Karen staring wide-eyed into the face of the moon, unaware that he was even there.

Confused, Sean began exploring Karen's body with his always hungry eyes. He noticed delicate, uneven patterns crisscrossing her stomach and down to where her hair curled to a stop against the gentle swell of her belly. He raised his head, pressing his chin on his chest, trying to focus in the dark. That's when he felt Karen ease down, forcing him to look up at her. She was watching him. "I could feel you this time," she said, swallowing her words. "Stay hard," she said, tightening around him, "please?"

"Too late." Sean laughed out of embarrassment. His movement forced Karen to lose her balance and fall forward onto his chest, spitting him out of her. And for the first time, Sean felt Karen's full weight pressing down on him, taking his breath away. He bit into her flesh with his lips, then his teeth, tasting her, a sweet-and-sour taste. They rolled sideways. When he looked down, Karen pulled him close to her. "You don't want to see it," she said sternly, and revealed a side of her Sean had not seen since meeting her.

"What is it?" he tried sliding free, but was unable to.

"Something that can't be explained."

"I only want to—"

"No," she ordered, wrapping her herself around him and devouring him like he was part of her, not him.

To Sean's surprise, they made love again, locked in each others arms. This time there was no beginning and no ending, as time melted away, inside and out. Exhausted, Sean wrapped the blanket around them, no longer two, but one, falling asleep as the moon fell to earth.

The first strokes of light painted the sky awake with streaks of pink. Rising, naked, their bodies bathed in the cool gray light drifting across the fields, they moved closer, feeling each other still warm from sleep. They made love, standing, hard and fast and good. The distant choking of a tractor's engine startled them apart. They dressed quickly, giggling like truant schoolchildren. Holding his breath, Sean asked Karen who she was and where he could find her. She sighed, then kissed him gently, more gently then she had before, giving him her silent answer, then turned, and started walking away. Something lying on the blanket caught his eye.

Picking it up, Sean smiled to himself and stuffed the clutch of black silk, embroidered with gold, into his shirt as he watched Karen walking away, the rising sun warming the cold white of her caftan, trying to slip inside like the moon, but unable to. Sean raced after her.

"Thank you," Karen sighed as she came to a stop at the edge of the field, whimsically kicking up the dirt with her bare foot. "You've made me feel beautiful and young again. You asked for nothing, yet gave me everything I demanded of you, even more than you thought you could." She smiled at this. Sean did, too. Karen asked him not to speak with a wipe of her fingertips over his lips. "I can feel you flowing through my body, I can taste you in my mouth, I can smell you on my skin. It's as if you became me, and I, you." Karen turned away, taking herself from him. "I've never felt like this," she whispered, but to herself, and slipped through the dew-soaked bushes back onto the narrow path leading to Sean's car.

Sean followed. "Please," he said, resting his hands on Karen's shoulders, pulling her to a stop. "Let me see your eyes?" He turned her around. "I was right," he said, kissing her on the mouth, then on each closed eyelid. "You *are* ageless."

"For the moment." Karen then looked at him, through him, and beyond, making him feel empty and cold once again. "I don't know how to say this,"—she was struggling to find the words she wanted—"but after the hunger in your belly was satisfied, a hunger too long ignored, even though you thought it was satisfied the night before"—Sean's face turned to ice at hearing Karen say this, but she melted it away with the touch of her hand on his cheek—"it was as if I was no longer with . . ." Karen shook her head. Her long hair, twisted into knots from their night of making love, flared out like the unkempt mane of a feral beast.

"As if you were no longer with what?" Sean asked. Karen looked away, refusing his penetrating gaze. "Karen?"

"As if I wasn't with a man," she replied, slipping out of his

Donald Beman

grasp. She quickly stepped back into his arms when she saw a pained look on his face. "I can't explain." She wound her arms around him, taking his breath away with her powerful embrace. "I shouldn't have said what I did. It wasn't fair of me. I'm sorry."

Sean's body appeared to collapse inward as he held Karen away from him and asked, "Wasn't I—"

Karen kissed Sean's anxious question away and said with renewed certainty, and a hint of leftover passion, "You were more than I can ever tell you. You gave me life"—she took his hands in hers—"and I gave you life, too." She sighed. "Now, I have to go. There's something I have to do." Karen tried slipping through Sean's grasp, but he held her to him. "No," she said with determination, "if I let you hold me again, I may never be able to let you go. And that would be a tragedy, for both of us." Karen pressed Sean's hands together and gave them back to him. "Now, go!" she said, pushing him away, nodding to his car, and waiting for him to do what she asked, what she commanded.

The smell of fresh coffee brewing filled the kitchen, reminding Sean of just how hungry he was. But he wanted the coffee first. He needed it, desperately. He pulled Karen's blanket up over his shoulders and around his naked body, and watched the water drip black and thick with caffeine. After pouring his mug full, he shuffled over to the chair near the window and eased himself down, laughing uncontrollably at the soreness in his whole being as he began taking short, steady sips, nursing what he had so he wouldn't have to get up for another cup, not yet.

Patches of the blanket were stiff. Some weren't even dry yet. He tried finding her, but the smell of coffee got in the way. He buried his face into what was left from their night together and waited, but the thought stayed a thought. He started twisting his neck around in circles, trying to stretch out the kinks from sleeping on the ground, and that's when he noticed a small folded-over piece of paper on the table, propped up against the wall, with his name on it. Reaching for it, grimacing at the tenderness in his ribs, but smiling with pleasure at its cause, Sean opened

108

the note and immediately recognized the small, swirling handwriting. "Damn."

Dear Sean

Your lights were on. I knocked, but there was no answer. The door was ajar, so I peeked in. It looked like the door at the top of the landing was open, too. I was worried, so I came in. Now we both know that you weren't home!

Thank you for having dinner with me. And thank you for staying the night. It's been a long time since I was with a man. I hope we can begin seeing each other again.

Your landlady came upstairs to see who was here. I told her we were colleagues. She said you were out on a date with a young lady. Is that right? Young? A date? I'm jealous!

I want you to know that I love you more than ever, and I ache to have you in me again.

—Patricia

Sean snarled, "Why didn't you stay away from her?" as he crumpled the note into a ball and threw it across the kitchen, not caring where it landed, resolving that instant to write to Patricia and end it all before it got out of hand. Again.

10

Friday, June 28, 1991

BODY FOUND
George Kraft
Staff Reporter

While plowing one of her fields early yesterday morning, Catherine Greene, owner of Greene Farms, in Red Hook, NY, made a grisly discovery when she came upon the naked and mutilated body of a man who, authorities say, had been dead for only a few hours.

Red Hook Police Chief Peter Kratz reports that the cause of death is as yet unknown, and that an autopsy is scheduled for later today. However, reliable sources in the department report that the county medical examiner has already commented (unofficially) on the cause of death since, according to our sources, the body was found with its chest split, or sliced open, and the heart cut out. They also report that the face and hands of the victim were burned beyond recognition, but by some sort of strong chemical, not a fire, forcing identification of the victim (who, the police say, was in his mid or late forties) to be made using dental records.

While still unconfirmed, inside sources also report that the victim's genitals were missing, possibly torn from the body.

While Ms. Greene declined to comment on what she found until the police have finished their initial investigation and left the site where she discovered the body, she did want the public to know that "This is the first time in the farm's 150-year history anything like this has ever happened, and I hope everyone will feel perfectly safe visiting the farm for the fresh fruits and vegetables we have become famous for in the Hudson Valley."

Chief Kratz has said it appears the body was "brought to this location, and the murder took place elsewhere. The murderer, or murderers, dropped the body in the field, well off the road, sometime just before dawn."

At this point, the police have no leads to go on, not even footprints around the body, since investigators at the scene have reported that everything appeared to have been brushed clean or blown away by a strong wind, but only within what sources say was a thirty-foot area surrounding the body.

When contacted, regional weather services advised that there were no high winds detected by them (or reported to them by private sources) anywhere in the area, and that in fact the air was "dead calm due to a stationary column of high-pressure air, which moved in late yesterday afternoon, accounting for the hot and muggy air in the valley."

11

Monday, July 8, 1991

Sean knew he wouldn't be able to pay attention to anything else until he'd satisfied his curiosity as to what was inside the large brown envelope. It was puffy and spongy in the center, the scratchy lines from an old fountain pen having bled into the coarse fibers of the foreign-made envelope, spinning a web of spidery veins around Oliver Shore's parsimonious handwriting, meticulously printing out the letters and numbers of Sean's name and address. "All right, my friend," Sean wondered aloud as he shook the envelope. "What piece of me do you want today?" A balled-up wad of paper hit the table and bounced into his lap. He squeezed his legs shut to keep it from falling onto the floor and held it there. After another shake, a clutch of papers dropped down onto the table, stood upright for a split second, then collapsed face down. A giant paper clip attaching a small, handwritten note to the sheaf of papers accounted for its weighted nosedive.

Sean—

These were in the files I collected from your office this past May. I opened and read the papers clipped to this note. The ball of paper has been left as I found it, since it seemed I might damage it if I tried to open it.

I had set them aside to give them to you, then forgot about

them. I found them on the floor behind my desk when I was packing to leave for England.

Oliver

Sean recognized the all-too-familiar papers attached to Oliver's note. He started to discard them without reading them for what easily would have been the thousandth time. But he found himself unable to do that, as he always had, and started reading the fuzzy words that had been typed with an old, cloth-ribbon typewriter. Some of the letters, like the upper-case "O" and the lower case "a," had punched through the original, causing holes that looked burned through in the faded photocopy of his wife's autopsy report. He started reading aloud, but quickly gave up and read silently, since he was still unable, even after all these years, to say the words out loud.

```
NAME: MacDonald, Janet (Peters)
CASE: 012774.06R

Female—White—Approximately 30 years.

    Autopsy    performed    on    the    above-
mentioned body at the Albany County Med-
ical Examiner's office by the undersigned
at the request of the Dutchess County
District Attorney's office.
    Present at the autopsy are: Assistant
D.A., Arnold Kratz (Dutchess County);
Dutchess County Sheriff, Peter W. Ander-
son; evidence personnel; two departmen-
tal photographers; and ACME diener, R.
Fried.

EXTERNAL EXAMINATION:

    The body is that of an adult white fe-
male approximately 30 years of age. The
```

body measures approximately 173 cm in length, is of a large but trim build, and weighs approximately 64 kg. The head is normocephalic. The head hair is long, reddish brown in color, and twisted with dried leaves and grass.

The eyes are wide open, more so than what is normal. The pupils are largely dilated. The irises are gray-black with spots of red. There are round contusions above the right and left eyebrows, both of which show signs of what appears to be charring of the skin. Similar contusions are on both cheekbones and the chin, all of which reveal the same blackish charring. The nostrils are not remarkable.

The external auditory meati are not remarkable. The oral cavity contains natural teeth in very good repair. The lips are swollen and cracked and cyanotic. The tongue is split and bitten between the upper and lower jaws. The anterior neck is symmetrical. The neck veins are engorged. The right and left arms are broken in numerous places and folded over across the chest. The right and left hands show a clubbing or clenching effect. The fingernails on both hands are splintered and broken and appear to have been forcefully pulled away from the nail beds with great force. There is a black fleshy substance under the nails. There are no tattoos on the body.

The left breast is completely destroyed due to a severe, and bizarre-

looking, injury, one I have never seen
before (to be described later). The
right breast is intact. The right nipple
is intact. There is an oblong birthmark,
measuring approximately 3 cm long and 1
cm wide, below and to the right of the
nipple.

There is a large, triangular, sliced-
open hole in the left side of the chest
measuring approximately 21 cm on each of
three sides, extending from the sternum,
the converging point of the triangle
(and which is cleanly severed through in
two places and partially torn out of the
chest), across the chest to below the
left armpit, or the base of the triangular opening. The severed tissue around
the edges of the wound, as well as the
cartilage and splintered bone, show the
same charring effect as on the face.
Like these areas, the charring here does
not smell of fire or burning of the flesh
from heat or a flame. The charring appears to have been caused by a very
strong acid of some sort. Samples of
charred soft tissue and bone will be
sent to the lab for testing.

There is little evidence of blood anywhere on the body or around the perimeter of the wound, which appears to be
the result of a cauterizing effect of
the severed arteries, veins, and surrounding soft tissue by the acidulous
substance.

The abdomen is intact. There is a
fairly recent surgical scar (horizontal
and measuring approximately 22 cm) due

to what appears to have been a recent (2 to 3 months) caesarian-section birth. Surrounding skin color and texture supports this conclusion. The external genitalia are that of an adult female. The pubic hair is of the same color as the head hair.

There is an object between the tightly closed thighs, a religious cross or crucifix, which is lodged in the vagina. Upon removal it can be clearly seen to be a crucifix, made of some sort of hard, black wood, with what appears to be a sterling silver figure of Christ mounted to it. It measures approximately 388 mm in overall length, 100 mm across, and 30 mm in shaft thickness (both limbs). There is dried and thickly clotted blood and soft tissue covering the crucifix, the opening of the vagina, the labia majora, and spotted on the interior sides of the upper thighs.

Rigor mortis is partially present and livor mortis is anterior. The back is not remarkable except for the presence of dried leaves and mud and grass sticking to and impressed into the skin.

There are large circular contusions on both thighs, one on the medial side and two on the lateral side, like huge fingerprints, each measuring approximately 5 cm in diameter, and with a deep gash running from the edge outward. Each one shows the same charring as with all other contusions. However these appear far more severe, and deeper, indicating possible forceful abduction of the legs. This may also account for the crushed muscle and surrounding soft tissue at the points of contact. The femur of both legs is broken directly beneath each of these points of contact, like a twig snapped between one's fingers.

Except for the surface cuts and scratches all over the body, but only on the anterior side, the body is very well preserved. When first brought to this office, it was still partially frozen, with only the face, upper-chest areas and hands and forearms showing signs of thawing.

INTERNAL EXAMINATION:

The body is opened in the usual Y-shaped incision, allowing for the large hole in the right side of the chest to remain undisturbed. The great vessels of the thorax and abdomen are identified and are not remarkable. There is evidence of the heart having been torn or ripped away from the aorta and pulmonary artery and forcefully removed from the body. There is no heart present. Surprisingly, there is very little evidence of blood in the pericardial cavity as would be expected in such a violent evisceration of the heart.

The left lung is severely and deeply lacerated. The right lung shows evidence of puncture. The . . .

Sean skipped over the next page of the autopsy report, not wanting to read the medical examiner's description of the condition and size of Janet's internal organs or the detailed description of her horribly mutilated vagina. He jumped down to the summary at the bottom of the last page, which had been circled so many times in blue, ballpoint pen—by him—that it was about to fall through the sheet like a crude, paper cutout.

```
ANATOMICAL & GENERAL DIAGNOSIS:

 1. Body found nude and frozen on night of
    January 23, 1974.
 2. Massive visceral congestion.
 3. Left breast completely mutilated.
 4. Hole ripped through left side of chest.
 5. Fractured and severed ribs on the left
    and right side.
 6. Evidence of (chemical) charring of the
    wounds.
 7. Heart ripped or cut or torn from the
    chest.
 8. Aorta and pulmonary artery severed.
 9. Left lung cut badly; right lung punc-
    tured.
10. Contusions on face, with evidence of
    charring.
11. Birthmark below nipple of right breast.
12. Crucifix found lodged in the vagina,
    ripping and tearing the walls, causing
    massive hemorrhaging.
Note: This was done prior to the forceful
    removal of the heart.
13. A recent history of marital prob-
    lems requiring counseling was reported
    by Duchess County Assistant D.A. pres-
    ent.
```

```
TOXICOLOGY: All samples sent to ACME lab
for analysis and toxicology report.
```

```
DATE & TIME OF DEATH: To be determined af-
ter examination and testing of stomach
contents. Presently estimated at approxi-
mately two weeks prior to the date of the
police report in our possession.
```

```
CAUSE OF DEATH: Forced removal of the
heart.
```

Sean slipped the coroner's report, along with Oliver's note, back into the envelope. He then scooped the tennis ball–sized wad of paper from between his thighs and tossed it into the air playfully, only to snatch his hand back to his chest when he realized what it was. He watched it bounce onto the table and come to rest teetering on the edge, directly in front of him. He sat staring at the blood-stained ball of crumpled-up paper. He had never opened it, even though he'd tried, wanting to, easily a hundred times. Picking it up, he examined it closely—turning it over and over like it was a Chinese puzzle ball—looking for some hidden key that would tell him how to open it; one he'd never been able to find before. When he dug his fingers into one of the folded crevices and pulled, it crackled like a wafer-thin sheet of ice covering a puddle of water after a first frost on an early winter morning, when you tap it with the toe of your shoe. He gingerly tugged another one open. Then a few more. The red was no longer red, but black, like caked-on ash. The lines of faded type, letterpressed into the old paper, were shattered by delicate cracks and fine fibrous tears.

Slowly, he read what he saw before him.

> For the heart whose woes are legion
> 'Tis a peaceful, soothing region—
> For the spirit that walks in shadow
> 'Tis—oh 'tis an Eldorado!

But the traveller, travelling through it,
May not—dare not openly view it;
Never its mysteries are exposed
To the weak human eye unclosed;
So wills its King, who hath forbid
The uplifting of the fringed lid;
And thus the sad Soul that here passes
Beholds it but through darkened glasses.

By a route obscure and lonely,
Haunted by ill angels only,
Where an Eidolon, named NIGHT,
On a black throne reigns upright,
I have wandered home but newly
From this ultimate dim Thule.

Written into the margins of the poem were curious combinations of numbers, simple equations, and cryptic notations in Hebrew and ancient Greek. The paper, old and yellowed and once water-swollen, made it impossible to decipher anything but the letters QSR NRWN, and the carefully, deliberately printed notation at the bottom, which read

Life divided by that persistent six,
LXX divided by 666 = .105105105105105 . . .
six, ad infinitum.

Without making a sound, and barely breathing, Sean stuffed the dried and crumbling sheet of paper back into the envelope, then started for the kitchen door. But he wasn't fast enough as the memories locked inside this forgotten piece of the past, like a genie bottled up in time, rose up just as bright and clear as they had been seventeen years ago, and suddenly he was there.

. . . *Running down the long corridor in Merrywood Hall, the slapping of his leather-soled shoes on the marble floor ricocheting off the walls. He ducked the silent questions thrown at him by one curious face after another when they stepped into the hall.*

The Taking

*They followed when he threw himself against the heavy oak doors
leading out to the patio and the snow-covered common. Blocking
the doors open, he stumbled out into the colorless dark of the
new moon, his feet punching through the thin crust of ice covering
the melting snow as he raced ...*

"No!" Sean cried, stumbling down the stairs, throwing the
screen door open—flinching when it sprung back, hitting him in
the head—then pitching over the porch railing, gasping for air.
"You raped her. You toyed with her. Why? *Why!*" he yelled,
pounding his hands on the railing. "And the poem. You think I
don't know. But you're wrong, I do. But you will never have me,
never! You goddamn fucking—"

"Sean?" Jean Murphy called as she rushed out onto the porch,
her hands, her whole body shaking with fright. "Are you all right,
son? *Sean?*"

12

Friday, July 12, 1991

There was a tasty summer breeze tumbling down out of the Catskills and splashing across the Hudson. It was mountain cool and
pine sweet and all-over clean. Cathy was standing on the edge of
the circular driveway in front of her house, directly across from
the porch steps, looking up into the sky, chasing the clouds with
her eyes. One hand was stuffed into the back pocket of her jeans;
the other hung at her side, clutching a sweater falling down into
the uncut grass. Sean pulled up around the drive, squeaking to a
stop in front of her. Before he could say anything, Cathy tossed
her sweater into the car, hitting him with it, and climbed in. Sean

folded the baby-blue cardigan into a store-bought bundle and set it on her lap. "Am I late?"

"No!" followed the same path as the sweater, only hitting him harder.

With an innocent blink of his eyes, Sean coasted down the drive and pulled out onto Molly Lane. He moved through the gears smoothly, quietly, listening for something, something that was wrong, but not with the car. With a furious shuffle of her hands, Cathy shook her hair loose, giving it to the wind to twist into knots. When she looked settled, Sean asked in a made-up milquetoast voice, trying his best not to push some invisible button, "Any news about the identity of that poor bastard you found in the fields two weeks ago?"

"No."

Feeling brave, or foolish, Sean tried again. "Want to talk about it?" he asked, resting his hand on her arm.

Cathy swept away his offer with a brusque wave of her hand.

When they entered the center of Red Hook, Sean took a sudden left onto Route 199, heading east and back out of town, ignoring Cathy's square-jawed challenge of his decision. Not a word was spoken as they drove through Rock City, Milan, and past the Taconic Parkway, wandering over and around miles of shaded country roads, before doubling back to Red Hook from the south, driving north up Route 9. Finding a parking spot on Broadway, Sean lowered his head and zipped in, making believe he didn't see the Mercedes in front of him about to back into it, a risky move for a car as small as his. He smiled sheepishly when the driver leaned on the irritating European horn. When he was gone, leaving behind the smell of burned rubber, Sean tipped sideways and kissed Cathy on the cheek before she could pull herself away from him. "Come on," he said softly, forcing himself to forget how hungry he was. "Let's wander around town and window-shop for a while."

Cathy yanked him to her with a one-armed hug. "I don't need a walk," she said quietly. "Not anymore. Besides, I'm starving. And you must be, too." She hopped out, skipping over the cracks in the sidewalk with a playful laugh, suddenly free of whatever it was that had infected her. She was like that, and she'd been showing Sean how to be that way, too. "Let's go to my place." Cathy started primping her shirt and smoothing out her jeans.

Sean climbed out and walked around the car, trying without success to keep himself beyond the reach of Cathy's rediscovered playfulness until he was sure she was no longer infected. "And where's 'your' place?" he asked with a skeptical, but curious and willing, smile.

Cathy nudged him along ahead of her, gesturing to a white wooden sign rising up out of a cluster of flowering red azaleas, the words RED HOOK INN painted in black above a large, cast-iron rigger's hook bolted to the wood, staining the white brown with rust. "It's nothing fancy," Cathy said, urging Sean to hurry up with an excited tug of his arm. "Just good food and good people. Besides, I know the bartender." Sean's eyes lit up. Cathy took aim with her finger at an imaginary target on Sean's chest. "And no wisecracks when you meet him, Dr. MacDonald." She chucked him under his chin when he looked down at her hand.

Sean scratched an X over his heart. "I promise."

Laughing, Cathy pushed Sean up the creaking steps of the porch and through the front door. The ceiling of the two-hundred-year-old colonial building was low, barely seven feet tall, its sagging rough-cut beams held up at either end by tree-trunk posts still showing the stubs of branches axed off. The palmed-plaster ceiling and windowless walls gave it the look of a revolutionary fort, not a wayside colonial tavern. The tarnished-brass and clouded-glass lanterns, their candles having been replaced with tiny bulbs, gave off just enough light to see. The wide-planked floor rose and fell like wooden waves. The musty earth seeping up through the split seams mixed with the smell of stale beer and cigarette smoke, creating a muddy puddle.

Cathy steered Sean away from the main dining room on the right and guided him into the taproom on their left. "This is where I come when—"

"Hey!" someone snarled in a drunken slur. "It's that dike." Two men in a group of three pushed themselves away from the bar. One shoved past Sean, reaching out for Cathy; the other locked Sean's arms behind his back, jamming a knee into the base of his spine. Pain shot up his back, pounding his eyes shut, as wet beer and hot breath were spit all over him. Sean broke free, smashing the man in the mouth with his fist, snapping his head around. He hit him again, ripping his face open. Blood burst out as he dropped to the floor, motionless. Sean spun around, his hands out in front of him, balled into fists, searching for Cathy. The second man was lying on the floor, face up, eyes shut, arm twisted at his side as if it didn't have a bone in it, a bone-white splinter piercing his dirty denim shirt, staining it red. Another man rushed out of nowhere, screaming obscenities. The bartender yelled a strange word. Cathy spun around and took a wild punch that glanced off her cheek. Her leg shot out; the man bellowed and fell to his knees, gagging. She was on him, filling her fist with his hair, ramming her knee into his back, smashing his face into the rough wooden floor. A hideous crack shattered the breathless silence in the room. She raised his head out of the blood pooling on the floor, seeping down into the cracks. His nose was gone, pushed into his face. Letting go, she stepped away, quiet and calm and barely breathing.

Sean stood staring at her, speechless. A sharp pain stung his hand. He glanced down to see blood dripping onto the floor and his ring finger bent sideways. Something was sticking out of the back of his hand between his knuckles. He smiled with relief when it flicked out onto the floor, and he realized that it was a piece of tooth, not bone—and not his. He lowered his arm, then instantly wished he hadn't when the pain pounded his fingers into a throbbing fist that he covered with his other hand in a futile attempt to comfort it.

Cathy reached out. "Let me see," she said, taking hold of his wrist and raising his hand to the light, then gently feeling his finger. "Nothing's broken," she said convincingly. "Your finger's just out of joint." There was a curious, detached smile on her face. Sean shrugged his shoulders. Cathy did, too, then wrapped her hand around his crooked finger. Before he could protest, she squeezed and pushed. There was a dull popping sound. It hurt, but he was damned if he was going to show it, not after what he'd just witnessed. "It'll be fine in a few days," she assured him. "A little swelling, but nothing more." She turned and called, "Bobby, fill one of your champagne buckets with ice and bring it over, would you please?" With Sean in tow, holding his hand up like it was a prize, Cathy led them to the closest open table, arriving barely two steps ahead of the bucket of ice, which was carried effortlessly in one hand by the person she'd called Bobby, a huge hulk of a man with a thick neck, who made the bucket look like a tin cup.

"You OK, Cath?" he asked gently, sounding nothing like he looked.

Cathy put her hand on his massive forearm. "Thanks, McCarthy." She turned to Sean. "And thank *you*. You impressed me for . . ."

Sean could see it coming and beat her to it. "For a man my age?" he said jokingly, then found himself smiling at what the sound of his own words brought to mind as the voices around them in the taproom grew steadily louder, like a rising wind.

Cathy looked wounded. "No, silly." She rubbed his arm. "You impressed me for someone without training." Sean felt stupid and wished the Bobby-person wasn't there. Someone without training? he thought as Cathy turned to Bobby and asked, "Bring us a platter of sandwiches, OK?"

Two police officers appeared in the doorway. One broke for the man stumbling into the kitchen. The other one took a position standing over the two men lying on the floor, then looked over at Cathy and nodded his head smartly. "Captain."

"Captain?" Sean whispered to himself, and looked around for another police officer.

"Hi, Pete," Cathy replied in a friendly sort of way. When she looked back, there was a question mark on Sean's face.

"Care to tell me what this is all about? *Captain?*" Sean made a sweeping gesture in the direction of the three men, who were now sitting up on the floor, back to back, in a circle.

For the first time since he'd picked her up, Cathy breathed a sigh of relief. But it was Sean who now felt uncomfortable, and he tried hiding it. "Who's this Bobby-person?" he asked, ticking his head in the direction of the bar. "And what is this all about?" He made a dispensatory gesture toward the men now being helped to their feet by the two young officers.

An amused smile wormed its way across Cathy's smooth, tanned face. "McCarthy? We were in the service together," Cathy replied as if nothing had happened.

"Service?" Sean heard himself ask.

Cathy reached out, gently tapping Sean's chin, turning him back to face her. "It's not polite to stare," she teased.

"That's all, you two were in the service? Who are these men?"

Before Cathy could say anything, another police officer arrived, one much older than the others, and began asking everyone lots of questions. He knew Cathy and her family. The other two officers knew her, too, but in a different way. There was respect in how they all spoke to her. It was the kind of respect a man shows for another man, and it made Sean proud to be with her, yet somehow jealous at the same time. The questions were all directed to Cathy, even when they were about him. He soon felt left out, and tried not to feel hurt. But he did, and was sure it showed, even when he buried his face in the mug of beer Bobby McCarthy brought over without having been asked.

Standing up, easily a few inches taller than the older man, Cathy said, "Thank you, Chief Kratz," and shook his hand briskly.

Sean spun around, his body wired, his eyes sparking with energy as he waited for the police officer to leave. "Did you say Kratz?" he asked, fighting to keep himself in his seat.

"Why are you staring at me like that?" Cathy asked.

"Is he related to Judge Arnold Kratz?"

"Yes." Cathy sat down. "But Peter doesn't talk with his brother if he can help it. I think it's because the judge is gay." Cathy drained her glass. "Why do you ask?" Sean was drumming his fingernails on the table. "What's Arnold Kratz to you?" she asked, clamping her hand over his, silencing it.

Sean threw himself back in his chair. "He was the asshole assistant D.A. investigating my wife's murder."

"That was a long time ago, Sean. What's your problem now?"

"My problem is that that bastard made my life miserable! He was convinced that I'd killed my wife, in spite of the evidence, or lack of it, I should say. And I'm certain he still believes it. That son-of-a—" Sean abruptly stopped and slammed his hands down on the table, making Cathy jump. He winced and grabbed hold of his swollen hand. "Forget it," he said, standing up. "Forget I even brought it up." He started to leave.

Cathy reached out, grabbing his shirt sleeve, tugging him back down into his chair. "Let it go, Sean."

Sean looked down at Cathy's hand on his arm, and everything started rewinding, then fast-forwarding—she raised his head out of the blood pooling on the floor . . . his nose was gone, pushed into his face . . . she stepped away, quiet and calm, and barely breathing—Sean stood up again. "I'm not hungry anymore."

"Sean? Are you all right?"

"I just want some fresh air," he said, walking away, one frame replaying itself in his head . . . quiet and calm and barely breathing . . . quiet and calm and barely breathing . . . quiet . . .

13

Sunday, July 14, 1991

Dear Oliver,

I hope my letter finds you comfortably settled in England for the summer. And before I forget to ask, who is this "lady friend" my landlady told me that you were going to see? Is she that doctoral candidate at Columbia, the one with Irish-red hair, just like yours? Come on, fess up, my friend.

Donald Beman

Although I wasn't going to play along, I'm sending you the schedule of events and corresponding dates in my life you asked me to put together for you. The "unabridged" listing, setting forth graduations, marriages, awards, other people's birth and death dates, etc, etc, etc, can be found on the hand-written schedule enclosed with this letter. I've highlighted a few of the key dates below for a quick look at this patient's life, "Doctor" Shore. Have fun, my friend.

BIRTH DATES—immediate family:

Robert MacDonald	(father)	07/13/16
Eileen (Merritt) MacDonald	(mother)	12/28/17
Sean MacDonald		09/23/43
Janet (Peters) MacDonald	(wife)	08/25/45
John MacDonald	(son)	12/10/73

DEATH DATES—immediate family:

	Cause of Death	
Mother	(childbirth?)	12/24/50
Sister	(stillborn?)	12/24/50
Father	(stroke)	07/16/62
Wife	(murder)	01/08/74
Son	(unknown)	11/22/80
Me?	(you!)	??/??/??

OTHER DATES—important to me—good or bad:

Marriage	05/23/68
The Quill—first issue	04/28/72
Raven's Quill Prize—first awards	04/12/79
Problem Short Story Published	04/24/86
Patricia Jennings (start)	05/08/86
Patricia Jennings (end!)	06/07/86
The Strawberry Moon (see below)	06/26/91

The Taking

In case you want details for the rest of my family (uncles, aunts, cousins, grandparents, and other ancestors), I've included a copy of the genealogist's report on my family, most of which was taken from the *Encyclopedia of American Quaker Genealogy,* as well as records on file at the Historical Society of Pennsylvania.

Except for Bruce, whose birth date is on the schedule, I don't know the birth dates for any of our colleagues, so you're on your own there. Good luck with Sarah Potter and Ruth Stein! As for Patricia Jennings, that one I do happen to know; It's 12/31/52, which makes her 39 this year.

The other papers I've enclosed provide a summary of names and birth dates for my students, including the dates they attended Hart. Ones who transferred or dropped out have the ending date circled. Any who I learned had died are noted with an asterisk in front of their name.

Now, for reality. I'm writing with abandon! And the story-line, you ask? I'll tell you all about it when you get back, but it directly relates to the date I listed above after the heading "Strawberry Moon," which I think will also be the title of my story. At the rate I'm going, I could be finished by the end of August, maybe mid-September—the end of summer.

And speaking of summer, if you're back before the end of August, I'd like you to come to The Thomas Cole House (under Bruce's invitation and auspices) for an old-fashioned, Victorian croquet party. I'm told there will be some very interesting people there, including the eccentric (according to Bruce) director of the Thomas Cole Foundation. The date is the 24th. Bruce also said something about a British sports car club rally, so maybe everyone will be driving one to Catskill. I'll fit right in! Why don't you buy one while you're over there and bring it back with you?

Oh, I almost forgot: I'm also enclosing a poem I received at the end of the 1986 academic year. At the time I thought it was just an anonymous gift from one of my students, since it was left on my desk, gift-wrapped and nicely framed. But as time wore on, I came to doubt that it was a gift. What do you think?

Sean

After opening the back of the small frame, Sean removed the dried-out corrugated backing, then tried to slip the poem out of its matting. But he tore the top of the old page that it was printed on when the rice-paper hinges refused to let go. Tossing the useless frame into the wastebasket, wincing at the jarring shatter of glass, he sat back, reading the poem one last time. It was like seeing an old friend for the first time in years—or perhaps an enemy.

Evening Star

'Twas noontide of summer,
And mid-time of night;
And stars, in their orbits,
Shone pale, thro' the light
Of the brighter, cold moon,
'Mid planets her slaves,
Herself in the Heavens,
Her beam on the waves.
I gaz'd awhile
On her cold smile;
Too cold—too cold for me—
There pass'd, as a shroud,
A fleecy cloud,
And I turn'd away to thee,
Proud Evening Star,
In thy glory afar,
And dearer thy beam shall be;
For joy to my heart
Is the proud part
Thou bearest in Heav'n at night,
And more I admire

The Taking

Thy distant fire,
Than that colder, lowly light.

Leaving the printer nibbling back and forth across the paper like a hungry caterpillar, Sean turned the light out in his study, stepped out into the darkened hallway, and started for the kitchen. "Cathy!" he yelped, jumping backward. "What are you doing here?"

Cathy pushed him up against the wall, holding him there with a jab of her finger. "We had a date, remember!" She poked him again. "You, Sean MacDonald, were supposed to be ready at eight-thirty sharp. And it's almost ten now!" Spinning away, Cathy stormed into the kitchen. "I've been sitting out here for over an hour," she said, folding her arms and sitting down and trying her best to look upset. She was wearing a flower-print skirt and white cotton tank top—without a bra—instead of her uniform of jeans, work shirt, and heavy boots. The skirt was splashed with yellows and pinks and violets, and it fell loosely through her bare legs, which were spread apart like a tomboy's. Sean couldn't help smiling. Looking down, seeing what he was staring at, Cathy frowned and reached for her skirt. But Sean was there before she could pull it down, lifting her up out of the chair and onto the edge of the kitchen table in one powerful move.

Cathy pushed Sean away, but held onto him, then reached up and grabbed the pull string hanging down from the ceiling light, clicking them into the dark. She gathered up the hem of her skirt and slipped off her panties. She tried sliding back onto the table, but her skin stuck to the summer night that had glued itself to the lacquered wood, grabbing, then letting go of her moist flesh with gentle squeaks. Sean's pants dropped to the floor. The buckle clanked. He kicked them aside. Cathy reached down, touching him for the first time. He pitched forward into her hand. Kicking off her sandals, Cathy raised her legs and braced her heels on the table's edge as she leaned back onto her elbows. Sean slipped his hands under her hips, lifting her up, pulling her to him. She wasn't ready. He eased back, watching the moonlight play with the colors buried in the folds of her skirt, slip down into the velvet black

131

between her thighs, then spill over onto the table, repainting the stenciled-on flowers beneath the lacquered finish, curling up around her hips.

Suddenly, Sean felt nauseated. He tried swallowing it away, but it bubbled back up into his throat, thick and bitter. He began fighting for air. Cathy raised her head. "I'm sorry," she said, feeling to see where her skirt was, then pulling it back down over her. "I thought it was dark enough to hide them."

Sean put his hand on her leg, rubbing it gently, trying to clear his throat. "It's not you. It's me," he said, swallowing hard. "I suddenly felt this fire raging in my stomach and burning my chest. Then I felt dizzy and cold. And frightened. And angry! All at the same time. But I don't know why. Or at what." Cathy's hand was there, covering his. Sean pulled her to him, wrapping his arms around her as far as they would go, holding her to him. "Cathy?" he asked, his voice thin, frail. "Will you stay with me tonight? I don't want to be alone; I don't even want to fall asleep." He was shaking like a frightened child woken up from a bad dream.

Cathy threaded her arms around his waist. "Of course."

With a nervous shake of his head, Sean pulled himself loose and started for the hallway. Stepping down off the table, straightening her skirt, Cathy crossed the kitchen, locked the door, then followed Sean down the hall. They smiled at each other in the dark when they found the bed not made and the sheets falling off onto the floor. Sean slipped his shirt off as Cathy untied her skirt, letting it fall to the floor around her ankles, but she kept her blouse on as she crawled into bed. Sean followed, not giving it a second thought.

Nothing but the cottony-soft sounds of them slipping beneath the sheets, moving about, finding each other, could be heard in the quiet of Sean's bedroom. Cathy rolled onto her side, facing away from him. Sean fitted himself into the curves of her body and slid his arm around her, filling his hand with her breast.

Cathy held onto his arm, refusing to let his hand move down when he tried, and squirmed herself back into his soft embrace, then smiled at the sound of sleep in her ear as a bewildered look settled down over her face.

14

Monday, July 15, 1991

Dear Bruce,

Is your offer still good to read and edit anything new that I write? Presuming it is, I'm sending you—on diskette—a draft of the first twelve chapters from a story that I started at the end of last month. Using diskettes should make everything easier, no schlepping papers back and forth.

You'll find two diskettes enclosed, one for you to make your comments on and send back to me, the other for you to hold onto for reference. This second one I will replace with an updated version of the manuscript as we go along. Sound simple enough?

I've titled the story *The Strawberry Moon*. But that may change as the storyline develops. I didn't prepare an outline or a synopsis, its just stream of consciousness. Exactly what I told my students never to do. Fuck it!

When you write, tell me what you're doing. And I want to know how your new book is coming along. And one more thing, a bit of advice; move cautiously when it comes to Patricia Jennings. OK?

I miss you, my friend. Give my love to Betty.

Sean

15

Friday, July 19, 1991

Sean glanced up into the rearview mirror without moving his head. The satin-black Porsche was still there, less than a hundred yards behind him, keeping its distance. Not wanting his brake lights to give him away, Sean took his foot off the gas, letting the drag of the engine slow him down. He looked again. The Porsche had matched his move. Without signaling or downshifting, he swerved left into Cathy's driveway, coasting up the sharp incline in third gear. The roar ripping past behind him startled him into stalling out just as he reached the front porch, where Cathy was waiting.

Cathy tipped up onto her toes to see what was no longer on the other side of the wall of forsythia bushes. "It was her, wasn't it?" she asked, walking around the front of the car, peering at Sean through the windscreen with a made-up scowl. He shrugged his shoulders and began tapping his fingers on the wood-rimmed steering wheel in time with the music falling out of the radio in the dash. "Well?" she asked, climbing in, fully expecting—wanting him—to say something about Patricia Jennings.

"I feel like swimming. How about you?" He kept tapping.

This obviously wasn't what Cathy wanted to hear. She snatched his hand off the steering wheel. "I don't have a suit," she said, then tossed his hand back to him, but affectionately.

"Good." He smiled. There was a devilish glint in his eyes as he restarted the engine and pulled down the drive, then out onto

134

Molly Lane, heading west, unable to keep from looking into the rearview mirror every few seconds.

The afternoon rush-hour traffic slowed to a crawl on the Kingston-Rhinebeck Bridge crossing the Hudson from Dutchess to Ulster County. The river was busy, too, filled with powerboats plowing up and down the narrow channel, while little runabouts darted back and forth from shore to shore, bouncing over the deep wakes crisscrossing the river in a frothy herringbone pattern. From high up on the bridge, looking south down the river, the sailboats racing in Kingston Bay, tacking and reaching for the wind, looked like a swarm of multicolored bugs skittering over the water in slow motion from mark to mark.

Suddenly, Patricia was there again, matching his speed as the traffic fanned out onto Route 209 after the tollbooth. Sean pushed his foot to the floor, knowing it was futile, but doing it anyway. Again she mirrored his move. He pulled into the left lane, pushing his little Healy as fast as it would go, flying right past the exit for Route 9W. ''When was the last time you were in Woodstock?'' Sean asked, jumping lanes without warning and rocketing down the exit ramp for Sawkill Road at almost eighty miles an hour.

''Are you planning on driving to it?'' Cathy asked, pinning her feet to the floorboards and bracing herself against the dash. ''Or *over* it!'' She tried a laugh, but it didn't work.

''That depends,'' Sean answered, pumping the brakes, his eyes bouncing back and forth between the rearview mirror and the stop sign racing toward them.

''She missed the exit,'' Cathy said with assurance after glancing up and seeing the Porsche shoot past them on the overpass. Sean skidded through the stop sign, then backed up and slipped the car into neutral, giving his little engine a chance to catch its breath—and him, too. Cathy was sitting perfectly still, her eyes, her whole body tracking the sound of the Porsche as it accelerated down Route 209. Without waiting to find out what Patricia Jennings was going to do, Sean pulled onto Sawkill Road, his rear wheels spinning out on the leftover winter sand, then chirping playfully when they found the road again. He held the tach at 2500, not once touching the brakes, shifting his way through the five miles of winding road hugging the banks of the Sawkill Creek all the way to Route 212, where he turned west, heading into Woodstock.

The center of Woodstock was choked to a summer standstill with bodies and cars fighting each other for the right of way. It was so unlike the early mornings in Woodstock that Sean was used to. At that hour, the village green had been swept broom-clean of every last one of the wannabe hippies, clearing the streets for the sour-faced joggers to jiggle through the common in their trendy designer sweats, while the real hippies, the ones living here long before the concert that never was, raced past the joggers in their baggy jeans and threadbare sweatshirts, chasing after the smell of fresh coffee like it was ganja smoke.

The joggers in Woodstock are called weekenders by the locals, who refer to themselves as "Woodstockians," and do so with a high-pitched, haughty voice. In their own defense, since no one else in Woodstock will come to it, the year-round weekenders are a cut or two above the summer stockers, who only visit during July and August—between Fourth of July and Labor Day week-end to be exact. Not surprisingly, the weekenders and summer stockers are looked upon with equal disdain by the Woodstocki-ans. They don't come right out and say anything; it's the way they look at each other, mouths turned down, eyebrows raised, holding up their permanently wrinkled foreheads, as they glide past these outsiders in the aisles of the falling-down Grand Union on Tinker Street, which always looks like it needs to be swept up and washed down, not unlike the real Woodstockians.

The funny thing is that the weekenders and summer stockers spend most of the money in the overpriced, cutesy shops in town, the ones renovated to look wasted and washed-out, selling out-of-date health food, stale art, imported leather, organic Mexican food for their inorganic patrons, gayly scented candles from San Francisco, bags of harmless incense, and every possible silk-screened T-shirt one could possibly imagine, each one of them made to look socially conscious. However, no one spends as much money in Woodstock as the day-trippers, who visit once, maybe twice every ten years, faithfully keeping the dream alive of a place that never was, except for those real painters and poets and writers, and the real hippies, the Bohemians, the ones with money now, and manners, and nice clothes.

Sitting in traffic, exchanging silent glances that said *Let's get out of here,* Sean pulled down Tannery Brook Road, slowing just long enough to point out Julian's Bakery, "The home of the best scones outside of Glasgow, but not at this time of the day, because they're stale by now," before crossing the metal-grate bridge he hated to go over with his car, and turning left onto Millstream Road. But before he could get out of third gear, he slowed down and pulled over to the opposite side of the road to show Cathy Hippo Hollow.

Hippo Hollow wasn't the real name for this stretch of the old mill stream. It was a made-up name, Sean's made-up name, for a small pond lying at the foot of a low waterfall, halfway between the steel bridge at Tannery Brook and the ugly concrete overpass at West Hurley Road. Sean had noticed the pond on his way to Julian's early one morning on a sultry July day. The water was emerald clear, with pint-sized fish snapping hungrily at wiry-legged bugs skittering over the surface. Everything was whisper quiet, except for the sleepy splash and gurgle of the stream. When he returned thirty minutes later, hot coffee and a scone in hand, the virgin calm had been violated by three very large people; two burly men with long bushy beards, and an even bigger woman. The men appeared to be naked, and if they weren't, it looked that way because of the folds of fat swallowing up anything that might have been considered a bathing suit, as well as their manhood. The woman, with her large, rolling breasts floating in the water like pink pontoons, left little doubt that she was naked, at least from the waist up. But they weren't swimming; They were bathing, soap and all. Wallowing and bobbing about, ducking down to rinse off, then rolling over and rising to the surface, their mountainous bellies breaking through the bubbly film as they slapped themselves like seals. When they finally pulled themselves out of the water, revealing that they were, in fact, naked, and waddled slowly up the hill to their psychedelic, rusted-through VW van, all Sean could think of was a family of hippos.

* * *

It was now almost 8:30. With the hot, gooey sun having dripped down through the cracks in the horizon, it should have started cooling down, but it didn't. It actually seemed to be growing hotter and stickier, making it even harder to breathe than before. Cathy plucked at her shirt, fluffing it off of her skin. "We'll be there soon," Sean assured her, pointing aimlessly through the windscreen. But there wasn't anything to see except road and trees and bushes creeping out of the woods from both sides. "It's across from the old Snyder Estate, in Rosendale." Cathy's head nodded, snapped up, then slowly rocked down again. "Are you too tired to go swimming?" Sean asked, rubbing Cathy's arm, deliberately brushing the back of his fingers against the rounded swell of her breast, testing to see just how tired she really was.

"No," Cathy drawled, leaning into his touch, then snuggling down into the undersized bucket seat just as Sean turned left and pulled up a crunchy gravel drive that was so narrow she had to pull her arm inside the car to keep from being hit by the branches of the wisteria bushes crowding the entrance. They came to a gentle stop in front of an old stone stable.

"Let's go," Sean said, stretching the drive out of his body. He hopped out and started to back down the overgrown driveway. Pushing the door open, Cathy rolled out of her seat and began shuffling over the pebbles to catch up. She curled her fingers under Sean's belt, pulling him back to her sleepy pace. He spun free and dashed away, leaving behind a nasty, older-brother laugh. Cathy caught him and looped her fingers through his belt again, laughing victoriously as he towed her down an abandoned service road to a well house. Circling around back, he stopped when his path was blocked by a dense and threatening row of wild raspberry bushes, ripe with fruit, bordering the top of a steep ridge. "It's down there," he said proudly with a stiff-armed point down the rocky embankment. He jauntily picked a few raspberries and tossed them into his mouth.

Cathy peered over the edge. "And just how do we get down there, Tom Sawyer?" she asked sarcastically. "Fly?"

Matching Cathy's challenge with a smirk of his own, Sean

reached beneath the undergrowth, fished around, and pulled out a fat hemp rope covered with wet earth and choked with vines. "We use this," he said, holding it up, grinning. "Think you can handle it, 'Captain'?"

Cathy let go of Sean's belt with a shove. "She can if you can," she teased, but seriously, and began nudging Sean closer to the edge with a steady poking of her fingers. "You go first," she said, pulling away when he grabbed for her.

Sticking his tongue out, Sean wrapped both hands around the thick rope and backed into the prickly bushes, kicking at the thorny branches snagging his pants. Then, looking serious, he began working his way down the sheer cliff, using as toeholds the mortarless seams in the huge blocks of fractured limestone peering out like Mayan gods from behind twisted vines and roots growing down over their ancient faces. Close to the bottom, the rope swung free above a handful of jagged fingers of stone, clawing their way out into the stream. Pushing off, Sean jumped the last few feet, stumbling and falling backward. When he looked up, he saw Cathy swing out over the ledge and land gracefully beside him without making a sound, except for the muffled slap of her hands on her jeans, dusting off the dirt.

With a smile that said *I'm impressed,* which Cathy was quick to acknowledge with a confident nod of her head, Sean scrambled to his feet and led them out onto one of the moss-covered granite pathways to the very end, where he stopped and kicked his shoes off. "Like it?" he asked, spreading his arms out, inviting Cathy to share in his hidden secret. Before he could turn around, a pair of jeans flew past his head, landing barely a foot from the water's edge. Coins tumbled out of the pockets, a few dancing to a stop in the crevices, others rolling into the water, flickering silver and copper, before disappearing beneath the surface. Panties followed, floating wide of the mark, and were quickly snatched away by the water. Sean stepped out of his jeans, revealing that he wasn't wearing briefs. Cathy's response was unspoken, throaty. When Sean turned back, he smiled at what he found waiting for him. Long bare legs, offering a delicious contrast to the harsh gray stone beneath her feet, and the crisp blue of her new denim shirt, hanging down below her hips, hiding her from him. Avoiding his probing gaze, Cathy shrugged the shirt off her shoulders, keeping the lower half closed with a clenched fist. Taking his own shirt off, Sean dropped it without a care as to where it fell. "Are we shy?" he teased, standing naked, waiting for Cathy to join him.

Dusk was rapidly filling the dense wooded glen, painting everything around them a thousand shades of green and gray. The air was thick and heavy and still. Cathy hadn't moved, and her hand appeared to be shaking. Sean took a step toward her. She told him to stay where he was with a closed-eyed shake of her head, then let the shirt fall off her shoulders onto the ground. And there, in the lost twilight of the warm summer night, Sean saw what Cathy had been hiding from him all this time. Some of the scars were long and thin, others short and thick, all were raw and pink and looking still tender to the touch. Cathy stood anchored to the stone, as if she was now part of it.

Knowing one second too many would tell her what she expected to hear, what the fear in her eyes flashed at him across the expanding abyss between them, Sean rushed forward and scooped her up in his arms, curling her into his chest. Cathy buried herself against him, trying to hide. Sean felt the wet from her eyes and wanted to say a thousand things, but nothing felt right. He shifted his weight. She lifted her head, thinking he was losing his hold. But it was only to raise her higher so he could kiss her there, tenderly, once, then again and again and again, until he had kissed them all away. Her mouth pressed against his neck, her teeth broke his skin, but he felt the pain of her tears more as they burned through his flesh, deep into his heart.

Cathy found his face and kissed him, hungrily biting his lips, pressing herself around him. Then, without warning, she stepped down, only to turn back to see what had pushed hard against her. She was back, sliding her thighs around his rising erection, feeling him growing harder between her legs.

Sean wrapped his arms around Cathy, pulling her to him and lifting her off her feet as he stepped off the ledge, plunging them into the waiting pool. Their bodies sucked in from the cold. Sean held her in his embrace as they sank down, suspended in time.

The Taking

Cathy spread her legs around him and pulled him to her. She was water wet, and tight. He pushed hard, slipping inside. The rush of water ripping against rock drowned out Cathy's close-mouthed cries as he brought them up to the surface with powerful sweeps of his arms, gasping the hot night air into his lungs. Bracing against the splintered granite at the water's edge, he held them up, tethered to the stone, moving in and out of each other, unaware that they were no longer alone.

"Sean?"

"Yes?"

"Were you pleased?"

He hesitated. "Not yet," he said, burying his face in her flesh, sucking on her nipples.

"Why not?"

"Is it really important?"

"Is it because of what I look like?" she asked anxiously.

"No," he said, trying to free himself from her embrace.

Cathy closed her legs around him and squeezed until he protested with a breathless sigh. She then took his face in her hands, pressing her fingers deep into his thoughts. "I love you," she whispered, and repeated her words over and over and over again, but with her body, until he came, arching his back, thrusting hard, losing himself in her, to her.

16

For Sean, seconds sprouted into minutes, minutes grew into hours, and hours flowered, slowing their seasonal pace as days hurried past and the world around him slipped silently by. He didn't watch. It was as if he didn't even care, as the days became nameless, numberless, unhurried, sweet, and delicious. He awoke without the rude prodding of an alarm, long before the sun, clear-eyed and rested, no longer damp and cold from the invisible dreams that once danced wildly through the night just beyond his reach. His days were simple, uncluttered; coffee, sunrise, a few passages from his Bible, the one he read religiously every day, *The Old Farmer's Almanac*. He wrote until he was empty, or blind, or both, which could take all day, and often did. He then ran, sweating, untying the worded knots he'd twisted himself into. Then he found Cathy, and long before most, Sean found sleep, which came easy to him now, perhaps because it was no longer feared.

Sean told himself when he was a young boy, and too soon tired of the soil he was forced to work in, that he would never, ever again, kneel down and put his hands in dirt, a determination that drove him to become what he was. Yet that's exactly what he found himself doing, working at Cathy's side under the lukewarm glare of the late-afternoon summer sun, breaking a dry sweat since there was little left for him to give by that time of day.

When he found her, somewhere out in the fields, or hidden amongst the trees in the orchards, she was bone tired in spite of her strength and unusual stamina, which never failed to impress him. He would call her down from the tractor, steal the weary smile off her face with a fresh kiss, then climb up and replace her at the wheel. But that wasn't something she let him do at first. He had to take a test of sorts before she would let him drive the tractor, her tractor, the green one with the yellow deer jumping over the engine. She laughed more than he did that first time, watching and listening to him tell her, "It's like riding a bicycle, you never forget," as he jerked and chugged his way across the open field. But then he got to the end of the row and tried turning on a dime, something you can't do with an old pinch-wheel tractor. The nose stuck in the ground, and the tractor heeled over. Cathy was there in a breath, kneeling beside him, frightened and worried, then angry when he started laughing and tried pulling her down on top of him.

Sean succeeded in getting Cathy to stop working before the sun fell off the other side of day. It wasn't easy; she'd become accustomed to staying out until it was so dark she had to turn the tractor's lights on to see, and in the summer that meant she was working until after nine o'clock. She didn't have a reason why she did it, she just did. Sally Curtis said it was because Cathy didn't have any place to go (but not because no one ever asked—they did, and often—she just never said yes to anyone).

Before Sean, when Cathy was forced out of the fields by the dark instead of him, she would drag herself back the house and collapse into a hot bath, one of those deep, cast-iron kind with claw feet. The tub was easily large enough for two, with room left over for lots of suds. Sometimes she steeped in it for an hour, now and then draining a little bit out, then adding more hot water with a practiced curl of her toes and twist of her foot, slowly cooking herself clean.

"How can you just sit there and soak in your own dirt?" Sean once asked when he walked in on her after he'd waited downstairs for more than an hour, the dinner that he'd made for them cold and tasteless.

"Because girls don't get dirty the way boys do," had been her flippant reply. "And we don't pee in the water!" she added with a tomboy smirk, tossing a handful of wet suds at him, hitting him in the face, then jumping up when he couldn't see, pulling him down into the tub with her, clothes and all. After that, Sean never said anything to Cathy about her long baths, and he never walked in on her again, either. He knocked first, and entered only after she invited him in. But even then the closest he would get was the bathroom door, which—and he'd made certain of it—was well out of suds range.

The relentless summer heat often drove them across the Hudson, back to Sean's secret swimming hole, which was Cathy's now, too, so it was no longer a secret. Every time they went, Sean was peppered with Cathy's surreptitious questions trying to find out if he'd ever been there with anyone else besides her. "No," he said, giving in to her one evening after they'd stripped their clothes off and were standing naked, side by side, waiting to see who would jump in first. "Never with another woman," he protested.

"Any girls?" she asked, standing ready to push him into the water if he gave her the wrong, or right, answer.

"Nope," he replied with feigned disappointment.

"And just how did you find this buried treasure?" she asked.

He smiled. "Bruce Fanning and I came upon it one blistering hot summer afternoon, when we were driving around in my car with the top down, trying to match up a painting he was authenticating for what he said was a 'demanding woman dealer in the city.' When we found it, we were like little boys, scrambling down the hill, scratching our hands and faces on the pricker bushes, tearing our clothes, and not even caring! Then stripping down and jumping into the water without the slightest concern for how deep it was." He started laughing.

"What's so funny?" Cathy asked, her hands at the ready.

"We weren't alone! Only we didn't know it until after we climbed out and started walking around, naked as a pair of jaybirds, and checking things out like a couple of stray dogs."

"And just who was here?" Cathy asked slyly, anticipating his reply because of his widening smirk.

"Just two other jaybirds!" Sean answered with a wide-eyed grin, and skipped beyond her reach.

"And did their plumes match yours?" Cathy asked, inching closer, her fingers wriggling, ready to tickle.

144

"Nope!" Sean replied, jumping into the stream before Cathy could push him in.

If it was cool in the evening, they would sneak up into the hayloft with an old cotton sheet, stomp the hay flat, and spread the sheet out. But it proved too thin, so they added a second one, then a third for the top to keep the chill off them when the night air snuck in through the loft door, looking for a place to hide. They talked until the sun crept over the horizon and peeked into the hayloft. But mostly Cathy listened, after nudging Sean with a question that didn't sound like a question, something she learned to do with him from the very start. Questions such as, "I can't possibly imagine, no one can, what it was like for you then. It had to be devastating." Or, "I simply don't know how you got through it." Or, "You were very fortunate to have someone close to you, like Bruce, to help." And, "I always thought you were such a good father to him." But that was only once. After the first time, Cathy never mentioned his son again.

Sean leaned back against the rough wooden post shooting up out of the hay to brace the rafters overhead. "I wanted it to be symbolic of nineteenth-century American literature," he said, responding to Cathy's comments about the literary competition he'd started years ago for the prestigious Raven's Quill prize. "The quill represented writing in its simplest form. The oak plaque it was mounted on was my way of symbolizing the Victorian Era, the rise of aestheticism, and a symbolic link between the writers of the past and the towering literary giants of the early twentieth century, who cast a shadow over everything and everyone with their strident, and fundamentally new, writing styles. As for the small gold rings holding the quill to the plaque, the gold was intended to give the award a biblical spirit, not unlike the golden idols referred to in the Old Testament. It was my way of implying that writers should never lose sight of what writing was all about. The rings were cast in the form of scarabs, which symbolize immortality. A rebirth and continuing renewal of sorts for man's creative spirit, just like the dung beetle, which is what the scarab is, that lays its eggs in a ball of camel dung. The Egyptians saw the young beetles breaking free, as if reborn out of the excrement of life, and made them a sacred symbol of resurrection and eternal life. As for the personalized inscriptions I wrote on the plagues in red ink, then lacquered over before the ink had dried so that they would bleed a little, they were simply my bizarre side showing through.'' Sean laughed at himself out loud, which was something he was doing more now.

The Red Hook Inn soon became their dining room, and Sean's office, since he claimed it was halfway between the post office and his apartment—if you bent a straight line into a horseshoe—offering him a place to stop, open and read his mail, all while enjoying Bobby McCarthy's company and a cold beer or two. Or three or four. It was something he had never allowed himself to do, just talk without some definite purpose, some objective, some driven need, and he found that he liked it.

''I don't know why the trustees went after you when no one showed up to claim the Raven's Quill that year,'' Cathy said, matching Sean sip for sip of cold beer. ''I mean, it wasn't like you planned the whole thing!''

Sean doubled his pace and watched to see if Cathy would do the same. She quickly chugged the mug empty, then winked. He couldn't do that, never could, and bowed his head in respect. ''Well, that's not what they thought. If I wasn't responding to the rumor that had me writing the damn story myself under a pen name, I was answering a barrage of asinine questions from one of the bright-eyed, bushy-tailed reporters from *The Spectrum* about my covering up for whoever had written it and refused to come forward because of the furor the story had caused on campus.'' Sean sat back, unfurling a perplexed look down his face. ''I just thought that it was a damn good short story, plain and simple, which is why I published it in *The Quill*. Yes, the language was rough. But no stronger than what Kerouac and his café cronies had spewed forth three decades earlier. And yes, the theme was sort of sacrilegious, but so what. Look at what Arthur Miller gave us. Thank God! Even to this day, I can't honestly say why I was attracted to it. There was some sort of kinship that, I might add, was shared by every member of the editorial board, all of whom served as jurors for the competition.'' Sean appeared to be talking more to himself, or someone else, but certainly not to Cathy. "And I suppose that damned affair I had with—" He stopped abruptly and glanced cautiously over at Cathy. She wasn't looking at him. She was sort of listening with one ear while eating. "There's no question in my mind, now at least, that it was poor judgment on my part to publish that story, only I didn't see it as that back then. Sometimes I think I was just tired of hearing all of the stories about myself. Either I was a 'hermit,' who locked himself away in his office and never went near women. Or I was afraid of them. One of the stories even had me being a closet queen, which amazed me! The simple fact was—"

"It's all behind you," Cathy interrupted, revealing that she was paying far closer attention to what Sean was saying than he thought. "And I think that is the best place to keep it." She still hadn't looked at him. "Unless you don't want to?"

Keep "what" there? Sean asked himself. Janet's murder? My son's death? The short story fiasco? Or is it Patricia Jennings you want me to put behind me? He flagged Bobby McCarthy for another beer. Then, as if trying to mollify Cathy, or simply to get her to look at him, Sean said, "I suppose what really fueled most of the rumors, and contributed to my growing isolation over the years, which my colleagues tried their best to pull me out of, was my preoccupation with the way my wife had been killed. I had become obsessed with the symbolic meaning of it all, and was convinced that there was a message of some sort hidden in the ritualistic way she had been killed. When my son died, I guess I went off the deep end, which, without Bruce, I might never have been able to climb out of. In a way, he kept me from drowning."

Cathy was now listening with every part of her being, and Sean saw that, only now it was he who couldn't look her in the eye. "And your celibate life?" Cathy asked, setting her hands down onto the table from where they had been pressed together, palm to palm, like she was praying.

Sean inched his hands across the table, covering her fingers with his. "I don't know why." He began tracing the outline of her hands and following the lazy movement of his own fingers with his eyes. "Maybe I was . . ." He stopped again in mid-sentence, unable, or perhaps unwilling, to finish what he'd started to say, and he refused to give Cathy his eyes to tell which it was. She'd slipped and asked a direct question, begging a direct answer, and it was too late now to do anything about it.

"It must have been very lonely for you," she said softly, hoping to undo what she'd done.

But Sean was now buried deep inside himself, unable to dig his way out.

17

Monday, July 29, 1991

Bruce,

I took your suggestions at face value. The revisions are here, along with what I wrote since then. Your thoughts and recommendations have also been carried into the new work. I think everything reads much better now. You're a genius! Thanks.

The 24th and 25th of August are blanked out on my calendar for the Cole House gathering. Cathy Greene will be accompanying me. When I wrote Oliver, I invited him, too—on your invitation—which I hope was all right. I'm fairly certain that he'll bring a new lady friend. I think her name is Hazel Kent. Be sure to let me know the exact day and time.

I look forward to reading your reactions to the rewrite. And above all, knowing what your thoughts are on the new stuff.

Sean

18

Tuesday, August 20, 1991

Twisting all around and turning upside down, looking like a human pretzel, Sean collected the mail scattered on the floor of his car from his madcap ride from the post office to the Red Hook Inn. Clutching the swirl of envelopes to his chest, he sprinted through the back parking lot to the side entrance, laughing to himself at some suddenly remembered boyhood game as he slipped inside. "Safe!" he whispered and stole himself to a seat in the back of the room, where he sat down and began sorting and stacking and primping the envelopes into neat piles.

"Doc!" rang out across the room, making Sean jump. You're caught, Sean told himself, and reluctantly gave up yesterday for today as Bobby McCarthy walked up and set a foamy draft down in front of him. "What are you doing out this early in the day?" Sean didn't answer right away. He just sat there, sucking the head off his mug of ice-cold beer and peering past Bobby at the multicolored words printed on the dusty chalkboard over the bar. "What are you grinning at?" Bobby asked, then looked back over his shoulder and began checking off with a reassuring nod of his head each of the words that he'd written.

"I'll have a ham and swiss on rye," Sean ordered. "With mustard and lettuce and sliced onion. And another beer," he pronounced, then set about draining the mug.

"You got it," Bobby replied smartly and left.

Sean went back to playing with his mail. Junk mail got tossed onto an empty chair beside him as he built up a pair of side-by-

149

side stacks in front of him. He ceremoniously split them into three for no apparent reason, then looked around the room, smiling at himself and shaking his head discreetly. "You've got to stop that," he whispered. Using the knife rolled up in the napkin at his place, wincing at the metallic clanking when the fork and spoon slipped out onto the table, Sean slit open one envelope and unfolded the letter inside without looking at it, then ran his thumbnail over the creases, pressing them flat, before turning the typewritten letter over and reading it.

Sean,

My editorial comments on your most recent chapters will follow under separate cover. You're writing faster than I can give you feedback. But it's good, and I like it, so keep it up.

From what I hear, mostly from Sarah Potter, you and Catherine Greene are getting along wonderfully. Other than seeing her at Sarah's party for the faculty last June, I honestly don't remember her as a student. I'm looking forward to meeting her again.

As you may have heard by now, Betty has left me, and I don't expect that she'll be returning. Yes, it's over between us. Patricia Jennings has been very supportive in this whole thing. Quite frankly, Sean, I think you misjudged her.

When you see Oliver, tell him that he can attend the Cole House party. As it turns out, the director already knows him from a book the two of them worked on a few years ago as contributing authors. Small world, isn't it?

See you all in a few days.

Bruce

Bruce's letter was undated. The postmark was August thirteenth, and the mailer for the diskette, which had been stuffed into the envelope, wasn't addressed in Bruce's hand, but Patricia Jennings' precise, controlled handwriting. With a sharp snap of his wrist, Sean tossed the letter into the center of the table, causing it to spin around and around like a paper top. He then slapped the diskette on top of it in disgust.

"You're losing it, my friend," Sean snapped. "Cathy wasn't at the reception,"—he paused—"at least I didn't see her. You must be thinking of someone else, you old letch."

The next envelope didn't have a return address, so he was about to add it to the junk pile, but it was hand-addressed, and the postmark was Gramercy Park, making it too tempting not to open, which he did with a sense of mystery. It was handwritten like the envelope, with a confident yet casual swirl to the letters, making it inviting and easy to read. There wasn't a signature, just a large, solitary upper-case letter struck boldly at the bottom, as if penned by a calligrapher.

My Dear Sean,

I'm in Manhattan, preparing to fly home. Although my business was finished yesterday, I stayed over because I wanted to drive up and see you. However, after renting a car and starting out, I turned back, realizing that you cannot, and must not be, no matter how I feel about you.

For reasons I can never explain, I wish I had never met you. But I wouldn't have it any other way, not after what you gave me. No, what I took from you, even after your body said no. Then again, after you were asleep. Yes, Sean, asleep. But then, men never know about that.

There are so many things I wish I could tell you, but can't. There are also things that I now know that I wish I hadn't found out. In a way, a way that you can't possibly understand, you gave me a new life. I believe I did the same for you, but I pray, for the both of us, you never have to put it to the test.

I really don't know why I'm writing, since I shouldn't be. Maybe it's so I can be done with it, done with you! But that's silly, since I realize that I will never be done with you. And

you will never be done with me, never, even though you may
think so.

K

"Fan mail?" The sound of Cathy's voice gave Sean a start.
For a second he felt guilty, then stupid at thinking that. She was
covered with dust from head to toe, and her shirt was ringed with
sweat stains. Bending down, she kissed him on the cheek. The
heavy aroma of hard work tumbled down off her body and settled
over Sean, arousing him instantly. He slid his hand up between
her legs, grabbing hold of a handful of fabric and flesh on the
inside of her thigh. She squeezed her legs shut, stopping him.
"You're amazing!" she said, shaking her head more with delight
than disapproval. "Mind if I join you?"

Sean's hand retreated back down Cathy's thigh. "Of course
not." He let go and turned to look for Bobby McCarthy, only to
bump into his oversized biceps. The pair of frosted mugs sitting
in the center of the cork-lined tray, which was balanced in the
flat of his huge, open hand, began sloshing back and forth.

"He's already had two, Cath," Bobby announced. "OK to give
him a third?"

Cathy punched Bobby in the arm, but the way a man would,
not a woman, causing the beer to start rocking all over again, this
time losing its head. Ignoring it, and Cathy, too, Bobby set the
mugs down, then turned and walked away, but not before giving
Sean a stone-faced wink.

"How's the writing going?" Cathy asked.

"Fast, unbelievably fast. I'm working my way through the last
chapter. But then I know there will be dozens of rewrites after
that." Sean snatched up Bruce's letter. "Speaking of which"—
he waved it over the table—"I heard from Bruce."

Taking the letter, Cathy scanned it over the rim of her glass as
she sipped. She then read it again, slowly. "What do you think
about his feelings toward Patricia Jennings?" she asked without
a trace of emotion in her voice, or on her face.

Not that, Sean thought to himself, and regretted having given

Cathy the letter. "I don't think he wrote the letter." Sean tapped the mailer on the table in front of him with his index finger. "We've been using diskettes to write back and forth. The letter doesn't make sense. Besides, he doesn't have a carbon-ribbon typewriter, at least not that I know of. As for his feelings about Jennings? I think he's wrong, dead wrong, and I only hope that it doesn't—" Sean cut himself off.

"Doesn't what?" Cathy asked, sitting up, then tipping back and slipping her fingers into the waist of her jeans.

"Nothing," Sean replied.

"You've slept with her, haven't you?" Cathy asked out of the blue, then buried her eyes deep into Sean's, waiting for his answer. Not that she needed him to tell her what he already had by the ashen look on his face.

Sean sat up stiff as a rod. "Yes," he said, but with a great deal of difficulty. He then braced himself for the other shoe to drop, her wanting to know when.

"When she was an undergraduate? Or in '86, when she came back to finish up her degree after her marriage to Ira Jennings? Or haven't you stopped sleeping with her?"

Sean was pinned back in his chair. "How did you . . ."

Standing up, slapping at the dust on her clothes, Cathy said softly, "I made arrangements to get away this coming Saturday."

"Do you still want to go with me?"

"Yes," Cathy said without hesitation. She then pointed at the letter lying open on the table. "I give you odds that Bruce shows up with her, and I want to meet her." Cathy turned and left, leaving unanswered what she really wanted to know.

19

Sean's feet sank into a pile of clothing crumpled on the floor
beside his bed, next to his own pajamas, which he'd thrown off
sometime during the night because it was so hot and muggy.
Turning around, he found Cathy scrunched up against the wall,
sound asleep. Falling back, he buried his face in the sheets
wrapped loosely around her naked body, filling his lungs, his
heart, with the pillowy-sweet smell of sleep. He got an instant
rush and felt himself becoming delightfully aroused. No! he told
himself, knowing that she had to have gotten in well after he'd
gone to bed and after a long hard day. He rocked back up and
tiptoed quietly out of the room, gently pulling the door closed
behind him.

Once in the kitchen, Sean moved about as if everything was
made of sugared lace, even the linoleum floor, which he skated
over in his bare feet, trying to keep it from crackling too loud.
While waiting for the water to boil, thinking about the caffeine
comfort soon to be coursing through his veins, Sean stepped into
the center of the kitchen, into the sunlight creeping over the horizon and sneaking in through the windows, letting it warm his
naked body. The porch downstairs creaked, freezing him. He held
his breath, listening. "It must be Jean at this hour," he told himself.

Footsteps took his breath away again. There was a scratching
at the kitchen door. Turning his head, he saw Patricia Jennings,
smiling at him through the lace curtains, tickling the glass with

her fingernails, asking to be let in. Her smile widened when he turned all the way around, and she looked down. With a furious shake of his head, Sean mouthed, No!

Patricia countered with a playful up-and-down nodding of her head as she leaned against the door with her hands. It popped open an inch or two and stuttered to a stop. Before he could get over and close it, Patricia was inside. "Hi!" She closed the door behind her with a hidden hand.

Sean asked through a hushed whisper, "What do you think you're doing here?"

Stepping forward, Patricia brushed her fingers through the hair on his chest. "I've got fresh croissants," she announced proudly, and held up a small white paper bag. "And one still-hot blueberry scone." Patricia gestured to the empty glass pot on the stove with the filter balanced on top and fresh ground coffee nestled inside. "From the looks of it, you're right on time with the coffee." She winked, then sauntered over and put the bag down on the kitchen table. When she turned back, she had the look in her eyes of a cat, a very large cat, one that had just cornered her prey.

"Patricia," Sean said, holding his arms outstretched, "please leave."

Patricia shut her eyes and shook off Sean's request. She then plucked at the bow tied behind her neck, shrugged her tanned shoulders, and watched Sean's eyes follow her yellow shirtwaist dress as it slid down over her bare breasts, paused on her hips, then collapsed into a puddle of color on the floor around her feet. "There!" she quipped, standing stark naked. "You're not alone anymore."

"No!" Sean pleaded, inching backward when Patricia stepped out of her sandals and started moving toward him. But the other part of him, the part he never had any control over, told her something completely different, and he suddenly felt more than just naked. When she took another determined step, he hurried his retreat across the kitchen.

Patricia reached out, shaking her head and pointing at him. This only made Sean pull back that much faster. "Ow!" he yelped, lurching away from the hot stove and into Patricia's outstretched arms.

A sleep-filled voice called, "Sean? Are you all right?" He broke free, pushing Patricia away. "What the hell are you doing here!" Cathy demanded as she walked into the kitchen. Her body was instantly carved up into twisted ribbons of pink and orange by the raking sunlight slicing through the windows. Patricia stepped back, her eyes bursting open on her face. Cathy followed Patricia's horror-stricken gaze, giving her the time she needed to snatch her dress off the floor and start for the door. Cathy moved at her, her hand reaching out, forcing Patricia to jump back and hit her head on the wall. Her eyes banged shut, then popped back open. She grabbed the kitchen door, threw it open, and darted out into the darkened hallway. The sound of bare feet pounding into the steps was followed by a screen door swinging open and slamming against the house, then slapping shut. There was the thunk of a car door, followed by the roar of an engine, rattling the brittle glass in the windows as tires screeched the day awake.

As if in a trance, Cathy drifted past Sean, tripping over Patricia's sandals, and closed the door. She locked it with a determined twist of her wrist, then turned back, her eyes filled with tears. She tried laughing, but couldn't. She stood there forever, then slowly walked over and picked up Patricia's sandals, handing them to Sean, refusing to look at him as she walked out of the kitchen and down the hall, into the bathroom.

She let the shower run until the air was filled with billowing clouds of steam. When she stepped in, her hair melted down her neck and over her shoulders in rivulets of honey and gold. Sean slipped into the bathroom unnoticed, hiding beneath the noisy splash of water. He stepped in behind her, gently pressing himself against her. Cathy arched away from him. Sean took hold of her waist, pulling her back to him. Cathy placed her hands on the tiled wall, her fingers spread wide, her whole body rigid, and leaned forward, bracing herself. Sean eased himself inside her. She was tight and cold and dry. Water started pooling in the small of her back. Sliding deeper, Sean grew harder as Cathy answered him beat for beat and measure for measure, until he knew that he no longer mattered.

The hot, muggy air in the kitchen was thick, too thick even to squeeze through the open windows, leaving the room to bake in the glare of the hot sun. Sean wiped the beads of sweat off his brow with the damp towel, then dropped it over the back of the chair. The faint sound of a car idling, then stopping, pulled him to the window just in time to see Oliver stepping out of a large black car and stand on the running board.

"Oliver," Sean called down, "what are doing with that Rolls?"

Looking up, Oliver waved. "Know what it is?" He was hardly able to contain his excitement.

Sean leaned out the window, stretching his neck, his whole body, trying to get a better look. "Where did you steal that from?"

Cathy walked into the kitchen, looking cool and powder dry as only a woman could in this heat. "What is it?" she asked, straightening the pair of ponytails that she'd split her long blond hair into, looking like a grown-up pixie, a very tall pixie. Sean rushed past her, dragging his bright-eyed smile into a blur in front of her face, and raced downstairs. Throwing open the screen door, he vaulted off the porch and darted across the lawn, coming to rest squarely in front of Ollie's car, mimicking the toothy grin of the massive chrome grill with one of his own.

Oliver beamed like a proud father as Sean walked around the car on his silent inspection tour. A woman was stretched out on the expansive rear seat, sound asleep. She didn't budge when the front end was rocked up and down, making everything squeak. But the opening and closing of the doors, first the front, then back, earned Sean and Oliver a sleepy-eyed scowl when she sat up, then yawned and tipped back down out of sight.

"She's beautiful, Ollie!" There was a twinge of adolescent envy in Sean's voice. He was fighting to keep his hands off the graceful, ski-jump slope of the rear boot. "These James Young coach-built bodies are the most stylish of all of the postwar Rolls

Royces.'' Sean let his fingers caress the air over the car, feeling the dry heat rising up from the liquid black skin.

"She was a state car," Oliver said proudly. "She was placed into service sometime during the summer of 1956, at Balmoral Castle. The London dealer I purchased her from said that he acquired it just this past winter, directly from the royal family. He said they traded it in for a new Phantom.''

The tires of the Rolls Royce were tall and fat and white from the hubcap to the tread. The body was soft and smooth, as if sculpted out of black clay, not stamped out of aluminum. The hand-rubbed lacquer finish was so deep that it swallowed up the clouds overhead. The front-bench seat was fitted with leather, while the rear compartment was upholstered in a gray felted wool. The burl-walnut trim filling the dash and wrapping around the inside of the car appeared to be coated with glass, not polish. The divider was electric and slow. Stately was a kinder term. And it was whisper quiet as it raised and lowered the transparent wall of class between driver and driven. The faint smells inside were pungent and spicy, with a hint of sweet and sour that brought to mind images of moist skin, while the delicate stains on the headliner told of champagne having been opened with regal excitement. But everything else remained silent, as it should.

Oliver opened the driver's-side door and offered Sean the keys. But Sean declined with a shake of his head, then locked his hands behind his back to make sure he couldn't change his mind as he peered inside, listening to Ollie run on about all of the little idiosyncrasies he'd found so far. "I couldn't help myself," Oliver confessed. "It was love at first sight!"

"Was it always chauffeur driven?" Sean asked, rubbing his hand over the leather on the driver's side seat.

"As far as I can tell, yes." Oliver pointed to the passenger side. "But those scratches there have me confused."

Sean crawled halfway in and rubbed his fingers over the barely visible hatch marks. "My guess is that they're from a dog." He backed out of the front seat and stood on the running board. "Something small, like a Cavalier King Charles Spaniel."

Agreeing with an amused grumpfh, Oliver reached in and gestured at the floorboard. "What's that extra pedal for? The little one, to the left of the clutch and few inches higher?"

"Oiler," Sean said without looking. Oliver pushed himself closer to get a better look. "The chauffeur would pump it when he felt the chassis needed lubrication." Sean had pushed the word "chassis" through his teeth, making it sound like shhha-sea, instead of chopping it up the way it's done on this side of the Atlantic. A smile wriggled itself into Oliver's beard.

But before he could ask what he wanted to know, the crack of the screen door ended Sean's little lecture, much to Oliver's disappointment. "Dr. Shore!" Cathy stepped down off the porch and walked smartly across the lawn. "It fits you like a glove."

Oliver looked at Sean with an expectant gaze. "Oliver Shore," Sean said with a melodramatic sweep of his arm and a deep bow at the waist. "I'd like you to meet Ms. Catherine Greene." He turned to Cathy, standing as stiffly as he possible could and puckering a goofy grin. "Ms. Greene," he said, turning back to Oliver, crossing his eyes, looking silly, "this is Oliver Shore."

Ignoring Sean's clowning, Oliver stepped forward and said in his best baritone, which was now seasoned with a British accent, "My pleasure, Miss Greene. I'm honored to meet you." He offered his hand.

"I've heard a lot about you, Oliver," Cathy said with a charming smile.

A bright, sunny voice added to the stilted Victorianesque ceremony. "Hi! I'm Hazel."

Oliver quickly added, "Kent," and stepped aside.

A perky redhead, speckled head-to-toe with rusty brown freckles, was standing on the running board, looking wide awake. She wasn't more than five feet tall, nor more than a hundred pounds. But she had a grown-up woman's figure that might easily be called busty, if you were a woman. A man would have said it differently, and thought it still another way.

"Hello, Hazel Kent," Cathy said cheerfully and extended her hand. "I'm Catherine Greene. Please call me Cathy." Cathy then herded the two men out of the way. "Let's leave them to play with their toy." With a protective sweep of her arm around Hazel's shoulders, Cathy turned and led Hazel back to the house.

The moment they were out of sight, Oliver and Sean climbed into the rear passenger compartment of the seven-passenger Rolls Royce, raised the fold-down footrests, propped their feet up, and stretched out, looking every bit the gentlemen that their boyish smirks said they couldn't possibly be. "Want to talk numbers?" Oliver asked, slipping his hand into the top of his wool blazer, which was wilted and wrinkled from the heat and humidity.

Sean groaned and grabbed hold of Oliver's wrist. "Just leave whatever it is you have tucked inside that ancient blazer of yours." He pulled Oliver's hand out of his inside pocket and rested it on top of his formidable midsection.

Staring at Sean as if surveying his change of mood, Oliver backed himself into the corner of the rear seat, out of Sean's reach, and retrieved what it was he wanted. "His royal highness can look at it whenever it pleases him," Oliver said pompously, sounding like the Lord High Chamberlain himself. Then, with his cherublike cheeks glowing red, and his large round eyes bulging with mischief, Oliver broke into a bearlike roar, startling Sean, and lunged across the seat, his manly laugh breaking up into a high-pitched schoolboy cackle as he pinned Sean in place and stuffed the small gray envelope into Sean's shirt before he knew what was happening to him. Rolling off onto the floor, his cackle having cooled to a snicker, Oliver crawled out of the car onto the lawn, where he raised himself to one knee and paused to catch his breath.

"What in the world are you two doing?" Cathy sang out from the kitchen window. Hazel wedged herself into what little space she could find, a baby chick squeezing beside its mother hen.

Bursting out of the car, batting Cathy's meddlesome query away with a slap of his hand, Sean tackled Oliver from behind with a loud cheer. It started them tumbling arm in arm and belly over backside across the lawn. With Oliver's bushy red beard, rotund girth, and oversized hands pawing at Sean, matched against Sean's height, muscular shoulders, and longer arms, the two men looked like a recalcitrant circus bear and its irate handler wrestling about on the lawn, laughing and coughing and bickering between gasps for air.

"Stop that this minute!" Jean Murphy demanded with a stomp of her foot on the porch. "I said, stop it!"

Splitting apart, rolling onto their backs and breathing heavily through self-satisfied sighs, Sean and Oliver pushed themselves up into split-legged sitting positions. They started laughing all over again when they looked at each other, and fell backward onto the grass, their arms and legs splayed out like angels without snow.

Hazel took a breath to yell something down to Oliver. Cathy tapped her on the arm, then smiled when Hazel turned to see what she wanted. "Let them be," she said affectionately. "I don't know about Oliver, but Sean needs this more than he knows."

Still laughing, the two men helped each other to their feet and began brushing themselves off without saying a word as they ambled across the lawn to the Rolls, drifting apart, then back, bumping, then apart again, looking like a pair of disheveled vagrants. They climbed back into the Rolls, each from the other side, their faces lighting up as they pulled the big doors shut behind them, and collapsed into the plush gray of their elegant clubhouse to plan their day.

20

Saturday Afternoon

Pockets of puffy black and white clouds kept rushing up, stomping their thunderous hooves overhead, then galloping away as if spooked, giving back the sun. And now and then it rained, but Sean didn't seem to care; the top was staying down. Besides, as long as he didn't let his speed drop below thirty, he and Cathy stayed dry as they drove north along Route 32 from Woodstock to Catskill. Double-bagged and tucked behind the seats in the boot, staying fresh and warm, was their admission to the party at The Cole House: an armful of baguettes, three dozen *petit pain*, four large *pain de campagne*, a gaggle of brioches, and two dozen croissants, which were dripping with so much butter that they'd stained through the bags by the time Sean and Cathy walked from the back door of Julian's and climbed into the car. For dessert there were strawberry, raspberry, and blueberry linzer tortes.

Cathy reached out and put her hand on Sean's leg. "You surprised me this morning in the shower." She began scratching the smooth fabric of his light-blue slacks with her fingernails, as if digging for something. When Sean didn't say anything, Cathy worked her way along his leg and up his arm, wriggling her fingers like a spider, popping open a button and slipping into his shirt. The twitching of his muscles asked her to stop, but not. She wandered over his chest, ruffling the hair then smoothing it, before settling on one small spot when a quick breath told her what she'd found. His nipple hardened like a pebble between her fingers. Sean shook his head and started smiling to himself as he let

162

The Taking

the car coast to a stop beside a grassy meadow lying at the foot of a dense cluster of oak trees separating two just-plowed fields. The air was damp and the soil sweet from the fresh wounds carved into the rich dark earth.

Looking up and down the deserted country road, then over to Sean, Cathy asked, "What are you doing?"

"What we both want." He gestured for her to get of the car, then pushed himself up onto the back of the seat and stepped over the door without bothering to open it. Taking Cathy's hand, Sean dove into the lake of waist-high grass bordering the field. The two of them laughed at the feel of it splashing around them as they waded through to the other side, where it drained away to ankle height, tickling their bare skin as they hurried into the woods. Hidden behind a lush ceiling of green, sunbeams of gold and dust were shooting holes through the branches, forcing the dried leaves on the ground to dance with the daylight. Sean slipped his shirt off and spread it out on the ground. Cathy sat down on the soft patch of dark blue, circled by wispy-thin sprays of green grass, and raised her hips. She slipped off her slacks and panties in a single, graceful move, and leaned back, watching Sean unzip his jeans, struggle with them, and laugh at himself before letting them drop to the ground around his feet. Cathy braced herself on her elbows. Sean knelt down between her legs, pressing gently, then sliding, falling deep inside her, shattering the pastoral silence surrounding them as he came before touching bottom, and for the first time, before Cathy.

The entrance to the early-nineteenth-century homestead of painter Thomas Cole, in Catskill, wound its way back and forth up the steep, wooded hillside from the recently paved county road. Once the original carriage path, it was now little more than a pair of narrow dirt ruts hiding beneath a scraggly cover of tenacious crab-grass. On one side of the meandering drive was a falling-down wooden fence, splashed with whitewash and held up in the thorny embrace of rosebushes gone wild. On the other side was a regimented column of ancient oak trees, old enough to have been drawn as saplings by the artist himself, and recorded in his sketch-

Donald Beman

book. Where the path met the corner of the house it leveled off and turned into gravel, then passed beneath the sagging steps of the weathered porch surrounding the brick-and-frame Federal-style house that Thomas Cole and his family of women once lived, and died, in. A few yards beyond the porch, the drive underwent another metamorphosis, changing from pea-sized crushed stone into dirt and grass. It then circled around Cole's studio, now a modest cottage, before disappearing behind wavy rows of aging grapevines, their bony arms heavy with clusters of luscious green and purple grapes, each one tethered to rusting wires with carefully tied bows of sun-bleached twine.

Cars were parked everywhere, some slipped beneath painted but barren trellises, others tucked between overgrown flower beds. A few were lined up side by side on the edge of the uncut lower lawn, rafting like a fleet of classic wooden runabouts. There were four basic colors—red, white, green, and black—except for an old MG TF, looking barely able to stand up on its spindly, wood-spoked wheels, that proudly wore its wartime coat of olive-drab over its thin tin skin, and an XJ-6 Jaguar sedan, which was dark burgundy and sporting Connecticut license plates that read LA TACHE.

Perched on top of the wooded hillside, circled by flowering forsythia bushes bowing elegantly low to the ground, were sunlit patches of lawn. Each carpet of green was pinned in place with lacquered wooden poles hammered into the ground behind curving wire wickets, their skinny necks ringed with red and white and blue and green. The fragile woodland grass had likely been cut with an old-fashioned wood-handled mower, the heavy cast-iron kind that you push, pull back, then push again, leaving behind feathery blades of grass.

People were milling about, talking and nodding, holding brightly colored croquet mallets in one hand while balancing long-stemmed glasses in the other. The men had their mallets hoisted over their shoulders, trying their masculine best to look comfortable with their impotent wooden-headed axes. The women let theirs swing lazily at their sides as they glided over the lawn

164

in their ankle-length dresses, blown from point to point by a gentle summer breeze.

"Oliver!" someone called. "Oliver Shore. Welcome to the Thomas Cole House." Not wanting to reach in front of Cathy and Hazel, Julian Davidson stepped around behind them and held out both hands to Oliver. But not to be shaken, to be taken and held, as if he didn't want Oliver to get too close to him. "And you must be Dr. MacDonald." Pulling back one of his hands before Oliver could take it, Julian Davidson gave it to Sean. "Dear Bruce has spoken highly of you, Dr. MacDonald." A sense of pleasure filled the air, making what Julian Davidson said wholly believable. But then something in his face changed, as if to say, Brace yourself. "Bruce was even kind enough to share with me your personal views on Thomas Cole's paintings."

Sean sighed, "He didn't!" and dropped his shoulders, looking like a sinful supplicant about to receive a reprimand.

"He most certainly did," Julian replied with a theatrical sweep of his arms. But there was no malice to be found in the way he played his role.

Julian Davidson could have been a character drawn with the creative quill of Washington Irving, an Ichabod Crane, but with a few more pounds. He was taller than Sean, and he towered over Oliver. His hands were wide and weathered and worn rough, exposing him as being more than just an academic. His skin was drawn tight over his flesh. His hair was straight, decrying the need for a comb or a brush as it fell in thin silken layers to both sides of his head, barely covering his Ichabodian ears. He had chocolate brown eyes. But the most curious thing was that he didn't have to shave, which made guessing his age that much more difficult than it already was.

Sean brought his hands together in mock prayer. "I hope you'll allow me to explain," he said with a solicitous bow of his head.

"There's really no need to, Dr. MacDonald," Julian replied through a friendly, inviting laugh. "Knowing Bruce, as I'm sure we both do, I guarantee that he conveniently forgot to tell you that I, too, think Cole painted by numbers." Julian feigned an indignant manner. "But melted crayons!" he exclaimed, laughing. Then, stepping backward, refusing to take his eyes off Sean, Julian retrieved an empty glass and open bottle of wine from the makeshift buffet table behind him. The table was the folding aluminum kind found at backyard parties. After handing Sean the glass, Julian poured it half full. "Bruce also told me that you know your wines." He held the bottle up to the sun and peered into it. "I'd like to know what you think of my Chateau Cole." He leveled his gaze at Sean and tightened the muscles in his jaw.

Seeing that he was on trial, Sean raised the glass to his nose, paused, breathed in ever so gently, then took the tiniest of sips and held it on his tongue. He rinsed it about in his mouth, pitched his head back, gargled discreetly, and swallowed.

"Well?" Julian asked, leaning forward into Sean's reply.

Sean hesitated, selfishly hoarding what he knew and giving it up only when Julian appeared about to burst with anticipation. "It's young," he said decisively, accepting Julian's expectant stare. "And it's a bit foxy, but that's the true nature of the Concord grape, which is what I taste. And it's a little tired." Julian's face puddled into disappointment. "But it's fresh and happy, the perfect summer wine for an occasion such as this, and it will have no trouble standing up to anything we can throw at it. I like it. I like it a lot." Julian's face percolated back to life. With Julian beaming still, Sean turned to introduce Cathy, only to find her circling around another table with Hazel in tow, balancing a paper plate in one hand, happily filling it with anything that would break loose with a twist or tug of her free hand.

The table was rough-sawn planking laid across wooden horses hidden beneath a five-and-dime, red-checked tablecloth. But there was nothing simple about what had been set out on top of the country tablecloth. There were plates melting down under the hot sun into pools of creamy Brie and Camembert. Only the extra-sharp Vermont cheddar was still standing firm. The loaves of bread created a floured obstacle course, offering the choice of breaking the end off of a baguette sticking its skinny neck into the air, slicing up the sesame seed–covered Italian loaf, tearing off a chunk of dark pumpernickel, or deciding where to cut into the powdered mound of crusty peasant bread, sitting as yet un-

touched in the center of the table and daring anyone to try. The
pâté was easy; One simply chiseled a chunk off of the heavy brick
filled with goose liver, fresh veal, country pork, and truffles,
wrapped in bacon and sprinkled with black and white pepper. The
salmon mousse was pressed into the shape of a one-eyed fish,
looking more like a flounder than a salmon, lying on a bed of
rapidly melting crushed ice. No one bothered with the pasta, except for one rather heavy man who grimaced in pain with each
dollop he dropped onto his barren plate, while devouring everything around him with his gluttonous gaze, including the mound
of garden-fresh colors smothered under gobs of chunky blue
cheese, sprinkled with crisp bacon, and topped with croutons.

Sean gestured across the lawn. "The tall lady with the tan
slacks and sandy-blond hair is Catherine Greene." He paused,
smiling at the sight of grass stains on the back of Cathy's slacks,
so faint that only he could tell what they were. "She's mine."
Looking back at Julian, who raised his glass and his eyebrows in
a mock toast, Sean instantly regretted having said what he did,
the way he did. "And the petite redhead with the fiery look in
her eyes, standing beside her, is Hazel Kent. She's with Oliver."
Sean turned to Oliver, who all this while had been listening patiently and prodded him to say something.

Oliver grumbled, "Where's the ale, Davidson?"

Sean and Julian exchanged private glances, knotted with a twist
of confusion. Julian pointed to a red plastic cooler sitting under
the aluminum picnic table. "You'll find what you want in there.
It's Bass, not Whitbread. I hope it will do."

"It will do just fine, thank you." Oliver beamed and made his
way to the white-handled treasure chest a dozen paces away.

Julian stepped closer to Sean when Oliver began digging noisily through the ice. "I hope your croquet game is up to par," he
said secretively. "We've got a few money players in our midst
today, so be wary—they'll try getting you to wager. And not for
nickels and dimes, either." He gestured with a nod of his head,
and said in an even quieter voice, "Be particularly careful of
those two men standing near the path leading up to Cole's old
studio, which is my pied-à-terre from June to September while

we're open to the public. The tall one with the condescending scowl is a painting dealer from the city. Rumor has it that he has more money than any man should be allowed to possess. The short one is an artist who, I'm told, aside from being the best contemporary trompe l'oeil still life painter on the scene today, has a nasty temper.''

Julian's advice had a clandestine air about it and made Sean feel honored in some perverse way at having been taken into his confidence. Sean moved a little closer to Julian. ''Thanks for the warning,'' he said in a near whisper, which he pushed out of the side of his mouth. ''But my guess is they're the ones who will have to watch out, but for Oliver, not me. He practically lives the game when he's in England, and he just returned from a summer-long stay, so he should be in fine form.''

Julian stiffened. ''Canterbury?'' Sean nodded. ''Could it be for another one of his harebrained projects?'' Julian had spoken deliberately loud enough for Oliver to hear, which he did, but said nothing.

Sean swallowed the sip of wine in his mouth. ''Yes, how did you know?'' he asked, before noticing Julian's soured look and realizing his words were meant to do real harm, not just tease.

Julian tightened his sarcastic noose. ''What else does the little man have to do? Was he chasing the Devil, or does he still think Satan is after him?''

Sean wasn't sure if he wanted to get into this, not today, but he was sorely tempted to accept Julian's challenge, if nothing else but to say something in Ollie's defense. Not that Oliver Shore needed anyone to speak up for him. ''Both, in a way,'' Sean finally said, trying not to sound defensive. ''He took over my work in numerical mysticism and merged it with his own research into somewhat of a similar bent, which I'm not really that familiar with. From what little I know, I think his focus is more on history, nonfiction so to speak, as compared with my work, which dealt with literary fiction.''

Julian tried beating a graceful retreat from his assault on Oliver. ''Oh. I see. And what, exactly, were you working on?''

''Nothing original,'' Sean responded in a less-guarded manner.

"I toyed for quite a number of years with mystical numerology and its symbolic presence in nineteenth-century American literature and art. My focus was primarily on the literary side, because of my limited knowledge of fine art from that period."

Sean's reply must have sparked something inside Julian, for he suddenly came alive. "Right!" He held up his hand, shaking his finger. "Bruce mentioned that." Julian extended an inviting hand to Sean, once again without any expectation of it actually being taken. "We'll have to talk some time." His offer had a feeling of insincerity written all over it, like the kisses socially chic women give everyone that never, ever, touch their cheeks.

Relieved, Sean seconded Julian. "Great!" He then matched Julian's empty-glass toast to their vague understanding of sorts.

Julian asked, "Have you been inside the Cole House yet?" He followed up with that curious look of his.

But for some reason Sean no longer felt any need to be cautious with him. "No," he replied openly. "Is the director himself offering to give me a personal tour?"

With a polite nod of his head, Julian set out across the lawn, walking straight through a croquet match in progress, waving for Sean to follow. Sean deferred, choosing instead to scurry around the players in spite of their polite invitations for him to follow Julian's lead.

The interior of the Thomas Cole House creaked with voices from the past with each uninvited footstep, no matter how gentle, as it landed on the tired old hardwood floors. They were unhappy voices, strained by sacrifice from unfulfilled promises abridged by the death of patrons whose commissions were left unpaid. Then came the death of an artist whose worldly dreams were left unfulfilled, whose family was left wanting in a world he was anxious to leave, and whose work was ignored by generations in favor of the brighter and tighter paintings by others of lesser inspiration, but more often greater talent.

The walls were cracked and swollen and patched. The doors and windows were trimmed with grooved wood, painted bisque white. The floors had split open and erupted underfoot. Decades of dirt now filled the open seams, which were stained dark with age, matching the coarse grain of the young oak felled far too soon in the surrounding forest.

Except for paintings, there was only one of everything, even when a pair was called for. A drop-leaf table; a saber-legged chair; an Empire loveseat, tattered and frayed; a white marble wash basin; an empty pitcher, glazed and cracked all over; and one linen hand towel. A small round mirror hung above the mantle, its single glass eye bulging out beneath a carved mahogany eagle, its gilded feathers molting back to walnut. Threadbare oriental carpets, their patterns worn under foot, their fringes eaten by time, were set out in the center of each room. The stairway rising to the second floor was guarded by a thick velvet rope, the darkened landing at the top filled with mysterious silence.

Holding a dripping-wet bottle of ale in one hand, Oliver walked up and wedged himself between Sean and Julian as they stepped off the porch onto the paved section of the driveway, prompting Julian to stop what he was saying and flash an irritated scowl down at Oliver. He then tossed what was left of it over to Sean, inviting him to do the same. As if he could feel what he hadn't seen, Oliver said, "You were saying, Davidson?" then returned to nursing his bottle of Bass ale.

There was a long deliberate pause, a half-dozen strides long, taking them across the drive and onto the lawn, before Julian consented to continue. "I really don't think the fact that Cole chose to paint four canvases in the *Voyage of Life* series you just viewed inside was intended to carry any great significance, Dr. MacDonald. I think Cole simply saw man's journey through his life in four stages of growth, undoubtedly taking his cue from the biblical allegory of man's life here on earth." Julian looked askance at Sean, but his words were direct. "After all, as I'm sure you know, four is viewed as the number of the created world. Since Cole was a very religious man, four may also have represented the four Gospels, which are regarded as signifying the universality of the word of the Lord, while marking the beginning of the Christian epoch on earth." Resting his arm on Oliver's shoulder, Sean tried grabbing the bottle of ale away from him. Oliver held fast, turning Sean's move into a playful tug of war.

The Taking

Their behavior heightened Julian's disdainful glare, which was now directed at Sean. "Perhaps you were referring to the literal number of canvases, not the metaphorical elements in the series," Julian added, as if replying to an unspoken response from Sean.

"Is there a difference?" Sean batted back, certain that Julian knew very well what he'd meant in the first place, and waited for an explanation. Given the time it took for Julian to respond, Sean knew that he was taking the conversation seriously.

Before Julian could reply, a familiar voice called out loudly, "Sean!" Sean spun around to see Bruce Fanning pushing his way through the crowd gathered around a group of arguing croquet players that included the painting dealer and his artist friend.

"Bruce!" Sean called back, beside himself with delight. "Where the hell have you been?" Sean and Bruce gave each other a bear hug, laughing loudly at the pleasure of seeing each other. "Are you alone?' Sean asked, looking around, but not really.

"Of course not." Bruce held his hand out. "Trish is with me." As if waiting in the wings for her cue, Patricia Jennings walked slowly, deliberately, to Bruce's side. A hushed silence fell over the small gathering as the bright afternoon sun burned through the thin lace of her long white dress, evaporating the sheer lining beneath it, tracing the graceful outline of her taut body with its sultry summer touch. Bruce threaded his arm around Patricia's waist, pulling her to him, holding her there as if against her will.

Oliver said politely, "Good afternoon, Dr. Jennings," then stepped away and kept right on stepping backward until he bumped to a stop against Hazel's outstretched hands.

Bruce glanced past Sean. "And this must be Miss Greene." He looked from Cathy to Patricia, back to Cathy, then scrunched his face down into a perplexed frown before giving it up and smiling, but with reserve. Sean hadn't noticed. But Oliver had, making note of it with a bite of his lip, causing the wiry red whiskers of his beard to twitch.

Cathy offered her hand to Bruce. "I didn't think you would recognize me, Dr. Fanning."

"Please, call me Bruce," he asked, taking Cathy's hand, then holding it up, as if offering it to Patricia. "Trish, this is Sean's new lady friend, the one I've told you so much about." He kissed Patricia on her cheek, unaware of the subtle stiffening of her body as he passed Cathy's hand to her.

"Hello, Dr. Jennings," Cathy said with a steady, clear-eyed smile. "It's a pleasure to meet you."

Shaking Cathy's hand, feeling her sure grip, returning the gesture, Patricia said coolly, "Good afternoon, Catherine." She said this as if it hurt her mouth to form the letters of Cathy's name. Patricia pulled free of Cathy's grip and turned to Bruce. "How about a tour of the house?" she asked, as if Cathy no longer existed.

Looking around, Bruce found Julian. "Mind if I do the honors?" He held Patricia's hand in the air and pointed to the Cole House. Julian shooed them both away. "Come on, Trish," Bruce said, putting a lively snap into his step and leading Patricia away. Patricia opened her stride, moving ahead of him. Her dress grabbed at her hips and thighs and firm ass with every step. She whispered something to Bruce. He laughed and let his hand slide down below her waist. This time she didn't pull away. Instead, she pulled him close to her.

Unable to wait one second longer, the brooding August sky burst open with a loud thunderous clap, startling everyone, freezing them in place, then chasing them, laughing, to the safety of the wraparound porch of the Cole House as the rain poured down in unrelenting sheets. It was thick and hot, and there was no wind, so it just hung there, filling the air.

Cathy seemed to be in no real hurry as she crossed the open lawn. Racing up behind her, Sean grabbed her hand, pulling her with him, only to be yanked back when she didn't follow his lead. He tried letting go, but found himself bound tightly to her hand. "Cathy?" She didn't move. "Cath?" Still nothing. He shook her hand, trying to break her free of whatever was holding her there. Her white silk blouse was dissolving into a translucent film, clinging to the ridges stitched across her abdomen.

Sean could hear questions being batted nervously back and forth on the porch behind him, and he moved to shield her from prying eyes. Cathy pulled back, refusing to let him touch her, as she looked into his face for one, eternal second, then released her hold on him and walked away. Sean stood there, wondering what was wrong, asking himself if she wanted to be alone. Then his chest burst open, flooding his brain, washing his every thought away as he ran after her.

One, then another, turned over and coughed up puffs of powder-blue smoke. Julian was sitting on the porch steps, his elbow stuck into his knee, balancing a freshly lit cigar between his thumb and index finger. Oliver and Hazel waved as they passed in front of the porch, ceremoniously pulling the train of creaking and rattling cars behind them as each driver tossed a curt and very British wave to Julian. Once past Cole's studio, Oliver started honking his horn. The others followed suit, making it sound like a flight of stuffy-nosed geese taking off.

As they died away, Julian placed his hand on the shoulder of the woman sitting one step below him. "Are you sure I can't get you a glass of wine, Alex?" he asked in an unusually soft and caring voice. "You must be parched after that drive up from the city, especially on a day like today." Bending down, Julian buried his face in her hair, kissing her tenderly.

"Not just yet, thank you," Alex said quietly. "I want to relax for a few minutes and let that nerve-racking drive drain out of me." She rested her arm on Julian's leg, inviting him to switch the cigar to his other hand with a disdainful wave at the smoke, then put her head down. This brought Julian's free hand to her face, fussing with the loose strands of hair falling down around her face and spilling over onto the nape of her neck.

Alexandra Hayes was plain in her manner of dress, but elegant in her finely chiseled features. Her chestnut brown hair sparkled with hints of burgundy and gold. There wasn't a lick of makeup on her face, not even a quick slash of lipstick. She wasn't noticeably tall or short; she was that middle height that easily fit any man. Her figure was whatever you wanted it to be, because the loose-fitting shirtwaist dress she was wearing wouldn't grab hold of her long enough to see if she was large or small, wide or narrow, firm or soft. Curiously, Alex and Julian had the same English-looking skin, just short of appearing forever wind blown. The wisps of auburn hair tucked under her arms seemed like they should be there, unlike many women. There was a sense of poetic peace about the two of them as they sat pressed together, staring out over the wet lawn, which was glistening under the fading afternoon sun.

At that very moment, pine-fresh Catskill mountain air stirred up the stillness of the Cole House, pushing the musty smells of a century past out of the open front door and down the steps. Alex stood up, rubbing her arms, as if chilled. Her hair fell down her back, below her waist. She shook it wildly as she walked across the drive onto the lawn, where she kicked off her sandals. "I'm going to take a shower," she said, scooping the sandals up by the straps and letting them dangle from her fingers as she ambled toward the rear entrance of Julian's cottage, lazily scuffing her feet through the wet grass.

When she was out of sight, Julian turned and crossed his legs. "Sean," he said inquisitively, "I understand you're writing a novel dealing with the numerical mysticism we touched on earlier. Care to talk about it?"

Sean was taken by surprise with Julian's sudden change of manner, but more so by the subject chosen. His thoughts stuttered inside his head. Somehow, his silence made Cathy uncomfortable. "Sean?" She put her hand on his leg, bridging the gap that had been growing between them ever since Patricia Jenning's arrival. "You feel all right?"

He patted Cathy's hand, then held onto it. "It's just a story about life and death," Sean replied casually, as if trying to distance himself from Julian's curiosity. He let his eyes follow the path of Alex's meandering steps through the soft wet grass. "Same old shit."

Cathy looked bothered by his cavalier attitude. But before she could say something to him, Julian disarmed Sean with a friendly tapping of his finger on the toe of his loafer. "That's not quite what I've been told." There was a gentle, almost seductive rhythm in his voice. "According to Bruce, it's a story about a very lonely man and his struggle with reality, with life itself, and a woman that he meets who changes everything."

Julian's convincing description pulled Cathy deeper into the discussion. "Is that true?" she asked, looking first to Julian, then to Sean.

Sean gave up on Alex's footprints when the determined blades of grass sprung back to life, erasing them. "That's certainly an interesting perspective."

Julian zeroed in on Sean's evasive eyes. "Bruce believes, and I hope I'm not speaking out of line, and getting dear Bruce in any sort of trouble, that it's autobiographical." Julian cleared his throat. "In a metaphorical sense, of course. But he wasn't really clear about that when we spoke." Sean sat up as if pricked by a pin. "Can this be true?" Julian asked, making it sound as if he already knew the answer.

Sean's reply was hollow and echoed with indifference. "I have no idea what he's talking about."

Julian twisted his words tighter as he leaned back, resting his elbows on the step behind him. "Well, from what I've read, I think there may be a thread of truth to what Bruce says, now that we've met." He tipped his head back, staring lazily up into the cracked and peeling rafters of the porch roof.

"What you've read?" Sean asked, without a doubt surprised at what Julian had said. "I take it that Bruce gave you a diskette with my story on it."

"No," Julian replied, "he gave me a typed manuscript."

Sensing something was wrong, seeing it in Sean's eyes, Cathy stood up and suggested, "Let's go for a walk before it gets too dark." Then, putting her hands to the top button on her blouse, she slipped it open, leaving a bright, inviting laugh dancing on the lawn behind her as she headed for the woods behind the house.

Sean looked over to Julian, trying without success to hide the grin creeping across his face. "It seems we're going for a walk. See you in an hour or so."

"Careful, MacDonald," Julian warned playfully. "She could be the death of you."

Alex sang out, "Not death, Julian, life!" preempting whatever Sean was about to say in his own defense, or Cathy's.

Taking advantage of Alex's intervention, Sean raced after Cathy. Julian turned to find Alex standing beneath the flowered trellis on the other side of the lawn, holding a half-filled bottle of wine with her fingertips, swinging it back and forth at her side, brushing against the folds of her dress. He waved for her to join him. Shaking her head, Alex pulled at the spaghetti straps cinching her dress to her shoulders, letting the fabric inch down her shower-moistened skin until it caught on the upturned slope of her firm breasts and the points of her small pink nipples. Looking down, she pinched the dress with her fingers, tugging it gently, exposing one breast. Glancing up, she smiled at Julian, who was now walking across the lawn toward her. With a sensuous turn of her shoulders, Alex freed herself of the dress. The upside-down triangle of auburn hair was still wet from her shower and matted down against her ivory-white skin. When Julian was within arm's reach, Alex turned and skipped down the grassy path leading to the entrance of the cool earthen cellar beneath the cottage.

It rained again. When it stopped, a breeze flew out of the north, chasing clouds ahead of it, blowing out the sun. The air grew summer cool and quiet.

Cathy was walking behind Sean, holding her hand on his back while looking down and slipping her feet into the depressions left in the rain-soaked grass with his every step. "Your feet are bigger than mine." There was a note of disappointment in her voice. "But my legs are longer than yours." She tickled the back of his neck. "Want to go back and check our legs?" Cathy asked, taking a playful nip out of Sean's ear.

"Damn." Sean came to an abrupt halt. "I thought they left."

"Who?" Cathy asked, bumping into him. She wriggled her face into a squint and peered over his shoulder, making believe she was trying to see.

"Bruce and Patricia. They're with Julian, over by the water-logged buffet tables."

The Taking

"Maybe they forgot something," Cathy said quizzically as she tiptoed over the steamy blacktop, then hopped onto the safety of the grass to wait for him.

Julian pointed and said something to Bruce, who turned and walked with a determined pace to where Sean and Cathy were standing. "I'm sorry." He extended his hands, waiting for Sean to take them. "It was rude of me to leave and not say anything. But Trish wasn't feeling well."

"Too bad," Cathy whispered.

"Forget it." Sean gave Bruce a gentle pat on the arm.

"Dr. Fanning,"—Cathy caught herself—"Bruce. You and Mrs. Jennings should go for a walk before it gets too dark. The woods are all quiet and deliciously cool from the rain." Cathy smiled when Bruce did. "You can find dry patches under the yellow pines. Just watch out for the needles." She laughed, rubbing her backside.

Patricia appeared out of nowhere, locking her fiery gaze on Cathy, raking her body with her eyes, disgust twisting her mouth into a knot. "Was it good?" she asked, turning to face Sean, positioning herself directly in front of him. "Well? Was she?" Sean leaned back. Patricia grabbed hold of him, digging her nails into his wrists. "Does she please you?" There was a storm raging in her eyes. "How can you even stand to touch her?"

"You're making a mistake," Sean told Patricia as he pulled free of her grasp and started to turn away.

The crack of skin on skin shattered the evening's calm. Sean's head spun around, his eyes slammed shut, his face flared red as water filled his eyes.

"Trish!" Bruce screamed.

Patricia swung at Sean again, but this time he saw it coming and pulled back, which only enraged her.

Julian reached out, grabbing at the air. "Dr. Jennings!"

Patricia threw her arm out, holding them back. "Stay out of this." She moved to within inches of Sean. "I thought that when we were together again that you wanted me, and not anyone else." Patricia was fighting to keep herself from grabbing hold of him.

Sean raised his hands.

"No," Cathy said calmly.

He lowered his hands. "Stay the hell out of my life," he snarled, then threw his arms out, brushing Patricia back.

She went for him again. Bruce rushed between them. "Trish, please. I told you. It's over."

With a sweep of her arm, Patricia dispensed with Bruce and went for Cathy.

"I wouldn't if I were you," Cathy warned.

Patricia pulled herself to a stop. "Aren't you going to protect him?" she taunted, her fingers curling into bony rocks.

Cathy's reply was steady, measured, her eyes bullets on her face. "I don't think he needs anyone to protect him."

"You're wrong, dead wrong." Patricia's chilling words froze the warm night air.

21

Sunday, August 25, 1991

Saturday's rain returned with a vengeance, blocking out the sun, throwing summer hail the size of gumballs against the house, and pounding Sean out of a deep sleep. He could feel Cathy outlining his face with the tips of her fingers, as if etching his every feature into her brain. He started to get up but turned over and flopped back down, burying his face in his pillow. "What time is it?" he asked.

Cathy propped herself up onto her elbow and peered over his head at the digital clock on the nightstand. "It will be exactly eleven-hundred hours. Now.'' She pecked Sean's ear playfully, marking the hour precisely.

''Ow!'' Sean cupped his hand over his ear.

Cathy dug her nails into Sean's flesh, pinching him, making him flinch. ''Don't get so close next time,'' she whispered through her teeth, and gave Sean a playful but firm slap on his backside.

''There won't be any next time.''

Cathy started pushing Sean out of bed. ''I'm not so sure she would agree with you.'' She watched him roll off onto the floor.

Standing up, Sean yawned into a lethargic stretch and started down the hall, gingerly feeling his ear. With a sweep of her arm, Cathy threw the sheet off and jumped out of bed, naked, telling herself, ''You really don't want to get dressed yet.'' She walked over to Sean's dresser and with a mischievous smile began leafing through one of the drawers. The fuzzy feel of cotton flannel clung to her hand. She pulled whatever it was out. It was a faded plaid shirt with a green background and thin blue and yellow stripes running up and down and side to side. It looked more like a Scottish tartan than plain old plaid. The buttons were cracked, and the tails were frayed all around the bottom edges. Smelling it, Cathy smiled with her eyes when she found a different Sean, a wintery smell. She tried shaking the wrinkles out. Something dropped to the floor, black and silky, with elegant initials embroidered in gold peeking out from inside the soft folds. ''It's none of your business, Catherine,'' she scolded, and quickly stuffed the black panties back into the drawer, knowing she was dying to look, to read the letters and check the size, all the while laughing at her own feminine curiosity and fighting the twinge of insecurity nibbling at her.

Spinning away, she wrapped herself inside Sean's tired old shirt, took another sniff, then checked the length to be sure it covered all of her. She was in the kitchen before all of the buttons were holed, opening and closing the cupboard doors, rummaging around, hoping to ferret out something to make for them for breakfast. She noticed dirt smudged on her fingers. Where did that come from? she wondered, wiping her hands on the shirt out of habit, then looking around the kitchen, mentally checking everything she'd touched. *What's that?* She bent down, sweeping her hand underneath the stove, scooping out a crumpled-up wad of paper. She peeled it open.

Dear Sean,

Your lights were on. I knocked, but there was no answer. The door was ajar, so I peeked in. It looked like the door at the top of the landing was open, too. I was worried, so I came in. Now we both know that you weren't home!

Thank you for having dinner with me. And thank you for staying the night. It's been a long time since I was with a man. I hope . . .

22

Friday, September 13, 1991

Dear Bruce,

Here are the last three chapters of my story. I think the ending will be a surprise for you. At least I hope it will.

I guess with Betty leaving, and your getting ready for the fall semester, you've been too busy to get anything back to me lately. I hope you'll have a chance to catch up soon, since I've come to rely upon your feedback.

I was sorry you weren't with Oliver and me when we were sparring with Julian earlier in the day at the party. But in a

The Taking

way you were, since he kept referring to things he said you
had told him I said. Later, he also told me you let him read
my manuscript. Needless to say, I was surprised, as well as
curious as to why you had it typed. Care to share your thoughts
with me?

As for the incident with Patricia, I'm sure it was just as
disturbing for you as it was for me. I only hope that you're
never the target of her anger the way I've been. I'm not just
talking about last Saturday, either, and you know what I mean.

But looking on the brighter side of life: My 48th birthday
is coming up on the 23rd of September. I plan on being with
Cathy that night, so what about the three of us getting together? Maybe I'll ask Oliver and Hazel, too. Bringing Patricia
would pose a problem, to say the least. What about one of
your many divorced alumnae in the area?

Let me know. And thanks again for everything,

Sean.

As the letter to Bruce began printing out, Sean sat staring at
the dove-gray envelope that he'd tacked up on the wall over the
credenza, the envelope Oliver had given him after getting back
from London, which he was still yet to open. It was wrinkled and
creased from having been through their wrestling match.

You know you don't want to read it, he told himself, plucking
it off the wall and tossing it at the wastepaper basket beside his
desk. It pitched up, stalled, and dropped to the floor, short of its
mark. "Tails!" He laughed to himself when he saw it land face
down.

Snatching it up, Sean knifed his finger under the flap, then
ripped it open with a snap of his wrist.

Dear Sean:

Please forgive me for not responding sooner to your letter
of 14 July. I'm afraid I was so engrossed in my work here,
and occupied—wonderfully so—by Hazel every free moment

181

the two of us had, that I let it slide.

I took a few moments to convert the names in your letter just to get you thinking about what I've said during our two recent discussions. I also started a simple time line, which begins with your mother's death. But you did this already, right?

The initial numbers and patterns, while inconclusive, are fascinating, wouldn't you agree? Of greatest interest to me was what Patricia Jennings's name worked out to, which I did for both her married and maiden name (I got it from the student records). What do you think it means? Anything?

Naturally, this will have to be done for everyone closely associated with your life. And it must start with your birth date. This may then allow me to determine what your Unlock Date is, which is critical if we are to stop this from happening . . .

"Unlock Date? Stop what from happening?" Sean spun Oliver's letter into the air and took a look at the hand-printed schedule.

```
1 2 3 4 5 6 7 8 9
A B C D E F G H I
J K L M N O P Q R
S T U V W X Y Z
```

E I L E E N   M E R R I T T (MACDONALD)   *Aura*
5 9 3 5 5 5   4 5 9 9 9 2 2 = 72 7+2 =   [9]

R O B E R T   M A C D O N A L D
9 6 2 5 9 2   4 1 3 4 6 5 1 3 4 = 64 = 6+4 = 10 = [1]

J A N E T   P E T E R S (MACDONALD)
1 1 5 4 2   7 5 2 5 9 1 = 42 = 4+2 =   [6]

S E A N   M A C D O N A L D
1 5 1 5   4 1 3 4 6 5 1 3 4 = 43 = 4+3 =   [7]

J O H N   M A C D O N A L D
1 6 8 5   4 1 3 4 6 5 1 3 4 = 51 = 5+1 =   [6]

The Taking

```
P A T R I C I A   J E N N I N G S
7 1 2 9 9 3 9 1  1 5 5 5 9 5 7 1 = 79 = 7+9 = 16 =   [7]

P A T R I C I A   H A W L E Y
7 1 2 9 9 3 9 1  8 1 5 3 5 7 = 70 = 7+0 =            [7]

P A T R I C I A   H A W L E Y   J E N N I N G S
7 1 2 9 9 3 9 1  8 1 5 3 5 7  1 5 5 5 9 5 7 1 =      [9]

C A T H E R I N E   G R E E N E
3 1 2 8 5 9 9 5 5  7 9 5 5 5 5 = 83 = 8+3 = 11 = [2]

O L I V E R   S H O R E
6 3 9 4 5 9  1 8 6 9 5 = 65 = 6+5 = 11 =             [2]

B R U C E   F A N N I N G
2 9 3 3 5  6 1 5 5 9 5 7 = 60 = 6+0 =                [6]

S A R A H   P O T T E R
1 1 9 1 8  7 6 2 2 5 9 = 51 = 5+1=                   [6]

K A R E N   LAST NAME UNKNOWN
2 1 9 5 5 =                                          [?]


1950:   MOTHER'S DEATH            =  0 / BASE YEAR
        SISTER'S DEATH            =  0 / BASE YEAR

1962:   FATHER'S DEATH            = 12-YEAR INTERVAL
                                  = 12-YEAR SPAN
                                    [FROM 1950]

1974:   WIFE'S DEATH              = 12-YEAR INTERVAL
                                  = 24-YEAR SPAN

1980:   SON'S DEATH               =  6-YEAR INTERVAL
                                  = 30-YEAR SPAN

1986:   SEAN'S ''NEAR DEATH''     =  6-YEAR INTERVAL
                                  = 36-YEAR SPAN

1992:                             =  6-YEAR INTERVAL
                                  = 42-YEAR SPAN
```

Sean folded the schedule back up. "So far you haven't done anything that I didn't already do, my friend, and at least a dozen times. I'm afraid you're going to have to come up with something far more convincing to get me to play your game again."

23

Sunday, September 15, 1991

Bobby McCarthy marched up, sat down directly across from Sean, and ceremoniously set a dripping-wet mug of beer in front of each of them without saying a word. Bobby wasn't just sitting in the chair; he had obliterated it with his hulking frame, the way a parent does when sitting in a child's little kindergarten chair. His forearms shrunk the mug down to dollhouse size, matching the lost chair. Sean eyed his frosty gift suspiciously. "Is this a bribe of some sort?" he asked, his hand at the ready, waiting for Bobby's assurance that it wasn't.

"No, sir." Bobby snapped the word "sir" to attention, his thick neck tightening for an instant, filling his shirt and holding the collar pressed stiffly to his skin even though it wasn't buttoned closed.

"What's the occasion?" Sean's hand inched closed.

Bobby started patting his hands on the table, playing the bongo drums, making everything shake and rattle and jump up and down. "You've done it," he said. "You've stolen her away from us." Bobby slid the mug into Sean's waiting hand, then drowned his smirk in his own beer.

Taking his cue from Bobby, Sean dove into the frothy foam. When he came up for air, he asked, "What are you talking about?"

Bobby started to say something, but his eyes narrowed and drew a tight focus on something behind Sean. Sean twisted around. "Sharon!" The name was said with a hollow suck of air.

A thin smile parted Sharon Lucien's lips as she turned to a taller, thinner, and darker-skinned woman standing a step behind her. "Aster,"—she sounded like she was talking to a complete stranger—"would you mind?" The woman nodded. Her coarse, salt-and-pepper, shoulder-length hair stayed in place as if it were glued to the sides of her head, her face wrinkled beneath her skin, her dark amber eyes didn't move. Reaching out, she took the thin leather valise Sharon was clutching under one arm and turned to find a table of her own. Aster pulled to a stop, listening, but not turning back. "On second thought, perhaps it's best you return to the office. I'll meet you back there when I'm finished here." Aster nodded and walked away.

Amused with what he'd just seen, Bobby stood up and turned to leave, but not before saying, "She's a beautiful woman, Doc. And you're perfect for her. You've made her feel—" Sean's raised hand and stern gaze asked Bobby not to finish. "Later," Bobby said, dragging his eyes over Sharon's face and body before walking away, his shoulders and head held as straight and strong as a granite column. Sharon followed him, her head turning like it was gimbled on her neck, the needle of a compass, until he disappeared into the kitchen.

Say something, MacDonald, Sean told himself. "What a surprise to see you." *You bet your sweet ass it is.* "Join me?" His eyes began flitting back and forth between Sharon and the empty chair across the table from him, while he fought to keep her from getting inside him. But she did, and all too easily. He could feel her scraping around inside for something to pick off his bones. He moved around the table in what felt like slow motion to him, pulling the chair out, casting his eyes down, gesturing, then looking up. Sharon placed her hands on the arms of the chair and

185

eased herself down into it. You act like an old woman, Sean thought to himself. Then, fighting it every inch of the way, he leaned down as close as he dared and breathed in. The heat of the evening and the damp close air in the bar made sure that he found what he was looking for. But it was different than he remembered, stronger and sharper, pushing his head away, then jerking it back down for more until he caught himself.

"The sandwiches are great." He felt uneasy. He quickly put the false security of the table between them and sat down.

Bobby was back. "You folks having dinner?" His words were relaxed and casual, but his body was rigidly formal.

"I think so," Sean said tentatively. He looked at Sharon, who was waiting for him. At that moment, something, and he didn't know what, broke loose inside him and started sliding toward her. Stop it, you jerk, he told himself, locking his hands on the edge of the table and pushing himself back.

Sharon said bluntly, "Turkey. White meat. On rye toast. No butter or mayonnaise. And hearts of lettuce on the side, with oil and vinegar." She tried grabbing hold of Bobby with her piercing black eyes but couldn't penetrate his armor and gave up. "And a glass of whatever you have on tap." Bobby took Sean's order and left.

This is ridiculous, Sean thought, and dove into Sharon's face. It was like falling through a hole in the ice on a frozen lake in the dead of winter. He fought back a freezing shiver. I hate this shit! he screamed inside his head, and dove back in.

You're much thinner than I remember, was the first thing that came to mind. And she was. Her neck was drawn taut, and no longer soft on his eyes. Her skin was coarse and dry—not sun dried or weathered—time dried. And her lips were thicker, but to his surprise they still asked to be tasted. He fought back the urge to run his tongue over his own lips to see how they felt, to see if they had changed, too, perhaps when he wasn't looking. He then found himself wondering whether or not he'd actually done it.

"How's your book coming?" Sharon folded her arms in front

of her, ending Sean's scrutiny, which she seemed to have been allowing him to do, patiently, tolerantly, while doing the same to him.

How the hell did you know about my book? "I'm pleased with it," he said happily. But his words were guarded, and he knew it the instant he felt them stick in his throat. "It's done. I'm just reworking the dialogue. I hope to be finished sometime next week, since I want to be done with it before the end of the month." Sean took a nervous breath, not knowing why. "And you?" he asked. Go ahead, say it, he told himself. "How's business?"

Sharon ignored his question, choosing instead to ask another one of her own, which he answered quickly and without hesitation, then wished he hadn't when she smiled back. He tried others, but she would only give him questions in return, questions about himself and what he was doing now. When he answered, she acted like she already knew, which made him uneasy all over again, then irritated, then indifferent, all in the blink of an eye. He tried getting inside her again, but the hole had frozen over. He looked down; she blocked his move. Their sandwiches were set on the table, along with her beer. Sean watched her take a sip, then swallow. Sharp, rapid pulses flickered back at him from under her skin. She scratched the meat out of the sandwich, discarded the bread, and ate it slowly.

They began talking again, but at each other, not with each other, stuffing questions one behind the other, with only Sean giving up answers. Sharon became impatient with his bright and overly enthusiastic replies, and sped up her demands. Thinking he had to compete, Sean jumped ahead of her and held the lead through dinner.

Sharon pushed her plate to one side and leaned forward, her hands coming to rest on the table, palms down. "Who is she?" she asked. Sean found himself looking for her pencil and pad, then laughing at himself. Sharon ticked her head in the direction of the bar. "The woman that mesomorph mentioned when I came in earlier."

Sean forced a smile. "A friend." He held on to it.

"Is this 'friend' older or younger than you?"

Something was begging him not to tell her, but he ignored it. "Younger." He smiled.

"Much?"

Fuck you! started flashing in front of him in big bold letters. "Not really, there's only a twelve-year difference, as of my birthday."

"You haven't found that to be a problem?"

He repeated to himself, Fuck you! then worried if his thought had found its way to his lips when Sharon pulled back in her chair, scowling. "Why would it be a problem?" he asked.

Sharon asked with rapierlike speed, "At forty-eight, are you able to keep up?"

You'll never give it a rest, will you? he thought, and let her loose inside him, defying her to find something, anything to grab hold of. "I'm surprised you'd say something like that." *No you're not, you jerk.* "You know very well that my life had been empty for years. Besides, I love her. And she loves me." It sounded like a confession, and he knew it.

"Love?"

Without knowing why, Sean reached out, unfolded Sharon's tightly closed hands and held them in his. She yanked herself free with startling ease. He watched with curiosity as she slid her hands off the table and down into her lap. "Yes, love, even for me," he replied calmly.

"What's her name?"

Don't be a fool clanged like a fire alarm in his head. What's wrong with you? he asked himself. "Sharon," he said in a conciliatory, almost submissive, but firm voice. "Let's just be friends." He sat back, feeling safe.

"What are you hiding from?" she asked, her words flying across the table at him like a diving hawk. He felt himself ducking, and hoped he only thought it. "Does she know?"

Know what? He suddenly wanted to smash Sharon in the face with his fist. "You know," he said, blinking away that thought, "I think our problem was that you couldn't, or wouldn't accept the fact that I was finished and didn't need you anymore."

The Taking

With a puzzled look on her face, Sharon stood up and set her napkin down beside her plate. "It was selfish of me to interrupt you," she said politely, turning the look of amusement into one of disappointment. "I'm sorry. I'd hoped otherwise."

Hi!

   I came by around 11:30, but you weren't here. I went over to the inn. Bobby told me you'd just left. He said a "real hard-looking woman" invited herself to have dinner with you.
  · I came back to see if we had passed one another, which explains this note. I'm sorry I missed you. I wanted to be with you tonight. Stop by tomorrow. I'll be busy, but I can take time for lunch.

Love you,
Cathy

Exhausted, Sean dropped the note on the floor beside his bed and let his clothes fall on top of it. He climbed into bed, wanting sleep, but afraid of it at the same time. He could feel her on him, trying to get inside again. Why does she do this to you? he asked as he lay awake, fighting her. He felt himself slipping, losing. Or was he winning? He couldn't tell anymore, and gave up.

. . . He folded his shoulders around himself. "It's nothing," he said quietly, as if talking to himself.
"I think it is." Sharon slipped past the anxious blinking of his eyes. "You've got to say it, you've got to get it out in the open so others can hear it, and know what you know."
"I can't." He tried shaking her loose.
She lowered her voice. "I think you can," she replied, rejecting his frail excuse with a gentle touch of her hand on his. Then, leaning closer, she said softly, "Trust me, Sean. Only you must be prepared for what may follow." She hesitated, as if pondering her own words. "And it's not from Janet."
He seized her steady gaze. "What are you saying?"

"I think you know." He stood up. She glanced down, then up into his face, fighting back a curious smile. He turned away, shoving his hands into his pockets. *"I'm sorry,"* she said in a deep, almost masculine voice.

He turned back to find her not bothering to button her blouse, and there wasn't a blush of pink anywhere on her. She looked up at him, but said nothing. Straddling the ottoman, he sat down and leaned forward, kissing the patch of soft white skin, then the top of her breast. She grabbed a fistful of his hair, scratching her nails into his scalp. There was a knock on the door, freezing them into silence. Words sliced through the solid wood like it was paper. He listened. She said nothing. The stairs creaked, slowly, one step at time. The front door clicked open, then yawned shut. A car started and pulled away.

He stood up, pulling her with him, kissing her. She sucked the air out of his lungs. He slid his hand under her dress and between her thighs, grabbing a handful of warm flesh, then slipping his fingers inside her panties. Pushing him away, she reached beneath her skirt, tugging her panties down and off, then fell back into the chair. He dropped to his knees and rolled her skirt up. Her hips were broad, her legs firm, almost muscular, but soft and fleshy on the inside, and whiter than ivory. He could smell her in the warm humid air, honey sweet. She pulled him down to her, burying his face in her, saying nothing. Standing up, he unzipped his pants and tugged them down and off, releasing the pressure knotted inside. He was half soft, half hard, and pouting out delicate drops of clear liquid with every rising beat of his heart. She reached for him, twirling the sticky fluid onto her fingertip, then brought it to her lips, her tongue. Her eyes glowed like molten pitch when he did the same. She put her fingers inside herself, and held them up for him. He licked them dry, then pushed himself into her face. She slid her hand down his blood-engorged shaft, squeezing hard at the base, making him swell up even larger, filling her mouth. She bit down, gently, then harder, making him wince, but not pull away.

The phone on the desk started ringing, its harsh electronic stutter ratcheting them apart. The answering machine clicked to *life, unwinding her familiar voice into the air. There was a beep, then another voice. Her body tightened with each anxious word, then relaxed when they were clicked back into silence.*

She raised her legs, propping her feet on the edge of her chair. He knelt down, pressing into her. She was tight and dry, surprising him. He pulled back. She wrapped her legs around his waist, guiding him back down, then forcing him inside her, crying out. He winced at the pain pinching his flesh. She dug her heels into his sides, stopping him, pushing him out, then rubbing her fingers all over him.

"Are you ready?" she asked, taking his testicles in her hand, squeezing them.

"No, not yet." He smiled, covering her other hand with his as she stroked him with the very tips of her long fingers.

She took him back in, this time all the way, holding him inside her, squeezing the breath out of him, then thrusting her hips up, taking him even deeper. "Can you feel that?" she asked.

"I've never felt anything like it." She pulled him to her, pressing his face into her breasts, smothering him in the thick oily sweat seeping out of her pores. "No," he cried, trying to pull out of her. "Stop. Please!" Suddenly, violently, she drove her heels into him, kicking him out of her. Looking down, his eyes exploded on his face at the sight of blood everywhere—on him, on her, dripping out of her, staining the floor, her belly heaving . . .

Sean bolted up in bed, his body soaking wet and smelling sour, his heart pounding him deaf. Kicking the sheets off, he jumped out of bed and stumbled down the hallway to the bathroom.

"This has got to stop," he told himself, stepping into the shower, turning the water on, not caring if it was hot or cold.

24

The orange September sun was falling out of the cloudless azure sky. Sean slowed down, looking for a spot to squeeze into, but cars were parked on both sides of Molly Lane, bumper to bumper, and were even blocking Cathy's driveway. And both lots in front of the farm stand were crammed full. Giving up, he sped down Molly Lane, swerving off the road onto a tractor path and squeaking beneath a rope drawn taut from apple tree to apple tree, and hung with a sign warning everyone—but him—ORCHARD NOT OPEN. With a self-satisfied smile pinned to his face, ignoring the scowls and a few angry horns from the cars inching along the side of the road, Sean jogged the mile back to the farm stand.

Cathy was carrying a half-bushel of apples under her arm, with a short, flat-faced Oriental woman following two steps behind. She gave Sean a glancing kiss on her way to the cash register. "It's been like this since we opened." She sighed. "People were queued up and waiting to get into the raspberry and blackberry fields when I arrived with Sally at six-thirty!" Handing the woman her apples, Cathy added her to the end of the checkout line and turned back to Sean, who was stealing an apple out of one of the bins. "What time is it?" She looked at her bare wrist. "I even forgot to put my watch on this morning."

Sean didn't bother to look. "A little after four."

Cathy snatched the apple out of his hand just as he was about to take a bite out of it. "Get me out of here!" she shrieked playfully, pulling Sean through the crush of bodies crowding the entrance and out into the parking lot. Circling around to the back of the stand, Cathy made a beeline for the barn. Not the red barn, but one of the weathered gray barns.

Inside, and out of the glare of the dying summer sun, the air was dry and barn cool. Although horses hadn't seen the inside of the stable-turned-barn since the farm reluctantly made the conversion to tractors during the early eighties, everything had been left intact. The double-thick bridles and sweat-stained reins, drawn taut and cracked by the weight of their heavy workhorse bits, hung from sturdy wooden pegs like tarnished tinsel. Decades of undisturbed cobwebs were spun around the dried leather skeletons, creating the illusion there was something inside, waiting to be reborn. Even though the stalls were all clean now, heady smells lingered in the open pores of the cracked and worn wooden timbers, needing only the brush of a loving hand, or a stiff, wet breeze sneaking through the widening slits of the up-and-down siding to free them, filling the air with memories of fresh oats and molasses and wintergreen, and wet leather and saddle soap, memories that gasoline and Red Devil touch-up paint could never replace. High above the stalls, bales of hay and scratchy straw filled the lofts, tipping precariously on the edge, threatening to come crashing down with the slightest provocation.

In the center of the barn, a cut-down barrel was turned upside down, topped with one-half of a Dutch door, and covered with a blue-and-white-checked tablecloth. A pair of wooden milk crates, the kind with galvanized wire dividers and handles worn smooth by calloused hands, were turned on end, bracketing the barrel, serving as chairs.

With a sweep of her hand, Cathy removed the red plastic sheet covering the makeshift table and stood to one side, a blue-jeaned toreador, inviting Sean to have a seat. "Nothing fancy," she said with a proud smile. "Just a simple country buffet." She began pointing at the things on the table. "Our own cheddar cheese, not Brie. Smoked ham, not pâté. Sourdough bread instead of baguettes. And a freshly baked apple pie in lieu of a linzer torte."

Sean charged the table and proceeded to create a sandwich with the skill of Dagwood Bumstead. Carrying it like it was heavy and tippy and might fall over, playing at juggling it, he walked over to one of the locked stalls, kicked some loose straw into a pile at the foot of the door, and sat down with his prize.

"Prefer the ground?" Cathy asked with a curious frown.

A precious blush took hold of him. "Childhood," he murmured, and looked away.

This drew an affectionate smile from Cathy as she reached for the glass pitcher covered with condensation. "Lemonade?"

"Yes, please," Sean replied, just before sinking his teeth into his double-decker sandwich.

After making one herself, but only a single story high, Cathy handed Sean a quart-sized glass of lemonade and slid down beside him. He tapped her foot with his to get her attention, then looked over to the table filled with food. "Yours is better." He winked, then turned back to his sandwich, eyeing it, trying to decide where to bite next.

Leaning back, Cathy lowered her hands into her lap and crossed her legs. "Sean?" He turned, motioning to his puffy cheeks. Cathy nodded and smiled politely. "That woman, the one Bobby told me about. Who is she?" Cathy began fussing with her sandwich, tucking in the loose ends of lettuce, pulling off the edges of ham, then stuffing them back between the slices of bread, trying to make everything fit just so.

"Woman?"

"The one you had dinner with at the inn the other night."

"Oh." Sean laughed uncomfortably. "She was my therapist, Dr. Sharon Lucien."

Cathy cast her eyes around the inside of the darkened barn, as if searching for something. "I didn't know." She sounded like she was apologizing for something. "You don't have to talk about it if you don't want to." She bit into her sandwich.

Sean patted her leg reassuringly. "I don't mind." He settled back and began talking quietly between small bites of his sandwich and lazy sips of lemonade, beginning with his early sessions with Sharon Lucien, the ones with his wife. But not once did he refer to his wife by name. Cathy said nothing; she just listened with her whole body. Sean made note of every one of those first few sessions, as if they were still fresh in his mind, although he accorded each of them no more than a few cryptic sentences, spoken like he was reading an epitaph—someone else's. The words were handed over to Cathy as if he were counting out change to some stranger who had just purchased something from him, something he was relieved finally to sell and be rid of. "Then, after I buried her, Sharon told me that it would be advisable for me to remain in therapy 'for my own benefit,' so I did. At first, I went purely out of guilt, even though I denied it back then. But I soon began to see what was happening, in spite of my resistance to the whole thing, and stayed with it." Sean shook his head. "For six long years the first time around."

"Why did you finally stop?"

"I almost split in the very beginning," Sean said quickly. "Then again about two years later. I think the urge to bolt was motivated by fear, which was a feeling I couldn't admit to, at least not then." Sean set his plate down between them, leaving his sandwich only half-eaten, and rested his head against the door, staring up into the rafters. "She was getting too close."

Cathy reached out, trying to find someplace to touch him, someplace that wasn't all-over prickly and hackled, but gave up. "Too close?" she asked cautiously.

"Yes, too close to whatever it was that I couldn't deal with after Janet's murder." Cathy nodded at hearing Sean finally say his wife's name. "Or perhaps things from before I even knew Janet." "Then, after maybe four or five years into it—into the 'process'—I realized the less I fought, the better I got." Reaching down, Sean began dusting his jeans off with lazy slaps of his hand.

"End of therapy?"

Sean laughed, but not at Cathy. "Far from it! But things came to a screeching halt after a series of hypnosis sessions I let her talk me into." Cathy became very still at hearing this. "However, I started seeing her again in the fall of 1980, shortly after John died." Sean paused, waiting for what he expected would happen at the mention of his son's name. But there was nothing there. He slumped back, looking relieved. "I desperately needed someone after that, and besides Bruce, she was the only one I thought might be able to help me deal with John's death. But I should have known better." Cathy was following every unconscious twist of Sean's body and awkward jerk of his hands, which he seemed completely unaware of, and which were out of synch with his words. "That lasted for all of two months."

"Did it help?" Cathy asked carefully.

"No. At least I don't think so. But it was probably more my fault than hers. I still haven't come to terms with it, but that's not important now." Sean turned and looked at Cathy for the longest time, then said with some difficulty, "I also went back after my misguided affair with Patricia Jennings, just as soon as I was out of the hospital."

"Hospital?" Cathy whispered to herself.

Sean shrugged his shoulders and fingered his side where his scars were, but didn't offer Cathy anything more in the way of an explanation. Cathy's expression turned from a little surprised and curious to angry. "That time I stopped because she started getting mean."

"But she was your therapist, Sean. Why would—"

Wrapped up in his own thoughts, Sean interrupted Cathy's question. "She told me that it was me, and not her. She also said that I was hiding something, or hiding *from* something, I don't remember her exact words." Sean took a deep breath. "Which is exactly what she harped on that night at the inn."

Cathy finally found a spot on Sean's leg that seemed safe for her to touch. "Did she frighten you? You know, because of what she knew about you, and you were now seeing her in a different setting?"

"Frighten?" Sean laughed, making it sound as if Cathy's question was silly. But when he saw the pained look on her face, he gently rested his hand on hers. "Yes," he admitted to his own surprise. "Now that I think about it, that's what I felt. That must be why, when I got home and fell asleep . . ." Sean stopped and made an effort to stand up, but slid back down, rubbing his legs like they'd fallen asleep. "I had gone back to see her last December. Why, I sure as hell don't know." He waved his hands, erasing what he'd just said. "That's not true. I went back to get copies of the transcripts that she never gave me from my hypnosis sessions." Sean appeared pensive. "At least that's what I thought was why I went back, but I'm not so sure anymore."

There was an awkward, protracted silence. "Sean?" Cathy finally asked. He didn't seem to hear her; he was off in his own world. "Sean?" He nodded his head, acknowledging her, but still didn't look like he was paying attention. "I don't understand why you went back to her." Sean turned to face her, his eyes covered with a film of tears, but still said nothing. "Do you think there could have been something that drew you back to her?"

"Me!" he snapped, and climbed to his feet, offering Cathy his hand.

Cathy got up on her own. "I still don't understand." Her words were honed with a sharp edge of impatience.

Sean deliberately put distance between them. "I couldn't stay away from her. There was something about her I couldn't get out of my system. On the one hand, the woman had the ability to drive me up the wall with her questions and her not-so-subtle implications about my sanity. Or lack of it! Yet there were other times that she was dead right. And there were times when I wanted to smash her in the face." This brought an apprehensive frown to Cathy's face. "And there were other times when I wanted to—" Sean spun around to face Cathy. "I don't ever want to go back," he said anxiously.

"Go back? To her?"

"No," he replied, needlessly dusting his pants off again. "Back to where I was."

"You've lost me."

"No, Catherine, I didn't lose you." Sean pulled Cathy to him, wrapping his arms around her, holding her tight. "I found you, and I found me, too. I think. Ever since this past June, when I—" Sean abruptly let go of that thought.

Cathy hadn't been listening closely to what Sean said after he told her "I found you, and I found me, too." She was struggling with something else. "I think you know what it was that made you go back to her. Why can't you—" Cathy turned her head aside when Sean tried kissing her question away. "Why can't you tell me?" Grabbing hold of Sean's wrists, Cathy pushed him away and held him at arm's length. "I want to know," she demanded.

Sean looked down at her hands, then up into her eyes. "Let go of me," he said quietly, "please."

Cathy tightened her grip. "No." She halved the distance between them. "I want to know. I'm tired of this," she said.

Sean's face turned to stone, his eyes became hard, his body rigid. He spoke through his teeth. "One second I hated the bitch, I guess because she was right, and the next second I wanted to fuck her brains out, and that infuriated me, because I couldn't stop myself from feeling that way. Is that a good enough explanation for you, Catherine?"

Cathy released her hold of Sean with a deliberate shove. He stumbled backward, then caught his balance. "And did you?" she asked, but something in her eyes said she knew, and Sean knew it.

Sean wanted to explain, to tell her it wasn't anything like she thought, but he knew if he told her what really happened, it would only make things worse. He watched as Cathy walked out of the barn, into the lost sunlight, wishing he'd never said a word about Sharon, about what happened, and about his feelings, yet at the same time wishing he could tell her everything. Everything.

You can't tell anyone everything, Sean told himself as he watched Cathy walk away. Haven't you learned that yet?

Jean Murphy watched as Sean walked slowly across the lawn, but not in a straight line; he drifted from side to side as if he was lost. What Jean didn't see was that he had his eyes closed. After climbing the porch steps with heavy feet, he flopped down into the squeaky wicker rocker beside her.

"She was here again," Jean announced with an "I-told-you-so" clang to her words.

"She?" Sean asked in a lazy daze.

"The tall dark-skinned one with the jet black hair and fancy sports car. The one who always seems to stop by when you're not here." Jean picked up the book that was lying in her lap and wrapped her arms around it, clutching it to her chest. "I don't know why you're avoiding her. She's a very elegant and well-spoken woman. A real lady.''

"She has that effect on people," Sean mumbled, staring out across the road. He then asked, and from as far away as he could get from Jean's reach, "How long was Dr. Jennings here?"

"An hour, maybe an hour-and-a-half. I lost track of time talking to her." Sean grimaced. "She told me all about herself, and about her ex-husband, the art dealer." Jean sat back. "She told me that he married her for show." Jean rose up in her chair and bore down on Sean as if he'd done something horrible. "Did you know that she caught him in bed with another man, doing it! And in their bedroom!" Jean made a choking noise that sounded real. "It makes me sick to my stomach just to think about it."

"Then don't," Sean said with detachment laced with contempt.

Jean got up and walked to the front of the porch, watching cars pass, her head snapping from side to side. "Do you know what he said when she walked in on them?"

Sean gave her a cold and disinterested, "No, Jean, I don't."

Jean stormed back, "He told her that she could watch!"

Something suddenly erupted inside Sean's gut. He tried choking it down, but it came back up, gagging him.

. . . *She was over him, her body glistening with sweat in the soft candlelight of his bedroom, sliding down, her burning flesh wrapping around his throbbing cock, swallowing him up. He felt himself about to explode, when a sharp pain knifed into his side. His eyes burst open to a room pitch black, her face, a stranger's face, twisting into his, her hot breath scalding him with words he couldn't understand, growling a name not his. He felt the wet spreading beneath him, warm and thick, and sticking to his skin. She struck again, folding him into a scream . . .*

Dropping his glass, deaf to its shatter, Sean flew off the porch.

Jean sat perfectly still, watching him stumble across the lawn, out into the fields, a mask of cold, feminine indifference freezing itself onto her face as she kicked the porch with short hard jabs of her feet, driving the squeaking wicker rocking chair back and forth like a rusted metronome.

25

"Sean!" Cathy called excitedly from the kitchen window. "Come see!" She waved secretly to Oliver and Hazel, who were standing side by side, in chauffeur's uniforms, shoulders thrown back, arms stuck to their sides, looking like painted wooden soldiers beside Oliver's just-polished Silver Wraith, trying to wipe the impish smirks off their faces before Sean appeared at the window. Sean rushed into the kitchen holding a shoe in each hand, and slid across the shiny linoleum floor in his stocking feet, bumping to a stop against the windowsill beside Cathy. "Look!" she said with rehearsed surprise, and pointed outside.

Without moving his head or eyes, staring earnestly into the side of the house, Oliver announced, "Your car is ready, sir."

"Let's go!" Sean hopped across the kitchen while trying to put his shoes on, clomped noisily down the stairs with them still only half on, and barged out onto the porch. "Come on, Cathy!" he called up through the screen door, stomping his feet into his loafers, barely able to contain himself as he waited for her.

Hazel was fighting back a giggle as they approached the car. She opened the rear door, but only after fidgeting with the handle, which was hidden beneath a neatly tied white satin bow, its long tails reaching down, barely touching the running board. Red carnations were in each of the crystal bud vases mounted to the quarterdecks inside. Small sterling silver trays with tiny clawed feet were crouching low on each of the fold-down burl tables, holding an assortment of canapés on their silver backs. The top of a champagne bottle, its fat mushroom-shaped cork having already been removed, then twisted back in, was poking its neck up through the white linen towel, which was wrapped like a cleric's collar around the dented silver bucket sitting on the carpeted floor between the pair of jump seats.

Oliver clicked the heels of his high-topped leather boots, forcing his jodhpurs to puff out like an elephant's ears. "Sir!" echoed from deep inside his prodigious chest, which was covered with the charcoal-blue gaberdine coat of his Victorian British chauffeur's uniform. "Reservations are for eight, so we best be on our way." Closing the door once Sean and Cathy were inside, he sighed, letting go of the breath he was holding his stomach in with. The parallel rows of polished black buttons stitched to his uniform promptly bent into opposing columns around each side of his portly midsection.

"Don't say anything," Cathy whispered, pulling Sean back into the seat. "You'll only hurt his feelings."

The faint scent of a match having been lit, then blown out before it could get started, revealed that the champagne had been opened only moments earlier. Tulip-shaped hollow-stemmed goblets were hanging upside down from wooden slots on the inside of the bar doors. Light and dark chocolates were buried beneath tissue papers and tucked inside a frosted Lalique dish decorated with puffy-cheeked cherubs. The tan wool headliner, its stains barely visible, had been cleaned, making Sean smile at the thought.

The ride was fun. Drivers waved and beeped. Some followed close behind in silent procession. Others pulled alongside, gawking to see who the regal passengers might be, before racing away from their own embarrassment. Oliver drove south on the Taconic Parkway for nearly an hour, turned east somewhere below Yorktown Heights, in Westchester, then slipped unnoticed out of New York, into Connecticut, on Route 35.

Pulling into the main entrance of The Ridgefield Inn, Oliver announced, "It's seven-fifty-five, sir," and guided his horseless carriage to a squeaky stop beneath the canopied entrance of the old country inn. He waited, eyeing Hazel imperiously. She stared

back at him with a perplexed and pleasant smile on her face,
having completely forgotten her assignment. With a disapproving
harrumph, he was out of the car and at Cathy's door just as she
started opening it. "Mademoiselle." He bowed politely, inviting
an affectionate graze of Cathy's hand against his cheek, which
brought him back to a stiff upright position. Sean stepped out and
nodded, graciously playing the role he was cast in. "Sir," Oliver
said in a marble-mouthed British mumble, and gestured to the
front entrance of The Ridgefield Inn, where a tuxedoed maître d'
was waiting with the door held open. Sean fought back the urge
to put his arms around his dear friend and hug him.

The second Sean and Cathy disappeared into the darkened
foyer, Oliver and Hazel dashed around back, laughing and fumbling with the buttons on their uniforms, bursting into the kitchen
through the service entrance, startling the busy staff into frozen,
open-mouthed stares. "Monsieur Oliver!" the statuesque, toque-
headed chef exclaimed as he sprinkled fresh dill over the poached
salmon that he'd just drowned in a creamy white sauce. "You're
right on time!" A double-clap of his hands started everyone racing around the kitchen again as Oliver and Hazel peeled their
costumes off without an ounce of modesty, then set about replacing them with the evening clothes suspended from wooden pegs
lining the wall of the rear entrance to the kitchen.

"You're a saint, Henri." Oliver was teetering on his tiptoes,
peering into the small round shaving mirror mounted on the wall,
threading his plaid wool tie into a bulky Windsor knot.

"You'll be hanged in that some day," Hazel teased, and
knocked him off balance with a peck on his check, making him
blush.

"Merci, mon ami," Henri blustered, smoothing out the collar
of Oliver's blazer. He stepped over and zipped up Hazel's knee-
length, blue satin evening dress, turning his head away from her
voluptuous cleavage, but discretely leaving his eyes behind. "An-
dre is waiting for you just outside the kitchen doors to seat you
with your guests." Henri guided Oliver and Hazel through the
steamy kitchen to the dining room doors, which kept sweeping in
and out as waiters flew into the kitchen empty-handed, chattered

excitedly, then raced back out, balancing dishes on their hands and arms. *"Bon appétit."* Henri smiled as he nudged them both on their way with an affectionate pat on their derrieres.

The pungent smell of curried lamb filled the dining room with mysterious anticipation, forcing the other patrons to look around, ask their waiters, "What's that?" then want the very same thing, only to be disappointed upon hearing, "It was prepared by Henri just for that table over there, sir. Sorry." The curry was by no means an easy service for the orthodox French kitchen. The saffron-gold sauce was accented with bold dashes of paprika and generous pinches of finely chopped fresh cilantro. Oliver had chosen a young Puligny-Montrachet, which was risky, and he knew it. But the white burgundy held its own under the assault of the more experienced Indian dish. Shimmering jellies, mint greens, pimiento reds, chutney browns, and pickled relishes of every shade of orange and red and yellow gaily circled the fluffy bed of steaming-hot rice. The Coquille St. Jacques, which had misled everyone at the start of the meal, as it was intended to do, made the curry an even greater surprise, and a more delicious taste treat.

"MacDonald!" Oliver's announcement was loud enough for the entire dining room to hear. Heads bobbed up and looked around. "You were born on September 23, 1943, which makes you forty-eight today." Oliver took a deep breath. Sean winced and shut his eyes. "After a great deal of work, and my success in finding some, but not by any means all, of the material I was looking for while in England, I have come to belief that you are marked for The Taking."

Sean collared Oliver with a baleful stare. "Don't get started with that, not here, not tonight. Do you understand?"

Sean was summarily discharged with a sweeping backhand. "Your birthing date adds up to twenty-one." Oliver pulled a pen and small notepad from his inside blazer pocket and began writing, adding to notes already carefully organized on the pages. After a moment of silence, he triumphantly held up his handiwork in front of Sean. "Look."

Cathy glanced at the writing, line after line of tiny words and numbers, then at Oliver. "What is a 'birthing date'?" she asked.

Oliver appeared not to have heard her, or didn't want to. Cathy raised her voice, just short of sounding loud. "Oliver, I asked you a question. What is a birthing date?"

Oliver hunched his shoulders up around his neck. Sean braced himself, knowing, or thinking he did, what Oliver was going to say. "One's birthing date is the date upon which he was born, but it means far more than that from a numerological standpoint." He gestured to Sean, but didn't look at him. "My dear colleague here found references to this by the Egyptians of the third millennia, specifically ascribing a significance to birthing dates equaling twenty-one. The Sumerians, a little less than fifteen-hundred years earlier, wrote about the same thing. And in virtually every one of the Middle Eastern cultures, even the Greeks during the Homeric period, while it may have been called by some other name, a man's numerological birth date was viewed as being prophetic from the standpoint of what his life held for him. This was especially true for the Jews, even as late as the Cabala. Coupled with the numerology of a man's name, this was seen as a bellwether for his future." Oliver nodded curtly to Cathy, having answered her, and turned back to Sean, shaking the notebook at him, waiting for him to take it.

But Cathy wasn't finished with him. "There's got to be hundreds, if not thousands, of dates that add up to twenty-one. So what's the big deal?"

"No," Oliver said with absolute certainty, but without looking at Cathy, "there are not. And taking into account the fact that Sean was born under the autumnal equinox, we have a paired even which occurs only twenty-one times in this century. I've checked," he said with complete confidence, "thanks to the wonderful books you gave me, Sean." Oliver waited for Sean to say something, but gave up after an awkward silence. "What I found particularly interesting was the fact that the dates for the events in your life, ones which you see as happy, resulted in numerical values that are all multiples or combinations of the prime numbers three and seven, which, curiously enough, ties into my research. On the other hand, the dates for those events in your past which you saw as unhappy or tragic, such as your wife's murder in 1974, all appear to be combinations of other numbers.'' Oliver shook his head slowly. "I can't believe that you, Sean, of all people, never made any connection between the numbers in your own life, and your research, numbers which you were ascribing to good and evil in both ancient and modern literature."

There was an expressionless mask covering Sean's face. "So, Dr. Shore, what, pray tell us, are these bad numbers?" Sean asked derisively.

"Six of course," Oliver said with matter-of-fact surety. "And multiples of six, such as twelve, eighteen, twenty-four, and forty-eight." Oliver appeared to become irritated when he saw Sean mooning him with a sleepy-eyed expression. "Don't be so damned cavalier, MacDonald," he barked. "This is important!"

Sean wasn't accustomed to hearing Oliver talk like this, and it surprised him. "Would you mind telling me exactly why this is so damned important? At least to anyone else besides yourself."

Oliver appeared chagrined. "I can't, at least not yet. There are still too many things I need to know about your life, and the lives of those who are, or were, close to you." Cathy shifted around impatiently, catching Oliver's eye. But he blinked it off. "There are also things which my own research will have to verify, presuming it can, when I find the diary I'm looking for."

Sean asked with a sardonic grin, "Is this that satanic thing of yours?"

At hearing this, Cathy leaned forward, putting herself back into the conversation. "What 'satanic thing'?" she asked.

Oliver's face was puffing up with mottled patches of red. "It's not satanic," he replied indignantly to both of them.

Sean matched his pique, but only for effect. "But it really is, isn't it!"

Oliver folded his arms over his stomach. "Somewhat."

Sean relented, softening his words. He sighed. "Oliver, be reasonable. What could all of this possibly have to do with Janet's death? Or my son, John's, for that matter?" Sean reached across the table and stuck a finger into Oliver's chest. "Before you go one step farther, you must tell me about this ritual of yours." Oliver half-heartedly slapped at his hand. "You never did explain it, not really. Whenever I tried getting a straight answer out of you, you gave me some silly, sacrosanct reply, and changed the subject." Sean released his hold on Oliver's chest. "And keep it short."

Oliver beamed. "In my earlier research at Oxford . . ." he began, making it sound like he was telling a bedtime story. As much as he didn't want to risk encouraging Oliver, Sean couldn't help smiling. ". . . I found that for some unexplained reason there were certain men and women who were, and as yet I still don't know exactly why, considered special." He paused and looked to Sean. "Remember the references we both found to this?" Sean wouldn't give him the "yes" he was looking for. "Anyway, it appears to have started centuries before the birth of Christ, just how long before it, I can't tell for sure. But I do know for sure that it began crystalizing into a discernable pattern in the century immediately following the crucifixion, with numerous references cropping up in writings during Nero's reign, the last of the Julio-Claudian emperors."

"Is this going to be a catechism lesson?" Sean taunted. There was an undeniable air of tension settling over the table.

Oliver forced himself to brush aside Sean's belligerent mood. "It's my belief, based upon the research I've done, that what makes these people different, so to speak, is that they rejected God, or the concept of a god, and I mean this in the purest sense, without any conscious theological basis. For this reason, their souls have great value if they can be taken, in this case by Satan. I think, but I'm not sure since I haven't been able to document it properly as yet, the belief is that if the Devil can somehow force them to renounce God in his presence, then capture their soul at that instant before death seizes their body, that they must serve him for an eternity, doomed, if you will, to seek out the souls of others so marked for The Taking." Oliver took a quick breath, which he needed, and smiled at Sean.

"This is all starting to sound really stupid." Sean snorted.

The Taking

"Shhh," Cathy told him with a pat of her hand on his. "I want to hear what Oliver has to say."

Oliver smiled and gave Cathy an appreciative nod of his head, then turned back to Sean. "I realize I don't know yet how the dates are figured in order to predict when The Taking will occur, or where, but I think I can determine who has been chosen. When I was in England this past summer, I finally, after years of searching, found documented evidence in the Church of England's archives of the diaries that were kept by Father Reeves Knight, who was the recording secretary to the Archbishop of Canterbury until shortly after the turn of the century. If my translations from the Greek are accurate, which I found odd being used by anyone in the Anglican Church in the nineteenth century, Father Knight was found impaled on an iron gate in a small cemetery outside London, horribly mutilated, but still alive." It was now Oliver who looked away to gather his composure. "His eyes had been plucked from their sockets, his tongue ripped out, his eardrums pierced, and the poor wretch's fingers had been pulled off." Oliver sat staring at nothing. "Not cut off, Sean, but ripped off his hands!" Oliver leaned forward and whispered softly. "I only pray that I can find Father Knight's diaries when I'm in England over the winter break, before it's too late."

Cathy reached out, took the notebook out from underneath Oliver' hands, and scanned what he'd written. She looked up, made a clown's face at Hazel, then glanced back down, reading slowly, and aloud, using her finger to underscore each line.

```
S E A N   M A C D O N A L D
1 5 1 5   4 1 3 4 6 5 1 3 4 = 43 = 4+3       = 7

Sean's Birthing Date (9-23-43) = 9+2+3+4+3  = 21

Sean was born on the exact date
of the autumnal equinox in 1943 = 9+2+3+4+3  = 21

The date for the full moon
that month was 9-14-43, which = 9+1+4+4+3 = 21
```

Donald Beman

The incidence of a numbered birth date equaling
21, and falling under the equinox or solstice,
occurs only 21 times in a century.

She flipped the page and continued reading.

Sean's age this birthday = 48 = 4+8 $\qquad$ = 12

September 23, 1991 [9/23/91] = 9+2+3+9+1 = 24
24 = 2+4 $\qquad$ = 6

9/23/91 is the date of the full
moon, which is also the date of
the autumnal equinox, and $\qquad$ = 24

48 can be reduced by $\qquad$ 6
24 can be reduced by $\qquad$ 6
12 can be reduced by $\qquad$ 6
6 can be reduced by $\qquad$ 6

None of these numbers can be reduced by Sean = 7

Could the 48th birthday be (another) Unlock
Date?

Although there was more, Cathy stopped and looked up. Hazel was staring back at her in comic disbelief. Oliver was sitting back, wide-eyed and innocent. Sean was seething. "What does it mean for Sean's name to equal seven?" Cathy asked, organizing her thoughts, sorting out all of the questions begging to be asked. "Or for anyone's name to equal a numeric value for that matter?"

"Everything!" Oliver responded instantaneously, his face lighting up.

"Oliver," Sean interjected, "why are you doing this?" Seeing Oliver's face grow brighter, Sean realized what he'd done and wished that he hadn't said anything at all.

"No, it's all right," Cathy said, rubbing Sean's arm reassur-

ingly, trying to calm him down. Then, giving a fiercely determined snap to each of her words, she turned to Oliver, and said,
"I want to play."

Oliver appeared confused. "I beg your pardon?"

"I said," holding her hand up, she spoke slowly "I want to
play. Tell me what my name adds up to in your little game."

Frowning, Oliver hesitated, then answered her. "I'd have to
figure it out," he replied offhandedly, refusing to look at her,
which told Cathy what she wanted to know.

"I think you already know it," she said, reaching out and dropping her large hand onto Oliver's stocky forearm, which startled
him into looking at her.

"You're a two," he said reluctantly.

"And just exactly what is a 'two'?" she asked doggedly.

"It's more complicated than you might realize." There was a
flicker or anxiety burning in Oliver's amber-red eyes. He turned
to Sean, but got no help whatsoever.

"Then make it uncomplicated," Cathy told him with a tap of
her finger on his arm. She sat back, folding her hands in her lap,
looking anything but contrite as she waited for Oliver to answer
her.

Oliver gave a compliant nod of his head. "The number two
represents duality and the natural tension found in the mortal
world. People whose given and surname add up to the number
two are destined to live a life filled with conflict, either within
themselves, with others, or both. Twos are also incomplete beings,
since they can never be resolved by themselves. Someone who is
a two needs another force, another person, or spiritual entity, to
balance out their lives. But those other persons must be the right
number themselves in order to relieve the tension, thereby elim-
inating the continuous push and pull of that person's dualistic
nature. A one, a five, or a seven can do this, unlike another two,
or a four, numbers which, when combined with the number two,
would only make that person's life that much more difficult, perhaps even dangerous." Oliver stopped and looked over to Sean
for help, but came up empty-handed again.

"What does the number nine signify?" Cathy asked skeptically, but at the same time revealing that she fully understood what he was driving at.

Looking as if he had just been let off the hook, Oliver went on. "Nine is the ultimate number of completeness. To some that means spiritual completeness. Nine is the sum of three threes, which signifies the infinite unity of the trinity. In some philosophical circles, it's seen as the metaphysical opposite of the number six, which is the number of ultimate incompleteness and infinite duality. Within Christianity, they speak of nine orders of angels, and Dante saw his Beatrice as the embodiment of nine. Nine is also an odd number, therefore lucky, offsetting the unlucky and disquieting qualities of the even number six. Nine is considered to be more powerful than seven, which is the first number of completeness. The use of the number nine is widely connected with Celtic peoples, such as the Druids. And the traditions about King Arthur show an abundance of nines, which probably arose from the Nordic preoccupation with nine, resulting from the nine long months of winter in the northernmost hemisphere. Although nine does occur frequently in the more southerly lore of the Greeks." Oliver took a chest-filling breath. "Nine also has one rather unique characteristic, for when you combine the number with itself in simple arithmetic progression, the sum of the digits of each and every resulting number equals nine, ad infinitum."

Oliver could see Cathy struggling with his explanation, and said slowly, "Nine plus nine equals eighteen. And eighteen is one plus eight, which equals nine. Then eighteen plus nine equals twenty-seven, and two plus seven equals nine. It works with all numbers that are multiples of the number nine, such as ninehundred-ninety-nine, the sum of which is twenty-seven, and that sum is nine. In all cases, the sum of the digits of these numbers will reduce down to the number nine, and no other root number possesses this mystical property." Looking across the table, Oliver tried pulling Sean into the conversation with a smile and a wink of his eye. "Sean sees the number nine as symbolizing immortality, which he bases on its regenerative properties. But I don't quite agree, not yet."

The Taking

"Is nine seen as good or evil?" Cathy asked, ignoring Sean's repeated shaking of his head, asking her to drop the whole thing.

"According to Dr. MacDonald," Oliver said stiffly, as if trying to shift the responsibility for what had happened to the evening onto Sean's shoulders, "it can be either good or evil. It depends wholly upon the origin of its component numbers. But whichever it is, Sean is convinced that it's a very powerful force, and one which little is known about. It's also a number that does not occur frequently in nature, or in name numerology, much like the number one, which I find curious."

Cathy was struggling to accept what Oliver had said. "Are you implying that when individuals marry, people whose names equate to certain numbers, such as a two and a seven, that their life together is subject to the numerology of that union?"

Oliver replied without hesitating so much as a second. "Precisely. Each one of them contributes to, and becomes part of, the sum total of their combined metaphysical spirit, their collective aura. But it doesn't only result from marriage; it arise from any contact, intimate or casual." Oliver's face flared up at the sight of Cathy's disbelieving smirk. "If you doubt me," he said, pounding the table with his open hand, surprising everyone, but not Sean, "just look around at the people you know, and check out the numerology of their names, and a few selected events in their lives, and see what you get. I guarantee that they will be reflections of their numerological spirits, both individually and as a couple."

Cathy wouldn't let him go. "Accepting for a moment that what you say is true, then what do the numbers six and twelve signify, since you seem to have made such a fuss about them?"

Oliver pointed at Sean. "Since my dear colleague doesn't fully agree with my viewpoints on these numbers, even though his own research does, I suggest that you ask him for an explanation. But I don't think he's interested in getting involved with all of this anymore, since he claims that he no longer believes any of it, and says it's all no more than 'silly superstition.' "

"Fair enough," Cathy said. Her casual, almost flippant response was followed by a period of silence, which Oliver appeared to relish. As did Sean, but for different reasons. However, Cathy's thoughts were by no means quiet as they shouted back and forth to each from one eye to the other. "Patricia Jennings is a seven, isn't she?" Cathy asked, tying Oliver back up into a knot. Sean muffled a laugh, which Cathy clearly didn't appreciate.

Oliver was not accustomed to dealing with such a formidable woman, one he couldn't just brush aside like one of his students, and looked like he wished that he could hide from her. "Yes."

"And exactly what does that mean?" she asked, sensing his discomfort, and zeroing in on him. "As concerns Sean, that is."

Again, Oliver looked to Sean for support. But Sean just sat there, staring blankly into the cluttered table waiting to be bussed. "Taken alone?" Oliver finally said. "Sean and Dr. Jennings are equals in a manner of speaking. But in light of their relationship as I know it"—Sean sat up stiffly, Cathy smiled nervously—"and from all of the numbers and dates and events, at least the ones I know about, it would seem that they are on opposite, but connected, poles of a powerful push and pull, a battle of wills, of personalities, male versus female, the ultimate duality, a conflict from which only one of them can hope to—"

"And Dr. Fanning?" Cathy asked, cutting Oliver off, not wanting to hear another word about Patricia Jennings.

"A six," he said quickly, obviously happy to be off the subject of Patricia Jennings. "I think," he added. "Yes, a six." For some reason Oliver looked proud as a peacock as he foraged through the uneaten rice on his plate for overlooked pieces of lamb. Finding none, he peered over at Hazel's plate, then reached for it.

Within minutes of pulling out of the parking lot of The Ridgefield Inn, the wine took its toll on Sean. He tipped over onto Cathy's shoulder and fell sound asleep. Besides, by one o'clock in the morning, he was only a few hours away from getting up. It was late for Cathy, too, rising with the sun, but not ahead of it like Sean. However, she was kept wide awake by Oliver's tantalizing stories about his "dear friend, Sean," and other tales that told of his "dear colleague, Dr. MacDonald." Oliver spoke as if they were two different people, which made Cathy realize that she, too, saw Sean in much the same light.

Sinking back into the deep wool seats of the Rolls, listening to Oliver go on and on about his research, "our research" as he referred to it with a nod of his head in Sean's direction, Cathy became fixed on his every word, especially whenever the subject of The Taking came up, or the mention of Father Reeves Knight. When she tried pinning him down to exactly what Sean had to do with it all, Oliver abruptly stopped talking, looked into the rearview mirror, then out into the night.

Lifting Sean's head off her shoulder, laying him down gently on the armrest between them, Cathy climbed forward and sat on the jump seat behind Oliver, but only after twisting around sideways because of her long legs. She then rested her arms on top of the divider separating the front driver's seat from the rear, and locked onto the reflection of Oliver's dark red eyes in the rearview mirror. "What is the 'unlock date'?" she asked.

Oliver, preoccupied with the traffic, which was surprisingly heavy given to the hour, didn't answer her, at least not as quickly as Cathy might have liked. So she asked again. "The unlock date, Oliver. What does it mean?"

Shifting around to get comfortable, but still looking uncomfortable, even though he wasn't wearing his chauffeur's uniform anymore, Oliver replied, "The unlock date marks what I call a window in time, which remains open for a very definite and inflexible period. It is, I believe, a window through which Satan, or whatever you're comfortable calling evil, is able to pass through into this world and seize the souls of those persons so marked."

"And Sean's forty-eighth birthday, why is it, or how is it you think this is his unlock date?"

A whimsical smile lighted Oliver's face. "From what I've been able to extract from Sean's work, and from my own research, only in a very different field, the unlock date is somehow tied into a date, or dates, in one's life which yield numerical values that can all be reduced by the root number six, while at the same time that date, and all of the interrelated numbers associated with one's life at that time, cannot be reduced by the numerology of their own name. In other words, they cannot defend themselves from Satan, numerological speaking, and must rely wholly upon their faith in God, whatever that means. There also appears to be a key, for lack of a better term, which I believe is a common integer tied into a specific event in time, and which correlates mathematically to the events in this person's life. My belief is that if we can unravel the numerology of our lives, using this 'key,' we can somehow, but I don't know how, change the outcome.''

With a curious frown, Cathy asked, "Is this thing that passes through your window in time male or female?"

Fussing about as if the traffic was too heavy for him to pay attention to her, Oliver didn't answer. Cathy stuck her head over the divider and just stared at him. He tried avoiding her, but finally gave in to her persistence. "I don't know what form it actually takes, other than possessing the body of a mortal, a host if you will. But even that is conjecture on my part. It could be a spirit of some sort, for all I know.''

"Does the 'host' know who, or what, they are?"

"I don't know that, either," Oliver replied impatiently, and pulled his head away from Cathy's penetrating gaze.

Cathy wasn't buying Oliver's answer. "And how long did you say that you've been working on this project, Dr. Shore?''

"Twenty years, perhaps longer." The seriousness of Oliver's reply revealed that he hadn't felt the prick of Cathy's sarcasm.

"And its gender?" she asked, not wanting to let go of this.

Oliver drew quiet. "I never gave any thought to gender, although Sean seems certain about it, if not fixated. I suppose I just accepted it as manifesting itself in the form of a man. But now that you bring it up, I have never found any specific references in the literature to a man or a woman. For that matter, it could be genderless! But Sean feels otherwise.''

Cathy seemed put off with this answer. "You still haven't explained the significance of the number twenty-one as it relates to Sean's birth date. Actually, when I think about it, you haven't really *explained* one damn thing about the relationship of those numbers you wrote down.'' Dispensing with a secondhand piece of him in the mirror, Cathy slid closer, as if trying to look through his skull and into his brain for the answers that she wanted. "I can't believe someone with your knowledge and education would get involved with this." She pulled away, leaving Oliver's thoughts to himself.

"We're all superstitious in some way, Catherine"—when Oliver called her Catherine it didn't appear to bother her the way it did when Sean called her that—"regardless of whether we admit it or not. And even if we aren't, that doesn't change what is. Do you think someone who believes in one God, their God, would accept that someone who doesn't believe in any god is free from their God?" Oliver promptly answered his own question. "Of course not. They believe their God has absolute control over everything, and everyone, including those who don't believe."

"Does Sean know how strongly you feel about all of this?"

Oliver coughed up a laugh. "Sean doesn't take this seriously, at least not anymore."

"Have you told him what you've found?"

"I tried, and I'm not confronting him again until I have hard facts lined up to show him. I have to go back to England to find Father Knight's journal, his personal diary, not the one he kept for the church. I'm certain that the clues—"

"Oliver?" Cathy interrupted. "Could this really have anything to do with the death of Sean's wife?" Oliver didn't answer. More accurately, he wouldn't, and Cathy knew it. "Oliver?" she repeated, adding a sharp poke of his arm.

"I think so. But Sean has refused to let himself believe any of this anymore, even though he went into the meanings associated with the metaphor of the poems."

"Poems?"

"Yes, the poems left behind at the scene of Janet's murder, and the one he found in his son's bedroom. There was even one he discovered in his mother's hospital room, the morning after she died. And there's one he received during his affair—" Oliver caught himself.

But Cathy knew what he was about to say, and finished it for him, much to his surprise. "With Patricia?"

The car turned, then jerked to a stop, tossing Sean off the seat and onto the floor before Cathy could grab him. "I go right past the driveway at night myself." Sean laughed, climbing back up, giving Cathy a sleepy peck on the cheek. He then opened the door and pulled her out of the car with him.

Házel popped up in the front seat like a redheaded jack-in-the-box. "Are we home?" she asked, yawning and stretching.

"I didn't leave the kitchen window open," Cathy noted, waving good-bye to Hazel as Oliver backed out of the driveway.

Sean slipped his arm around Cathy's waist. "Wasn't it open when I ran downstairs with my shoes half on?" he asked.

"I closed it," Cathy replied, looking up to the open window as they started across the lawn, kicking their way through the puddles of moonlight flooding the yard and drowning the lawn. "That's what took so me long to come down. It was stuck, and I had to work it loose. Didn't you hear me?"

"Nope," Sean said with a sleepy shake of his head. "Maybe Jean went up for something," he suggested, scooping Cathy into his arms and carrying her up the porch steps as easily as if she was no heavier than his own breath. "I love you, Catherine." He kissed her tenderly on the lips before setting her down. This time, for the first time, Catherine meant Cathy, not something, or someone else.

Cathy climbed the stairs ahead of Sean, who stopped to lock the door behind him. "What's that smell?" Cathy asked when she reached the landing.

"Don't open that door!" Sean yelled, racing up the stairs and pushing her aside. "Stay here," he ordered, slipping into the kitchen. Ignoring him, Cathy was at his side in two steps. The odor grew stronger and thicker and colder as they moved through the darkened kitchen to the long hallway, which was pitch black from end to end, except for the block of moonlight falling out of his bedroom onto the floor in the hall. Sean felt his way along the wall. He hit his arm on the open attic door. Cathy started to say something. He hushed her with his hand over her mouth and closed the door without making a sound. The air had turned foul, like the stench from the rotting carcass of a dead animal left lying

216

in the sun, crawling with maggots and buzzing with flies.

Bracing his arms in front of him, Sean stepped into the doorway. The window over his bed was thrown open. The air was dead calm and thick, even though the wind could be heard scratching over the roof. He hit the light switch with a slapping sweep of his hand. The room had exploded into a shambles. The sheets were ripped into shreds and thrown about like tissue paper. The mattress was torn apart, disemboweled. The pillows had burst open like blisters filled with puss; the feathers were sticking to oily clumps of yellow and brown, like clotted gore. The walls and floor were spattered with spots of black, still wet. "Happy birthday," Sean whispered, slumping against the doorjamb, his body seized by a violent shiver.

Early Tuesday Morning

Cathy looked up from the kitchen table long enough to say, "Good morning, sleepyhead," then bobbed back down and continued playing with the scraps of paper spread out in front of her.

Sean draped his arms over her shoulders. "Good morning." He yawned and gave her a lingering kiss on the top of her head. He then shuffled across the kitchen with his hand outstretched, reaching for the coffee pot on the stove. "How's your back from sleeping on the floor?" he asked, filling his mug to the rim.

"It feels like I spent a night on the parade grounds at Parris Island," she said dryly, fitting the final few pieces of her papered puzzle into place with a tap of her finger. "Well, here it is," she said proudly. "But there's no title. Want me to read it to you?"

"Sure, why not," he replied, slurping his coffee down so that it wouldn't slosh out as he walked back. "This ought to be interesting."

Cathy stood up so she could look down on the wrinkled patches of torn paper that she'd glued to the back of a notebook. Taking a deep breath, she read aloud, "The night, though clear, shall frown ... and the stars shall not look down from their high thrones in the Heaven with light like hope to mortals given ..."

" 'Spirits of the Dead,' " Sean interrupted, slipping his arm around Cathy's waist and pulling her to him as if he needed the support. "Is that all of the pieces?" he asked, devouring with his eyes the chewed-up words lying on the table in front of him.

"It's everything that was in the room. Why do you ask?"

"Because the first two stanzas are missing."

Picking the notebook up, looking at it curiously, then over at Cathy, he asked, "Where did you get this notebook?"

"It was on the floor in the hall. Why do you ask?"

"Because it was packed away upstairs, that's why," he said with a shrug of his shoulders, and began circling the kitchen, sipping his coffee while reading to himself what was on the back of the notebook.

> Thy soul shall find itself alone
> 'Mid dark thoughts of the gray tomb-stone—
> Not one, of all the crowd, to pry
> Into thine hour of secrecy:
>
> Be silent in that solitude,
> Which is not loneliness—for then
> The spirits of the dead are again who stood
> In life before thee
> In death around thee—and their will
> Shall overshadow thee; be still.
>
> The night—tho' clear—shall frown—
> And the stars shall look not down
> From their high thrones in the Heaven,
> With light like hope to mortals given—
>
> But their red orbs, without beam,
> To thy weariness shall seem
> As a burning and a fever
> Which would cling to thee for ever
>
> Now are thoughts thou shalt not banish—
> Now are visions ne'er to vanish—

The Taking

From thy spirit shall they pass
No more—like dewdrops from the grass.

The breeze—the breath of God—is still—
And the mist upon the hill
Shadowy—shadowy—yet unbroken,
Is a symbol and a token—
How it hangs upon the trees,
A mystery of mysteries?—

"Someone made a mistake," he said, handing the poem back to Cathy, almost dropping it when he absentmindedly let go too soon. He then sat down across from her, staring out the window.

"What's been changed?"

"There should be an exclamation point at the end, not a question mark." He downed the last bit of coffee with a gulp.

"I'm going downstairs to use Jean Murphy's phone."

"Why?"

"To call the police."

"No!" Sean ordered, startling Cathy with his sharp command. "Please," he said more softly, tempering himself, but not her.

"What do you mean, no?" she asked.

"Because it's a waste of time," he told her, taking aim at the nearly empty pot of coffee on the stove. "Anyway, they won't believe you when you tell them what you found. Trust me."

In a sudden and unexpected move, Cathy blocked Sean's path to the stove. "What are you saying?" she asked, spreading her arms out when he tried slipping past her, holding him prisoner in front of her. "You're not making any sense. Talk to me."

Sean was tired and had little or no patience left for all of this. "Which word didn't you understand, Catherine?"

"Damn it, Sean! Don't 'Catherine' me!" she snapped angrily. When Sean tried stepping around her again, Cathy hooked his arm and spun him back. Sean stumbled into the kitchen table. "What the hell is wrong with you?" she demanded, pointing down the hall. "Do you realize what would have happened if you were in that bed last night when that person showed up?" Cathy was no longer the woman Sean knew; she was that other woman, the one he'd seen and felt in the air around him for those few fleeting seconds in the Red Hook Inn. He could see the man lying on the floor, his arm twisted and limp, the splintered end of a bone pushing through his shirt.

Leaning against the table, watching Cathy change back, Sean slid his hand up his arm, feeling with his fingers where she'd grabbed him. It was sore, as though he'd been punched, punched hard, and not by a woman. At least not any woman that he'd ever known. Not even Janet hit him that hard. "I think you should leave," he said, turning away from her, stepping over to the window. "I think it's best for the both us that you do."

"No," Cathy replied. She was standing behind him before he could argue with her. "What's wrong with you?" she asked, sounding more like Cathy now. Sean acted like she wasn't even there. "Sean?" She put her hand on his shoulder. He shrugged it off. "Why aren't you going to do anything about this?" she asked, gingerly pressing her open hand on his back. "Is there something you're not telling me?"

Sean turned around to face her. "It's what I don't know that I'm not telling you. As for doing something, what would you suggest, 'Captain'?" Cathy bristled at hearing him call her this. Sean appeared to smile, but more with his eyes than his mouth. "What is, is," he said, stepping past her. "Now, I asked you to leave. Please leave."

Cathy became still, then left without saying another word.

26

Sunday, October 13, 1991

Sean,

I got your diskette with the final chapters. You were right, I was surprised when I read the ending. But I think it works. Well done!

From what I see, you don't need me anymore, Sean, so don't bother sending me the rewrites. I'm also returning these two diskettes to you, since I don't see what I can say about the current work that will make any difference.

Although I've looked everywhere, I can't seem to find the duplicate you sent from last time, but I'll keep looking. I guess I must have misplaced it.

One last comment I will make, however, is about the way your character lets women use him, even push him around. He should be more of his own man, a man's man so to speak. Give it some thought, OK?

Because Trish and I were in the middle of finalizing the curriculum for a series of new courses combining American literature with art history—your idea, remember?—I wasn't able to make your party. I should have let you know beforehand, but we were in Manhattan every day last week, and it simply slipped my mind. Please accept my apologies.

And a belated, but very sincere Happy 48th Birthday, "old" man!

Bruce

Sean read and reread Bruce's letter. There was something missing—he could just feel it. He read it again, slowly, and out loud, and found it. But not in what Bruce had said, in the hundreds of things he didn't say. With angry pokes of his fingers, Sean deleted all of the files from the diskette, then did the same with the duplicate, and started another letter.

Dear Sarah,

I mailed out my first submissions to agents and publishers today. I feel like a kid sending away for his first Captain Midnight decoder ring!

I know the wait for me has been brief compared with most writers, but in reality, it's taken me more than twenty years to get here. While I will hope, I really don't expect anything to happen right away.

And I'm also preparing myself—I think—for a strikeout the first time at bat. But keep your fingers crossed for me anyway.

As always, thank you.

                                                                Sean

Just as Sean walked into the kitchen, the ship's clock on the wall began chiming. He grabbed his brown suede jacket off the back of the chair and started downstairs, counting each of the bells under his breath. When he reached the bottom, he waited for the last two, then yelled back up, "Eight!" as if having been in a race with time, and won.

He flew over the back roads on his way to the farm, laughing each time he took a turn too fast, and the tires chattered back at him in the crisp autumn air, instead of moaning and groaning as they'd done all summer when they dragged themselves over the soft macadam. Hints of fall were everywhere, staining the leaves honey gold and bitter orange and mocha brown. He drove faster and faster, writing and rewriting his apology to Cathy.

The porch wrapped around three sides of Cathy's two-story,

turn-of-the-century farmhouse. The back, facing north, was screened in with large sheets of metallic mesh, billowing out like tarnished aluminum sails filled with an invisible wind. Here and there, patches of shiny new screening were wire-tied over frayed finger holes. During the day, angry yellow jackets bounced off the screen, trying to get out, getting madder and madder with each futile attempt. Meanwhile, large wasps crawled in and out of their prisons of mud glued to the rafters with sticky saliva, snapping and flicking their shiny blue wings, appearing to have accepted their fate, until one of them dropped straight down, searching for someone, anyone, to sting. The cool of the evening quieted them all down in time for the legions of mosquitoes to mount their whining attack outside, trying to get inside.

Sean propped his elbows on the rickety wooden table opposite the kitchen window and scrunched his chin in his hands. "I just don't understand why Bruce mailed everything back and told me I didn't need him anymore. He also said that he was working with 'Trish' on a new curriculum." Sean's mouth tightened into a fleshless line as he swallowed his lips. "I developed that goddamn program years ago!" he complained, sitting back, peering out into the abandoned paddocks behind the house filling up with shadows. "But every time I tried talking with Potter about it, she gave me the runaround."

Cathy waited for Sean to stop gesturing, but his hands and head and eyes kept moving, even though the sound had been turned off. "Do you think it could be that you're jealous?" she asked.

Sean scowled. "Of Bruce? Absolutely not!"

"I meant of Patricia, *with* Bruce."

"Don't be ridiculous," Sean said, rejecting Cathy's suggestion with a distasteful frown and toss of his head.

Sean had never spoken to her this way, and it surprised her. She spoke with a sureness that forced Sean to look at her. "I think it's about Bruce rejecting you for her, and I think you're hurt. And I think you're expressing it with anger."

"Who the hell do you think you are, my fucking therapist?"

Cathy was surprised into silence. She sat looking at Sean, tilting her head first to one side, then the other, like a curious cat. Sean wanted to say he was sorry, but couldn't, or wouldn't. Nothing was going the way he'd rehearsed it on his drive over. He kept forgetting his lines, which only made things worse, because then he said what he felt without thinking. He went back to picking at the apple pie Sally had made for dessert, only the ice cream had melted and turned the crust into soggy cardboard. He could feel Cathy looking at him, trying to get inside. He wished that she somehow could, but knew it wasn't going to be easy, not anymore. He forced himself to finish the pie, as if eating it and not liking it was some sort of offering.

The sound of shuffling papers lifted his eyes. Cathy had returned to reading his manuscript, which is what she had been doing when he arrived a half-hour early for dinner. She had been quiet and soft-spoken, telling him she had just come downstairs after having taken what she said was "A deliciously hot, and much needed bath." She had been reserved, too, until he apologized to her. But even that hadn't gone the way he wanted. He kept losing the words he'd set aside for her, which wasn't like him.

"What do you think of my story?" He doubled up his question with a nervous smile, which he poked across the table at her.

Cathy didn't take her eyes off the page, although she was no longer reading. "Your descriptions of places have a bittersweet taste to them, especially those passages describing indoor places. When your characters are outside, I'm left feeling that they're lost, and you're trying to build walls around them to make them safe, only I don't know from what. At least not yet. The dialogue is a little rough for me at times." Cathy found herself struggling for the rest of what she felt, and only made it worse by trying to hide it when she said, "I don't have any difficulty with what is said; I have trouble with what's not said." The faint light that had begun to glow in Sean's eyes, lighting up his face, was dimming. "It leaves me feeling that there's a strong undercurrent of emotions that I can't sort out and that I'm afraid will pull me under with them if I'm not careful. But then, I suppose you're succeeding as a writer, since you're making me slow down and feel the way you want me to feel, in spite of what I want to feel, or what I want your characters to feel, or do. I probably just need to relax and accept what's happening, both in the story and in me.'' Cathy finally looked up and across the table at Sean. He was waiting for her, hungry for what he knew wasn't being given to him. "I'm also getting this uneasy sense that something is going to happen, but I don't know what it is. Or which one of your characters will be affected.''

Sean hadn't gotten what he wanted, what he needed. "And?'' he asked, sitting sideways and leaning his arm on the table.

Cathy folded her hands on top of the box holding his manuscript. "What do you mean, 'and'?'' she asked.

He sat up, looking hurt. "Do you like it?'' he asked out of desperation.

Cathy looked away, throwing her thoughts outside, beyond the darkened paddocks. With each passing second, the anticipation dripped down off of Sean's face, until he cast his empty eyes aside and sat back. Cathy's reply finally came, but from out there somewhere. "As I got deeper into the story, it became almost uncomfortable for me to read, so I put it down.''

"And why was that, Catherine?'' Sean asked, failing miserably in sweetening his bitter feelings of disappointment and disdain.

"Because I suddenly realized that I don't know you, Sean. And I also realized that I couldn't tell what was real and what wasn't. Everything felt . . .''

Sean couldn't help himself. "Surreal?''

Cathy inhaled the word, then stuck her finger into the table. "If that's what you wanted to achieve, then which side of the canvas are you on?'' Cathy took careful aim at him. "Do you know, I mean really know? Or have you buried yourself so deep in the pages of your fanciful imagination that I'm now talking to one of your characters? Is that who I've been sleeping with?'' she asked, surprising him with her anger.

Sean fired back, "I guess you'll just have to tough it out and finish the story, Captain Greene.''

Cathy's eyes turned ice cold. She drew her hands off the table and dropped them into her lap. There was a vaporous look about her; she was evaporating before his eyes. At that very instant, Sean knew something was different between them, something that could never be turned back, unlike the pages of a story that could be reread, then rewritten. He wished that he'd never said what he did. If he had any doubts of what he saw, the turn of Cathy's head, as if ducking a punch in slow motion, told him to forget it. As he watched, Sean saw something fold itself over and over, deep inside her, shutting out the light, and shutting him out, too. Standing up, Sean walked off the porch, slapping his hand at the whack of the screen door when it slammed shut behind him, and started down the drive with no intention of waiting for Cathy.

She followed, but at a distance, watching him gesturing to himself as he crossed the road, and abruptly bringing everything to an end with an explosive sweep of his arms, before wandering out into the fields. Without a moon, everything was pitch black.

Cathy caught up. "Sean?"

He quickened his pace. "Yes?"

She easily kept up with him. "What was Janet like?"

He slowed a little. "I wondered when you'd finally get around to asking me that."

Cathy stumbled on something in the dark and fell forward. Sean reached out, pulling her to him, then threading his arm around her waist, tying them together. They stayed that way, saying nothing, exchanging invisible explanations, apologies, back and forth as they walked deeper into the night. Cathy said softly, "I remember seeing your wife on campus, and then only at a distance. She always seemed to be in hurry. Did she have dark hair?"

"Sort of," Sean replied apprehensively. "It depended on what light she was in. I'd put it a few shades lighter than polished mahogany."

"What was she like?"

Sean started to answer, as if he didn't have to think, but stopped.

"If you don't want to talk about her, I understand."

Sean wound his pace down to a lazy walk. "It's odd, but for some reason, right this second, I can't remember what Janet looked like. I keep trying, but I can't see anything. Am I making any sense?" he asked anxiously.

"I'd like to say yes, but I'm not sure that I really know what you mean."

They were now walking in step, but very slowly.

"When I try looking back at the two of us, together, there aren't any clear images. There are only shadows, and silence. My brain knows what she looked like, I just can't describe her. Now am I making sense?"

"I'm afraid not."

Seeing the outline of the flatbed truck suddenly crystallize in front of them, they reached it together, patting the air, as if making sure the truck was real, before climbing up onto the rough wooden planks, scrunching side by side and leaning against each other like a pair of bookends. Sean started to tip his head down onto Cathy's shoulder, but she beat him to it, stealing his shoulder from him. Fresh hay had been spread over the planks, softening their splintery touch. Cornstalks, tied together and drained of color, were surrounded by a handful of would be jack-o'-lanterns, staring back at them, faceless.

"It's as if I wasn't ever there, and someone else was, someone I don't even know, a stranger." Falling back into the hay, Sean looked up. The night sky was brilliant with stars, each one sparkling brighter than the next, burning silvery holes through midnight into morning.

"Did you love her?"

Sean wanted to shiver, but couldn't, even when he tried. "Yes, I loved her in the beginning. But I *think* it now, I don't feel it. I've been told that I never really loved her, and that I was afraid to love anyone." Cathy held her breath. "For as long as I can remember, I was afraid to be truthful about how I felt, about anything, but especially how I felt about a woman."

Sean had nothing more to say, at least nothing he dared say. He waited for Cathy's next question, but her breathing told him she'd already started to slip away. He eased himself around, letting her face press into him, her breath warming his chest, restarting his heart. He tried again to find Janet, but Karen got in the way. He felt that his chest would burst open. There was nothing he could do to stop what was happening. But then, he didn't want to, and he knew it.

Cathy's hand started twitching, as if she was reaching out for him to join her in sleep. Sean closed his eyes, following her. But they weren't alone, and perhaps never would be again.

27

Friday, October 19, 1991

Sitting at his table in the Red Hook Inn, Sean hurried through the handful of form letters, letting each one float down on top of the one before it, until there was a sloppy pile of unsigned rejections scattered on the table around his empty mug of beer. He then turned his attention to the one envelope that he'd set aside, the one without a return address on it, as if knowing that it was somehow special.

My Dear Sean,

I like your story very much. It's a little rough in spots, but that's what editors are for. When you do tackle the rewrite, try and make things a little more "organic."

As I read the manuscript, I found I couldn't help thinking about your characters, the ones I don't know, and wanted to meet them. But then, I realized that wasn't possible; after all, it's fiction, right?

The ending was hard for me to accept. Are you really sure you want it that way? And why do you?

The Taking

I suppose about now you're wondering how your story came into my possession. It's really quite simple. I'm a literary agent, and you sent your manuscript to my office as part of a query package.

Unfortunately, and I mean that sincerely, I cannot take this on. Aside from the fact that I do not handle this type of work, my personal involvement with you would preclude it.

But if you don't mind, I'll pass it along to one or two agents I know, and who I think might very well be interested in it.

It's funny, but try as I might, I have been unable to get you out of my thoughts. You were unlike any man I ever made love with, and nothing like I thought you would be.

Good luck
K

Sean held the letter in his open hands, studying it like a rare book. " 'Unlike any man you ever made love with?' " Sean asked himself, and started rummaging through the mental files of his night with Karen, looking for something that might help him understand what she meant. Was it something I did? he asked himself. Or something I didn't do? He said aloud, "I was nothing like you thought I would be like? What was I, Karen, some sort of game for you?"

"Love letters?" Bobby McCarthy asked, looking down at the mess on the table and shaking his head as he replaced Sean's empty mug with a full one.

"Bobby?" Sean asked, stretching his leg underneath the table, and pushing out the chair across from him with a shove of his foot. "I need your help with something." Sean motioned for Bobby to have a seat.

Bobby happily sat down. "What can I do for you?"

"You were in the service with Cathy, right?"

"Yes, sir," Bobby snapped, then smiled at himself for the way he answered. "Yes, I was in the service with Cath," he repeated, only much more relaxed.

"You served in the Gulf, right?"

"Yes—" Bobby caught himself this time. "So did Cath."

Sean melted back into his chair. "Was she wounded?"

"Wounded? Cath?" There was suddenly a leathery stiffness about Bobby. He just sat there, expressionless, sizing up Sean.

"You were in her unit, weren't you?"

"I don't know what you're talking about." Bobby's reply was delivered across the table like a sniper's gunshot, hitting Sean squarely in the chest.

"But—"

"I'm afraid I can't help you, Dr. MacDonald." Bobby pushed his chair back and stood up.

"What are you two plotting?" Cathy asked, walking up behind Sean and putting her hands on his shoulders, but keeping her distance. Bobby nodded to Sean, smiled half-heartedly at Cathy, and left.

"What was *that* all about?" she asked.

"Nothing." Sean pulled Cathy's hands down and wrapped her arms around his neck. "I missed you." He kissed the palm of one hand, then the other. "And I'm sorry for being such a shit the other night." He could feel Cathy soften all over.

You finally got it right, MacDonald, he thought.

The evening was unhurried, the night hot, before melting into the morning. Still half asleep, Sean responded to Cathy's unseen touch and rolled over onto his side. She threaded her legs through his, tying their bodies into a knot, and took him inside her before he was ready, surprising him. She was warm and moist and creamy soft. They lay perfectly still. Cathy brushed the falling-down hair off his forehead and drew his eyes closed with the tips of her fingers. Then she sketched a smile onto his sleepy face.

"Be still," she whispered, and pressed her open hand flat on her tummy. "I want to memorize every delicious inch of you growing inside me, so that I can have you whenever I want."

Reaching out, Sean covered Cathy's hand with his, feeling her fingers pressing gently into her own flesh. Before he could do it, too, Cathy drained every last drop of leftover passion out of him, drinking him dry with sip after sip, and swallow after swallow of her body. As he grew soft, Cathy drifted back to sleep. When her hand slipped off her belly, sinking into the crumpled sheets lying around her naked body, Sean's hand fell onto the ribbons of skin, pink and hard, covering her firm stomach. He waited until he was certain she was fast asleep, then traced each and every scar with a feathery-light touch of his fingertips, as if searching for something, something he'd missed seeing in her eyes, or hearing in her voice.

28

Thursday, October 24, 1991

Dear Mr. MacDonald:

I'm returning your synopsis and manuscript. As I mentioned the first time you sent it to me, I specialize in nonfiction, so this isn't for me, even though I liked what little I read (my curiosity!).

By the way, your revised ending—I always take a peek at the ending—was a smart move. I think it will make all the difference. There also seemed to be a slight shift in the writing style with the revised ending. Was this intentional on your part?

Good luck finding an agent who can do justice to your work.

David Sandborne

Sean pushed the letter across the kitchen table to Cathy. "Cath?" he asked warily. "Take a look at this, and tell me what you think." Folding his arms, Sean rocked back in his chair.

Cathy's eyes scurried back and forth over the letter. "It says he thinks your revised ending was a smart move, that he liked what he read, and he doesn't handle fiction. It looks pretty straightforward to me." Cathy handed it back without bothering to look where Sean's outstretched hand was, and let go, forcing him to pitch forward and catch it in midflight on its way to the floor.

"But I only sent him one draft," he said, sitting up, balancing the note in his open hand like it was a paper tray, then thinking of Bobby McCarthy.

Taking it back, Cathy held it up to the window. "It's not a form letter," she said in a businesslike way. "Besides, he talks about your work specifically. What do those others you got today say?"

"Thanks, but no thanks," Sean replied with a discouraged grunt. "There's only a dozen, but it feels like a hundred." Giving David Sandborne's letter a less than gentle pat with his hand, Sean watched it puff up in the air, then flutter down to the floor. Then, shoving the handful of unopened letters out of the way, Sean returned to reading his *Almanac*, for October, the tenth month.

Sean ran his finger down the page to the twenty-third, the two-hundred-ninety-sixth day of the year, then slid it across to the opposite page, where he read to himself, *Full Hunter's Moon.*

A loud pounding downstairs made him jump and look up. "Sean!" a woman called out over the insistent hammering on the door. "It's me. Are you up there?"

Cathy frowned questioningly.

"Sarah Potter." He laughed.

Cathy began gathering up the papers scattered over the table, tidying them up. "Does she always knock that way?"

"Sean! Please! Let me in!" Sarah demanded.

Cathy shook her head in amazement. "You'd better answer the door before the woman pushes it down!"

"She could, too!" Sean laughed, dropping the almanac onto the kitchen table. "She packs quite a punch in those nicotine-stained fists of hers!'' The sound of feet pounding into the stairs told them Sarah Potter had let herself in. Sean made a comedic show of lunging for the kitchen door and pulling it open just as Sarah stumbled onto the landing, fighting for air. ''What a pleasant surprise, Sarah. What brings you out—''

Sarah exploded into the kitchen. ''He's dead!''

''Who?'' Sean whispered out of unknown respect.

''Bruce!''

Sean let go of the door, his arms falling away from him as if no longer attached to his body, and stumbled backward. Cathy shot up out of her chair. Sean took a step toward Sarah, looking like he was in a trance. Sarah stuck her arms straight out in front of her. ''No!'' She pushed him back without actually touching him. ''I must do this before you get near me, or I may not be able to finish.'' Sarah took a deep, rasping breath. ''We found him in your office.'' Sarah shut her eyes and shook her head. ''I mean *her* office.'' She tried calming herself with a nervous wiping of her hands. ''He was lying on the floor, naked! His wrists were tied to the legs of that old sofa of yours.'' Sean pitched against the kitchen door as Sarah continued with her grisly report between desperately needed gulps of air. With each cryptic, half-seen description of Bruce Fanning's mutilated body, Sean collapsed deeper and deeper into himself. ''It was horrible!'' Sarah gasped. Sean drifted across the kitchen to the window, where he appeared to lean through the glass, not against it. ''And there were these marks on his—'' Sarah slapped her hand over her mouth ''—I can't!'' She sounded like she was going to be sick. ''You'll have to speak with Oliver. He was the first one to come when I screamed.''

Cathy was there, guiding Sarah to the other window, opening it, letting the cool autumn air splash in over her. Walking around the table, Sean rested his hands on Sarah's shoulders, as if to comfort her. But he was leaning on her, and hard. Cathy asked, ''May I get you something, Dean Potter?'' She lifted Sean's hands off of Sarah and helped her down into the chair.

Sarah looked up. ''Miss Greene! Catherine. I didn't even realize you were here.'' She tried standing.

Cathy held her in place with a caring but firm hand. "Don't get up." Cathy turned her touch into a comforting caress.

The kitchen door clicked shut. Cathy spun around. "Sean?" The stairs groaned quietly. She raised her voice. "Sean! Wait! Please?" The screen door squeaked open, then closed with a whisper-soft clack. The porch steps moaned in mild protest. His car started. Cathy held her breath, listening as Sean pulled away.

29

Friday, October 25, 1991

A loud nasal honk startled Sean into glancing up into the rearview mirror, which was filled with the toothy chrome grin of Oliver's Silver Wraith. He killed the engine and got out. Oliver did the same, a large brown paper bag under one arm. As if answering a primordial signal, a scent hidden in the wind only they could smell, or a high-pitched sound only they could hear, Sean and Oliver began inspecting each other's cars in abject silence, not looking at one another, circling, then again, before coming together shoulder-to-shoulder and walking to the porch no more than a whisper apart, their hands stuffed down into their pockets, their eyes buried in the ground.

"How are you faring, my friend?" Oliver asked, reaching up and trying to put his short stocky arm around Sean's broad shoulders, but only getting his hand an inch past Sean's neck.

"Sean?" Jean Murphy asked before he could answer Oliver. Jean was standing on the porch, her feet wedged together, her hands clasped into a ball. Her eyes told him that what she had to say was private.

Oliver read her face before Sean did. "I'll be upstairs." Patting Sean on the arm, he stepped around Jean, acknowledging her curt nod of appreciation with a courteous smile, then disappeared inside the house. The sound of him clomping up the stairs wrinkled Jean's face into a web of hairline cracks that Sean had never noticed before. Her waited for her to finish disapproving of Oliver.

"Yes?"

While fidgeting for a place to put her hands, Jean whispered secretively, "There were two men here while you were out." She stuffed her bony fists into the pockets of her green moth-eaten cardigan. "They were from the sheriff's department." Her eyes popped open on her face. "They asked me all sorts of questions about you. Who visits you, what they look like, what kind of cars they drive, when you come and go, if anyone ever stays here with you, and if they do, who are they. And they showed me a photograph of a nice-looking man, almost bald, but not really, if you know what I mean. They asked if I had ever seen him here with you. I told them no. But they didn't look like they believed me." Jean stuck out her thin-skinned chin defiantly. "I wouldn't have told them even if I had seen him here!"

Sean was unfazed by Jean's anxious disclosure. "It sounds to me like they're just doing their job," he told her with an indifferent blink of his eyes. "I wouldn't let it bother you," he said with a tired smile and a reassuring pat of her hand.

Jean stepped down off the porch, forcing Sean to move back, then looked from side to side, as if checking to see if anyone was listening. "When they were walking back to their car, I heard them talking about someone named Katz."

Sean bristled instantly, then gave it up. "And what did they say about this 'Katz' person?" The expression on his face said, Now what?

"For one thing, they said they didn't like the 'faggot!'" Raising her eyebrows, Jean scampered backward up the steps. "That's their word, not mine!" she said defensively. Sean was growing weary of this, and let it show. Jean started speaking faster. "One of them also said they thought he was onto something, and that's

235

when the fat one, he's rude and fat, said that he didn't know what she saw in him."

"She? Him? Who are you talking about now?"

"I think they were talking about the Greene girl," Jean whispered, jamming her fists back into her sweater, punching the old cardigan out of shape.

When Sean walked into the kitchen, he saw the brown paper bag on the floor, and an open bottle of Whitbread ale sitting on the table in front of an empty chair. Oliver was slumped down in the other chair, his hands wrapped around a half-filled bottle of his own, looking like a wooden puppet taken out of service whose strings had been dropped down over him. Scooping up the waiting ale, Sean sat down opposite Oliver without saying anything and put the bottle to his mouth, sucking it dry in one long, thirsty breath. Still nothing was said. They just sat there, staring blankly out of their assigned windows, waiting for the tug of the marionette's fingers to start them moving again.

Oliver sat up and flopped his arms down onto the table, the bottle squeezed between his hands. "Dean Potter told me that Mrs. Fanning refused to attend the services we were planning to hold in Bruce's honor in Merrywood Garden."

"Why?" Sean asked, absentmindedly fingering the scars on his left side, which he could feel through his shirt and sweater.

"Sarah didn't say why when she told me this morning. She simply said that when she called Mrs. Fanning to tell her when it was, Mrs. Fanning told her she was going to have Bruce cremated just as soon as his body was released by the medical examiner. Based upon the way Sarah said it, it's my guess that she had strong words with Elizabeth."

Spinning around, startling Oliver, Sean pushed his face, his whole body across the table, forcing Oliver to retreat back into his chair. "I want to know exactly how Bruce was killed," Sean said, his eyes closing down like the muzzle of a double-barreled shotgun. "And don't leave out one single detail, understand?" He sat up, cocking his eyebrows, as if to make sure Oliver knew that he was serious.

"Didn't Sarah tell you?" Oliver sounded like he didn't want to get into it.

"She was too upset." Sean wouldn't lower his aim at Oliver.

"I see." Oliver began fidgeting with the tarnished brass buttons on his navy blue blazer. "Well," he said in a deep, formal voice, "Bruce was apparently late for a meeting with Sarah. I was working in my—"

Sean snapped angrily, "Just tell me what you found, damn it!"

It was apparent that Oliver was uneasy with Sean's darkening mood. He reached out, spread his fingers wide, then pressed his heavy hands on the table like he was trying to levitate it off the floor. "He was lying face up and completely naked. His torso was covered with deep slashes, but the wounds hadn't bled, which I thought was odd. There was a hole ripped in his chest like it was no more than a paper bag. And it was empty, Sean. Empty! The poor man's heart had been ripped out!" Oliver hesitated, giving Sean an opportunity to say something. But all he got was a silent stare. "There were two Raven's Quill plaques lying on the floor next to him, with each of the sharpened quills removed"—this pause was for Oliver's own benefit—"and stuck into his eyes. I knelt down to see if he was breathing, which was stupid of me, and I smelled something sour and soapy, but not soap, if you know what I mean. It was hard to tell for sure what it was, since the room was dank and damp. But then my sense of smell isn't very good, and it might simply have all been my imagination playing tricks on me." Sitting back, Oliver thread his thick fingers together and rested his hands on his stomach.

"Is that it?" Sean asked.

"No."

"Well?"

"I don't know why you must know every little detail."

Sean was losing his patience. "Just tell me, please," he pleaded, trying his best not to shout at Oliver.

"His genitals—" Oliver turned away from Sean's heated gaze as if embarrassed by what he had to say "—looked like he had been attacked by an animal. They were clawed to shreds." The horror staining Oliver's face was that which only a man could know. "Whoever or whatever killed him, Sean, had to be powerful beyond imagination!"

"Why is that?"

"There were bruises on his arms and thighs, like huge finger marks, crushing his flesh and bones." Oliver started to cave in. "They played with him, Sean." His head eased down onto his chest, his chin sank into his bushy beard, his eyes shuttered closed. "They watched him die, I just know it." Oliver slapped his mittlike hands down onto the table. "It's them. I know it."

"Have you seen Patricia yet?" Sean asked, erasing with a closed-eyed shake of his head the colorless images Oliver had sketched for him. But he couldn't, no matter how hard he tried, do anything about the ones that he'd painted for himself using the unforgettable palette burned into his brain years ago, as the imagined scene in his old office dripped with red.

Oliver had an incredulous look on his face. "Doesn't this upset you, even a little?"

Sean paused, sizing Oliver up, then spoke in a carefully modulated voice, wound up like a tight steel spring. "I asked you if you saw Patricia. Did you?"

"Yes!" Oliver threw back at him, and stood up. Sean pulled him back down. "I only want another ale," Oliver protested.

"That can wait," Sean barked, refusing to let go of Oliver's coat sleeve when he tried yanking himself free. "What was her reaction when you told her what happened?"

"She already knew."

"What! When did you see her?"

Oliver tapped his bearded chin. "We found Bruce just after noon, so it had to be later that afternoon. Yes, now that I think about it, it was soon after you called me. And it was dark, so I'd say it was about six o'clock."

"How could she have known?" Sean asked, discarding his fistful of Oliver's blazer. "I thought you said on the phone that she was in Manhattan."

"That's where she said she was going the day before." Oliver shrugged his stocky shoulders. "When I told her about Bruce, she walked right past me, whispering something to the effect that *they* all knew. She tried getting into her office, but couldn't."

"Why not?"

"It was sealed off because of the investigation."

"Then what?"

"She left."

"Thank you," Sean said without an ounce of emotion weighing down his words. "I appreciate this. I'm sure it wasn't easy."

Oliver grabbed hold of Sean's wrist before he could pull his hand away. "One more thing," he said, reaching into his blazer. "I found this."

Grabbing the bloodstained sheet of paper out of Oliver's hand, Sean shook out the folds with a snap of his wrist and read what was printed on the yellowed piece of old paper.

> Oh! that my young life were a lasting dream!
> My spirit not awak'ning till the beam
> Of an Eternity should bring the morrow:
> Yes! tho' that long dream were of hopeless sorrow,
> 'Twere better than the cold reality
> Of waking life to him whose heart must be,
> And hath been ever, on the chilly earth,
> A chaos of deep passion, from his birth! . . .

" 'Dream,' " Sean whispered without finishing it, and let the paper slip out of his hand, down onto the table.

"I thought you would recognize it." Oliver picked up the blood-stiffened sheet and read the rest of the poem.

> But should it be—that dreams eternally
> Continuing—as dreams have been to me
> In my young boyhood—should it thus be given,
> 'Twere folly still to hope for higher Heaven!
> For I have revell'd, when the sun was bright
> In the summer sky; in dreamy fields of light,
> And loveliness—And left unheedingly my very heart
> In climes of mine imaging—apart

Donald Beman

From mine own home, with beings that I have been
Of mine own thought—what more could I have seen?

'Twas once and *only* once and the wild hour
From my remembrance shall not pass—some power
Or spell had bound me—'twas the chilly wind
Came o'er me in the night, and left behind
Its image on my spirit, or the moon
Shone on my slumbers in her lofty noon
Too coldly—or the stars—howe'er it was
That dream was as that night wind—let it pass.

I have been happy, thou' in a dream.
I have been happy—and I love the theme . . .

Sean reached out, asking Oliver to stop with a tap of his finger
on Oliver's arm. When he looked up, Sean nodded and went on,
reciting from memory as if delivering a eulogy for Bruce.

Dreams! in their vivid coloring of life,
As in that fleeting, shadowy, misty strife
Of semblance with reality which brings
To the delirious eye more lovely things
Of Paradise and Love—and all our own!
Than young Hope in his sunniest hour hath known.

He stood up and threw himself against the window trim. "That
goddamn bitch!"

"Who?" Oliver asked.

Sean spun around and charged the refrigerator, snatching the
last two bottles of ale off the bottom shelf. Oliver began rereading
the poem to himself. "From *his* birth? When the *sun* was bright?
For higher *Heaven*? Some *power* bound me'?"

"What are you mumbling about?" Throwing himself into his
chair, Sean tipped back and propped his feet on the windowsill.

"May I keep this?" Oliver asked, mouthing other words and

phrases to himself as if trying to memorize them, or decipher them.

"It's not mine," Sean said indifferently. "Wait." He held his hand up. "How did you get it?" he asked. "Shouldn't it have been left as evidence?"

"I took it," Oliver admitted, his words echoing inside the bottle as he brought it to his mouth and buried it in his beard.

"Does anyone know you have it?"

"No," he replied proudly through a gasp for air. "It was underneath Bruce's arm, so Sarah couldn't possibly have seen it, since she ran out of the office before I knelt down beside him, or what was left of him, and saw an edge sticking out." Oliver carefully folded the paper closed and slipped it into the same pocket he'd retrieved it from. "This makes four, Sean, if my count is right." He pulled his tattered blazer around his belly, struggling to get a button holed.

"Five," Sean said, correcting him.

With rapid, side-to-side flicks of his eyes, as if scanning the titles of each of the previous poems, Oliver nodded his head four times in succession. "You have another?" He squinted one eye half-closed as only he could. "Sean?"

"Be right back." Sean disappeared down the hallway. When he returned, he was carrying the frayed puzzle Cathy had pieced together on the back of one of his journals. "Here." He dropped it on the table, making Oliver blink when it slapped crisply on the hardwood top. "Number five, one more to go!"

With his attention caught by what Sean had put in front of him, oblivious to what Sean had said, Oliver read the poem quickly, then put it down. "When did you get this?" he asked, wiping his hands on his pants as if he'd gotten something on them and wanted it off. "And why is it ripped into shreds? Did you lose your temper?"

Sean tried laughing. "No, Dr. Shore, I did not lose my temper. Cathy and I found it in my bedroom the night we returned from The Ridgefield Inn."

"That's all?" Oliver asked suspiciously.

"No." Sean drifted away from Oliver. "The room looked like

241

it had been put in a blender running at high speed. Everything—
my bed, the sheets, the pillows—was shredded to bits in what I
can only describe as a fit of blinding rage by someone, and someone with a razor-sharp knife of some sort.''

''Now do you believe me!'' Oliver bellowed piously as he sat
up, pinning his shoulder blades to the back of the rigid chair.

''Believe what?'' Sean asked scornfully. ''That there's some
raving lunatic running around out there?''

''A very old raving lunatic,'' Oliver noted cynically. ''At least
based upon how long this has been going on.'' This earned him
a disapproving scowl. ''And one other thing.'' Oliver was chewing on the ends of the untrimmed whiskers of his mustache.
''They found something underneath the sofa, but the older one
took it. It was a small leather bound book, which looked quite
old.''

''Older one?'' Sean asked, having lost Oliver's train of thought
when he'd run after his own. ''What are you talking about? What
older one?''

''He arrived after the detectives got there, and maybe twenty
minutes before the medical examiner showed up. He was in his
early sixties. He was not very nice, either. He was nasty to me,
the police officers, and even to the two detectives. But he was
disgustingly sweet to Sarah. I never heard anyone call him by
name. Just 'Yes, Your Honor' and 'No, Your Honor' and 'I don't
know, Your Honor.' It was evident that none of them liked 'his
honor' very much.''

Sean had been listening to every single word Oliver had said.
''How could Kratz have just come in and taken something?''

''Kratz?'' Oliver asked.

''Some other time,'' Sean told him.

''I don't know, Sean. But he told them it was yours.''

''Bullshit! Exactly what did he say?''

Closing his eyes, Oliver repeated what he had heard, slowly,
and in a computerized voice. '' 'This is his. It's MacDonald's. I
know it.' ''

''That can't be,'' Sean protested.

Oliver began miming what he had seen. ''He opened the book.

Thumbed through it. Stopped. Read some numbers off one of the pages.'' Oliver's eyes lit up. "I could see something written in the margins, but I couldn't make out what it was."

"No," Sean argued. "It's not possible." His voice was close to cracking.

"He sounded awfully certain to me."

"No!" Sean was vehement. "I didn't leave any books behind. Most certainly not any of my first editions, which is what this book sounds like. Everything was packed up. I did it myself. Besides, I never write in my books. Nothing, not even my name. So how would anyone know it was mine?" Sean stuck his hand into the air, fingering the ceiling. "They're all up in the attic."

"Are you sure about that?" Oliver asked.

Sean started to say yes, but stopped himself.

Oliver walked over to Sean and put his hands on Sean's shoulders. Sean didn't resist; he actually seemed to welcome Oliver's touch. He leaned back. His eyes had begun to water. "Sean," Oliver began calmly, almost paternally, "do you know what these poems mean? And I don't mean what each poem stands for from a poetic standpoint, but what you think they mean within the context of all that has happened, beginning with your mother's death, Janet's, the one you got the year you and Patricia had your fling"—Sean winced at Oliver's cavalier reference to his affair with Patricia—"your birthday, and now, what was left with poor Bruce." Oliver waited, his head ticking off seconds.

Stretching the knots out of his neck, Sean sighed, then leaned forward, resting his arms on the table. Oliver let go of him and wandered over to his chair, his eyes locked onto Sean's.

"From my perspective, and without all of the literary bullshit"—Sean snorted at what he'd just said—"each of the poems deals with a conflict between reality and fantasy, fact and fiction, the mortal and immortal worlds, and conflict between each of these entities, as well as between God and the Devil, in one form or another. And salvation. Strung together, they might be interpreted as an ongoing metaphor, an incomplete metaphor in search of subsequent poems to continue, or to complete the story. I often thought that if I could figure out which poem was next, and construct the metaphor, I would then be able to know what this mad-man"—Sean looked up, and into Oliver's eyes—"or woman, was going to do next, and to whom. But no matter how hard I tried, and I sure as hell did for years, I could not come up with anything that was plausible." Sean needed to clear his throat. "Maybe I was just too close, and my heart got in the way of my head and my years of schooling. Or maybe I'm too stupid!"

Oliver shook his head compassionately. "Stupid, my friend, you are not." Pulling his chair close to Sean, Oliver spoke softly. "Do you believe in God?" he asked. "Literally."

"No."

"Has that always been the case?"

"No."

"What about the Devil? And I'm not talking simply about man's evil nature, but a real devil."

Sean was not as quick to answer this question as he had Oliver's other two. "I thought so," Oliver answered for him. "Then you must truly believe in the mythology and numerology you spent half your life immersed in, even though you told me you didn't believe in it anymore. Don't you?"

Sean wouldn't let Oliver look into his eyes. "I told you, I don't know what to believe anymore. Except that I feel like I'm being stalked, and there's . . ."

Oliver answered again for him. "Nothing you can do about it?" Sean was still knotted into a ball and had no reply. But he did give Oliver a quick glance, which was all Oliver needed. "Sean," Oliver said ever so slowly, "how can you have one, the Devil, without the other, God?"

Sean stood up abruptly. "Theology 101 is over," he said sarcastically, and began gathering up the empty ale bottles.

"You're afraid to deal with it, aren't you?" Oliver asked.

Sean spun around, his eyes crackling with hate, driving Oliver back, his hands wrapped around the bottles, his knuckles turning white. "What do you know about fear!" he raged. "My entire family is gone. Every one of them was horribly murdered, except for my father, and no one could ever say for sure why he had a stroke. All because of me! Don't you think I figured that much out! So who the fuck do you think you are to tell me I'm afraid to deal with it? Deal with what? A dream? A nightmare! A ghost? A devil no one can see!'' Unable to breathe, Sean backed off. "Face it,'' he said with disgust, "you and I are no more than pieces of shit on this goddamn earth, and no matter—'' Sean's voice finally broke from yelling so loud.

Oliver walked over to Sean and put his arms around him. "I never knew how you felt,'' he said, holding Sean to him when he tried pulling away. "I'm sorry I said what I did.'' Giving Sean one last hug, Oliver walked across the kitchen and slowly went down the stairs.

30

Saturday, October 26, 1991

The heavy oak doors of Merrywood Hall were propped open with a pair of old broom handles, the broom part having been swept down to nothing but prickly nubs. Sean struggled with the thought of kicking one of them out, but spun away from the childish temptation and hopped over the brass saddle to a stop just inside the entrance. He waited for the stale dry air he knew was there to wrap itself around him before starting down the hallway on the soles of his shoes, refusing to let his leather heels clack on the marble floor and shatter the eerie silence.

When he turned the corner, he came face-to-face with a web of yellow plastic ribbons blocking the hall and covering the doorway of his old office like decorations at a Halloween dance. PO- LICE CRIME SCENE DO NOT CROSS were stamped in bold black letters on the flimsy yellow ribbon. Looking up and down the corridor, listening for someone, anyone, he ducked under the first barrier and headed straight for the second hurdle, two sagging strips of ribbon taped in an X over the open doorway of Patricia Jennings's office.

The drapes were drawn, casting the room into an unfamiliar darkness. A small brass-and-glass lamp gave a ghostly life to the chalky skeleton scratched into the carpet he'd left behind, then forgotten. Drawn inside the hideous cartoon caricature were squiggly circles, trapping fossilized remains on the top of the precise geometric patterns woven into the oriental rug. He looked away, then back, but it was still there. He thought he felt his heart stop and slapped his hand over his chest, moving it around, pressing a finger to his neck, searching for a beat. He exhaled a sigh of relief at the life he felt beating against his fingertip. He laughed and shut his eyes again. When he opened them, he wasn't alone anymore.

. . . He saw Bruce thrashing about on the sofa, but no matter how many different ways he tried folding and curling and bending his wiry-thin body over and around the withered leather cushions of the old Victorian sofa, he was unable to get back to sleep. So with a close-mouthed sigh, sounding like his last dying breath, he rolled over onto his side, flopping like a fish out of water, instead of turning over gingerly, causing the dried-out leather skin covering the old cushions, worn paper thin by time, to crackle to life in the wintry-dry air of Merrywood Hall. And to make matters worse, the ridges of his green corduroy pants scraped up dozens of crumbly brown flakes, leaving the cushions even more pockmarked than before.

Seeing what he'd done, Bruce licked his finger and began needling the tiny specks, frantically, comically trying to stitch them back into place. He quickly turned it into a game, until he saw that Sean was watching him and settled down.

And except for the occasional muffled conversation drifting up and down the corridor outside his office, the evening settled back to the stillness of a mid-winter's night, until the ship's clock over his desk played out six bells, slowly.

Hearing the tired old sofa complaining again, he looked over. Bruce sat up, his arms frozen in midair. "Did you hear that?" he asked, cocking his head to one side, listening.

"It was only the clock," he assured him.

"No!" Bruce snapped, batting his advice away with a swat of his hand. "I heard something outside." He leapt off the sofa and dashed to the window, pressing his face into the night, anxiously drumming his fingernails on the stained glass. "It sounded like a scream." Cupping his hand behind his ear, Bruce held it to the glass.

"Are you sure it wasn't the steam valve?"

"Shhh!" Bruce ordered.

He tried standing and pushing his chair out at the same time, but lost his balance and slipped onto the hardwood floor with a flurry and a thump.

Bruce peeled his face off the glass. "What the fuck are you doing on the floor!" he snarled, and started for the door. "Come on, get up, let's go!" he shouted, and darted out into the dimly lit hallway.

He followed Bruce, the slapping of his leather-soled shoes ricocheting off the marble walls . . .

Sean jumped when he heard "You can't go in there," then turned to see a young police officer approaching him, a steaming cup of coffee in one hand, gesturing for him to step away from the door with the other.

Shaking his head clear, Sean tried his very best to be respectful. "Do you mind if I just look while you drink your coffee? I won't touch anything."

"And you are, sir?" the officer asked, stiffening his resolve.

Sean answered slowly and clearly. "Sean MacDonald, Dr. Sean MacDonald. I taught here for twenty years, until only a few months ago, when I resigned." He gestured to the doorway of his old office, making an obvious effort to keep his hands close to his body to prove that he really wouldn't touch anything. "This office is, or was, mine."

The officer came to a stiff-legged stop. "I suppose it'll be all right, but don't go in." Sean shook his head eagerly, like that child who almost kicked the broom handle. "Did you know him?" the officer asked with a tick of his head and flick of his eyes in the direction of the empty skeleton lying on the floor.

"Yes." Sean took a much needed sip of air. "Very well." He felt as if he shouldn't have said this so willingly, unsure why, so he added quickly and nervously, "He and I started here at the college the same year."

"I was the first to respond when they called," the young officer said proudly. He took another gulp of coffee. "I've read about things like this." There was a sophomoric certainty to what he said. "But I never figured on seeing it firsthand, and not in a place like this!" His sweeping gesture sloshed drops of coffee onto the hardwood floor just inside the office.

"Do they have any idea who did it?"

The officer's reply was crisp and confident. "They think it may have been one of his lovers." Sean spun around. "And the guy was married, too! But his wife had just left him, we think because she found out about him. The D.A. has been talking with her about it, but no one knows what she told him."

Sean forced his body to go limp and the words "one of his lovers" to be thrown out of reach, afraid of what might happen if he didn't. Calm down, he told himself, just get what you want, and get out. "I heard there were a lot of people here from your department. Is that true?"

The officer cradled the white Styrofoam cup in both hands and leaned up against the doorjamb. "No more than usual."

Sean could feel himself leaning into the delicious smell of hot coffee. But he turned away just as quickly when the smell of stale cigarettes on the officer's breath slapped him in the face.

Stepping back discreetly, Sean asked through a hurried exhale, "Was Peter Kratz here?" hoping the use of the name would get him something more than another vacuous comment.

"Sure. He came, looked around, then left."

"This must not be that important to him if he didn't stay."

"He left when his cousin showed up."

"Arnold?" Sean deliberately let it slip out.

The Taking

The officer drawled, "Yeah, good old Arnie," with a snide, nasal twang. "The chief was really ticked off when he saw the judge push his way through everyone like the pompous ass he is. He wanted to know who had called him, but all the judge would tell him was that it was confidential court business and he couldn't talk about it."

Sean wanted the officer to keep talking, so he tried his best at being friendly, which was not how he felt just now. "They don't like each other very much, do they?" he said in a man-to-man sort of way, and smirked, trying his best to match the bitter taste that was left behind on the policeman's face.

"That's for sure!"

"Do you know why Judge Kratz was here? Unofficially, of course." Sean hoped he wasn't pushing his luck.

"Yup."

"Oh?"

"It's just a theory, mind you. But the judge isn't straight." He winked at Sean. "Know what I mean?" Sean forced himself to do the same. However, considering how he felt about Arnold Kratz, it wasn't really that hard. "And it didn't look to any of us like something a woman would have done, not any woman I know, thank God!"

Sean was forcing himself not to be impatient, but gave himself away when he asked tersely, "What are you trying to say?"

"Well, most of us think that this Fanning guy was a closet fairy and may have known Kratz." He smirked again. "Once, when I was on the night shift and driving through the parking lot at the Anonville train station, I saw—"

"Did you know him?" Sean shouted angrily, startling the officer into spilling his coffee down the front of his uniform.

"Well, no, I—"

"You don't know what you're talking about, you asshole!"

Sean suddenly found himself being shoved against the wall with a stiff-armed jab into the center of his chest. "Who the fuck do you think you are?"

The question was thrown on deaf ears as Sean pulled away and stormed down the hall, fists clenched, arms flailing about for something to hit. Turning the corner in a fury, he bumped into one of two men walking down the corridor, knocking him down.

"Shit, I'm really sorry," he said, helping the startled man to his feet.

"Dr. MacDonald?" the stranger asked, exchanging glances with the man beside him.

"That's me," Sean said, pushing his way past the two men.

"We'd like to speak with you, sir," the man replied, blocking Sean's exit. He held out a small wallet, which he let flap open in Sean's face. "We're with the sheriff's department," he said, pushing himself at Sean, forcing him to step back. "It won't take long, sir."

31

Friday, November 22, 1991

Sean bent down and lifted the two grocery bags off the front seat of his car. Standing up, he poked his face into one of them. "See," he told himself in a reassuring whisper that echoed softly inside the bag, "you didn't forget the cranberry sauce." He started jostling the bag and checking things off just to be sure he had everything he needed as he walked a crooked line across the stiff but not yet frozen lawn to the porch, keeping his face buried in the bag. "Fresh garlic, sage, thyme, turnips, chestnuts, shallots, mushrooms for the stuffing, flour, and—"

"Mr. MacDonald?" an unfamiliar voice called out, interrupting Sean's Thanksgiving dinner tally. He turned around to find a short pug-faced man, wearing a bulky sports coat two sizes too big for him, approaching from the road. His knee-jerk reaction was to start backing up. The man spoke again. "Are you Sean MacDonald?" he asked, holding one hand out, keeping the other close to his body, giving the impression that it was cocked and ready to swing into action.

Sean stopped his retreat at the porch. "Who are you?" He drew the bags in front of him, making them crinkle from the scrunching of the cellophane-covered contents.

"I have something for you, sir," the stranger said with a sarcastic bite to his words as he uncoiled his arm, making Sean flinch, then reached inside his coat and withdrew a large brown envelope. "Here," he said smartly, holding it out. Realizing Sean's hands were full, wavering for what seemed like forever, the stranger stuffed the envelope into the top of one of the shopping bags. "Thank you!" he said, hopping down and hurrying away into the dark to a car pulled off the road beyond the house.

Laughing at himself, Sean sat down on the top step, his knees weak and wobbly, and set the bags on the porch beside him. With his composure once again intact, he plucked the envelope out of the bag and boldly ripped it open from corner to corner. The contents dropped onto the step between his feet, then fell apart into two separate and slightly thinner packets, each backed with what looked like cobalt-blue construction paper. Picking up one of the packets, he held it up to catch the light shining over his shoulder from Jean's kitchen window, and started reading, then furiously began flipping the pages, tearing one or two, before coming to a scrawling signature, and began reading to himself through his teeth.

PENDING THE DETERMINATION of the instant Order to Show Cause, Defendant, Sean MacDonald, is hereby restrained from offering, entering into a contract to sell, distributing for the purposes of sale, agenting, or otherwise disposing of any story or manuscript titled *Strawberry Moon, The Strawberry Moon,* or *Under The Strawberry Moon,* with a storyline as set forth in the attached exhibit A, pending the determination of this application. . . .

Slapping the pages back to the beginning, Sean read the tight block of type in the upper right hand corner.

At a Special Term of the Supreme Court of the State of New York, held in the County of Dutchess, at the Courthouse thereof, on the 18th day of November, 1991.

He skipped down to the large print.

MANHATTAN PUBLISHERS, INC.
D/B/A GAZELLE BOOKS   Plaintiffs
                        —against—
SEAN MACDONALD   Defendant
ORDER TO SHOW CAUSE   Index No.:6066/91.

Sean began reading more slowly then he ever had in his life.

UPON READING AND FILING the annexed affidavit of Rosemary DeRiccio, duly sworn to on the 14th day of November, 1991; the Summons and Complaint to be served simultaneously herewith; and upon all the prior papers, pleadings and proceedings heretofore presented herein, let the Defendant or his attorney show cause before a Special Term Part of this Court to be held before the Hon. Arnold Kratz, on the 10th day of December, 1991, at the Dutchess County Courthouse, for an Order as follows: Granting the plaintiffs a preliminary injunction against Defendant, SEAN MACDONALD, his agents, servants, or employees, from distributing, offering for sale, entering into a contract of sale, or otherwise disposing of any story or manuscript titled *Strawberry Moon, The Strawberry Moon,* or *Under The Strawberry Moon* pending the determination of the above-captioned action.

The papers fell from Sean's hands, which were now shaking uncontrollably. His eyes wandered aimlessly out over the lawn, then blinked out into the cornfield, the useless stalks broken and falling to the ground. He was trying to think, to feel, to understand what was happening. A knot started tying itself in his gut, making him feel sick to his stomach. He tried swallowing, but couldn't. He choked the saliva up out of his throat, and tried spitting it out, only to feel it dribble off his lip and down into his beard. He tipped his head back at the sound of a door creaking open behind him.

"Did that nice man get you?" Jean Murphy asked with honest concern. Sean nodded, letting his chin bounce down onto his chest. "The poor thing," she clucked, wiping her wet hands on her hips. "He was waiting for hours. He told me that he had what you needed, and said he was very sorry he was late. Nice young man. I gave him a cup of hot cider and tried to get him to leave whatever it was he had for you with me. But he said he wanted to give it to you personally. Responsible of him, don't you think?" Jean asked, wanting Sean's approval. But all he had for her was a rocking horse nodding of his head. "Well, don't just sit there mooning, young man." Jean shivered and rubbed her arms. "You'll catch your death of a chill." And with a tousle of Sean's hair, Jean slipped back inside, humming loudly, sounding pleased as punch with herself.

Bending over, his joints suddenly feeling a hundred years old, Sean picked the two packets up off the steps with a swipe of his hand and jammed them under his arm. He then grabbed a fistful of brown paper in each hand and yanked the grocery bags off the porch. But before he could take a second step, they tore apart, spilling out their contents. Cans rolled in every which way, bonking to a stop against the house and the porch railing. One large can of pumpkin pie filling clunked down the steps. The bag of stuffing cracked open with a plastic pop when the carton of orange juice fell on top of it, scattering cubes of dried bread all around his feet. The bag of flour thumped down and burst open, powdering the gray porch and his brown shoes white. Onions tumbled down the steps, out onto the lawn, disappearing into the dark.

Looking around, all Sean could say was "Shit" as he dropped to his knees, then slumped back onto his heels, staring into nowhere, fighting back the sour lump pounding its way up his throat into his dry mouth.

32

Without bothering to look at him, the chubby young receptionist announced in a little girl's voice, "Mr. Allen is out of his meeting now, Dr. MacDonald," as she waved at the brass-handled glass doors behind her as if she were drying her nails. The doors were Windex clean and decorated with crinkly gold letters spelling out the name of the firm. Dropping the *Time* magazine he'd been holding, but not reading, just mindlessly flipping the pages, looking at the pictures, Sean started across the lobby. "Wait," she ordered, holding her fat little hand up. "Mr. Allen's secretary will be out to get you when he's ready, sir." She then pushed the receiver to her mouth and hissed something under her breath.

Feeling stupid, Sean stood with his back to the wall beside the doors, his hands folded in front of him, panning the waiting room. He found himself smiling, then biting his lip to keep it from showing, as nervous faces buried themselves back into their adult weekly readers.

"This way, Dr. MacDonald," Mary Alison called with a gracious sweep of her arm and inviting turn of her head, while struggling to hold one of the heavy glass doors open with her petite hip. Sean stepped through, then waited for Mary to jump free of the door and lead the way. He secretly imitated her rapid steps, forced on her by her tight straight skirt. They marched in tandem past rows of baked-enamel filing cabinets overflowing with manila folders stinking of stale cigar smoke, then hurried beneath oak-stained cliffs reaching to the ceiling with leather-bound books embedded in their sheer faces, showing no signs of ever having been climbed.

"Sean. Sean MacDonald," Neal Allen said with a serious, grown-up man's voice, which sounded odd coming from his little boy's body. "It's been a long time. Too long." While shaking Sean's hand, Neal gestured to the chair in front of his glass-topped desk. "Mind if I take this call?" he asked, and pulled away, not waiting for an answer. But then Neal never waited for answers to his questions, since he always seemed to have them.

Neal Allen had short wiry hair, and wide-open slate-blue eyes. His hands were small and manicured. His large head was balanced atop his narrow shoulders with a precarious pitch to it, giving the impression it could roll off and drop onto his desk with a loud thump if he was bumped too hard. Neal would have to have been well over six-feet tall, not the five-six he was, for his head to have looked right for his body. But his voice helped him look taller, until he got excited and it broke into a curious falsetto, which could sound male or female from breath to breath.

"Of course not," Sean replied politely, knowing that he had little choice in the matter. "Go right ahead." What else can I say? he thought. No, Neal, you can't take the fucking telephone call, you rude son-of-a-bitch? Stop it, he told himself.

Staring at the phone, his hands on his hips, Neal barked, "Mary! Which line is it?" It sounded more like a loud squeak. Hearing the number called back to him, but softly, Neal lifted the receiver, whacked one of the blinking red buttons with a slap of his finger, and sat down, grinning stupidly at Sean. He then began talking between up-and-down bobs of his head and periodic blinks of his eyes, creating the image of one of those dolls in the rear window of a jacked-up Chevy in the Bronx.

Sean had met Neal the summer he arrived at Hart College. He and Janet were looking for a house close to campus, one they could afford on his modest starting salary. When the time came to find an attorney to handle the closing, they were introduced to Neal by Margaret DeVoe, the real estate agent helping them. Margaret just happened to be Neal's fiancée. But Neal and Margaret never got married, although they came to within two months of a wedding. It seems Maggie was making too much money at the time, and Neal couldn't handle it, no matter what he told everyone. Sean's friendship continued with both of them after the breakup, until Maggie began seeing one of the senior partners in Neal's firm, and everything became too complicated.

Neal finally got married to someone who was the complete opposite of Maggie, or so everyone thought. But like most things in life, Andrea wasn't what she appeared to be on first blush. She blossomed, so to speak, into a woman who could have eaten Maggie for breakfast, and still have room left for Neal. She once tried taking a bite out of Sean at a dinner party, in front of the other guests, but found him to be more than she could swallow. Janet's death had provided a convenient excuse for Sean to decline their quarterly offerings of skinless chicken, uncooked green things, wine that was too young or too sweet—but always the right price—and niggardly portions of chocolate something-or-other. Sean and Neal stayed in touch after that through Sean's yearly visits, but that bond proved tenuous, since Sean had little to offer in the way of fees.

Choosing not to listen to Neal's monologue, Sean started reading the upside-down papers on Neal's desk. As he pecked around, he was snagged by the words twisting up off the pages like barbed wire. Accusing, defending, alleging, pleading, denying, countering. Uncommon words; old, archaic, and pompous, insulating, and protecting—the lawyers, of course, not their clients.

Neal dropped the receiver into the cradle and withdrew a fresh pencil from a peeling-apart paper mug, one with spindly stick figures running around the outside, and the word "Daddy" scrawled on it in red crayon. "Now," Neal said with a smile, his thin lips disappearing from his face, "tell me what the problem is."

Sean gave up fighting with his heavy chrome-and-leather chair, trying to pull it closer to the desk, and sat up straight, grabbing hold of the padded armrests. He looked like he was strapped into an art deco electric chair. "Did you read what I sent, including the background information?" he asked.

"Of course." Neal began shuffling through the disarray of papers on his desk. "And I've already called the plaintiff's attorney." Neal cranked his arm up into the air. "I got a monster judgment against one of their senior partners last year," he said slyly, snatching up what it was he was looking for. "What do you want to know?" He handed the blue-backed packet to Sean.

Sean pushed it back. "You're the lawyer; you read them. I just want to know what's going on. And I want to know how some judge, especially this judge, can decide that I can't sell *my* story. And tell me in English, not your lawyers' slang."

Neal pursed his lips at Sean's characterization. "It's really very simple!" he said with a flutter of his eyes.

Sean slumped back. "Good, explain it to me the same way."

Neal flipped through the papers Sean had sent him, but didn't really read them. "First, they claim you stole a story from them, a story that they allege they already paid someone a twenty-thousand-dollar advance for. Second, they want an injunction against you to keep you from selling their story, which means they want the court to order you not to do anything with it." Neal tossed the papers down. "And all of the usual boilerplate claims for relief and damages and punishment," he snickered, "and your firstborn child." Sean didn't find his humor amusing. "Now, my dear client, what can you tell me that will help me prove them wrong, and keep them from convincing some judge downtown to give them a permanent injunction, instead of the TRO they now have?"

Sean pointed at the papers Neal had dropped onto his desk. "Who do they claim wrote the story?" he asked.

"These don't say," Neal replied, tapping the papers with his small hand, breaking Sean's hypnotic trance. "But I talked with the lawyer handling this for Branden, Weiss, and she told me"—Neal held his hand up again—"purely as a courtesy, mind you, that the author is a woman by the name of Hawley."

Sean snapped to attention. "Patricia Hawley?"

Neal squinted at hearing the name, then dug through his notes. "Yes."

"That bitch!" Sean shot up out of his chair, forcing Neal to rock back in his. "That fucking bitch," he repeated, biting down on the word "bitch."

"Sean, please, sit down."

Sean responded to Neal's steady patting of the air. "When is she supposed to have written *her* story?"

"I was told"—Neal held up his hands and wiggled his fingers into imaginary quotation marks—"as a courtesy, that a treatment was copyrighted sometime in August." He dropped his hands. "She's sending me a copy of the verified application by the author from the Library of Congress."

"And what is the title of her book?" Sean asked, rising out of his seat again. He ignored Neal when he poked his finger at him, then pointed to the chair.

"It's here somewhere." Neal pushed the papers around, even though what he wanted was right in front of him. "Here it is. *Under the Strawberry Moon.*"

"Jesus Christ!" Sean threw himself into his chair, causing it to rock backward, then thump forward.

"Tell me about this woman, Karen, you wrote me about." Neal put a sheet of paper, already half-filled with scribbly notes, squarely in front of himself.

Seeing the long, yellow paper, Sean hesitated, then shook off the thought. "That's her real name." Sean's soft-spoken response forced Neal to cup his hand behind his ear so he could hear. "Not the name I used in my story."

"And what's 'Karen's' full name?" Neal pinned his pencil to the paper, holding it ready to be pressed into service.

"I don't know."

"Where does she live?"

"I don't know that either."

Neal dropped his pencil. "You expect me to believe that you spent all afternoon—and all night—with a woman, and you didn't even get her name?"

"It's the truth."

Neal rapped his knuckles on the desk. "These papers don't say anything about truth, Sean. I need facts." Neal placed both hands on his desk. "We're in a court of law, not a justice court," he said sternly, then folded his hands together.

"Don't you believe me?" Sean waited, wanting to hear Neal's answer. "I asked if you believe me, Neal."

Neal wouldn't let Sean have his way. "You've got to find this woman Karen, so you can prove she was the basis for your story, and that what took place between the two of you predates the filing of this other author's copyright. If you can, we have a very good chance at getting the TRO lifted."

"What about the letters and drafts to Dr. Fanning that I mentioned to you in my cover letter? I started sending him my manuscript in July."

"Good!" Neal fingered a fresh pencil out of the cardboard cup. "We can get his sworn testimony, along with his copies of the letters. Give me his phone number," Neal instructed. "I'll call him today and make the arrangements."

Sean folded himself up in the chair. "Don't bother."

"Why not?"

"Because he's dead."

"What!"

Sean threw himself at Neal's desk, slapping his hands on the glass top. "The diskettes!"

"What are you talking about now?"

"We mailed diskettes back and forth. I would send him what I'd written on a diskette, then he would send it back, with his comments, including any changes that he thought were called for." Sean pointed his finger, cocked his thumb, and fired. "Will that do?" he asked with a gunfighter's cocky grin.

"Are there dates on the files stored on the diskette?"

"Yes. It's automatic in the software." Sean looked relieved.

"Get them to me immediately. I'll have them transcribed by an independent expert, who can give us a notarized affidavit as to what he found." Sean flopped back in his chair, his hands lying limp in his lap, looking helpless. "What now?" Neal asked.

"I erased the disks Bruce sent back to me because I was upset over something he'd written. He . . ." Sean's words wound down to nothing.

"We've got a problem here, Sean."

Mary was in the doorway, knocking softly with the back of her hand on the open door. "Mr. Allen, there's a call for you on four. It's Judge Kratz's law clerk returning your call."

Neal pressed his finger over his lips for Sean to be quiet. But Sean didn't want to listen and walked out of the office, closing the door behind him to be sure nothing leaked out. His glances left and right told Mary what he wanted. She held up a key attached to a piece of carved wood, spelling out the word "Men." "Two rights and a left," she said with a cute smile, and pointed down the hall. "You have to jiggle the lock."

"Is this really necessary?" Sean asked, holding up the over-sized Cub Scout wood carving.

"It's so you don't forget and leave it there," she said with a shove of her hand at his elbow to get him started, which ended in a gentle tap of his arm.

"I see." He examined the key and its odd companion, which were connected with a six-inch length of braided lanyard, the kind kids make their first year in summer camp. "I figured it was so that it would float in case someone dropped it in."

"You haven't changed one bit, Dr. MacDonald." Leaning over her typewriter, Mary peered at Sean with a wrinkly-eyed smile. "Except that you look younger than when I last saw you, much younger. Are you seeing a younger woman?" she asked with a knowing wink. Beaming, Sean turned smartly on his heel and started down the hall, leaving behind an expression on Mary Alison's face that shifted from amused to curious.

The key didn't work at first, so he tried twisting and jiggling it just as Mary said he should. When the door didn't open, he grabbed the knob and rattled it. The door opened, pulled from inside. Sean stepped back, expecting someone to walk out, only to see a woman staring out at him. She bent forward at the waist and pointed down the hall. "Yours is on the left," she said curtly, and pushed the door shut.

When Sean returned, Neal's door was wide open, so he slipped in. "I got us a two-week adjournment," Neal announced. "The clerk gave it to me subject to Gazelle's lawyer consenting. She didn't, so I had to call and speak with the judge myself. He granted it after hearing me out. Nice fellow, that Kratz. I like him.'' Sean couldn't believe what he'd just heard, and was about to say something, to remind Neal who Arnold Kratz was, and what he had once put the both of them through, but Neal cut him off. ''We have to be in court on January ninth, which is a Thursday. The calendar call is nine-thirty. Be there no later than nine. I'll be waiting at the security check downstairs.'' Neal began making notes to himself.

''Do I have to be there?''

''Well, no, not really. My opposing motion, the supporting exhibits, and any pertinent affidavits are what the judge will rely upon in arriving at his decision. And the case law, of course, which is all over the ballpark in matters like this. But they do ask questions sometimes. And I'm sure the plaintiff's attorney will be there for that same reason, or at least one of her overpaid, Ivy League flunkies. So try and be there.''

''Isn't that what you're getting paid for?''

Neal looked up, his face blank. He glanced back down at the clutter covering his desk and began shifting the piles in a clockwise rotation by what amounted to one hour on the face of his imaginary clock. ''Now,'' he said, talking to his desk, while primping each freshly made stack of papers, ''I've got to prepare an answer to this motion. And in order to do that, you have to get together everything you can for me. Start with a chronology of events from the day you left Hart.'' Neal erased what he'd just said with a wave of his hand. ''On second thought, begin six months before that. There's always the chance that something may pop up that might prove important. And prepare a detailed list of names and addresses of everyone you've had contact with who might have known what you were writing about. And be sure to make a note of the dates, even the time of day you spoke with them, and where it was. With any luck, I can construct a plausible defense.'' Neal took square aim at Sean with his stone-gray eyes. ''But I want to be frank with you, Sean.'' Neal forced his voice to be as grown-up as possible. ''I don't think I will be able to get the stay lifted while the suit is pending.''

''What exactly does that mean to me, in layman's terms?''

"It means that you're fucked. Is that simple enough? It also means that you can't peddle your story to anyone." Turning away, Neal looked out the window of his office at the rows and columns of windows covering the building on the other side of Fifth Avenue, a patchwork quilt of glass and bronze and aluminum. "And if you lose this thing," he said ominously, "you'll have to kiss your story good-bye, since it won't be yours anymore as a matter of law." He turned back with a slight improvement in his outlook. "Unless, of course, we appeal. But that takes big bucks." Neal looked up at the ceiling, as if what he wanted was on the Swiss cheese tiles stapled up overhead. "At the very least, assuming there's only one or two motions, a few very short court appearances, and no protracted discovery, my guess is that it would come to twenty, maybe twenty-five thousand. But that's on top of—"

"Wait!" Sean interrupted, his eyes sparkling with hope. "I wrote Bruce a letter, by hand, just before going out with Karen. I'm pretty sure I told him about her. I think I even mentioned her name. I'm also certain I told him what we were going to be doing. Will that help?"

Sean slipped into the kitchen and shut the door behind him, then collapsed against it. Cathy was sitting at the table with her back to him, looking out the window. "Everything all right?" he asked, stepping away from the door, but leaving his hand pressed against it like he was unable, or unwilling, to let go.

Cathy pushed the chair around. In her lap was a green, mud-encrusted champagne bottle, empty. She set it on the table. Flakes of dirt fell off onto the lacquered surface. She squeezed the top of the heavy bottle with her fingertips and twisted it around so the label was facing him. She took a slow, shallow breath. "I found this yesterday afternoon," she said softly. "It was lying on the ground in the south field, near the red oak, not far from where you were lying down the first time you visited the farm. Remember?" Cathy rested one hand in her lap and set her other hand on the table beside the bottle, fingers spread wide, palm pressed flat.

Sean was unable to break free of her riveting gaze. "Yes."

The Taking

"Isn't this is the same champagne that I took out of the refrigerator to give to Oliver for your birthday?"

"Yes."

"Was that you I saw off in the distance, getting dressed, when I was plowing the field early one morning last June? It was the morning after I'd been in New York. You were with a woman, weren't you?" Sean's eyes began darting back and forth between the bottle and Cathy's rapidly solidifying face. Raising her arm slowly, as if it weighed a thousand pounds, Cathy pointed across the kitchen to the hallway. "Are those her panties I saw in your dresser?" Sean said nothing. Cathy absentmindedly wiped her hand on her jeans, as if there was something on it. Sean's eyes fell to the floor. "Was it Patricia Jennings?" He looked up and shook his head no, but was still unable to say anything.

Rising, moving as if her body was raked with pain, Cathy stepped in front of Sean. She pulled a folded-up sheet of paper, wrinkled and pressed flat, out of her pocket. "Are you sure?" she asked, unfolding the note and handing it to him. Sean held it, refusing to close his hand. Reaching out, Cathy brushed the hair off Sean's forehead with a lazy, almost whimsical flick of her fingers as she looked past his frozen gaze, into his heart. "Why?" she asked. Sean shut his eyes. "If it wasn't Patricia, then . . ." She stopped, her face turning to stone, and walked out.

33

Thursday, December 5, 1991

Dear Neal:

The information you asked for is enclosed with this letter. Because of the murder investigation, I'm unable to gain access to Dr. Fanning's things to look for the handwritten letter I wrote to him on the 26th of June, or the duplicate diskette I sent him, which I forgot to tell you about. Can you? Maybe your "good friend" Arnold Kratz can help you with this.

Upon checking, I've learned that there were a number of people Bruce showed my manuscript to. I've marked their names with a red asterisk. I also dropped a note to each of them, alerting them to the fact that you might be contacting them, and I also told them why. Now be nice—they're friends.

I know you that would have told me not to, which is precisely why I didn't bring it up, but I've tried reaching Patricia Jennings (aka Hawley) to talk with her about this. But it seems she's away on personal leave. How convenient.

Your retainer is enclosed. It's the last of my savings. Do I have to sign anything? Should I follow up? Or will you simply call me when you know what the court has decided? Let me know, OK?

Sean

After rereading the copy of the letter he'd mailed to Neal Allen, and double-checking the schedules sent along with it, Sean put

The Taking

aside the file he'd started for the papers he knew would soon be inundating him from Neal's office, and turned his attention to the journals that he'd dug out of the boxes Oliver brought back last June. Selecting the one with the Roman numeral VI printed on the cover with a black felt-tip marker, he pushed the others to the back of the kitchen table. He opened it to the last page with writing—his—and began jotting down everything he could remember Sarah and Oliver telling him about Bruce's murder and the condition of the body, using, out of habit, the very same outline format that he'd used throughout his research journals.

His notes were detailed and descriptive. He included his own vivid recollections, part reality and part imagination, from his visit to Merrywood Hall. He wrote out a description of the young police officer, including what had been said by both of them. It read like dialogue in a script. He reconstructed everything as best he could, taking pains to include every minute detail of what Oliver said Bruce looked like when he found him. He added a footnote about the poem, including where it had been found. He even made mention of the book Arnold Kratz had taken, and Oliver's report of what Kratz had said about the book, and whose it was. He then played with the numbered date of Bruce's murder, underlining the words *"Hunter Moon"* after printing them out neatly. He added other dates surrounding Bruce's life that came to mind, many of which he himself had been part of. He used the format Oliver started to summarize the dates that he prepared for the night of the birthday dinner at The Ridgefield Inn. A quick check of the numerology of Bruce's name, which he took the time to print out on the page, caused him to stop and think for a few minutes as he read it to himself.

```
B R U C E   F A N N I N G
2+9+3+3+5   6+1+5+5+9+5+7  =  60  =  6+0  =  6
```

Sean then wrote out the words Harvest Moon, which was the full moon that had risen on his own birthday this past September. He was unsure why he did it. He then set about listing each of the poems that had been received to date, taking care to place them in chronological order, then inserting each of the respective dates. This resulted in his repeating, yet expanding upon, Oliver's cyclical six-year summary, which had begun with December 24, 1950, the date of Sean's mother's death.

Sitting back, Sean read the schedule he'd created, playing with the patterns that had, and had not, taken form on the page, wondering what, if anything the relationships meant.

Date	Name	Aura	Poem Title	Cycle
12/24/50	Eileen Merritt	[9]	''A Dream within a Dream''	0/0
07/13/62	Robert MacDonald	[1]		12
01/08/74	Janet Peters	[6]	''Dream-Land''	24
11/22/80	John MacDonald	[6]	''Dream-Land''	30
05/23/86	Affair w/ Patricia	[7]	''Evening Star''	36
09/23/91	48th Birthday	[7]	''Spirits of the Dead''	41?
10/23/91	Bruce Fanning	[6]	''Dreams''	41

He ran his finger along the entry for 11/22/80, telling himself, ''You forgot to tell Oliver about finding the first four stanzas of 'Dream-Land' in John's bedroom. You'll have to say something the next time you see him.''

Shutting his eyes, Sean set the journal down on the table, covering his face with his hands, for even now, after eleven years, the memory of his son's death, and the images of what his child looked like on that peaceful fall morning, still took his breath away. He had found his son lying on the floor of his bedroom, his gentle face carved up with terror, his adoring eyes filled with tears, his arms suspended in the air, as if frozen in time, his hands, hands that only hours ago had held his father's face to his for a goodnight kiss, twisted into hideous knots. It was unlike Janet's death, which Sean had come to terms with. At least he thought he had. At that moment, Sean knew that Sharon Lucien had been right, and he had been wrong, very wrong, for not dealing with his son's sudden and unexplained death. He'd left the pain to simmer, day by day, then slowly boil into rage without his knowing it. Rage that had become so powerful and explosive that he was now terrified of what might happen, should it ever rise to the surface before he could catch it as he always did—as he did just now—and put it safely back inside the cage of scars he'd built for it over time.

The creaking of the porch steps, followed by a firm and steady knocking on the brand-new aluminum storm door, startled him upright in his chair. Looking at the clock, he saw that it was nearly seven. Before he could get to the kitchen door, the knock was repeated, a little harder and louder, making the glass chatter in the thin metal frame. The thought crossed his mind, Shit! I hope it's not her, as the chimes of the ship's clock started announcing the hour. He joined in, taking every other step down the stairs in time with each sound of the small, brass bell, ending at the bottom landing, waiting quietly for the seventh and final bell to toll before opening the door, then shielding his eyes from the glare of the rising sun sitting on the horizon.

"Are you Dr. Sean MacDonald?" a shadow asked, his body carving a silhouette into the face of the sun.

Sean answered brightly, "Yes, I am."

"Please step outside, sir."

Squinting through his fingers, seeing it was a police officer, Sean pushed the storm door open and stepped out onto the porch. "What is it?" he asked. "Is everything—" Someone grabbed him from behind, pulling his arms back, twisting them together. "What the fuck . . ."

"Sean MacDonald, you're under arrest for the murder of Bruce—" The words exploded inside Sean's head, deafening him to everything that was said after that, until he was pulled back to harsh reality by a sharp pain cutting through his wrists. "And for suspicion of the murder of Janet—" Out of the corner of his eye, Sean saw two men slouched against the side of the house, their suit coats draped over their folded arms, their shirtsleeves rolled up to their elbows, looking foolish in the biting cold of the early morning. "You have the right to remain silent. Anything—" Thumbs were pressed into his arms, between the muscles, drilling pain deep into his body.

Hands were all over him, pushing and grabbing and pulling him down the porch steps, out onto the lawn. Sean began shivering uncontrollably. A hand reached in front of him, opening a car door. Hot air exploded in his face, wet and thick with cigarette smoke and stale sweat and day-old vomit. Voices behind him turned his head just before it was pushed down inside the car.

"I say she's telling the truth, Tony."

"I don't agree, Rod, but the warrant says arrest him, so we arrest him."

"I think the other one, the one from the college, killed this one's wife so they could be lovers. And things were fine for years, until MacDonald here started up with that Greene woman, who I think is a lesbian." There was a dirty laugh. "I figure he and Fanning got into a fight after some faggoty sex, and—"

"Christ, your imagination amazes me."

"Wait! Listen to this. After giving him a blow job—"

"You're disgusting, Rodney!"

"But I can't figure out why he ripped the poor bastard's heart out. Or what he used to cut his chest open. Shit, man, that was scary, especially since the M.E. said the poor bastard was probably still alive when his heart was ripped out!"

"Come on, we can go upstairs now. He's in the car."

"Don't you want to hear the rest?"

"No! Now come on. We've got work to do."

34

Friday, December 20th, 1991

Sean took two steps inside Sharon Lucien's office, stopped, looked around, and started rubbing his arms, even though the room was hot and stuffy. Familiar smells filled the air, organic smells, sweet and sour and bitter, all in one breath.

"You don't want to be here, do you?" Sharon asked. There was a touch of compassion in her voice.

That's for sure, Sean thought, walking over and sitting down directly in front of her, peeking at her with his eyes. Her skin was thin, like antique bone china, with hairline cracks spreading beneath the surface. Her pitch-black eyes were clouded with a veil of white, turning them gray. Her hands were more bone than flesh. Yet she somehow seemed softer to him, perhaps because he wanted her to be, needed her to be. He gave up on her with a blink of his eyes and started feeding on the office, thinking to himself, *New drapes, new carpet, new chair—hers—but the same old ottoman.* He looked up into Sharon's patient gaze. Who are you? he thought, fitting himself into the rungs of his chair.

"It's a common feeling," Sharon noted, as if trying to relax him. "Especially when a patient's been away for as long as you have. Don't let it bother you. It'll pass in a little while."

No, it won't, Sean thought, his eyes sliding down her neck, into her blouse. Stop it! he told himself, but didn't listen.

Folding her arms over her chest, Sharon ended Sean's examination. "Where would you like to begin?" she asked, leaning to one side when the sunlight that was streaming in through the

269

window behind Sean splashed onto her face, forcing her to shut her eyes.

Looking back over his shoulder, Sean started to move to the chair next to him, but paused midway to examine the new drapes, their printed flames of pink and orange and coal-blue climbing the pleated folds of gun-metal gray all the way to the ceiling. "Let me just shift my chair around so that I can—"

Sharon pulled herself out of the light. "It's fine now. You can stay where you are." Surprised by her casual response, Sean turned back to find Sharon staring at him, her eyes focusing and refocusing, slowly, as if unable to stop. "My thoughts just wandered," she said, sitting back, but to one side, and as far away as possible from the sunlight slicing the shadows in her office into slivers of light and dark.

You? Wander? Sean thought, easing back down into his chair, finding the rigid wooden seat still too hard. "Let's see," he mused, toying with Sharon's offer. "Where do I want to start?" His face lit up. "How about where we left off?" he suggested, shifting around, trying to find a more comfortable position.

Sharon rejected his suggestion with a lazy flitting of her fingers. Out of habit, Sean sat up, bracing himself for what he thought would follow. "Don't be silly," she said with a soft smile. Sean didn't know whether to be relieved or surprised. "How did you make bail?" Sharon sounded like she really cared.

Is it me, or you? Sean wondered. "I didn't," he replied, still feeling confused. "Someone posted it for me. I think it was Dr. Jennings, the woman who took over my chair at the college, but I haven't been able to confirm that yet since she's still on personal leave. Besides, I don't know who else could have come up with that kind of cash, since two-hundred-and-fifty-thousand dollars is not what anyone I know has sitting in the bank. If she, or whoever did it, hadn't posted bail, I'd still be sitting in that stinking detention center, a goddamn pet for that warped Arnold Kratz to play with."

Sean had been held at the Dutchess County Detention Center for five days after his arrest, in spite of his protests, before being brought before the Honorable Arnold Kratz, JSC, for his arraign-

ment on the charge of second-degree murder in the death of Dr.
Bruce Fanning, an arraignment that was manipulated into a media
circus by Kratz. Surprisingly, no mention had been made of the
other charge, which had been included in his arrest warrant, that
of his alleged role in the death of his wife. Every member of the
press, print and broadcast, within a fifty mile radius of the college,
including the little country weeklies, had been sent a grossly in-
accurate, and poorly written, profile on one Dr. Sean MacDonald.
Adding to the burlesque atmosphere was Arnold Kratz's deliberate delay of reading the charges until the courtroom was
crammed full of reporters and curiosity seekers. There was even
a delegation from the college, headed by Sarah Potter.

In the confusion and embarrassment of being arrested, Sean
had forgotten to tell his court-appointed attorney, Daniel Ott,
about Kratz's involvement as the judge in the pending civil suit
with Gazelle Books. He had also overlooked mentioning that
Kratz was at the murder scene, and may have removed evidence,
or at the very least tampered with it. But he intentionally did not
say anything about the poem Oliver had secreted away. It wasn't
until he heard Arnold Kratz grant the district attorney's request
for a $250,000 cash bond, "For the safety of the people, Your
Honor," that Sean was shaken to his senses, and he promptly
revealed everything, except for the poem, to Daniel Ott, right
there in court, including Kratz's role in Janet's murder investigation seventeen years ago.

Visibly upset, and believing without a doubt that he could have
forced Arnold Kratz to excuse himself from the case, Ott had told
Sean that it would now be difficult, if not impossible, to reopen
the matter of bail. But he said he would try in light of this new,
and "substantive," information. He then added in a threatening
tone of voice, "But only after I *personally* verify for myself that
what you're telling me is, in fact, the truth," which had left Sean
with little hope of being released on bail while the investigation
proceeded. After all, he was a suspect—*the* suspect—in the sav-
age murder of his closest friend.

"Are you saying that you aren't positive who it was that came
forward with a quarter of a million dollars?" Sharon asked with

total disbelief. She did not in any way doubt Sean; she was just unable to believe it.

Sean smiled, enjoying what little pleasure he could extract from Sharon's amazement, and there was not much to be had. "My attorney subsequently got Kratz to recuse himself from the case, which is even more impressive than the bail in light of the way that idiot judge was carrying on in court. You'd think that Bruce was *his* best friend, not mine!"

"Why don't you try telling me how you feel," Sharon suggested.

"I feel fine," Sean replied with a lively bounce to his words, patting his face and chest and arms and legs, showing her that he was fit and healthy all over.

"Interesting," Sharon noted, and wrote something on her pad.

Sean wanted to stuff the word "interesting" down her throat, but when he tried visualizing it, thinking it, and feeling it, everything evaporated into the stale air. When he concentrated, trying to force himself to do it, the thought melted down into the back of his brain, and that's when he realized that he didn't care. Why did you come here? he asked himself.

Sharon appeared at loss for words. "How are you sleeping?" she finally asked after a thoughtful pause.

"Like a baby," Sean quipped, then remembered what she had once told him about people in institutions, "The insane sleep like babies," and waited for her to throw it up in his face.

But Sharon simply asked, "Do you feel angry about being arrested and held against your will?"

I'm out of shape for this shit, he thought. "It's more a sense of indignation," he replied doggedly, his confusion growing with every question Sharon asked, or comment she made.

Sharon rocked back. "Does it make you angry to read the things they're digging up about you?" She glanced down at her notes. "Such as the troubles you had back in 1986? And all of those stories about your former colleague who, according to the press, seems to have lived a double life?"

This is going nowhere, Sean decided. "Come on, Sharon, stop playing games with me." He was frustrated and sensing feelings he didn't want, feelings he thought no longer existed, rising up inside him. The words *"fuck you"* found their way into his mouth, but he chewed them up and swallowed them back down before they could get out. "Getting angry serves no useful purpose," he said. But Sean was really talking to himself, not Sharon, and he realized that after he'd snapped his reply back at her.

"And Dr. Fanning?" Sharon asked, overlooking his steadily rising resentment, which she appeared to expect of him.

"I miss him terribly," Sean replied instantly, forfeiting his newfound mood. "Except for the death of my son, I've never felt so empty. Never."

"More than when Janet died?"

This is insane, he thought, watching her watch him.

"You loved him, didn't you? Dr. Fanning, that is."

Fuck it, I can't take this, he thought, not today, not the way I feel. Just let her have her way, he told himself. Tell her whatever she wants to know. Tell her the truth! He laughed.

"Yes," Sean said with a sense of relief. "I loved him, and I didn't realize the full extent of my feelings until he was gone." Sean started folding up like he used to, but took a deep breath and sat up tall in his stiff chair. "In some ways," he said philosophically, "I feel responsible."

"Why is that?"

"Because I think he was asking me for help all those years, and I didn't see it. At least not the way he may have wanted me to help."

"Do you feel guilty?" Sharon sounded as though she'd just found something she'd lost.

Sean was unaware of the ice forming inside Sharon's eyes. "At first I did," he said quietly. "But I don't anymore." Sharon started writing. Sean just shook his head and went on. "I stopped feeling guilty when I realized that I never did anything to hurt him, even though he took whatever he wanted from me." Sean began playing with an effervescent chuckle. "My office, my sofa, my time at all hours of the night, my sleep, my sanity." He laughed. "And even my students." He let a bawdy private chuckle settle comfortably in his chest.

"Why are you suddenly acting so cavalier?"

"Why shouldn't the memories of a dear friend be happy?"

"Did you feel deceived—about his homosexuality, that is."

Sean felt his muscles, all of them, attached to every bone in his body, tighten like rubber bands. "Yes." It felt good to say this. "I accepted Bruce for what he was, and for what he wanted me to see him as." Sean looked away from Sharon for the first time, and said in a receding voice, "What more can a good friend do?"

"Just a friend?" Sharon asked with a prying twist to her words, matching the skeptical turn of her head.

Sean was all over her, tearing her apart with his eyes. She held him off easily, gracefully, which only added to his growing confusion of how he felt, and what he felt. He lowered his gaze, forcing her to draw her legs together. Her reaction pleased him.

Sharon made an entry in her notes. "Do you still feel any guilt about your wife's death?" Sharon asked without so much as a drop of sarcasm in her voice.

"I felt guilty as hell after her death, and you knew that, but for reasons I didn't understand back then. It took years for me to see that my emotions were painting over my thoughts and covering up the real problem. Me! Then it took just as many years to push the shit out of the way so I could get at the problem and extinguish the flames before they consumed me."

"You sound like you think you've healed yourself."

Sean ignored what he thought was Sharon's intended sarcasm, even though nothing about the way she looked confirmed his suspicion. "In a way, I have. But in reality, I simply finished what we started. I can say without an ounce of reservation"—his words were tempered—"that in a strange way, I love you for what you did for me." He slid back, flopping his hands down on the arms of the chair, creating the muffled slap of flesh on wood.

"Sit down," Sharon snapped, her eyes flashing and darting about, "and stop playing games with me. What's the real reason you came here?" she demanded angrily. Sean was startled at the sudden change in Sharon, but pleased with it at the same time.

Sharon crossed her legs, unconsciously mimicking Sean. "Why don't you stop sparring with me, Sean, and answer my questions. And you can start by telling me exactly why you're here."

Sean felt even more relaxed now, as if sedated by Sharon's turn of emotion. "I'm here because you wrote and asked me to come see you after I was released on bail, that's why. When I got your note in jail, I realized that I wanted and needed someone to talk to, someone who I felt knew me. I felt alone, and wanted to share that feeling." Sean shifted to the edge of his seat.

"Why didn't you turn to Catherine Greene?" Sharon asked, subtly pulling back from Sean's unintentional advance.

Sean was surprised at hearing Cathy's name. "I never mentioned Catherine's name to you," he said cautiously. "Not even when we had dinner."

Sharon pursed her lips into a knot of disappointment. "What are you hiding from?" she asked.

This is crazy! he told himself. Get out of here. "I'm not hiding from anything. I was just surprised to hear Cathy's name, that's all." He sat upright. "But since you asked, I did go to see her the first day I was out. But she'd gone into the city and left me a note." Sean sat very still. "She told me that she didn't want to see me anymore."

"That must have made you angry."

Deaf to Sharon's caring tone, Sean thought, Jesus Christ, give it a fucking rest, will you! He said calmly, even though he no longer felt that way, "It hurt, and it still does, and it made me very sad. But I'm not—"

Sharon stood up. "I'm sorry, Sean, but I've got to be at the hospital in twenty minutes, so we must end here. Let me check and see when I can fit you in again." Sean followed Sharon to her desk. "January thirtieth, at nine o'clock." She tapped the book on the desk in front of her. "Make a note of it."

"I'm not sure I want to return," Sean told her, bringing her to an unwanted stop as she was about to walk away. "I have to think about it."

"Suit yourself," Sharon replied diffidently, which is when Sean noticed that she'd slipped into a different voice. "You must do what you must do.'' Sharon closed the appointment book with an impatient flick of her wrist and moved to get her coat, knocking the book onto the floor with the spin of her hips and the flare of her heavy wool shirt. The thud of the journal turned her around to find Sean kneeling down and about to pick it up. ''Leave it!'' she ordered. He pulled up. ''Please pull the door shut behind you. It'll lock itself,'' she instructed, rushing out and hurrying down the stairs.

The diary had fallen face down. Taking hold of the long black ribbon snaking out of the binding, Sean slipped his hand underneath and turned the book over carefully. It was open to February, not December. He started flipping the pages forward with the intention of tucking the ribbon into the correct date, while trying his best to ignore the names, crammed between the ruled lines on the pages, bracketing every hour of every day.

''Bruce?'' he blurted out. It was May. Stopping, letting one page at a time flick off his thumb, he saw *Fanning, Bruce, Ph.D.* entered twice a week, sometimes three. There were no entries in June. He shuffled the pages to July. ''Patricia?'' He raced forward to the end of October, slapping at the pages, bending and creasing the thick glossy paper. He found Bruce's name crossed out twice in one week, but the name Jennings remained, entered regularly every week thereafter.

Setting the book down on the desk, pressing it open with the heel of his hand to December 20, 1991, Sean pinched the satin ribbon between his thumb and forefinger, pulling it taut into the seam of the binding as he scanned every entry. He stopped when he found what he wanted, or didn't want.

1:00 / Dr. Jennings / Double / Out by 3:00

Tuesday, December 24, 1991

Kicking the kitchen door closed behind him, Sean eyed the ring of plump pudding sitting on the kitchen table, staring back at him, brown and moist, with glistening chunks of citron and cherries and raisins prickling up through its porous skin. A white candle

The Taking

with a green ribbon tied around its neck was rising up from a spray of holly buried in the center of the Christmas treat. It made his heart smile.

Holding up the wreath he'd just purchased for the front door, eying it for size, he fit it over the pudding, tamping it snug to the table, and telling himself, "It looks better here."

He started rummaging through the drawer next to the stove and came up with the box of wooden matches he'd never used before. Yanking the overhead light off, he struck the match, watching the room flare back to life. He lit the candle and blew out the match with a wordless whisper as the room flickered down to a warm yellow glow. After slipping his coat off and dropping it over the back of the chair in front of the window, he sat down and untied the shiny red ribbon the post office had bundled his mail with, making it look like a hastily wrapped Christmas present. He squiggled the ribbon around the outside of the pudding, snaking it through the sprays of blue spruce wired into the wreath. He spread the envelopes out as though he were going to play solitaire and grabbed one envelope off the top, one of his own self-addressed, stamped envelopes, bearing a two-week-old postmark, and tossed it to the back of the kitchen table, along with all of the others like it, resolving not to bother opening them. Letters that were hand addressed, or extra-thick ones, he stacked directly in front of him, then threw everything else out, including the bills.

The letter from Neal Allen was cryptic and almost caustic in its attempt to be done with what had to be said. It contained a receipt for his retainer, and made mention of the fact that a post-ponement had been requested by the plaintiff's attorney, "Be-cause of vacation plans to Aruba," Neal had written. A personal note was scrawled at the bottom, informing him that "Gazelle isn't willing to discuss settlement just yet, but I think it's only posturing on their lawyers' part."

There was an assortment of Christmas party invitations, with an equal number of retractions, each one citing "a sudden change of plans," and postmarked the week he was in jail, making him snort at the irony.

277

He then opened one of the letters without a return address, expecting—hoping—to find a note from Karen.

Sean,

I received your letter about Bruce. I wasn't going to reply to it, but the things you wrote wouldn't go away.

It was hell living with that man those last few years. No one can know what it's like for a woman, a wife, to live with someone like that. I hate him for doing what he did to me, and to my life. I also have mixed feelings about his death. Part of me is sorry, but I'm not sure whether it's for him or myself. Yet another part isn't sorry in the least.

During one of our many fights this past year, Bruce told me that he preferred your company over mine. He also told me that he loved you more than me. The more I thought about it, the more it made me sick to my stomach. I hate you for that.

Bruce told me that you were writing a book, and he seemed truly happy for you, but upset at the same time. Until recently, I thought he was jealous of it. But I see now that it must have been the fact that you had started up with women again. Did Janet find out about you two? Is that why you killed her?

From what I've read lately, prison will be heaven for you. That's if you don't die from AIDS. But maybe that's God's way of punishing you.

Elizabeth Turner

Sean drew the expensive notepaper between his thumb and index finger, feeling the strokes of Betty Fanning's signature, which were embossed deep into the paper beneath her typewritten maiden name. Beginning with a large expressive *E,* it dug down through the bottom of the *r,* scratching the paper open.

She had never liked being called Betty, Sean thought. In the beginning, that first heady year on campus, when everyone and everything was new, which now seemed so very long ago, she would introduce herself as "Elizabeth." But she soon gave up when Bruce kept calling her Betty, and everyone followed his lead.

Rereading her note, Sean thought it unkind, almost hypocritical of her not to sign her married name now. But then, it was in keeping with her letter. Puffing his words at the flame struggling to stay lit on the candle, Sean whispered, "You forgot to say, *'Merry Christmas, Sean.'*" He then turned his chair around, raised the bottom sash of the kitchen window halfway up, and sat directly in front of it, letting the bitter cold knife into the room, cutting through him, his hands and feet growing numb as he watched the night paint his reflection onto the glass in transparent shades of silver and black.

35

Monday, December 30, 1991

Sharon wrapped her arms around her pad, embracing it, and pushed the door closed with a light-hearted, almost feminine swing of her hip. "You left me with the distinct impression you didn't want to see me anymore," she said, leaning back against the door, playing with a smile. "I'm surprised that you're here."

Sean wanted to know—right that second—about Bruce and Patricia. But he knew he couldn't come right out and ask, so he found himself staring back at her, his own feelings blinding him to Sharon's inviting manner. "Sharon?" He waited until she acknowledged him with a nod of her head. "Will you answer a few questions for me?"

Her reply was cautious, but open. "That depends."

"Why did you treat me the way you did in the beginning?"

"Exactly what and when are you referring to?" she asked, ironing a look of resignation onto her face as she arched her back and pushed herself off the door.

"I'm referring to the very beginning, when Janet and I first began seeing you. I always felt that you were attacking me, either because of the way I spoke, how I tried expressing myself, or my inability to tell you what I felt. Even how fast, actually how slowly, I answered you."

Sharon replied nonchalantly, "You were highly defensive in the beginning, and overreacted to virtually everything I said, as if it threatened your very existence in some way. It left me with the perception that you were hiding from something, which only made me that much more suspicious, as it should."

"Suspicious?" Sean wondered. Of what? He spoke as if defending himself. "I have nothing to hide anymore."

After circling the office, Sharon sat down. "I find it interesting that you would say that now, after all these years." She started writing.

"Say what?" Sean asked, confused.

"You said that you had nothing to hide *anymore*."

"Well, it's true." Sean seemed to protest. "I don't."

Sharon began drumming the point of her sharpened pencil on the pad, but not impatiently, creating clusters of tiny gray dots, which she blew at to get rid of the graphite dust. "You seem a little tense today." Sharon stole a quick look at Sean, she thought without his knowing it, but he caught her. "Any special reason?" she asked.

Just let it go, he told himself, there's nothing she can do, not anymore. "Now that you mention it, yes. I feel isolated, and alone"—he was quick to correct himself—"but not lonely. I feel like I've been abandoned by everyone and left for dead."

Sharon put her pencil down and threaded her fingers together, tying her hands into a soft knot. "Do you think it's possible that you're the one who's withdrawing from everyone around you?"

Sean shook his head without giving her question a second thought. "Absolutely not." But he didn't sound very convincing.

Sharon stood up, disappointment dripping from her face, and tossed her pad down onto the seat of her chair, taking care to make sure it was face down. "I've got an opening in two weeks," she said, walking over to her desk and opening her diary. "Is Friday, January tenth, at five o'clock OK?" Sharon pushed herself around to face Sean. He nodded. "But before you come, Sean, make sure you're ready to stop fighting me. Do I make myself clear, Dr. MacDonald?"

"Sharon, I wasn't—"

Sharon held up her hand. "And give some thought to what I've been trying to say, without hitting you over the head with it. You may very well be back in jail soon, and I won't be able to help you then." With this said, Sharon picked up the phone and tapped a number on the buttons, making it clear that she was finished with him.

Nearly eight inches of fresh snow had fallen since yesterday morning, and it was still coming down. It was a slow, steady, peaceful snowfall, with big fat flakes falling straight down, sticking to the first thing they touched. As Sean walked out of Sharon's office and out onto the snow-covered lawn, he began kicking his feet through the fluffy powder. It quickly melted through his pants and his shoes, soaking his feet. But he kept doing it, wanting to feel the cold and the wet. He buried his feet in the deepest spot he could find and bent down, scooping up two handfuls of snow, pressing them over his eyes as he tipped his head back, waiting for the cold to knife into his brain. The snow melted into his beard, then dribbled down his neck. He waited to feel the chill on his chest, but couldn't, because right now he couldn't feel anything. He didn't wipe his face when he looked down, and he stopped himself from stomping off the snow clumping to his wool pants, letting everything get wetter.

When he walked across the small parking lot, Sean thought he could feel Sharon watching him from the window of her office on the second floor, trying to get inside. Again. But when he looked up, she wasn't there.

Donald Beman

Sean was writing for the first time in weeks, not having to think, and not having to stop and read what he'd written before going on. It felt good; he felt good. It was a story about the art world, and about Bruce. It would be his way of vindicating himself in case he lost the fight with Gazelle Books, which Neal Allen kept telling him he probably would. Neal didn't say it in so many words; it was the way he phrased his little notes at the bottom of the letters, letters that Sean knew Mary Alison penned for him, her gentle style trying, but failing, to sweeten Neal's bitter rancor.

Sean looked up at the calendar, then walked over to the brown wicker basket stuffed full of what he'd been getting from the post office each day, but left unopened. He began digging through the basket for something that would magically say to him, "Hey! Open me!"

One small envelope found him, one that he couldn't believe he missed when he saw Cathy's graceful and easy-to-read handwriting. Tearing it open, he raced through the brief, handwritten note, reading it aloud in a single breath, "Would you please come for Christmas Eve dinner? It will be just the two of us. Seven-thirty. If you don't, I'll understand."

Pulling around the front of Cathy's house far too fast, Sean slid off the icy driveway and right through the plowed-up bank of snow. Laughing at himself, he threw the door open, slammed it shut, and ran across the snow-covered lawn, jumping up onto the porch steps, only to have to hop back down so he could open the useless screen door. He let himself in through the unlocked back door, shushing the startled look off Sally's face with a finger pressed to his lips, while ignoring the shaking of her head as he tiptoed past the kitchen table, which was stacked with bowls bearing remnants of creamed onions and chopped spinach and mashed potatoes and brown sugar–coated yams, all surrounding a carved-up honey-glazed ham, stuck with cloves and covered with rings of oven-charred pineapple. With a thankful wave of his hand to Sally, Sean slipped quietly into the dimly lit hallway leading to

The Taking

the front rooms. The air was filled with the crisp smell of ever-green and burning apple wood and just-brewed coffee. The fire in the living room crackled with excitement as it threw shadows onto the polished hardwood floor in the hall. A gentle murmur of voices bubbled up out of the dining room across the hall. Sean recognized Cathy's voice. The other, male or female (he wasn't sure) was soft-spoken. For an instant, he thought, What if she's with someone else? He pulled back, his heart beating faster. But then he heard Cathy say with reassuring determination, "I don't care. It must be done. It's your last chance." Sean took a deep breath, straightened himself in front of a mirror that wasn't there, and stepped silently into the arched doorway of the dining room.

"Sean!" Cathy exclaimed, glancing anxiously across the table at her dinner guest. "I didn't hear you come in." Rising, she walked around the table, forcing herself not to look at her guest, who, as yet, hadn't moved. "What a coincidence." She extended her hands, and with a nervous flicker of fingers, invited Sean to join her.

"I'm sorry," he whispered, suddenly feeling uncomfortable, then stepped backward into the hallway. "I really shouldn't have. I'm sorry for disturbing you two." He started to leave. Cathy invited him back into the candlelit room with an impatient wave of her hand just as her guest rose, standing as tall as she was, and turned to face him. Her hair was long and straight and solid gray, and brushed to a silken sheen. Her eyes were black-green, like emerald ash, and alive, as if the fire that once formed the priceless jewels set in her beautiful face still burned hot. Her skin was like liquid ivory, thick and deep and creamy soft, inviting him to slip beneath the surface. Again. She smiled, warming the air, warming him. "Karen?" he whispered.

36

Saturday, January 4, 1992

With a powerful sweep of his arm, Sean collected Hazel out of the frigid night air and held her close to him. "Where's Ollie?" he asked, peering over the top of her cold red hair and out into the night. The only thing he found was his own breath, clouding his view of the Silver Wraith hiding in the dark.

"He didn't return with me from London," Hazel replied, burying her face in the warm folds of Sean's cashmere sweater, shivering the cold out of her body. She slipped out of Sean's grasp and raced upstairs to the landing, laughing like a little girl. "Close that door before you freeze to death," she yelled down, then darted into the warmth of the kitchen.

Sean sniffed away the smell of stale cigarette smoke and jet fuel left behind by her travel-weary hair. He dashed up after her, making far more noise than she had in the process. He grabbed hold of the molding around the doorway and swung himself into the kitchen like he was playing snap-the-whip. "Everything OK?" he asked, bumping into Hazel, then having to catch her before she fell backward from the impact.

Pushing herself free, Hazel stuck a clutch of papers close to his face, so close that Sean could feel the cold on his nose. "I found these," she said, taking his hand, slapping the papers into it, making them crinkle like dried leaves. "They were on the bed in our room. Read them," she ordered with a convincing point of her finger.

Looking down, Sean recognized Oliver's meticulous, up-and-down handwriting, and started reading. When he smiled broadly, Hazel put her tiny hand over the page, pushing his eyes off the paper. "Yes?" he asked, looking up, finding her staring at him, her face squiggled into a disapproving knot.

"Not the personal stuff," Hazel said with a freckled blush. "Just what I highlighted." She nudged Sean toward the kitchen table. "You go sit down and read. I'm standing over there." She backed up to the cast-iron stove and the four gas burners that were turned all the way up. "Well? Go ahead," she said, warming her hands over the clear blue flames. Sean obeyed with a smirk.

Good news, my love! I located Father Knight's diary. But Father Hillary—he's the archivist for the chapel library—will not meet with me until after Epiphany Monday, so I can make arrangements to have it transcribed by one of his calligraphers, since he will not permit me to expose the old paper and ink to the light of a photocopy machine. I must also get some help with the translations, since Father Knight used an odd form of the Vulgate, one I have never seen. It's almost a completely different tongue.

Tell Sean about this the moment you get back. And make sure that he agrees not to see Patricia Jennings or Catherine before I return. Tell him I'll explain everything. And ask him to read pages 45 through 90 in Book II of his notes, and also 32 through 67, in Book VI. I will need him to explain how he got some of the numbers he came up with. He'll argue with you, but you must get him to do it, even if you have to sit on him. He's like that now about his old work, since he's given up on it and no longer believes in any of it. Or so he says.

Then, first thing Monday morning, go see Dean Potter and tell her that I was taken ill. Tell her it was bad mutton—the thought of my discomfort will probably make the woman happy, and she'll forget all about how angry she is about my not being back for the start of classes—and don't let her reaction bother you. It's all an act.

As soon as I finish here, I'll fly home immediately. I will—

no, I must—be back before the 19th. Also, the papers accompanying this note are things I jotted down for Sean to start checking out, so please see that he gets them.

Hazel was waiting, arms folded, but not from the cold, when Sean looked up. "Now," she said sternly, "if this is just another one of his research projects, why is he doing this?" She leaned into her next question. "I can understand his asking you not to see that Jennings woman, not that I can imagine you would want to see her after what Oliver told me she's done to you! But why doesn't he want you to see Catherine?"

Sean smiled at hearing Hazel call her Catherine, not Cathy. "It doesn't make any difference," he mumbled, barely loud enough for her to hear him. "I don't think Cathy and I will be seeing each other anymore." Sean then began talking to himself while looking at the calendar on the wall over the kitchen table, ticking his head, counting off days. "No one but clerics living in the past pay any attention to that silly Holy Day anymore. Do they?" he asked, but not Hazel.

Hazel looked worried. "What's with you and Catherine?" she asked, giving up the warmth of the stove to walk across the kitchen to Sean and put her hand on his shoulder.

A smile, half-wry, half-curious, twisted itself onto Sean's face, while his eyes remained fixed on the calendar. "Not even closet Papists in the Anglican Church!" he said, still talking to himself.

"Did you hear what I said?" Hazel asked, sticking her hands on her hips, jutting her delicate jaw out, looking like an irate Irish pixie.

"Twelve," Sean said, burying himself deeper into his own thoughts. "The mystical twelve nights between the birth of Christ and the arrival of the three Magi, bearing their three gifts. Talk about superstition!" He glanced down at Ollie's note. "He wants me to read one section from my early work, and one from the later period. I wonder where I put those journals after I got out of jail?" Sean went back to staring at the calendar, only now he was focused on something else, something far on the other side of the wall.

The Taking

"Sean MacDonald!" Hazel stamped her foot. "Answer me."

"What's the matter?" he asked absentmindedly as he reached up, tapping the square on the calendar for the sixth of January.

"You're not listening to me, that's what's the matter. And what are you mumbling about?"

"Sorry." Sean blinked away from the calendar to look at her. "It's just that none of this makes any sense whatsoever." But he wasn't speaking to her; it was more like he was talking around her. And he didn't sound at all like he was confused. To the contrary, he sounded like he knew exactly what Oliver meant and was somehow worried about it, or about him. "I think Oliver is taking this whole thing entirely too seriously," he finally said to her. "As for Patricia Jennings, he doesn't have to worry about her. She isn't going to want to see me anymore, not after what I've said and written to her, and how I've treated her." Standing up, Sean put his arm around Hazel. "You've had a long flight," he said, trying to comfort her. "Why don't you go home and get a good night's sleep. I'll dig out those old notes of mine and read them. Then, after you see Sarah on Monday, come back, and I'll tell you what I think Ollie might be trying to tell us. How's that sound?"

Hazel button-holed Sean to a stop when he tried ushering her out of the kitchen onto the landing. "What about Catherine?" she asked. The pained look on his face, followed by his softening grip on her shoulder, asked her not to pry. "Sean," she asked apprehensively, "you aren't patronizing me, are you? I mean about what Oliver's doing, and what he may have found out?"

Sean waved for Hazel to follow him as he started down the stairs. "You've got to understand something, Hazel," he said thoughtfully. "What Oliver is talking about is all a fuzzy dream for me. Besides, I'm having trouble taking anything seriously anymore, not just this. What with Bruce's death, the problems with my story, being arrested, and now Catherine, I'm not sure that I even care, to be perfectly honest with you. So let's not get into what I think. Let's just take one thing at a time, OK?" Hazel's head bobbed up and down, but her body moved side to side in silent disagreement. "Now—"Sean blocked the stairs—"didn't

Ollie's note say something about some papers for me?''

Hazel slipped her hand down into her sweater, fished around, and pulled out a folded-over sheaf of faded white papers, along with a blush, and stuffed them into Sean's open shirt with a prankish smile. "Good night," she said with a gentle rub of his arm. She then blocked him out of her way and started downstairs.

"Drive safely," Sean called after her, and retrieved the papers. Unlike the others she'd given to him earlier, these were warm and soft and smelled of Hazel, not airports and strangers. He started to bring them to his face, but stopped himself.

"Sean?" Hazel asked as she pulled the outside door open.

"Yes?" he answered, holding the kitchen door ajar, waiting to shut it.

"Did you know that Oliver was an Anglican priest?"

"What!"

"I thought so," she said to herself, darting outside and dancing down the icy porch steps, then running across the lawn, laughing at the cold trying to catch her and slip inside her open coat. Looking like a little girl sneaking into her father's car, Hazel stepped up onto the running board and climbed into the Silver Wraith, needing two hands to pull the door shut. She sat shivering behind the huge steering wheel, as if wondering what to do next. Seeing Sean approaching with confusion written all over his face, Hazel cranked the window down. "I was just as surprised as you look right now when I found out," she said, her breath masking her face.

"When?" Sean asked.

"He told me he 'went over the wall' right after his wife was murdered, and said there was 'no longer any reason to keep up the charade.' " Hazel waited for Sean to say something, but he just stood there, feet frozen to the ground, breath frosting the night air, the words "I don't care, it must be done, it's your last chance" for some reason racing with abandon through his brain.

Sunday Evening, January 5, 1992

Sean typed *The Lost Balloon*, and sat back, reading aloud the title of the synopsis he'd just rewritten for the umpteenth time, playing with the sound of the words to see how they fell on his ears. He decided he liked what he heard. He saved the text, then went looking for something to eat in the kitchen.

Outside, an engine started, pulling him to the window. A late-model mid-sized car, white or beige, with its lights off, was backing out of the drive. Karen? he thought, and started downstairs, his eyes bright with anticipation.

The sight of an envelope wedged into the aluminum grill guarding the storm door brought him to a disappointing stop. He tried reading it where he was, but it was too dark. He ran up the stairs, two at a time, and back into light of the kitchen.

My Dear Sean,

I'm writing this letter before flying back to San Francisco. Yes, I'm Catherine's mother. You have no idea how I felt when I learned from her letters that she was seeing you. However, judging from what I saw on your face when you saw me, perhaps you do.

Your sudden departure, and your knowing my name, made things extremely uncomfortable for me. And for Catherine, too. I didn't say anything—what could I!—except to tell her that we had met once when I was visiting Sarah Potter, and that she's lucky to have you in her life. But I could see in her eyes she knew there was something more between us.

I think it wise you not return to see her, at least not until she contacts you herself. But I do not hold out much hope for that now, so I suggest you prepare yourself for the worst should she decide never to see you again. As for your book, I only pray that she does not see what I see when she reads it, that's if it gets published in light of what's happening with Gazelle Books.

Sadly, I cannot step forward and testify on your behalf in the litigation, as I had hoped to do after learning of your predicament through the trade grapevine following the indiscreet inquiries being made by your attorney in New York. It would surely break Catherine's heart when everything got out, as we both know it would, no matter what assurances we were given.

You see, Sean, I've been responsible for breaking Catherine's heart once already, when her father divorced me for things that happened before we were married, things that I never told him about, and that I never should have, even after he found about the baby. It's all so complicated and bizarre, and even though you're probably the one person who might understand, and believe what happened, I must never tell.

I will be returning to the East Coast on Friday, the 17th of this month, for a meeting with one of my clients and her new publisher. While I don't want to give you false hopes, there is something that I may be able to do about the Gazelle matter.

So at that time, I plan on following up on an inquiry I made this past week on your behalf. I will be staying at the farm that weekend, but do not try to see me.

And please, do not try contacting me on the West Coast, as I know you already have, not if you truly love Catherine.

Karen

Monday, January 6, 1992

"Sean? Are you here?" Jean Murphy called as she cracked open the kitchen door just enough to stick her head inside. "It's me. Jean."

"I'll be out in a second," Sean answered. He saved what he was working on, then walked out of his study and down the hall into the kitchen.

Jean smiled. "What are you doing still in your pajamas!" She gestured to the window. He followed her point. It was dark all over again; he'd missed another day. "And what are these doing on, young man!" she barked, pushing her way into the kitchen and stepping stiff-legged over to the stove, twisting each of the burners off with an indignant snap of her wrist. Sean just shrugged his shoulders, knowing there was nothing to be gained from telling a woman Jean Murphy's age that he was cold, when her apartment was even colder than his, even though she kept it that way by choice. "There's a young lady downstairs, a pretty Irish lass, who says her name is Hazel Kent. I remember seeing her with that portly professor friend of yours the night they took you out for your birthday in that old car of his." Jean walked over and turned Sean around. "Go get dressed." She aimed him down the hall and got him started with a maternal pat on his backside.

"Give me ten minutes. I want to take a shower first."

Sean was sitting at the kitchen table, playing with a sheepish grin, when Hazel tiptoed in. "I thought Mrs. Murphy said you were sleeping," she said softly, as if there was someone still asleep and she might wake him up by speaking too loudly.

"No." Sean smiled. "I had just lost track of time." He stood up and pulled a chair out for her. "It's been happening a lot lately." He shrugged his shoulders as if to say, so what.

Hazel dropped the papers she was carrying in her arms onto the table in front of him, then clapped her hands like they were dusty or dirty. "These are the pages Oliver referred to. I dug them out of the file cabinet in his office, after I met with Dean Potter, just in case you conveniently weren't able to find yours." Hazel rapped her knuckles on the table, making a noise louder than she was big. "That woman was not at all happy when I told her Oliver was delayed in London." She spun around on her heels. "I'm going out to get us both something to eat. You stay put and read what I brought you," she ordered, and departed just as quietly as she had arrived.

The date on the top of the first page, December 10, 1974, made Sean wince and want to hide. But he sat down and started reading, knowing that he had better be finished, or damn close to it, before Hazel returned. At first he found it difficult to stay focused on the disjointed entries, because he didn't want to do this. He had to force himself through one page after another, prodding himself along with the thought of Hazel sitting on him, as Oliver had told her to.

* * *

"Are you done?" Hazel asked, startling Sean when she slipped into the kitchen without his having heard her come up the stairs. She had a grease-stained brown paper bag in one hand, and a small envelope in the other, which she stuck in his face. "This was in the door," she said in a huff. "I don't remember seeing it when I went out, but then I wasn't looking for it either." Sean groaned at seeing his name handwritten on the front. Hazel asked, "Who's it from?"

Sean turned Hazel's groan into a moan of his own. "You don't want to know." She held up a six-pack, swinging it back and forth, peering over, grinning. "You and Ollie are made for one another," Sean told her.

She winked and nodded in agreement, then held out a can of beer for him, but snatched it back when he grabbed for it. "No, no, no," she teased, "you first have to tell Hazel who the note's from." When Sean tried again for it; she put it behind her back.

"Patricia Jennings," he said, and stuck his hand out for his reward. Reaching past his outstretched arm, Hazel snatched the note out of his hand. "Hazel!" he protested.

But it was to no avail as she handed him his payment, then tore open the small envelope. Her eyes flashed back and forth. "She says that she's truly sorry about Bruce. Right! And that it was horrible. And that she couldn't bear to look. And she goes on to beg you with all of her body and soul." Hazel threw the note at Sean. "Here," she said, "you read it. It makes me sick."

Dear Sean,

I know it's been over two months since Bruce's death, but I wanted to write and tell you how truly sorry I am about what happened. It was horrible! I couldn't bear to look. I know I should have come to see you right after it happened, but I couldn't. I couldn't face anyone afterward, especially you.

I think I was the first woman who knew about him from the start, and told him so up front. He was actually relieved, and from that point on was himself when he was in my company. Perhaps it was because he no longer had to keep up the deception? We developed a loving friendship, unlike the contentious one we had years earlier, when I was still in the trade, and he was working with some of my good clients.

And speaking of the past, when I saw my ex-husband recently to resolve some old business, he said that he met, and "got to know" Catherine Greene "quite well" last summer. It also seems that he told her why I came back to Hart. He shouldn't have, even though it's true, but he likes doing things like that. I presume she promptly told you like a good little girl.

I need you, Sean, now more than ever. It's like it was in my senior year, only now I know what it's like to be with you, and have to fantasize. Back then, I couldn't bear seeing you with another woman one day longer, which is why I left.

Please, let me have you in me again. I beg you with all my body and soul.

                                                           Patricia

"I have to see her," Sean said without thinking.

Hazel couldn't believe her ears. "Are you crazy!"

"She needs someone. She's hurting; I can't just ignore her."

Hazel made a fist, a small delicate ball of fingers, then waved it menacingly in front of Sean's face. "You just try seeing that woman, and I'll break your nose, Sean MacDonald." She slapped the side of his head to make her point. "Whatever made Oliver decide that he had to stay behind, and make a point of having me tell you not to see her, is well worth waiting for him to explain. Saturday night I was just worried. Now I'm frightened, and I don't know why, or about what." Hazel no longer had the look of demanding taskmaster. "It's been like this ever since he got those files from you, and it got worse after your birthday. He acts like he's possessed."

Sean was staring at the note and pinching at it with his fingers. "She says here that she 'couldn't bear to look'?"

"So?"

"She also says it's like it was in her senior year." Sean

293

glanced away, his eyes jumping around inside his face, then all around the kitchen. "If I remember correctly, she didn't return after the Christmas break that year. Then Janet was murdered the very next month."

"What are you talking about?"

"January 1974," he replied. "Eighteen years ago this month, as a matter of fact." He tossed Patricia Jennings's note onto the table. "I'll be right back," he told Hazel, walking out of the kitchen and down the hallway.

Sitting down, Hazel unwrapped one of the sandwiches she'd brought back. Sean was still talking, but to himself, not her, as he started up the attic stairs. But it wasn't quite loud enough for her to understand him. "You're starting to act like Oliver," she called back over her shoulder, then took a bite out of her sandwich. And not a ladylike bite either.

"Is that bad?" Sean yelled down.

With her mouth full of food, Hazel could only nod in agreement as she began reading the photocopies that she'd brought for Sean. Now and then she zeroed in on a word with her finger, or ran it under a complete sentence. "Sean?" Hazel tamped the papers into an orderly pile.

"I'll be down in a minute, Hazel."

"Sean?"

"What!" came rolling down the attic stairs, through the hall, and out into the kitchen.

"Do you know what Oliver's birth date is?"

"No. Don't you?"

Friday, January 10, 1992

Pulling his white cashmere scarf up around his neck, Sean kicked the folding door in the phone booth closed for added protection against the cold. He tucked the receiver under his arm to warm it up before sticking it to his ear, then pressed the frozen buttons down with his thumb and waited.

"Mary? Hi, Sean MacDonald. May I please speak with Neal?" Sean smiled warmly. "Thank you. Happy New Year to you, too."

Burying himself into one corner of the booth, Sean started breathing on the glass, building up a crispy layer of frost, then scratching figure eights into it with his fingernail. "He is? How long will he be tied up?" Sean covered everything up with a hollow, open-mouthed exhale. "Well, you tell him I'm standing in a telephone booth freezing my you-know-whats off!" He switched hands, blowing into the cold one before sticking it into his coat pocket.

"Neal? How did it go in court yesterday?" He made a face. "No, I didn't get a copy of your opposing motion." Sean's mouth screwed itself deeper into his face. "No, don't bother mailing it. Just read it to me, OK?" As he listened intently, his eyes repeated every word. "Are you telling me that I can't do a fucking thing with my story until after the goddamn lawsuit is settled?" He tried listening, but broke in, asking, "Why would they want to drag it out? It'll cost a goddamn fortune." He wedged the receiver between his neck and shoulder and blew into his hands. "Yes, you're right," he answered quietly, "*they* can afford it." His face reddened. "For the publicity?" There was a barely noticeable tick of his head. "You mean that they can actually stall this whole thing until it's published?" Sean squeezed the receiver, turning his knuckles as white as the frost on the glass. "What the fuck good are you if you can't cut it short!" He bit down hard, forcing himself to listen. "Then I'll just go see her myself!" he yelled, slamming the phone back and pulling the door open.

The blast of arctic air made Sean gasp and hold his breath as he ran to his car. Looking at his watch, seeing it was almost noon, he realized that he had less than ten minutes to make his appointment with Sharon. He threw the car into gear and spun out of the parking lot, fishtailing down the icy road until he finally let off the gas.

Sharon Lucien was flying around her office like an angry wasp looking for someone to sting. Sean sat perfectly still, waiting for her to land someplace where she wouldn't hurt herself, or him. When it looked like she might finally listen, although she was still moving about, he asked, "Don't you think that it's more of an ethical question than a legal one?''

Sharon looked as if she might lift off again. "You stole from me!" She threw herself into her chair. "And that's wrong," she said, pounding her fist into the wooden armrest, "no matter how you try rationalizing it."

Sean was trying his best not to let Sharon see that he was enjoying this. He stole a breath and said calmly, "The fact that you scheduled me on the very same days is more than just a coincidence, and I think you owe me an explanation."

Sharon's body suddenly appeared to be electrified. "What gave you the right to read my appointment diary?" she demanded, slapping the top of the leather-bound book lying closed in her lap. "Just who do you think you are, anyway?"

Sean had never seen Sharon like this. She was seething, but in a controlled way, and he realized that he liked it. But he decided it was best to try appeasing her. "I suppose I shouldn't have read it," he said, forcing himself to sound remorseful. "But it was lying on the floor after you rushed out, so I picked it up to put it back, which is when I saw that the bookmark had fallen out, and I started flipping to the right date. And that's when I saw the names."

"Don't ever do something like that again," she threatened. Sean nodded. They were quiet for a minute or two. He watched her look around, but not at him. She was still angry when she started speaking again. "You were beginning to tell me about your relationship with Dr. Jennings. Why don't you go on."

Sean smiled and frowned at the same time. "I wasn't telling you about Patricia," he said, a perplexed frown finding its way onto his face. "You were asking me about women in my life, and you brought her name up, not me."

"You're wrong," Sharon said emphatically, looking at her pad, which was underneath her diary. "My notes are quite clear."

Not this again, he thought. "This is silly, Sharon. We've been through this very same scenario before." He leaned forward, holding his hands out in a gesture of reconciliation.

"Stay where you are," Sharon snapped, clutching the pad and the diary to her chest, and sinking back into her chair.

The Taking

Sean was surprised by her reaction. "I wasn't going to take anything," he said with an amused smile. "But if I was, your actions certainly would have told me what I wanted to know."

"You bastard."

"Dr. Lucien!"

Sharon stood up, obviously still angry with what Sean had done. "You've been lying to me for years." Hearing this left Sean not knowing what to say. "And to yourself, too." Sharon was at her desk, slamming her diary down. "I'll see you next Friday at four." She hesitated. "No, make it eight. I've got a dinner engagement with an old friend."

Sean stepped beside her. "I don't like being treated this way." He deliberately moved closer, watching her stiffen and enjoying it. "I'll be here next Friday night, but only because I want to resolve some things between us, and now is obviously not the time for that." He put his hand on her arm and felt her become rigid. He waited for her to relax, but her arm only grew stiffer with each passing second. Not muscle hard—bone hard.

Slowing to a bumpy crawl because the roads were frozen into icy ruts from not having been plowed, Sean bounced his way to Merrywood Hall. Patricia's Porsche was there, along with most everyone else's car, forcing him to pull all the way to the end of the parking lot and walk back through the snow.

"Hi, Sean," Ruth Stein called out as she flew past him in the hall, clutching papers in one hand, blowing him a kiss with the other. "Faculty meeting," she spat out. "Potter's on a rampage, can't stop, good to see you, bye!"

"I figured as much," he said, speaking as fast as he possibly could to keep up with Ruthie's furious pace. "Would you please tell—"

"Jennings is already in there. I'll tell her you came by," Ruth rattled just before disappearing into the wall.

Leaving a note tacked on Oliver's door, which was locked, asking him to come over as soon as he was back and settled in, Sean left, wondering to himself, What made Ruthie think I was here to see Patricia? This made him want to go back and find out, but the thought of seeing Sarah changed his mind for him.

Sean held the flap of the corrugated carton open with his elbow and counted out five linen-backed journals, adding them, one at a time, to the one he'd already set down on the unfinished floor of the attic beside the file box labeled JOURNALS, but in Oliver's handwriting, not his. Taking these, and the three-ring binder labeled STUDENTS, which he'd dug out of another box, he went back downstairs into the kitchen, where he spread everything out in numerical order, left to right, I through VI. He then set the student binder directly in front of him and turned the pages until he came to Greene, Catherine (1977). He wrote down Cathy's birth date, December 29, 1955, and her age, 36, in the back of Book VI, where he had begun summarizing the information on Bruce the morning he was arrested. He turned to Jennings, Patricia H. (1986). The page was blank except for an address, which he was surprised to see was the same one for her house in Rhinebeck. At the bottom was the instruction *See Hawley*.

Turning back, he found the page for Patricia Hawley, which was completely filled in. Dividing the page in his journal into three columns, Sean wrote out Patricia's full name, Patricia Hawley Jennings, at the top of the first column. His entries were quick transferring her birth date, December 31, 1952, and 39 for her current age, noting to himself cynically, "You missed her birthday, MacDonald!" He penciled in the date for what would have been her original graduation, May 21, 1974. Then, using Oliver's guidelines, he entered Patricia's age on each line for every year since her birth date. He then began filling in the dates for any events, or occasions, that came to mind. He did the same thing for Cathy.

Curious beyond what he knew Oliver would want to know when he came over, Sean started reading Cathy's student information sheet. He stopped when he came to the entry for *Family Address*. There were two post office boxes listed, one in New York City, the other in San Francisco, each noted as being c/o *The Phoenix Agency*. On a hunch, and not knowing why, he went

The Taking

into his study and brought back his copy of *Writer's Market*. He turned to the section for author's agents, flipping the pages and speed-reading with his finger, until he found the entry he was looking for.

The Phoenix Agency, Inc.
PO Box 231
San Francisco, California 94104
Tel: (415) 555-7522
Year Est: 1970
New York Office: PO Box 312, New York, New York 10179

Not bothering with the rest of the listing, Sean began playing with the all of the numbers in anticipation of Oliver's questions. He entered the reduced sum of each number on the page, then laughed to himself. "You're going to have fun with these." Thinking he may have misread something, he double-checked his arithmetic. "Nope!" he chirped. "Right on."

He was sure that he'd sent a query to this agent and looked to see why he'd never received a reply, reading the agency profile.

Agency Commission: 15% US & Canada; 20% foreign. Foreign Representatives: all major markets. Agency Policies: Does not encourage new writers. Does not read unsolicited queries or submissions. Charges a reading and evaluation fee (Synopsis + 3 chapters, $250. Full MSS to 100,000 words, $350; up to 200,000, $450; Over 200,000, $750.00) MSS Categories: novel-length fiction, personal experience nonfiction, short story collections and poetry anthologies. Comments: Agency prefers work by women writers, writing about women and their struggle in contemporary American life for sexual and social freedom.

"The place is probably run by a covey of lesbians," he told himself, and started to put the book aside. But the very last entry leapt off the page at him. He read the words aloud and slowly, unable to believe what he was reading. "Founder and Consulting

Editor, Karen Hawley-Greene. Formally of Karen Sutherland & Associates. Agents in New York, Toronto, London, and Paris. Established 1926.''

Hawley? Sean read the entry once more, refusing to believe what he saw. That means Cathy and Patricia are sisters. What have you done? He returned to the entry, as if for some sort of solace. Nineteen-twenty-six? Can't be. It must be a typo, he told himself, leaning back, staring up into the endless pattern stamped into the tin ceiling, letting the pages of the book fan through his fingers until the cover flapped shut and the book slid off his lap onto the floor.

37

Thursday, January 16, 1992

Dear Sean,

How nice of you to have stopped by Merrywood Hall to see me last week. Unfortunately, Ruth Stein didn't tell me until today.

I came right over, but didn't find you at home, so this note must serve in my stead. I'm writing it while sitting in my car, with your landlady peeking out through the curtains in her kitchen, watching me like a hawk.

I heard about Catherine Greene. What with Bruce gone, Oliver out of the country, the pressures from all of your legal problems, and now this, you must feel terribly alone.

So, as the students say these days, let's do dinner. I have a doctor's appointment tomorrow afternoon, and won't have

The Taking

time to prepare anything, but Saturday night is clear for me. How about something simple—fresh baguette, ripe Brie, a wilted-spinach salad, filet mignon, a bottle of wine (I have two bottles of '84 Volnay that should be good) and then a very special dessert. Sound tempting?

As you know, the view of the Hudson from my living room can be simply exquisite, and even more so at this time of year. Especially when there's a full moon overhead, turning the ice on the river into gold.

Tempting? I hope so. I miss you. If I don't hear anything to the contrary, I'll expect to see you around 6:00. We can celebrate my birthday, albeit a few weeks late. But just bring yourself. You're all the gift I need.

Patricia

How did you hear about Cathy? was the first thing that came to Sean's mind. Besides, what business is it of yours anyway? Without realizing it, Sean was picking at the note with his fingers, pressing his nails into and through the paper. He began playing with the lower-right-hand corner as he reread sections of the note, bending and creasing the paper until the corner got floppy and loose. "And just exactly what did you hear?" he asked, flicking the corner with his finger, sending a small triangle of paper skittering across the table, where it stuck to the wall for a second, peeled itself loose, then fluttered down out of sight. *I wonder if Hazel said something to Sarah when she was there last week covering for Oliver, and you somehow overheard her? Or maybe someone else did, and they told you? But who?*

Sean was fixated with figuring out how Patricia learned about Cathy. Sarah? he wondered. Absolutely not! he decided with a resounding slap of his hand on the table. You are the last person she would say something to about me. "Pressures from all of my legal problems?" he wondered, rereading Patricia's words. *You're the cause of my legal problems, woman, and you act like it's no big deal. How can you expect me to have dinner with you? You stole my goddamn story from me!* "Oliver was right," he snarled,

301

folding the note closed, squashing it flat under the weight of his hand. "Someone should drown you."

But he reopened Patricia's letter with a sinister sparkle in his eyes. Two bottles of Volnay? And something "special" for dessert? On second thought, Patricia Hawley Jennings, I think I will have dinner with you, in spite of what Oliver said. Then maybe I can get some straight answers out of you. Sean began bouncing Patricia's missive in his open palm, passing it from one hand to the other with soft underhanded pats. *Besides, it's time I cleared up a few things between us, once and for all.* Giving Patricia's note a final smack, he watched it jump up, then start slicing back and forth like a pendulum as it floated down onto the table, upside down.

Friday, January 17, 1992

If Sean had ever harbored any doubts that the stairwell leading up to Sharon's office on the second floor of the converted two-family house in Red Hook was unheated, the loud creaking of the fat handrail as he pulled himself up the steps in the dark completely eliminated that uncertainty. While the dry, splintery cries of the bare wooden steps, reluctantly yielding to his weight, added their voices to the lament, his own whispered counting of each tread made the eerie chorus that much more melodramatic, especially when he deepened his voice to a slow Gregorian chant. "Eight, nine, ten, eleven, and twelve." He came to a stop on the first landing, turned, then started up the second flight of stairs. At the top, plugged into an outlet close to the floor, was a small security light, its crimson glow no brighter than a cluster of fireflies, and no match for the darkened hallway outside Sharon's office. I'm early, he thought.

Standing perfectly still, Sean took delicate breaths through his nose, trying to find her. It's too cold, he decided, then watched with amusement as his breath hung in the air, motionless, until he blew it away. Smiling, he began turning around in place, blowing gently, twirling his breath around his head. That's when he saw the patch of white on Sharon's door and wound himself down to a stop. He felt the outline of a small piece of paper. Running his fingers around the edges, catching his nail on the thumbtack holding it to the wood, he pried it loose, then knelt down close to the tiny light, as if praying.

Sean

I'm afraid that our session will have to be rescheduled. Something urgent came up. Monday at 5:00 is open. Please confirm.

Sharon

Sean patted his coat pockets for a pen. Finding one, one he thought he'd lost long ago, he printed his reply, *Fine with me!* and signed it. After rubbing around in the dark with his fingers, trying unsuccessfully to find the small pinhole in the door, he pushed the tack into a fresh spot, leaning his weight into his thumb in order to get it to stick into the hard wood. The door popped open. "Sharon?" he called out anxiously as he fell into her office. "Are you here?" She wasn't.

In two steps, he was at her diary without an ounce of guilt holding him back, trying to read the names sandwiched between the thin blue lines on the page it had been left open to. Needing more light, he moved to the floor lamp behind her chair. Tugging the chain, holding the book under the glass shade, he found what he wanted.

3:00 Dr. Jennings / double session / $150.00

Seeing that each of the succeeding entries had been crossed out, including his own appointment for eight o'clock, Sean started to close the book. But he stopped himself and walked back to the desk, thinking, *Now, where was it?* as he set the diary down and played with it until he was sure it was exactly the way he had found it.

When he turned to leave, he noticed that the top drawer of the small metal file cabinet beside Sharon's desk was pulled open. He started pushing it closed with his knee, but stopped and knelt down, pulling it back open. His moves were slow and sure and fingertip soft, as he flipped through the files until he came to *Fanning, Bruce (Ph.D.)*. He pried it open. There was nothing but an assortment of newspaper clippings telling of Bruce's death. Moving farther back, he found *Jennings, Patricia H. (Ph.D.)*. It was empty. Confused, he reached into the back of the drawer, cramming the files forward, and found *MacDonald, Sean (Ph.D.) & Janet (wife)*. It was thicker than most of the others. And there was a line drawn through Janet's name, followed by the date 1/8/74, which had been penciled in a long time ago. Wanting to open it, but oddly afraid at the very same time, Sean settled back onto his heels, waited, then spread the folder open on the floor. On top were long yellow pages scribbled with notes, which were illegible in the dark. A thick sheaf of neatly trimmed papers on the bottom protruded beyond the edges of the others. Fingering it, he withdrew a small booklet with a clear plastic cover and held it above his head for better light. A label was typed in black, the letters slightly smudged.

Hypnosis Session: MacDonald, Sean (Ph.D.)
Referred by: S. T. LUCIEN, MSW, Ph.D.
Session Date: 11/20/77
Conducted by: Werner Kaplan, Ph.D., M.D.

Remembering there were other sessions early the following year, Sean rocked back onto his knees and reached deep into the file cabinet, retrieving two more packets that had fallen down behind the file folders in the back of the drawer, along with a thin, unmarked manila folder. Opening the folder first, he found a collection of newspaper clippings, but nothing more. They were yellowed and gray and faded, making it impossible to read the small type in the dim light. Unwilling to take the time, he closed the folder and slipped it back where he'd found it. He then stacked the three transcripts in a pile on the floor, slid himself back to Sharon's chair, and started thumbing through endless sheets of notes, all arranged in chronological order. It was like turning back the pages of time. He flipped his way backward to the fall of 1973, where he found the long questionnaires he and Janet had been asked to fill out on their very first visit to Sharon's office. He started reading what he had written about why he thought he needed marriage counseling. The words brought back unpleasant memories, so he stopped. Then, seeing Janet's handwriting, without even reading the words, was all that was needed to fill his eyes with tears, which surprised him. He slumped back, the papers falling against his chest, as he lowered his head to let his feelings pass.

Scotch-taped to the back of his questionnaire were a pair of newspaper clippings, which piqued his curiosity. "Are you sure you want to know?" he heard himself asking in a hesitant whisper, and sat up, clearing his throat. But it was a foolish question, as he raised the long printed form up to the light and read one of the clippings.

MacDonald, Eileen M. (nee Merritt), December 24, 1950, of Mount Vernon, New York. Beloved wife of Robert MacDonald, loving mother of Sean, age 7. Born December 28, 1917. Of complications during childbirth at Davies Memorial Hospital. No service is planned by the family.

The next one was slightly longer.

MacDonald, Robert, July 16, 1962, of Mount Vernon, New York. Of a stroke. Husband of the late Eileen (Merritt) MacDonald, who died December 24, 1950, in childbirth. Beloved father of Sean, age 19, presently attending the University of Buffalo. Private services to be held at All Saints Episcopal Church, Valley Cottage Road, Mt. Vernon, at 9:30 A.M. Cremation immediately following the services.

"I wonder why no mention was made of the baby?" he asked himself, running his finger back and forth over the oddly written listing of his mother's death, which he couldn't remember ever having read. He started to touch his father's death notice, but his hand stopped above the curling-up block of newsprint. "I miss you," he said softly in the quiet of Sharon's office, then had to lean his head back to keep the tears from falling out onto the papers lying in his lap. That's really funny, he thought, putting everything back without paying attention to what he was doing. I don't think I ever said that to Sharon, no matter how many times she asked me. With a clap of his hands, Sean closed the thick folder, only to have a small square of paper puff out and float to the floor beside the base of the cast-metal lamp.

One of them must have come loose, he thought, pinching it off the floor with his fingers. He opened the folder again and flipped to the back. But both clippings were taped securely to the back of the questionnaire, prompting him to sit up and read the one he was holding.

MacDonald, John—November 22, 1980. Suddenly, and of unknown causes, at home, in Anonville-on-Hudson, New York. Age 7. Beloved son of Dr. Sean MacDonald, Professor of American Literature at Hart College. Contributions may be sent to the Children's . . .

Sean was unable to go on. Placing the notice of his son's death beside those of his mother and father, he closed the folder with a solemn press of his hand. He then crawled over to the cabinet and tucked the folder back into the overstuffed file drawer, making doubly sure that he had it in the correct alphabetical order. I'm surprised Janet's notice isn't in there, too, he thought as he gathered up the transcripts, slipping the bundle of uncertain memories under his arm. I don't know why Sharon would feel a need to include things like that in my file.

Having what he wanted, part of him started to leave, but there was a part that couldn't wait to read the transcripts, a strong part, strong enough to pull him back beneath the soft light of the lamp. Propping his knees up like a kid hiding in the dark, Sean started reading the first transcript. Suddenly, he jerked his head up, holding his breath, listening. After what felt like a thousand electrified seconds, he laughed, thinking, *You'll hear her car pull in, and the door close, so just relax.*

The first session was easy and quick and almost humorous, which surprised him. It was sprinkled with unintelligible replies—his—to textbook questions. It ended with the footnote; "Patient's subconscious is fighting the process." The second one read more like a short story, one that he knew by heart only too well now. He dove headlong into the third and final transcript, and the thinnest of the three bound booklets, which was comprised of no more than a half-dozen pages. A flinch suddenly rippled through his body, up into his neck, and ended with a ticking of his head that wouldn't stop until he glanced up from what he was reading. Taking a deep breath, he forced himself to continue. His eyes began chewing on the words, then swallowing, choking on each one like they were pieces of rancid meat.

"Oh, my God!" Sean dropped his head, covering the words with his hands. Then, as if blind, he began brushing his fingertips over the page, through teardrops spotting the paper and smearing the inky words, reading each line, one painful word at a time.

[WK] Sean, now tell me again. How old were you?

[SM] Seven.

[WK] Alison, make sure you get everything down this time, no matter what he does, or what he says. Do you understand me?

[AG] Yes, Dr. Kaplan.

[WK] Sean, why was it that you decided not to go to the retreat?

[SM] I didn't want to, I hated them. They always chased me and grabbed me and made me do things to them. Disgusting things!

Donald Beman

[WK] Easy son, you don't have to tell me that again.

[SM] I hate them. Hate them all! They're all sick!

[WK] Them? Who are you talking about, Sean?

[SM] Them! All of them! The priests. And the brothers, too.

[WK] Can you remember what time it was?

[SM] Nighttime ... Father James, he's the only nice one ... he never touched me, not once ... he saw me walking home from the movies and gave me a ride home.

[WK] Are you sure it was Father James, Sean?

[SM] Yes. He was new in the parish, and he had a new car. A blue one, with air conditioning. I had never been in a car with air conditioning before. It was hot that night. Really hot.

[WK] Can you remember when during the summer it was?

[SM] June.

[WK] Are you sure?

[SM] Yes!

[WK] Easy, son. That's it. Now, how do you know it was June?

The Taking

[SM]   St. Catherine's always held a retreat for the boys a few weeks before the end of the school year. It was the church's way of trying to get us to sign up for one of the sleep-away camps, where they try and talk you into becoming a priest. And other things!

[WK]   Can you remember exactly what you saw when you got home? And don't worry, son, I'm right here with you.

[Sharon, would you please get me that empty waste-paper basket by my desk, just in case he does it again. Thanks.]

[WK]   Go ahead, Sean. And take your time, son.

[SM]   The lights in the house were all out. So was the light on the front porch. And it was dark out, too, since there was no moon out. But I love the sky when it's like that, I love how I feel. And I . . . No!

[WK]   It's OK, son. I'm right here. See, you can feel my hands. That's it, just let it out.

[Sharon, hold his legs down. Now!]

[SM]   I didn't want to wake her up. I used the back door. The kitchen door. Oh, God. No!

[WK]   I'm here, son. That's it, easy now, let me wipe them for you.

[SM]   No! Stop!

[WK]   Easy. Take a deep breath. That's it. And one more. Good. I've got a pan right here, let it go.

[Sharon, get me the towel from the lavatory down the hall, and please hurry.]

[SL]   Send Alison.

[WK]   Forget it, I'll use these tissues. Here, Sean, let me wipe your mouth. That's it, son. Good.

[SM]   I saw something move . . . her legs were apart . . . I saw it!

[WK]   Sharon, hold it near his mouth. I'll hold his head. Thanks. Now, take another breath, Sean. Good. And again. That's it.

[SM]   She was lying on the kitchen table. He was over her. She was crying! I think. I saw the wings. No! Stop!

[WK]   Wings? Did you say wings, Sean? No, Sean, don't swallow it. Spit it out. That's it. Good.

[SM]   I can't breathe! Help me!

[WK]   You're fine, son. You just think you can't. But you can.

[SM]   No! The smell. I can't breathe! Help me!

[WK]   Smell? What smell? Sean, what are you talking about?

[SM]   I saw it!

[WK]   What, Sean? What did you see?

[SM]   Can't you see it?

The Taking

[WK] Try to remember, Sean. What did you see?

[SL] That's enough, Werner. He's under too much stress.

[WK] What are you talking about? He's almost there. I'm sure that once I get him past these childhood hallucinations about wings, which are obviously symbolic of something, and the smell, which I'm sure is an intentional memory block of some sort, I can get to the root of what it is that's been so traumatic for this man. We can't stop now, Sharon. It wouldn't be right!

[SL] I said, that's enough!

[WK] But—

[SL] The session's over, Werner. We can talk about trying again some other time.

Sean tried standing, but doubled over onto the floor, his knees bent and pulled up to his chest, his hands over his head, covering his ears. But he was unable to quiet the roar in his head, as tears fell from his eyes like rain, drowning his heart.

38

Saturday, January 18, 1992

Sean opened his eyes to find his bedroom bathed in white light, without so much as a shadow creeping across the ceiling or over the walls, telling him that he'd slept right through the morning. He rolled out of bed, still dressed from the night before, including his shoes, and ambled down the hall. Blocking the attic door shut with his arm, he wondered, Did I go up there last night? as he walked into the kitchen and shut his eyes to bleached-bright sunlight pouring in through the windows. He shuffled across the room and pressed his face to the glass, feeling the cool on his forehead as he squinted past the sun's harsh glare. The ground was no longer hard and dry, but soft and wet and covered with tiny patches of water, rippling in the wind, that had been ice only last night. The wetness made him think of coffee. A pot was filled and on the stove in seconds, and he was in the shower thirty steps later, leaving a trail behind him of kicked-off shoes and sour, sweat-soaked clothes.

Standing naked in front of the stove, shaking off the memory of the morning Patricia had surprised him in the kitchen, Sean closed his eyes and bent down, breathing in the vapors billowing up from the pot of boiling water. He raised his head when the skin inside his nostrils burned from the sting of the steam, but was right back down again, inhaling the soothing mist through his open mouth, deep down into his lungs, feeling his chest growing warm and swollen and heavy, as his brain started pounding against the inside of his skull, demanding its already tardy fix.

312

The Taking

The overstuffed wicker basket of unopened letters sitting on the credenza beside his desk called to him before he could turn his computer on and start writing. "Go ahead," he told himself, "it doesn't matter anymore," as he ceremoniously dumped the contents of the basket out onto the floor. Sitting down, sipping his coffee with an addict's delight, while discarding with a wave of his hand the urge to put the unopened secrets into some sort of made-up order, Sean dove headlong into the past. The first few letters were old, having been mailed before everyone knew, before the lies. Then came Thanksgiving, followed by December, a span of only a week, but which brought silence with it.

One letter, postmarked Chelsea Station and dated the ninth of December, during the week he was in jail, was thick, but only in the middle. The return address was printed in glossy blue ink, the letters raised up and shiny, looking still wet and sticky to the touch. This ought to be good, he thought, ripping the thinnest possible strip off one edge of the envelope and slipping the letter out. A diskette fell into his lap.

"That's mine!" he squeaked, then laughed at the sound of his own voice.

Dear Dr. MacDonald:

It's not been easy locating you, sir. Your colleagues are most protective of you, most particularly your new associate, Dr. Jennings. If it wasn't for the private sunset service a few of us arranged for dear Bruce at Olana, and a friendly chap by the name of Oliver Shore, I might never have tracked you down.

Enclosed is a diskette Bruce sent us last July, when he wrote to me asking that I consider publishing your story, even though it wasn't finished at the time. He later wrote to say you had finished it, and included the remaining chapters. Those, however, were typed. He asked me to deal directly with you if there was any interest on my part, since he was busy with some personal matters.

Please accept my apologies for not getting back to you

sooner. Although Bruce did send me everything last summer, I took an extended vacation with a few close friends, and we did not return until mid-October. Soon after that, dear Bruce was murdered.

Let me say up front, that knowing you as I feel I do from how Bruce spoke about you over the years, especially of late, we all know you had nothing to do with his death.

Now, about your story. I like it and want to publish it, if it's still available. So, if you're not committed in any way, please get the completed manuscript to me as soon as you can. I will have my Senior Editor handle it personally to determine how we should proceed regarding any desired revisions. I will also assign one of our more experienced story editors to work with you, if needed.

In the meantime, have your agent contact me so we can work out the details, including an advance. Our standard advance on novels of your type for first-time authors is $10,000.00.

I look forward to meeting you and getting to know you personally. Bruce said you were his dearest friend.

> Very truly yours
> David W. Alders, President/Publisher

Sean tried laughing, but it hurt too much. Reaching behind him, he rolled a pen off the desk onto the floor beside him, then scratched a note across the bottom of David Alders's letter, reading it as he wrote it; "See, Neal, I was telling the truth!" He then signed it with a flurry.

Leaving the engine running and the radio blaring, Sean slipped through the January air, through the front door, then raced with abandon up the two flights of stairs to Sharon's office. "Yes!" he cheered, snatching the untouched note off the door. "I know you've got a pen in there," he told himself, grabbing the doorknob, knocking just to be safe, then pushing his way in. He went directly to her chair, fishing a pencil out of the cushions, boldly

314

struck out what he'd written the night before, and printed *Changed my mind after sleeping like a baby!* resigned the note, *Love, Sean.*

As he walked out of Sharon's office, Sean pulled the door shut behind him with a determined snap of his wrist and pinned the note back up, pounding the tack flat with the heel of hand.

A vaporous mist was rising up from the melting snow and wrapping itself around the dead cornstalks in the fields behind the house. The torn piece of paper impaled on the curled-up end of the aluminum grillwork guarding the glass on the storm door made Sean smile when he saw it. "You're back, my friend," he said, carefully lifting it off to keep from tearing it any more than it already was.

Sean,

Sorry for this note, but I simply could not wait for you to return since there's so very much to be done.

I hope you won't be too upset with me, but I let myself into your apartment again since there were more things I needed from the attic. I also have the transcripts from your hypnosis sessions, which I found in your study, along with what I came back for.

And please, I beg you, until we speak later today, do not, under any circumstances, see either Patricia Jennings or Catherine. On second thought, don't even go upstairs. Drive around for awhile, then come to my office.

With a little luck, and the grace of God, I should be done before dark.

Oliver

Sean stood at the entrance to Merrywood Hall, staring into the expressionless faces of the bronze lions, asking himself if he really wanted to go in, since he knew that by this time of day, they were all about to bolt out of Sarah's monthly faculty meeting and dash for freedom, in which case they would see him, and he wasn't ready for that. Climbing the steps, he pulled one of the doors open just enough to peek inside. The churchlike quiet told him the meeting was still in session.

"You poor bastards." He laughed quietly to himself and stepped inside, slipping off his wet loafers and scuffing over the cold marble floor in his wet socks as he hurried down the hall to the safety of Oliver's office. But he found himself slowing his pace, and it wasn't because his wet socks were sticking to the unwaxed floor. You miss it, don't you, he thought, slowing down almost to a crawl. And he did, too. He missed just being here, missed the Saturday faculty meetings, where he and Bruce took turns teeing off on Sarah about why she couldn't get Oliver to come, missed his colleagues—even Carol Mathews—and he missed the students, which surprised him, and the simple, perhaps meaningless things like the echo of his leather heels when he strode down the corridor on his way to his office, an office that he suddenly remembered was no longer his, which only made him miss everything that much more.

"Ollie?" Sean whispered, melting into the marble alcove of Oliver's doorway, then looking up and down the hall to see if anyone had seen him. "It's me, Sean." He held his ear to the door, expecting to hear the sound of castors squeaking over the hardwood floor, or Oliver's heavy steps, or the dull thump of a book being shoved back onto a shelf. Nothing. "Ollie, I know you're in there," he said, trying to sound convincing, while drumming his fingernails on the door. He tried the knob. It turned, but the door wouldn't budge, even when he leaned up against it.

"Well, well, well," Patricia Jennings said with a triumphant laugh in her words. Sean jumped and spun around, fidgeting like a little thief out of *Oliver Twist*. "What are you doing here?"

"Nothing!" he replied, looking for a place to put his hands. "I just wanted to talk to Oliver, that's all."

"Well, you'll be doing a lot better than any of us if you can!" Patricia pushed her way into the alcove beside him, mimicking his secretive crouch. "According to Andy Jensen, the janitor"— Sean pursed his lips as if to say, I know who Andy Jensen is—

The Taking

"Oliver has been holed up in there since Thursday. Except for last night, when, according to Andy, he was gone for a few hours. He came back carrying an armful of books and a canvas tote bag filled with what Andy said looked like litter. When he called to him, Oliver ran down the hall and locked himself back up in his office"—Patricia smiled—"tight as a bug in a rug." Sean couldn't help smiling with her at the image of Oliver doing just that. "It seems that he's even unplugged his phone. At least we think he has, since we haven't heard it ring, and Potter must have tried calling every ten minutes." Reaching out, Patricia caressed the side of Sean's face with her open hand. "I haven't seen you look so rested in months," she said, searching for the invisible lines around his eyes. "What's your secret?"

He was about to say "a younger woman," but lost his train of thought, or his courage, when her touch slipped beneath his skin and did what it always did to him, drawing his eyes shut, pulling him to her. That's when he realized that for the first time since that night in June, six years ago, he wasn't afraid of her touch, and it surprised him.

Patricia must have sensed what he was thinking, because she took up the last few inches between them. "Sean," she asked. "Can you make it at eight tonight, instead of six? I have to run into Manhattan, which is where I was going when I saw you. I may not be back until seven or seven-thirty, depending upon traffic." She started to leave, walking backward. "If I'm not there when you arrive, just let yourself in. I'll leave the sliding doors on the back deck unlocked. OK?"

Sean answered with a nod of his head and watched her walk, almost saunter, down the hall. The thought of being with her, and the ambivalent feelings accompanying those thoughts (but always after he was with her, never before, like now), told him what he wanted more than anything else, but what he was most afraid of, and that was seeing Cathy. Even though Karen's words had been a constant warning to him, he decided that very second he was willing to risk everything to see her, in spite of what she might say to him. Or worse yet, what she might not say, because he now knew it was the one thing that he dreaded the most, what he

317

himself had dealt out all his life: silence.

Resolving to stop back to see Oliver on his way to Patricia's—
if you go there for dinner, he told himself—Sean left Merrywood
Hall to find Cathy.

The barn doors, which had been braced shut against winter, were
flung open, inviting the bittersweet air to tease its way through
the lofts, drying the hay. There was mud everywhere, oozing up
out of the earth, gluing itself to the tractors as they rumbled from
barn to barn, pulling hastily filled wagons of hay and straw and
bags of feed behind them. He drove too fast down Molly Lane
on his first pass, turning the figures—their boots sinking into the
ground, their blue-jeaned legs spattered to the knees—into a blur.
He swung around and made a second pass a little more slowly,
this time checking the heads instead of the bodies. But he failed
to find any blond hair falling down onto the autumn reds and
hunter greens of the woolen shirts. The third time he coasted, and
that's when he realized Cathy's white pickup truck wasn't anywhere to be found, not even pulled around behind the farm stand.
With a slap of the gearshift, he dropped it into second and pulled
away.

The Red Hook Inn was next. Bobby McCarthy acted as if he
was expecting him, which surprised Sean for all of ten seconds.
Then Bobby said coolly, and with a curt nod, "Dr. MacDonald."
His usually clear cerulean-blue eyes were brooding, clouded over
with gray. His easy smile was buried deep in the craggy features
of his square jaw. He turned his back on Sean.

"Know where Cathy is?" Sean asked nicely.

"Can't help you, sir," Bobby tossed back over his shoulder,
making Sean want to duck to keep from getting hit.

Their conversation quickly turned into a tactical battle, a battle
between Sean's determined guile and Bobby's iron will, until
Sean finally raised his hands like he was surrendering, and asked,
"May I please have a beer?" and watched Bobby walk away
from him as if he didn't even exist.

*   *   *

The Taking

There was no answer to his soft knock. Sean tried again, only a little harder. Still no response. Laughing to himself, making sure it was loud enough for Oliver to hear, Sean knelt down and pushed his face close to the crack at the bottom of the door so he could call to Oliver. "Damn!" he gasped, snorting the foul-smelling air out of his nose as he jumped up. "Oliver! Answer me!" he demanded, and began fighting with the door. It cracked open, surprising him. He pushed it another inch or two, enough to see that it was blocked by something on the other side. Stepping back, he shoved as hard as he could, slipping on the polished marble floor and dropping to one knee, but forcing the door open enough to poke his head inside and peer over the top of Oliver's rolltop desk, which was pushed up against the door.

"Ollie, answer me!" Sean begged, squirming sideways through the door and into the office. "You crazy son-of-a—" He froze in place. "What the hell?" Everything was pushed against the walls, or shoved in front of the bookcases—his wing chair, two end tables, the small brass table lamps, countless corrugated file boxes (half of them bearing Sean's name), an overfilled canterbury, the silk tapestry, and the huge rolltop desk, which Sean was now leaning against—exposing a crater of never-before-walked-on oak flooring in the center of the room. Arranged in a circle no less than eight feet across and looking like a giant game board were twelve piles of papers placed where each number would have been on the face of an imaginary clock, one without hands. Starting with one o'clock, circling down to six, they rose to midnight in ever decreasing thickness. And set in the center of the shiny patch of wood was a brass table lamp, its shade removed, an unfrosted bulb glaring bright, its tendriled filaments casting spidery shadows all around the room.

A stiff breeze pushed its way through the open window into the already chilly room, rustling the papers on the floor like dried leaves. Sean looked up to see that the drapes were pulled outside. Reaching back, groping at the air, he closed the door with a slap of his hand, killing the breeze, but not before it had succeeded in swirling the papers into disarray, and stirring up the stale air, which smelled of tea and dried leather, and the trace of something else, something Sean knew only too well, but which he chose to ignore, or was simply unwilling to accept.

"What in the world were you doing here?" Sean bent down, grabbing a few of the papers. He shot back up. "Wait!" He spun around, facing the door. "How did you get out?" he asked. As if to answer his question, a faltering draft curled around his neck. Turning back, he stepped gingerly over and around the fluttering papers, trying his best not to disturb them, but the wind did it for him when he spread the drapes open and looked out. The steel casement sashes had been pushed so far out that the brackets holding them to the frame mortared into the stone had been bent, top and bottom, making it impossible for him to close them.

"This must be how you got out, you strange little man," Sean told himself with obvious affection as he plucked a fragment of cloth off the window latch. Feeling the biting cold, he pulled the drapes back into the room and drew them shut with a sharp snap of the heavy fabric. One of the spartan wooden chairs offered an excellent weight to hold them closed. Squeezing and opening his right hand, then doing it again, he looked down into his palm to see what it was that felt thick and sticky.

It can't be, he thought, stepping through the leafy mess to the lamp and holding his hand up to the bulb. "It is!" he told himself, spitting into his palm, rubbing his hands together, then wiping them off on his pants. *He must have cut himself on the latch when he jumped to the ground. Why he left that way, I don't know. Maybe it was so he could avoid Sarah.*

Sean put the shade back onto the lamp, balanced it in place since there was no finial to be found anywhere, then kicked open a spot for himself in the midst of the windblown litter and sat down, eying the papers, every one of which was covered with Oliver's bold, open-faced handwriting. Closing his eyes, as if making a game of it, Sean drew his first bit of reading material out of the unruly pile as if he were selecting the winning ticket for a church raffle. Before starting, he looked around to check the time. A small squat-faced clock suspended on the wall over the spot where Oliver's desk had been squinted back at him. But it was too dark for him to read. Holding the shade, he tipped the

The Taking

lamp, spotlighting the tarnished ivory face and the Roman numerals painted onto the aging dial.

"Plenty of time," he told himself. "It's not even six yet." He turned back to the paper in his hand, which was filled with a vaguely familiar mix of quotations, each one meticulously printed in Oliver's hand.

And he said unto them, I beheld Satan as lightning fall from heaven.

Luke 10:18

. . . I will ascend into heaven, I will exalt my throne above the [seven] stars of God . . . how art thou fallen from heaven, O Lucifer, son of the morning [star] . . .

Isaiah 14 12–13

. . . for Satan himself is transformed into an angel of light.

Corinthians

. . . and the angels, the sons of the heavens, saw and lusted after them . . . and begat children . . .

Enoch 6:2

. . . here will stand the angels who have connected themselves with women . . . til the days of the great judgment . . .

Enoch 19:1

. . . they sacrificed their daughters unto devils.

Psalm 106:37

. . . there are two women . . . daughters of one mother . . .

Ezekial 23:2

. . . I will raise up thy lovers against thee . . . and I will bring them against thee on every side.

Ezekial 23:22

"What is this shit?" Sean asked himself, turning the page over. But he knew only too well what it was, and what Oliver was trying to say. He read what was printed verso after putting on his most convincing mask of indifference, as if someone was here watching him.

... I did not die, and I did not remain alive ... the emperor of the Dolorous Realm stood forth from ice ... I saw three faces ... under each there issued forth two mighty wings, no plumes had they; but were in form and texture like a bat's ... he was flapping them, so three winds went forth ...

Dante's *Inferno*

... and I stood upon the sand of the sea, and saw a beast rise up ... and I beheld another ... and he spake as a dragon ... let him who understands count the number [name] of the man [the second beast] ... six hundred three score and six [666]

Revelation 13:1–18

... above it stood the seraphims: each one had six wings ... and the house [of the Lord] was filled with smoke [fog] ...

Isaiah 6:2–4

... for the wickedness burns as the fire ... it shall mount up like the lifting of smoke [fog] ...

Isaiah 9:18

... the vapor of the fire wasteth his flesh ...

Ecclesiasticus 38:28

... for what is your life, but a vapor ...

James 4:14

There were others, some older, others centuries younger. Sean tossed the paper aside and sat staring into the sea of paper lapping at his legs. He drew his arm back, looking as though he was gong to sweep everything away, then shook his head and started pawing through the waves of paper. Seeing two alike, then three more, he gathered them up and slipped them into the numbered order written in the corner. He started reading with a steady nodding of his head, which quickly turned into a slow rocking of his whole body without his realizing it before he was halfway down the page.

```
S A R A H   P O T T E R
1 1 9 1 8   7 6 2 2 5 9        =51=5+1=              6
F R A N K   S T E A R N S
6 9 1 5 2   1 2 5 1 9 5 1      =47=11=1+1=           2
R U T H   S T E I N
9 3 2 0   1 2 5 9 5            =44=4+4=              8
Z O E   B E R N S T E I N
8 6 5   2 5 9 5 1 2 5 9 5      =62=6+2=              8
A N D R E W   J E N S E N
1 5 4 9 5 5   1 5 5 9 1 5 5    =50=5+0=              5
```

Scanning the second page, which was a continued listing of faculty and staff, Sean flipped over to the titles. The first entry made him laugh.

```
A R N O L D   K R A T Z
1 9 5 6 3 4   2 1 1 2 8        =42=4+2=              6
```

"Couldn't happen to a nicer guy," he said, biting his teeth with his mouth open, then again, just to hear the snap. "And better sooner than later."

The others on the page were listed without any sense of order, as if jotted down in haste. The writing looked hurried.

```
N E A L   A L L E N
5 5 1 3   1 3 3 5 5            =31=3+1=              4
H A Z E L   K E N T
8 1 8 5 3   2 5 5 2            =39=12=1+2=           3
```

Donald Beman

"Lucky match, Ollie," he noted when he saw Hazel's name and corresponding number. "You two equal five. Couldn't ask for a more peaceful joining, now could you." He laughed. "I guess I should have known that I would fall in love with someone like Cathy, or get mixed up with a woman who's more than my equal in Patricia!" He read on.

```
J U L I A N   D A V I D S O N
1 3 3 9 1 5   4 1 4 9 4 1 6 5     =56=5+6=11=1+1=     2
I R A   J E N N I N G S
9 9 1   1 5 5 5 9 5 7 1           =57=5+7=12=1+2=    · 3
E I L E E N   M E R R I T T
5 9 3 5 5 5   4 5 9 9 9 2 2       =72=7+2=             9
K A R E N   S U T H E R L A N D
2 1 9 5 5   1 3 2 8 5 9 3 1 5 4   =63=6+3=             9
S H A R O N   L U C I E N
1 8 1 9 6 5   3 3 3 9 5 5         =58=5+8=13=1+3=      4
```

Sutherland? Sean thought, How did you know her maiden name? He then pressed his thumb alongside the number for his mother, then did the same for Karen. "Nine. Interesting," he mused barely above a whisper. "Sharon would have a ball with that!" Sean put the pages back into order, then set them down carefully.

One random page, printed boldly in felt-tip marker, something Oliver never used, caught his eye. Continuing his unchallenged game of pickup sticks, he slipped it out from underneath a clutch of papers forming a fragile bridge.

```
1   12/24/1950   ''A Dream within a Dream''      #1
    DEATH        Eileen (Merritt) MacDonald      [9]

2   07/16/1962
    DEATH        Robert MacDonald                [1]

3   01/08/1974   ''Dream-Land'' [last 18 lines]  #2
    DEATH        Janet (Peters) MacDonald         [6]
```

4	11/22/1980	''Dream-Land'' [first 4 stan-zas]	
	DEATH	John MacDonald	[6]
5	05/23/1986	''Evening Star''	#3
	NEAR DEATH	Sean MacDonald	[7]
6	09/23/1991	''Spirits of the Dead''	#4
	NEAR DEATH	Sean MacDonald	[7]
7	10/23/1991	''Dreams''	#5
	DEATH	Bruce Fanning	[6]
8	?	?	#6?
	DEATH	Sean MacDonald	[7]

''There's no poem of his I know of that's titled *Death*.'' Sean laughed uncomfortably as he fitted the sheet back where he'd gotten it, only to have the bridge collapse down around his hand.

Sean had grown tired of his little game, and disappointed with what he found. Arching his back, stretching his neck, he started pushing himself up off his knees, but stopped when he saw a long yellow sheet of ruled paper, unlike all the others, trapped beneath the heel of his shoe. Sean leaned forward and grabbed it. His new find was torn across the bottom. He started pawing his way through the clutter around him, searching for what he thought he'd torn off when he snatched the sheet out from underneath his foot. But there wasn't a match to be found.

In the upper-left-hand corner, printed in letters barely readable, was repeated the last two lines of the quotation from Revelations, but with an additional line.

666 = QSR NRWN = KAISAR NERON = BEAST = SATAN = 666

The rest of what Oliver had written fell into place down the wrinkled page like a cascading waterfall, sweeping Sean with it.

Donald Beman

```
06/15/1950  RAPE/MOTHER         NEW MOON   1950−666=1284 AD
06/15/1284                      NEW MOON


12/24/1950  DEATH/MOTHER        FULL MOON  1950−666=1284 AD


12/24/1950  DEATH/SISTER        FULL MOON  1950−666=1284 AD
12/24/1284                      FULL MOON


07/16/1962  DEATH/FATHER        FULL MOON  1962−666=1296 AD
07/16/1296                      FULL MOON


01/08/1974  DEATH/WIFE          FULL MOON  1974−666=1308 AD
01/08/1308                      FULL MOON


11/22/1980  DEATH/SON           FULL MOON  1980−666=1314 AD
11/22/1314                      FULL MOON


05/23/1986  NEAR DEATH/SEAN     FULL MOON  1986−666=1320 AD
05/23/1320                      FULL MOON


09/23/1991  48TH BIRTHDAY       FULL MOON  1991−666=1325 AD
            ''UNLOCK DATE''
09/23/1325                      FULL MOON


10/23/1991  DEATH/BRUCE         FULL MOON  1991−666=1325 AD
10/23/1325                      FULL MOON
```

"Well, old friend," Sean said with a sigh of resignation. "It appears that you've found the key and solved the puzzle, and that you were right all along." Sean's hand was now shaking, forcing him to use two hands to steady the long summary, but it was to no avail. Bracing himself on the rolled-up oriental rug draped over the top of Ollie's desk, he turned to one side to get out of his own shadow and scanned the last few lines.

```
12/28/1917  BIRTH: EILEEN MERRITT        [9]  13TH FULL MOON


12/30/1925  BIRTH: KAREN SUTHERLAND      [9]  13TH FULL MOON


09/23/1943  BIRTH: SEAN MACDONALD        [7]  AUTUMNAL EQUINOX


06/21/1948  BIRTH: OLIVER KNIGHT SHORE   [8]  SUMMER SOLSTICE


12/24/1950  BIRTH: SHARON LUCIEN         [4]  13TH FULL MOON


12/31/1952  BIRTH: PATRICIA HAWLEY       [7]  13TH FULL MOON


12/29/1955  BIRTH: CATHERINE GREENE      [2]  13TH FULL MOON
```

That's interesting, he thought, tapping the entry for Sharon Lucien's name. You made the same mistake twice. Her full name is Sharon *Teresa* Lucien. He then started, but gave up, trying to refigure the aural number for Sharon's name. There was one last line, a hurried entry, broken up by the tear at the bottom of the page and blurred by what appeared to be red ink dripped onto the words. You won't give up your old fountain pens, will you? Sean thought, and was about to scratch off the blotches.

327

But he was suddenly no longer interested, or perhaps he was just tired of it all, or perhaps he knew all he needed to know, and there was no use going on. Dropping the paper onto the floor, he switched off the light, never having read the last few lines, which glowed in the dark with a life all their own as Sean groped his way to the chair beneath the window without waiting for his eyes to adjust to the dark, bumping his shin as a reward for his impatience. He stepped up onto the seat of the chair and slipped through the drapes out onto the stone ledge, where he paused, then jumped to the ground into the waiting arms of the mountain laurel growing beneath the window.

Pushing his way out, he walked with a heavy step over the rapidly hardening ground, shivering. But he wasn't shivering from the frigid wind blowing out of the mountains across the river; he was shivering from the haunting replay of what Oliver had written out, the names and the dates and the numbers, coursing through his veins like ice water, and the one number he'd known all along, but had refused to accept or work out as Oliver had in order to know the final date, his final date. That's if it was all true.

"But it's not," Sean heard himself saying. "It's simply a self-fulfilling prophecy from making the numbers work the way *you* want them to. Stay at it long enough, and you'll eventually get exactly what you want. Any fool can see that," he argued, but without the conviction that he'd always had. "Anyway, you still don't know who the hell is doing this, or"—Sean almost added "or what," but he slapped that thought away as he circled around Merrywood Hall, hurrying to his car, the rising fog closing in around him with each step he took.

39

Folding his arms over the top of the wood-rimmed steering wheel and resting his chin on top of his hands, Sean sat looking out through the fogged-up windshield, tracing the simple yet elegant lines of Patricia Jennings's house with his anxious gaze, as if inspecting the building for some defect that would give him a reason not to enter because it wasn't safe. Not that he didn't already have good enough cause.

He forced himself out of the car. "You're letting the stuff he did get to you, MacDonald," he told himself as he marched up to the front door, rang the bell with a bold jab of his finger, and stepped back, listening to the chimes inside play out their muted rhymes. After a minute, he did it again, then tried peeking around through the dense evergreens covering the picture window, only to be blocked by a curtained wall of black from the heavy drapes. She must not be back from the city, Sean thought, and started around the side of the house, slipping on the patches of ice-covered flagstone hidden beneath the fog. Just before he reached the deck, he looped his arm around a small birch tree and kicked clumps of frozen snow off the ledge, listening to them tumble down the sheer face of the cliff and splash into the water like powdered stones.

Spinning full circle, Sean was on the deck in three sure steps, pressing his face against the sliding glass door. The kitchen was bursting with garden-fresh colors, red and green peppers waiting to be sliced, a pile of fat white mushrooms, a bunch of fresh basil, scallions, cloves of garlic and shallots, and a solitary peppermill, scattered around the butcher block countertop like someone was

329

playing jacks. A just-washed head of lettuce was held prisoner
inside a wire cage suspended over the stainless steel sink, draining. Lined up on the counter along one wall was a row of small
cutting boards; the first held a wedge of brie, its creamy insides
oozing out all over, the second cradled a thick cut of pâté, filled
with peppercorns and pistachios, and a third was covered with a
mound of crumbled Roquefort cheese. Close by, lying beside a
lighted gas grill, was a full tenderloin. Nearby, the skinny end of
a baguette was protruding from a long paper bag. Beside it was
a bottle of red burgundy, its cork out, standing upright on the
serving shelf opening to the living room, which was alive with
orange and red flames dancing on the pristine white walls.

She's got to be here, he told himself, sliding the door open and
sticking his head inside. "Patricia? It's me, Sean. Sorry I'm late."
The musty smell of cheese pulled him inside. Walking past the
brie, he ran his finger through the thick goo and stuck it in his
mouth as he leaned into the living room. "Anyone home?" he
mumbled, licking the cheese off his finger. "Trish?" he said with
some difficulty.

"Up here." Sean followed the sound of Patricia's voice to the
balcony above the living room. She was standing a foot back from
the railing, holding the edge of a pink terry cloth towel that was
wrapped loosely around her. "I was just about to step into the
shower," she said. "Care to join me?"

Sean gave her a weak-handed wave as he walked into the living
room while trying unsuccessfully to look away. "I just took one
myself," he lied. "I'll just flop down in front of the fire and wait
for you." He threaded his way around the furniture to the brown
suede sofa in front of the fieldstone hearth, all the while looking
up at her.

"Suit yourself," Patricia said, then unwrapped herself with the
flare of a magician, tossing the towel off the balcony. She stepped
forward and leaned over the railing, watching the towel float
down and collapse into a bundle of rose-colored folds on top of
the plush beige carpeting. "Last chance," she teased, and smiled
broadly when she found Sean's eyes all over her. She then
stepped back and spread her arms in a gesture inviting him up-

stairs. This time he didn't try to look away. Perhaps it was the soft amber light of the fire, which was the only light in the room, or maybe it was his tired eyes, but Patricia's skin was much darker than he remembered, almost like wet slate after a rain. She waited for him to finish, giving no hint that she was in a hurry to shower, or in any way self-conscious at being naked, while he stood below her, dressed, sliding his eyes over, around, and inside her body.

"I hope it's not my last chance," he called up without thinking. Patricia said something he couldn't make out, laughed to herself, and walked away.

Sean collapsed into the puffy cushions of the sofa and shut his eyes, letting the heat from the fire melt the day away. Stay focused, he thought. And stay awake! He forced his eyes back open and stared into the flames. The sound of water running told him she'd left the bathroom door open. As hard as he tried, he couldn't quite make everything work the way it should, the way it always had when it came to Patricia, and he settled for the heat of the roaring fire. "Later," he told himself, and let his head fold over onto his shoulder.

A brightly wrapped package sitting on the coffee table, a table made from the cross section of a redwood tree trunk and topped with an inch-thick slab of amoeba-shaped glass, pried his eyes open wide. It was the size of a box of candy, a sampler, and covered with gold wrapping paper tied loosely with a shiny kelly green ribbon, its loose ends scraped with scissors into a cluster of curls in the center of the box.

Sean shut his eyes, telling himself in no uncertain terms, "It's not for you, so leave it alone." But it didn't work; there was too much boy in the man. His left eye popped back open, then his right eye joined in as he fell onto his side, as if hiding in the deep cushions, and lifted the box onto the sofa directly in front of his face. Well, it's not candy, he thought, sniffing one corner. A sudden flush of guilt made him sit up and look where Patricia had been standing, only to hear the water still running.

Sean wriggled his finger under the fold of wrapping paper on one corner and watched with impish delight as the end pulled open, allowing a gray cardboard box to slide out, with a little extra help from him. With Christmas-morning anticipation, he carefully lifted the top off to find a thin gilded frame with a poem, handwritten and on old yellowed paper, locked safely beneath the crystal-clear glass. As he read, his lips moved in a breathless whisper.

> From childhood's hour I have not been
> As others were: I have not seen
> As others saw; I could not bring
> My passions from a common spring.
> From the same source I have not taken
> My sorrow; I could not awaken
> My heart to joy at the same tone;
> And all I loved, I loved alone.
> Then—in my childhood, in the dawn
> Of a most stormy life—was drawn
> From every depth of good and ill
> The mystery which binds me still:
> From the torrent, or the fountain,
> From the red cliff of the mountain,
> From the sun that round me rolled
> In its autumn tint of gold,
> From the lightning in the sky
> As it pass'd me flying by,
> And the cloud that took the form
> (When the rest of Heaven was blue)
> Of a demon in my view.

Sean drew his fingers over the signature locked away from his touch—E. Poe, Baltimore, March 17, 1829. Sean closed his eyes. "Alone." He sighed. "I never thought to look at this one, because it was never considered to be by Poe." He laughed. "But it's so obvious, and it fits perfectly. You fool."

Trying not to make a sound, Sean placed the gilded frame back into its spartan box, deftly fitting the box back into the hollow shell of paper, then setting the unrequited gift back down onto

The Taking

he glass-topped table. Then, as if in a trance, he got up and
walked into the kitchen and slipped outside onto the deck. The
iver was now sleeping beneath a blanket of fog, which was
climbing the sheer face of the granite cliff. The rush of cold air
on his face, hot and dry from the fire, cleared his head.

"It can't be," he said, stepping into the snow, walking, then
unning, along the flagstone path back to his car.

'Now what!" he asked himself, withdrawing the stiff fold of
paper from the seam of the clapboard siding next to his door with
a pinch of his fingers. Leaning over the railing into the moonlight,
he opened the note, which was typed, not handwritten.

I must meet with you in private. It's very important. I may be
able to help with your lawsuit. Meet me in Merrywood Garden
shortly after midnight. It won't take long.

"I bet it won't!" Sean growled, yanking the storm door open
and kicking the heavy oak door, jamming it against the wall with
a loud crash. He was upstairs and in his study without having
closed any of the doors behind him, handwriting a reply.

Karen,

I'll meet you in Merrywood Garden at 12:00, just as you
asked.

Sean

Sean made a slow pass of Cathy's house with his lights off,
accelerating for a second, then letting his little sprite coast to a
top a few hundred yards beyond the farm stand. He jogged the
quarter-mile back to the house. Everything was pitch black; not
even the porch light was on. The windows on the second floor
glowed from the reflection of the early-rising moon. Sean snuck
around the drive and slipped the note under the windshield wiper
of Karen's car, then wondered how to let her know he was there.

Feeling he was being watched, he looked up to see a figure, naked, standing close to the second-floor bedroom window, shadows rippling over her body, her face guarded from the light of the full moon by the white lace curtains draped around the window, her long hair falling down below her shoulders, her breasts full, young, her nipples pink, her hips broad, her legs pressed together, caressing a delicious patch of black. He moved, chasing her away. When he looked back, he was startled to find Karen standing in the window, a white robe wrapped around her, looking down at him, smiling—but not.

Confused, he hesitated, then gave her a brusque wave and walked down the drive to the road. Then, and not knowing why, Sean ran down Molly Lane, holding his breath, leaving himself winded when he reached his car.

40

Midnight

Sean gave up fighting with the icy ruts and slush-filled potholes dotting Merrywood Lane, and pulled down the plowed-out blacktop drive leading to the cinder block maintenance building. Taking a deep breath, sucking up what little heat there was trapped inside his car, he climbed out and started back down the narrow service road to Merrywood Lane on his way to Merrywood Garden. But he felt less and less sure of himself with every step he took, and soon came to a wavering halt, looking around, as if the answers to his unasked questions were written on the dense walls of white surrounding him. He noticed the familiar steps kicked into the wall of snow, marking the heavily trodden shortcut through the woods.

Letting old habits have their way with him, Sean climbed to the top of the icy wall and jumped down, following the ragged line of half-frozen footprints as best he could in the fog. But his attempt at saving time quickly became an obstacle course in itself as he tripped and splashed his way along. His shoes quickly filled with cold water and prickly beads of ice, clouding his head with memories he didn't want. He tried hurrying, as if to flee the past, only to stumble and fall to his knees. "Shit!" he yelped, scrambling to his feet and slapping at the clumps of wet snow clinging to his thick wool pants like spiny burdocks. But it was too late; the ice-cold water had already soaked through, chilling him to the bone, and for the first time, Sean was aware of the frigid cold crushing the fragile January thaw all around him.

Growing impatient, he left the safety of the cratered path and veered off on his own through a maze of dense evergreens, their brittle branches snapping back at him whenever he brushed against one of them. A wall of Scotch pines was his last barricade. He wrapped his arms around himself and squeezed through sideways, wincing when the long thin needles pierced his sweater and shirt, pricking his skin. Once through, he stopped to extract the piney quills, which is when he noticed flickers of yellow and scarlet light dancing on the icy skin stretched over the frozen lawn.

Thinking the colors odd, he looked up to find the moon, glaring back at him through the barren branches of the leafless trees, its yellow face heated to a cardinal red by the fiery flames rising up from the distant horizon. He stood motionless, mesmerized by the moon's angry gaze, then nodded his head confidently, as if he knew what was afoot, and broke free into the moonlit clearing, shattering the eerie calm with the crunch of his feet punching through the frozen snow as he walked past Merrywood Hall. He turned his head when the light in Oliver's office caught his eye, but did not stop.

Karen's white compact, stained blood red by the moon, was sitting on the lawn beyond the parking lot, having been driven through the embankment. Sean brushed his hand over the hood as he walked past. It was still hot, inviting him to stop and warm his hands. Then, as if charged back up, he raced to the top of the hill overlooking the garden, only to be stopped by the cold wind slapping his face, pinching tears from his eyes. When he wiped them clear, a movement at the foot of the terraced knolls caught his eye before being swallowed up by the hungry fog.

"Karen?" he called, turning his ear into the unrelenting breeze. But no one answered. He inched his way to the very edge of the knoll and called again, louder. "Karen!"

"Is that you, Sean?" Karen called back softly, as if her words might wake the night.

Sean aimed his reply into the dark. "Yes!" He held his breath, listening to hear if it hit its mark.

"Down here, in the garden." The tranquil tone of her voice asked him to relax.

He tried, but failed, as he started down the sandstone steps notched into the earth. The scuffing of his leather-soled shoes were muffled by the blustery swirl of the winter's night. At the bottom, his heels dug into the pebbled path, the tiny stones and brittle shards of ice crunching and crackling as he walked to the archway, only to be stopped when the moon slipped behind the billowing clouds of an advancing winter storm, leaving him to face the walled-in black of the aging Victorian garden.

He braced his hands on the sides of the brick archway, waiting for his eyes to adjust to the dark. "Where are you?"

"Over here," Karen replied calmly, "near the fountain."

The fog was deeper and thicker inside the garden without a wind to drive it, slithering over and around him as he walked cautiously toward the sound of Karen's voice. Realizing that he couldn't see the ground, he knelt down to touch it, feeling the warm earth caressing his hand as the cold air above him weighed down on his shoulders like a yoke carved from a block of ice.

Suddenly, Karen was there, standing over him. Startled, Sean jumped up and back. Karen took up the distance. Moonlight leaked out through the jagged cracks in the clouds, painting her face yellow and gray and red. Then it was gone, pitching them back into darkness, save for the cottony twists of white writhing all around them. Karen reached out. "Are you all right?"

Sean held himself just beyond her reach. "I don't know." But the steely tension connecting each of his words said he did.

Karen moved closer. Sean held his ground this time. "Has the heat of passion from last June grown cold so soon?" she asked sadly, and took a half-step back, giving up her pursuit of him.

"No," Sean was quick to say. "That will never fade, Karen. It's just that I feel, well . . ." He clung to his thought, unsure if he should release it.

"What is it?" Karen tried for his arm, but missed when he stepped around her. "Sean?" He slowed his flight, but didn't stop. "Why are you treating me like this?" she asked.

Sean stopped and turned back. "It's not you," he said with a nervous clasp of his hands and looked away. Given the chance, Karen stole another few inches closer. "It's just that I feel uncomfortable." He paused. "No, I'm frightened, and I don't know why. Or maybe I do, and that only makes it worse."

"Are you afraid of me?" Karen asked, stepping still closer when Sean shut his eyes in embarrassment at what he'd admitted.

Sensing her reaching out to touch him, Sean started moving deeper into the garden. Karen matched his every step. Sean parried her advances, keeping his distance. They exchanged meaningless words for anxious thoughts. Reaching the marble portico above the Hudson, Sean stepped up onto the terrazzo floor and into the ghostly maw rising up from the river. Karen grabbed his wrist and turned him back. "You're shaking!" Pulling herself to him, she smiled when he didn't try slipping away from her.

"I'm cold," Sean stuttered, leaning back, bumping into one of the frozen columns, which held him for her in its stony grasp. He spoke in staccato fashion, as if trying to stop her with his words. "Your note said that you wanted—"

Karen raised her hand. "I didn't leave you a note," she said firmly. "You asked me to meet you here in the note *you* left for *me*." Her words were stitched together with a thread of impatience.

Hearing Karen say this, Sean saw the picture of her, of someone, standing in the window, shadows rippling over her body, long hair falling down below her shoulders, breasts full, young, nipples pink, legs pressed together, caressing a delicious patch of black. "You didn't have something to tell me about my lawsuit with Gazelle?" Sean asked, swallowing a cold breath of air, then shivering uncontrollably.

"No," Karen told him, relaxing her hold on him so that only her fingertips were grazing his skin. Still he didn't pull away.

"But your note said—" This time Karen silenced him with a kiss. Her lips were soft and moist against his, which were hard and dry and cracked. He responded to the heat of her delicious breath, drinking her in before he could tell himself not to.

Karen drew him to her. "It's not important," she whispered, looking deep into his eyes, taking the chill in his heart away. "I went to see someone who I thought would help. They couldn't, or should I say wouldn't."

"Don't worry; it's taken care of," he said, sounding distant and aloof and self-important. "I got a letter from a publisher in New York who told me that he received my manuscript last July from Bruce Fanning, who had sent it to him without my knowledge." Sean paused, then spoke with bitterness dripping from his lips. "*Before* Patricia Jennings, or Trish Hawley if you prefer, stole one of the diskettes I sent Bruce, and sold *my* story to Gazelle."

"No!" Karen argued, "Patricia would never steal anything, especially not from you."

Sean toyed with "Patricia" so that it had a doubtful ring to it. Then, with Karen's attention focused on his every word, her face inches from his, he asked in a biting and accusative tone of voice, "Does Catherine know Patricia is your daughter?" Karen tried pulling away, but it was Sean who held fast this time, denying her freedom. "Does she?" he asked again.

"How did you know Patricia was my daughter?"

"That's not important. I asked you if Catherine knows." Sean tightened his grip until Karen winced and pulled back.

"Yes," Karen snapped angrily, slamming the door shut on Sean's curiosity. She was no longer soft and warm. "I told her tonight, after I showed her your note and she demanded to know what was happening. Does that make you happy?''

"It's too late for my happiness," Sean told her. But he wanted more. "Why didn't you tell me when I first asked you?" There was a twist of irony laced with anguish in Sean's words. "Had I known, I never would have slept with you."

Karen replied with unquestioned conviction. "Yes, you would have. You had no choice. Nor did I. Besides, you couldn't have resisted me, Sean, no matter what you may think."

"You knew about Catherine and me, didn't you?" Sean asked, ignoring Karen's reply.

"No, I didn't know before I took you." A sadness suddenly filled Karen's heart. "But even if I had, I couldn't have done anything differently. Nor could you, Sean."

"What do you mean 'couldn't have'? What the hell would have stopped you?" The flames of Sean's rising anger appeared to have warmed him, for he was no longer shivering.

Karen slid her hands up his arms, grabbing hold of his shoulders, startling him with her strength. "If you care at all for me, Sean, or for Catherine, who loves you with all of her heart and only needs time for this to pass, just let everything lie buried in the past." Karen's face went dark, her eyes black. "And be thankful you're still alive." Turning away, she glanced around, as if looking for something. She then kissed Sean and said quietly, "You better leave now, before it's too late."

"I don't want to leave," he said defiantly, rejecting her evasive mood. "I want to know who you were going to see about helping me."

"It's not important anymore." Karen turned her iron-clad grasp of Sean into a velvet touch. "It didn't work out the way I hoped it might. And for my own sake, I wish now that I hadn't even tried." Karen's throat was dry, forcing her to scrape her words out for him. "It brought back terrible memories for me."

Sean pressed his hand against Karen's abdomen, just below the leather belt cinching closed the soft cashmere coat she was wearing. She didn't move. He slipped his hand inside. She held her breath. "Could those memories possibly have anything to do with

Donald Beman

these?'' he asked, holding his open hand over the gentle swell of
her stomach, then tracing the lines of the scars hidden beneath
her dress with the tips of his fingers. But what Sean felt wasn't
Karen, and he snatched his hand back, taking with him vivid
images of Cathy, a shirt falling off her shoulders onto the ground,
lost twilight lighting her naked body, and the scars, long and thin
and pink and looking still tender to the touch.

Karen wrapped her arms around Sean before he could withdraw
and fell into him, taking his chill away the instant her body met
his. Sean's heart told him to get away, to run, but his flesh said
no, and his head was clouded by Cathy's words, ''I want to memorize every delicious inch of you growing inside me so that I can
have you whenever I want.'' He found himself embracing her.

''You did see them.'' Karen sighed. ''I should have been more
careful.'' Resting her head on Sean's shoulder, she become very
still. ''You have no idea what you're asking me to tell . . .'' Her
words evaporated into the thin night air.

''What is it?'' Sean asked.

Karen buried her face in his sweater, then pulled back and
looked deep into his confused gaze. ''They were put there when
I was—'' Karen stopped and turned away. ''No, I can't,'' she
said with a shake of her head.

''Yes, you can!'' Sean demanded, spinning her around. ''You
must tell me.''

''I couldn't stop him,'' she said, her teeth grinding on the
words she'd found so hard to give up.

''Him? *Him!*'' Sean shouted, his voice cracking.

Karen was unaffected by his outburst. ''He tore me open when
I fought to stop him.'' Karen shivered, but not from the cold.
''He wanted me to take you that night we were together, but I
refused him.'' Karen hesitated. ''And I let you cast your seed in
me, which is forbidden, as is my own pleasure with a mortal man.
That night, Sean, I drank until I was full, and you were empty.''

'' 'Take me'?'' Sean whispered. His mouth was dry, forcing
him to swallow hard.

Karen shut her eyes, refusing to look at Sean. ''After you left,
I found another man and lured him into the woods, where I took

340

his life just before he entered me, as I was to have done with you. I then discarded his body in the field where we had been together." Karen tossed her head to one side, avoiding Sean's horrified gaze. "But it was you who should have been left there, and whose soul I should have taken, not some stranger whose time had not yet come."

Sean pushed Karen away from him. "It's you, isn't it!"

Karen wanted him back, to hold him, and to be held by him. She was there, slipping her arms around him without him having seen her move. He was speechless. "He will now take me for what I've done. And he will take you, too, my dear Sean. I'm sorry, I did not know there were two dates remaining. I thought I had let you pass beyond his reach. Unless you . . ."

Karen's words knifed through the thick air, cutting Sean free. He started running back through the garden, but he tripped on something buried beneath the fog and fell to the ground. "Oh, my God!" he screamed, scrambling to his feet. It was a body, a woman, face torn away, long hair dead white, arms spread wide, fingers curling up around spikes driven through her palms into the ground, chest hollowed out, empty.

Agonizing cries of pain suddenly pierced the brick walls surrounding them, followed by the sound of metal creaking and the thunk of iron hitting stone. At that instant, the clouds stopped, giving back the moon.

"Oliver!" Sean screamed, his cry echoing into the night when he saw Oliver suspended above the fog, hanging from the massive wrought-iron gate, his arms pulled wide, his hands pierced by the thick truncated spikes of the gate, his body hanging limp, his heavy leather shoes kicking about, hitting the bars, searching for something to stand on.

Sean spun around at sounds behind him, footsteps, his eyes darting about, his heart racing to keep him alive. He turned at another noise. Bursting out of the fog, larger than life, Karen pushed Sean aside with a powerful sweep of her arm, sending him reeling backward against the granite fountain. "Leave!" she ordered, slipping behind the curtain of white and disappearing from sight as the iron gate swung open with the slow painful screech of metal twisting into metal.

A shadow could be seen moving out into the garden, growing larger with every ponderous step, calling out, using words Sean couldn't understand, harsh and ancient sounding. Karen answered in the same foreign tongue, but clear and studied. Then he knew, and started to follow, answering her in kind, but awkwardly and faltering. Hands grabbed him from behind, pinning his shoulders back, holding him in place. Before he could turn to see who his silent captor was, Karen's screams froze him in place. There was a long crystal-clear silence, as if the wind had blown itself away. Then it was shattered when Karen cried, ''No! He's mine.''

With a violent swing of his arm, hitting someone or something with his clenched fist, Sean broke loose and ran toward the sounds of Karen shrieking in tortuous pain.

''I knew you would come,'' a voice, many voices, rasped in eerie harmony, piercing his heart like a thousand dying whispers, taking his breath away and spinning his head into a blur of forgotten memories.

Breathless, Sean inched closer to the shadow heaving about in the fog, then jerked back in horror at what he saw crouching over Karen's body. It was a huge creature—a beast!—its head bowed, licking the gored flesh of Karen's torn chest with its heavily bitten tongue, its enormous wings spread wide, casting a shadow over the earth, the claws of its powerful arms wrapped around her wrists and ankles, pinning her to the ground. Her eyes were staring up into the calloused face of the full moon.

''There is nothing you can do for her,'' the beast said without raising its scarred head, a head covered with the wiry nubs of hair singed by the same flames that had mutilated its skull, which was oddly small for its hulking frame, and burned its ears down to charred holes.

''She served me well,'' another voice said through a wet sucking sound. ''Until she failed with you.''

''But she will soon be part of us again,'' a third voice spoke out, only softer, but by no means gentle. ''She cannot live in this world any longer.'' With a deep-throated moan, sounding like it tasted of pleasure, the beast gave up on Karen and slumped back onto its haunches, wiping its hideous face, then licking its muscular arms clean with a methodical nodding of its head and slapping of its tongue.

"It can't be," Sean whispered, stepping back. "No."

"But I am," the voices replied as the beast raised its small ugly head to face him. Sean gasped in disgust. The face was that of a human, a woman, with lidless eyes, black as tar and bubbling hot, and shining bright. Her skin was wrinkled and cracked and old, older than anything he'd ever seen. Her lips were shrunken back from her mouth, exposing her teeth, porous and white like dried bones. Each time she breathed in, a hollow echo, a howling wind erupted from deep down inside her pendulous chest. When she exhaled, the stench of putrid flesh, covered with maggots and flies and rotting in the sun, boiled up out of her lungs, burning his eyes and throat, making him gag.

She smiled at him, as if pleased by his reaction. "But I am more than what you think, and more than what you believe, and much more than what you want to know." She stretched her long sinewy neck, biting and snapping at the air. "It is now your time," she growled. "I've come to usher you into our world." There was the hint of a smile tearing itself into the beast's distorted face. Before Sean could answer, she rocked forward, plunging her face into Karen's chest, shaking her head, growling, a nauseating gurgle of a growl. Karen kicked her legs, then was gone. Raising its head, its face covered with blood and splintered bone and pieces of torn flesh, the beast discarded Karen's lifeless form with a disdainful swipe of its arm and leaned forward, leering at Sean, blood dripping from its face.

"Forgive me, Sean," yet another voice said as the beast rose up, laughing, a loud thunderous laugh that shook the ground, before falling back onto its hindquarters and curling its arm over its face, wiping it up and down, then licking it clean with hungry jabs of its swollen tongue.

"Karen?" Sean choked.

The sounds of Oliver writhing in pain made him look past the beast. "Don't worry about him," she said. "It isn't his time." She then reached out, grabbing for Sean with her immense clawed hand. He slapped at her and was instantly thrown to the ground, his hands burning and blistering as if plunged into boiling acid.

"Was it Catherine's time?" he asked, struggling to his feet, gasping from the pain burning into his body. He pointed into the fog behind him. "Or is that Patricia, you grotesque disgusting bitch!" He was instantly hurled to the ground with a sweep of the beast's long arm, its razor-sharp claws whistling through the air, shredding his clothes, setting them on fire.

The smell of his own charred flesh filled Sean's nostrils as he crawled back and stood before her, angry, defiant, his clothes torn and blackened with the ash of his own flesh. "Was it Bruce's time?" he asked, taunting her, defying her to strike him again, as if denying that she could hurt him.

Swooping down, laughing her reply in his face, she asked, "You loved him, didn't you?" The spatter of hot saliva burned his eyes, blinding him.

"Why?" Sean asked, his shoulders slumping down, his body putting forth the same question as he held his hands out, red and raw and bleeding. "Why did you kill him?" His voice melted down into sorrow. "You shouldn't have."

"We? Shouldn't have? Don't be naive," the beast snarled contemptuously as it moved toward him.

Feeling the numbing cold leaking out of its body, Sean stepped aside, barely missing the clutch of its claws. He turned, unable to see clearly where he was going, and started moving away, tripping and stumbling, his body raked with pain. The beast didn't follow; its gaze held fixed on where Sean had been standing, its head turning from side to side, slowly, as if confused. It then started sweeping its long wings over the ground, like a reaper wielding a scythe, cutting the air down all around it.

Hearing the strange sounds behind him, Sean stopped and looked back through the stinging blur in his eyes. *You can't see me?* he thought as he watched the beast disappear into the fog.

When he turned to leave, thoughts of his wife—hair splayed out from her shattered skull, arms twisted and broken, chest ripped open, eyes blindly staring past him into the black of heaven—choked him to a stop. He spun around, muted by his

344

own rage, able only to think, *You disgusting fucking whore.*

Her head snapped around, the bottomless holes in her ugly face erupting with fire, burning through the fog, drilling into him. "I can see your anger." She laughed. "I always have."

Startled at the sound of a familiar voice, Sean asked without thinking, "Did you kill Janet, too?"

"What difference does it make now?" she growled, and began lumbering toward him, her cloven hooves digging into the frozen ground, splitting it open.

Raising his hands, clenching his fists, Sean demanded, "Tell me, God damn it!"

"There it is," she purred, then struck again in the blink of an eye, sweeping across his chest, cutting his flesh to the bone. Sean fell to his knees, his ravaged body jerking to a stop, his head dropping to his chest. Laughing, she tossed her head back. "Of course we did," she said with pride. "And we took your precious little son, too. Only he died before I could take his soul, so He has him now. Pity. He was so young, so pure."

"Oh, my God!" Sean cried out, sobbing, unable to hide his sorrow with his hideously deformed hands.

Another voice lashed out from inside the beast. "God? You have no God! You turned away from Him the night you saw me on the kitchen table and did nothing to help me. Nothing!"

"Mother?" Sean choked, looking up, trying to see, his eyes still burning. "Is that you?"

"Yes, my son," she said with disgust.

"Why? How?" Sean asked, standing up and leaning forward, struggling to see. Sean was unaware of the beast's growing excitement as he unknowingly moved closer and closer to its anxious quivering grasp.

"You abandoned me," she spit out with a venomous sting to her words. "His seed had not yet been left in me. You could have stopped him. But no, you ran away, leaving me to him, to them, to this!"

"No!" Sean roared, fighting back a torrent of rage pulling him ever closer to the beast. "No," he said with a sudden calm detachment, and stood firm where he was, his eyes swollen with tears, cleansing his sight. "I was nothing to you, nothing. You lived only for Him, and no one else but Him. Not me, not father. It was as if we didn't exist, as if we were nothing but steps upon which you climbed ever closer to Him."

"Oh, my son, how could you—"

"Stop!" the voice of Sharon Lucien ordered.

"Wait!" Sean pleaded, his emotions swirling into a tempest inside his chest, burning his heart. "I don't understand."

"She took her own life," Sharon said angrily, "damning herself forever. She was trying to keep me from entering this world. She broke the covenant." There was a sudden change in the beast's voice, turning frail and small and frightened. "I am her daughter," that other voice whimpered.

"Daughter?" Sean asked, his memories drowning him as they flooded his thoughts. "There was no child. My sister died."

"No!" she argued with infant's tears in her voice. "I am your sister. And she is my mother, *our* mother."

Sean was unable to utter a single word as he stared into the changing faces of the beast before him, knowing what he'd heard, but refusing to believe what was there before him. He found himself asking once again, as if what had been said, hadn't been said, therefore didn't exist, "Why did you kill Janet?"

"I was afraid of losing you," the reasoned voice of Sharon Lucien replied coolly. "The guilt, and the fear of their own death, always drives them back to us, even though they think it brings them closer to Him. But it didn't work with you. You had denied Him and were free, more free than all the others, for you truly did not believe." The beast turned to Oliver. "Most are like him," she sneered with contempt, "unable not to grasp hold of something, anything."

"And the crucifix?" Sean asked, falling, tripping to one side, then catching his balance.

She spread her wings wide as if to fly, then pushed the answer through her teeth, chewing on the words before spitting them at him. "It pleased me," the voice of Sharon Lucien snarled in bitter consonance, her words reaching out, wrapping themselves around Sean's neck and choking him back to his knees. "She was still

346

alive when I rammed it inside her.'' Sean tried, but was unable to cover his ears fast enough. "She screamed for you, but you didn't hear her. I saw to that."

"Why have you waited so long?" Sean asked, his energy, his very life draining away from him with every beat of his heart, but refusing to give in and give her what she wanted—and needed.

"It is He who sets the times. Not me, not us, not even him. They are six in number over the span of a lifetime. A few come on first call, most come on the second, which is only fitting. But with you, it is the sixth and final call." There was a long unearthly silence, as if the world had been hushed, then a deeper voice spoke. "The others have failed, so I am here."

"No!" Sean said, vehemently shaking his head in disbelief. "You aren't. I won't let you be." He fell to his knees again, slumping onto his heels, his body growing cold, his breathing growing fainter and fainter.

"*You* won't let me be!" the beast roared, rising up on its hind legs and reaching through the clouds, parting them, touching the stars with its long leathery wings, then dropping back to earth, shaking it, shaking everything in the garden, toppling the statues off their pedestals, cracking the marble columns and splitting the empty fountain open. It then pitched forward, balancing itself on its massive arms. "I am part of Him, and He is part of me. Without me, He cannot be. Nor can I, without Him. We are one. I will live to the end of time and beyond, as will He." The beast held its arms out, beckoning for Sean to come closer. "When you are finally with me, in me, you will learn that the spark of life must be held inside them to the very last second, just before the flame of hope is snuffed out." The beast paused for a useless breath. "This turns their fear into rage, embittering their soul for Him and giving them to me. And you, Sean, will fight more than all the others to stay alive, to stay in this world, your world, not mine, and not His." The beast's voice echoed with pride. "Your soul will be strong, stronger than those inside me now."

Forcing himself to his feet, Sean lunged for the beast, screaming, trying but unable to curl his horribly swollen fingers into a fist. Something wrapped its arms around him, pulling him back. "No!" he cried, half from the excruciating pain of being touched and half from blind rage, wanting to strike out at whatever was keeping him from it, from them.

The beast let out a shriek of delight and began thrashing about, talking, sounding like Sharon, then Karen. Sean stopped moving at the sound of her voice, which was filled with sorrow. "You've been empty and alone for too long," she called. "He will fill that emptiness. No one can make you feel like he can, not even Him." She became quiet. Sean tried leaning closer to hear her throaty whisper, but was held firm.

"Remember what you felt when you slid inside me?" the voice of Sharon Lucien asked. Sean shut his eyes, trying to block out the memories. "You told me it was like nothing you'd ever known." She growled from deep inside her poisonous belly. "It was really him you felt!" Sharon laughed triumphantly.

"No!" Sean cried, struggling to be free. But whatever it was held him fast, saying nothing, steadily pulling him away from the cruel taunts he was unable not to answer.

"And your mother," Sharon growled, her words dripping with crude sensuality. "When you were fucking me, you were fucking her!"

"Oh, God, no." Sean gagged, collapsing like a rag doll into the arms wrapped around him. Claws could be heard digging, scratching, tearing up the earth and slicing open the granite below. "Let me go," Sean begged. "I have no choice, not after what I've done. It's—"

"No!" came a harsh whisper, ignoring his cries of pain and breathless sobs of unfathomable agony.

"Catherine?" he choked. There was no answer, only the tightening of the grip around his chest, taking his breath away, driving the pain deeper into his body and filling his head with black. "Patricia?" Still no reply. The black turned blacker, then hard like glass, then cold like arctic ice.

Then there was nothing, except for a dead calm snow that began dropping giant flakes of white into the night, quieting the wind and quenching the fire in the sky. Vaporous swirls of black and gray were wrapping themselves around the beast as it lumbered clumsily through the garden in a blind rage, calling, taunting, jeering, trying to seduce Sean into believing, then ripping it out of him. But he could no longer answer in kind to the angry rasping of its many voices, to fuel its rage, or feel the razored edge of its cruel words, now dulled by the silence of sleep, and soothed by winter's cold night.

41

Sean lay perfectly still, his eyes shut, listening to the voice floating around him, humming, the deep-throated purring of a cat, unlike the harsh sibilance of angry whispers that he'd left behind in his dreams. He was trying to guess who it was, and where he was. And if he was. The nervous twitter of laughter echoed somewhere off in the distance, breaking his concentration. Giving up, he opened his eyes. The light was antiseptic bright and fluorescent clean. He was lying on his back, staring up at an old, painted-over plaster ceiling, the wafer-thin craters left behind from the scraped-off blisters of peeling paint forming an endless pattern of semicircles and misshapen crescents beneath the most recent skin of latex white.

How fitting, he thought, a heaven full of waxing and waning moons. He laughed at the irony. "Jesus Christ!" he groaned, grabbing for his chest, only to find that he couldn't move his arms.

"Well, well, well . . . look who's awake!" a woman sang out, her lyrical words bubbling with the effervescent bounce of a rich, Jamaican patois.

Sean flopped his head to one side. "Where am I?" he asked, trying to swallow away the soreness in his throat, but unable to.

Donald Beman

The nurse sitting in the chair opposite his bed, in front of a steel-casement window, was a large, smooth-skinned black woman with meticulous dreadlocks falling down around her face, the ends capped with gold. Her massive hands swallowed up the paperback book she was holding in her lap. The bleached white of her candy-crisp, tight-fitting uniform made the cobalt-blue nameplate pinned above her ample right breast appear to be flashing her name, MATTI WILLIAMS . . . MATTI WILLIAMS.

"Let me see now," Matti Williams said, a warm, ivory smile melting her chocolate-brown face. "The man is on the seventh floor of Harkness Pavilion, in Columbia Presbyterian Hospital, overlooking the mighty Hudson." Matti opened her big, white eyes, matching her inviting smile, and closed the book with a soft, papery clap, swallowing it up in her hands. "And where might you rather be?" she asked playfully, setting the book on the windowsill behind her chair and stepping to the side of Sean's bed. "Montego Bay? Sunny Ocho Rios? Or are you a wild Kingston man, looking for a bit of ganja smoke?" Matti chortled to herself as she fussed with Sean's sheets, ending with a nudge of her broad hip against the hospital bed, causing it to jiggle in place on its casters.

Sean tried laughing with her, but it hurt too much. With a gentle smile, Matti slipped her hand behind Sean's neck and lifted his head off the pillow while guiding a glass of water she'd snatched out of nowhere to his parched lips. The glass sat like a tiny crystal thimble perched between the fingers of her enormous black hand. "I win the pool," Matti said, tracking Sean's every move with her muddy white eyes. "You woke up on my shift." She took the water away too soon. Sean tried reaching for the plastic pitcher on the nightstand beside his bed, but he couldn't move his arm. When he looked down, he found that his left hand and forearm were wrapped in a ball of white gauze and tethered to the chrome-plated bar pulled up on the side of his bed. His right hand and arm were hidden inside the same neatly wrapped package, and lashed securely to the shiny metal gate raised up on that side as well.

"I'm still thirsty." He coughed, then swallowed, a dry,

scratchy swallow. "And hungry, too, for some strange reason."

Matti turned back with a refill in her hand. "That's to be expected." She tapped the base of the IV stand beside Sean's bed with a kick of her pink, rubber-soled white shoes. "All you've had is this sugar water," she chuckled to herself, "which where I come from is meant for hummingbirds, not humans!" Matti laughed again, this time a deep, chesty chortle, but still watched closely as Sean sucked the glass dry.

"What time is it?" he asked, glancing out the window, which afforded him a view of the top of an adjacent white-bricked building topped with an assortment of steaming cooling towers and galvanized steel tanks of varying sizes, all piped one to the other. He looked at Matti's thick wrists, but they were empty. "Time?" he asked meekly.

"It's here," she said, tapping a long, black finger near the watch, which was pinned upside down over her breast. "I keep it here so I can see it and still have both hands free for my patients." Matti bent down close so Sean could see the face of the small, gold lapel watch. "My daughter gave it to me," she said proudly. "She'll be a doctor come June. It's clear and easy to read. And it has plain numbers, not those silly Italian letters people think are so elegant. And the little second hand sweeps, doesn't tick, making it easy for me to take pulses."

Don't, Sean told himself, trying not to let the warm, buttery smells dripping off Matti's body drain down his throat and into his empty stomach. But he failed—or cheated—and found himself tasting an assortment of island spices, scented with the fragrance of a perfume that he'd never smelled before. It was thick and sugary sweet, but musky. He instantly thought of aki and rice. And dried fish and curried goat. And pan-fried plantains. This only started his mouth watering, forcing him to swallow the sticky saliva filling his mouth and gluing his tongue to his teeth. "I can't make out the numbers," he complained, blinking his eyes. Matti leaned closer. "No." He laughed, staring at her breast and not the watch. "They're even fuzzier now."

Standing up, Matti scrunched her chin back and looked down. "Ten after," she announced.

Sensing that she was toying with him, and trying his best to play along, Sean asked patiently, "Ten after what?"

"Noon," Matti said with impish pluck, and raised her head. The thin lines of pink, squeezed between firm rolls of flesh ribbing her thick neck when she scrunched her chin down to see the watch, were slowly fading back to black.

Sean yawned. "I feel like I've been asleep for hours."

A knowing smile spread across Matti's face and up into her big white eyes as she turned and started for the door. She stopped when she heard Sean groan. Looking back, she found him bracing his feet against the shiny bars on either side of him and pushing himself up, tears squeezing out of his eyes. Matti began chuckling to herself. When Sean looked, then followed her amused gaze, he found that he'd pulled the blue hospital gown down off his shoulders and below his knees, stripping himself naked except for his calves and feet. He started laughing at his predicament, then hunched over, a razor-sharp stabbing into his chest and knifing up into his skull, kicking his head back and slamming his eyes shut. "Damn!"

"I should just let you sit there like that!" Matti said, clucking her tongue at him. "Here you are, damn lucky to be alive—how, nobody knows, not even Dr. Jeffery, and you—"

"He's alive because he's blessed," Cathy said with a weary laugh in her voice as she walked into the room holding a book in her hand. She peered over Matti's shoulder at Sean, who was grinning sheepishly and blushing. "Only *he* won't admit it."

Sean started pitching backward, his eyes glassing over. Cathy was at his side before Matti could move, dropping the book on the bed and catching his head before it struck the corner of the table, taking the blow on the back of her hand for him. "He's bleeding!" she called to Matti, lowering Sean down onto the pillow. "Right over his heart, and it's seeping out the sides, too." She looked up, her face drawn and hollowed out from lack of sleep. "Get Dr. Jeffery, fast!" she yelled, the sleeves of her white silk blouse turning dark red.

Matti bellowed orders down the hall. There was an instant crush of silence, then a clatter of plastic and metal, followed by the stuttering skips and squeaks of rubber wheels, growing louder and louder until they burst into the room. Within seconds, the hastily marshaled team of two nurses and a young, female intern had the dressings on Sean's chest scissored open. Blood was oozing up between the sutures closing each of the lacerations sliced across his chest, which was shaved clean of hair.

Matti was quick to say under her breath, "Stubborn Scottish nature," adding, "too stubborn to stay lying down." She muttered this just as Dr. Robert Jeffery arrived, earning her an affectionate, half-hearted scowl as he stepped over and proceeded to examine Sean's wounds closely, while the pair of nurses worked to keep them clean for him.

Because of the nature of the blood flow, it was oozing, not pumping, and the color was a dark burgundy red. Dr. Jeffery decided that the bleeding was superficial—venous, not arterial—involving only the surgical lines closing the wounds over the severed intercostal muscle sheath covering Sean's rib cage. It had taken him more than three hours in surgery to stitch the interleaved layers of muscle and tissue back together. Once the sutures were cleaned and cauterized, the bleeding stopped, allowing the nurses to apply new dressings. With a wave of his hand, Dr. Jeffery instructed the young intern to take care of it, telling her, "It's good practice." She began without a second's hesitation, much to the guarded amusement of the two older, and more experienced, nurses.

Sean's wounds would have ended his life, according to Dr. Jeffery, had Cathy not stopped the bleeding and brought him to the hospital herself, rather than waiting for an ambulance. There were three deep horizontal slashes across his chest, starting at his left side, under his arm, and ending at the sternum, which was cut clean through where the claws had exited. It was not a blind, glancing blow, but a deliberate and well-aimed thrust, slicing through the leathery-tough layers of intercostal muscle and cartilage weaving the ribs and thoracic wall together, penetrating the pericardium and puncturing his left lung. The pulmonary artery was missed by no more than a few millimeters. It was obviously a blow intended to slice open Sean's chest and expose his heart, but leave it unscathed for the beast to devour it while it was still beating—and Sean's soul with it—all while he was alive and conscious: that microsecond of time it takes for the eyes to capture horror and burn it into the brain.

Because the claws were thin and razor sharp, the wounds were smooth and clean, making Dr. Jeffery's task of suturing the muscle and skin relatively easy. But Sean's ribs had to be stapled together, as did the separated sections of the sternum, to keep them from flexing and tearing apart the severed muscle sheath and soft tissue on top when he breathed or moved. The burns Sean sustained on his chest from the beast's first blow were third-degree burns and would leave behind severe, although localized, scarring, all of which, according to Dr. Jeffery, "will no doubt be hidden beneath the hair on his chest when it eventually grows back."

The only unusual problem facing the surgical team when Sean was brought in to the hospital was the rampant infection that had taken hold in the open wounds due to the rotting residue left behind by the beast's claws when they ripped through Sean's body. The same was the case with his hands and forearms, which had been burned and blistered by what Dr. Jeffery concluded was an unusually strong acid, something akin to the stomach acid from an animal such as a large constrictor, or an alligator, capable of digesting bone. Only this acid was far more concentrated, causing the skin to explode within seconds of contact, exposing raw flesh. Luckily, the acid had not been of sufficient quantity to work its way beneath the skin and attack the muscles and tendons, or irrevocably damage the nerves of his hands and forearms.

Sean regained consciousness just as the intern was taping down the edges of the dressing near his left armpit. He started giggling at the busy touch of her fingers, and was immediately admonished by her to "Sit still!" in her best, almost-doctor's voice.

The first thing he asked for, after having shown what was deemed to be sufficient remorse, was to have his hands cut loose. Dr. Jeffery consented with an understanding nod of his head from his vantage point at the foot of the bed, where he was engaged in a quiet and friendly conversation with Cathy. "And cut those bulky outer dressings off his hands while you're at it so he can start flexing and exercising his fingers a little to keep them from getting too stiff. Otherwise it'll be quite painful later on.''

After cleaning up, the nurses and intern left. So did Matti Williams. But Matti returned a few moments later carrying a large plastic container filled with fresh island fruit and holding a large, curved steel carving knife, more blunt than pointed at the end, not unlike a machete, only much smaller. She handed the container to Cathy and brandished the knife at Sean, who was quick to feign being frightened. ''Fill the man's stomach, and he'll settle down like a baby,'' she advised. ''And be careful with this knife, woman. It's sharp,'' she said in a stern but motherly voice as she handed Cathy the knife—handle first. Matti wouldn't release her grip until Cathy acknowledged that she had the knife firmly in hand. Matti then left again, but not before waving a menacing fist at Sean and ordering him not to try sitting up again, ''You stubborn man.''

Matti wasn't two steps out of the room when Cathy introduced Dr. Jeffery to Sean as, ''My very dear friend, Bob Jeffery, who saved my life.'' She sat beside Sean on the bed, setting the container of fruit on her lap, with her hands on top, holding the knife in place as she proceeded to tell Sean when and how she and Bob Jeffery had met. ''The first time I saw his face was in the intensive care unit of the field hospital in Saudi Arabia, a few days after my encounter with a very unfriendly enemy mortar, which left me with a body full of unladylike scars.'' Cathy hesitated and looked back over her shoulder at Bob Jeffery, as if for reassurance, then back to Sean. ''And also left me unable to ever have children.'' The startled, compassionate, and finally inquisitive expression unwinding itself onto Sean's face was left unanswered by Cathy, except for the satisfied smile she gave him, telling him that she knew what he was thinking about. And it was all he was going to get from her. For now at least.

Looking at Bob Jeffery, then Cathy, Sean realized there was an unspoken yet strong sense of camaraderie between the two of them, a bond much different than what Sean had sensed between

Donald Beman

Cathy and Bobby McCarthy, who, Sean was told, "was wounded in the same attack on our recon unit just outside of Kuwait City."

Upon hearing this, Bob Jeffery was quick to say, "A place where Captain Greene was not supposed to be, but went anyway, disobeying strict Marine Corp policy about women in combat, because she refused to permit a young sergeant to lead *her* unit." Bob Jeffrey softened his military bearing. "But if it hadn't been for Cathy, the entire unit would have been wiped out." He dug his eyes into Cathy, then jumped over to Sean. "She saved the lives of all but one man in her unit, and even carried one of her men to safety through enemy fire—a strapping hulk of a man."

Sean could readily see that their relationship was more congenial than the one between Cathy and Bobby, which had a competitive quality about it. It was also more respectful, which Sean attributed to what Bob Jeffery had done in saving Cathy's life, tempered, perhaps, by their equal rank. Sean found himself liking Bob Jeffery more and more as he listened to him and Cathy talk, reminisce, and catch up on mutual friends, all the while speaking around him, not with him. Before Sean had a chance to get involved, and get to know him better, Bob was beeped away.

Left alone so suddenly, Sean and Cathy found themselves surrounded by an awkward silence. Sean was only too aware of his actions the last time he saw Cathy, New Year's Eve, when he barged into her dining room to find Karen there, and bolted out of the house after revealing that he knew her. "Is Roger your stepfather?" Sean heard himself ask Cathy. He looked away, as if he wasn't the one speaking, but someone else.

Cathy rubbed Sean's cheek with the back of her hand. "You must have been listening to Jean Murphy." Sean nodded. Cathy locked onto his anxious gaze. "From what I understand, Jean and my father were an item before he met my mother. It seems that they were actually making plans to get married. As much as Jean tried—and from what I've been told she made quite a scene—she was unable to hold my father's eye once he met Mother."

Sean did all he could to keep from saying, "I know!"

"When I was born, my father told everyone I was premature, since he and mother had been married barely six months. It seems

356

that he even had the records at the hospital changed. Years later, he told me he did it to protect my mother's honor, which I always thought was gallant of him. And I still do. Anyway, no one ever questioned him since I was a puny kid when I was little.'' Looking at herself, Cathy laughed. So did Sean, but carefully while bracing his chest with his bandaged hands. ''No one, that is, but Jean, who, to this very day, believes that my mother tricked my father into marrying her by telling him she was pregnant with his child, when Jean believed—and made no bones about it apparently—that he wasn't the real father. *My* father.''

Sean had to know. ''Are you sure he is?' he asked bluntly, knowing that he was risking hurting Cathy's feelings.

Cathy replied without skipping a beat. ''Yes. I am.'' She then brushed the hair out of Sean's eyes. There was still a hint of skepticism clouding his face. Cathy kissed her finger and pressed it to Sean's lips, keeping him from asking the question on the tip of his tongue. ''Shortly after I was shipped back from the Gulf, an infection developed in my kidneys, which they didn't catch in time. I went into renal failure. Bob told me that I needed a transplant if I wanted to live. Well, Dr. MacDonald, for all of those doubting Thomases''—Cathy paused long enough to make her point—''led by Jean Murphy, my father was a perfect match. You might say that he gave me life a second time.''

Before Cathy could say anything more, Sean's eyes filled with tears, surprising her. And him, too. He then told her how much he loved her, and that he wanted her in his life forever, ''That's if you'll have me.'' There was a calm to his words, one that had never been there before. When he tried apologizing for all that had happened, ''everything I did wrong,'' he choked up.

Cathy took up the last few inches separating them and began cutting up the fruit—slices of ripe banana, wedges of fresh guava, and chunks of juicy mango—and feeding them to Sean. When he was full, she balanced the container on the windowsill, then ever-so-carefully wiped the knife off on the loose end of the sheets—unsuccessfully hiding a silly smile on her face when she realized what she was doing—before setting it down on the table beside the bed. ''Don't forget to make sure Matti gets it back,'' she said with a slap of her fingers on the table's edge. "It looks like something she brought with her from Jamaica."

The instant Cathy sat back down on the bed, the questions came one after the other in rapid-fire succession. And from both of them, although Sean was first to get things started. At first, he found it difficult to accept the fact that he'd been asleep for three days. He soon abandoned his skeptical, but playful, challenge, when Cathy told him that Oliver had said, "It would be fitting for *that* man to arise on the third day!" With Sean's mouth still forming the question, Cathy assured him that Oliver was doing well, "Especially considering what he'd been through, according to Bob Jeffery." The wounds to Oliver's chest were superficial compared with Sean's. However, the gaping holes punched through his hands had required an eight-hour operation with a team of micro-surgery specialists. Even then it would be weeks before they would know if Oliver would be able to use his hands again to write. Or have the dexterity to turn the pages of a book. "Other than that," Cathy said, trying to make light of it all, "Oliver is enjoying the comfort of his room just down the hall under Hazel's watchful eye." This only made Sean want to see him that very second, then just as quickly agree with Cathy that it was best they both rested.

A thought switched his eyes wide open. "Was that Patricia Jennings on the ground in Merrywood Garden?" he asked, and just as quickly had second thoughts about asking when he saw the pained, but not angry, look on Cathy's face.

Cathy became very still. "As of this morning, they still don't know who that was. The body was mutilated just like that middle-aged man they found in our south fields last June. And Peter Kratz told me—"

Sean started to say something, but stopped when he realized that he couldn't possibly tell Cathy what Karen had told him. For that matter, he couldn't tell anyone anything, and this started him laughing to himself at the irony of it. Cathy just sat there, too tired to ask what was so funny. Sean drew quiet and attentive as Cathy began answering his questions, such as how it was that she knew he was in Merrywood Garden.

"It was the note Mother showed me, the one she said you left for her. You ran away before she could open the window and call to you. Oliver had also stopped by late Friday night, after swinging by your apartment." Cathy mimicked Oliver's acquired British accent, and did a pretty good job of it. "He told us that when you didn't answer his repeated knocking, he 'roused that cantankerous Irish landlady of yours,' and convinced her to let him in. And that's when he found you 'thrashing about wildly in your bed, and talking gibberish in your sleep.' He said that Jean wanted him to call me that very instant. But Oliver, who had thumbed through the transcript he found half torn apart and thrown on the kitchen floor, told her not to bother. And that it was best to 'leave the poor man to work out in his sleep what was bothering him.'"

Cathy raised her arms over her head into a weary stretch. "Oliver left all three transcripts with me, along with some of his own notes, asking me to read them. I said I would, but I didn't, at least not until my mother arrived Saturday afternoon and found them in the living room. When she read them, she told me to sit down and read them, too." Cathy begrudgingly gave up a tiny smile. "She *ordered* me to read them is more like it. Oliver returned Saturday evening all in a twit, babbling on about three nines, and something about it being 'six-hundred-and-sixty-six years to the day,' whatever *that* meant. Before I could get him to calm down and explain himself, Mother came into the room. When I introduced her to Oliver, he immediately dropped the papers that he'd brought with him and bolted out of the house!"

Cathy stopped talking, got up, and walked to the window, where she stood motionless, staring out in silence, watching the twilight give way to night. Sean watched, aware of the fatigue weighing her down, and waited. After a few minutes, she began to speak again, but in a hoarse whisper, telling him of the long talk that she'd had with Karen. "Not a mother-to-daughter talk, a woman-to-woman talk. Almost as if we were strangers." Sean lay back and waited, expecting the worst. Cathy turned to face him. "She loved you, Sean, and that love cost her her life. But at the same time, it gave you yours."

Sean wasn't prepared to hear this, not from Cathy, and fought it off with a shake of his head. He waited for more. But there wasn't any more, at least nothing more Cathy wanted to say. She frowned as she explained, as if reading her answer off a cue card, "Mother also told me to tell you, 'In case I don't see him again, my dear,' that what you think happened between the two of you never did, not really, and that Oliver could explain it to you, since, as Mother put it, 'The man will never believe you.' "

"Oh?" Sean said, his face flushed clean of emotion, waiting, wanting Cathy to explain further. But she didn't; she just stared out the window for the longest time before saying softly, "I miss her already, Sean. And I know that I haven't even come close yet to admitting she's gone."

"She's not gone," Sean said under his breath, not intending Cathy to hear him.

But she did. "What?" she asked, a startled, yet curious look ironed onto her face, smoothing the fatigue away. "What is *that* supposed to mean?"

Sean didn't want to get into that, not now, not until his head was clear and he was sure of what he thought. And felt. Ignoring Cathy's question, he asked, "Is that all she had to say? Nothing more?"

"No," Cathy replied, collapsing into the chair near the window, where Matti Williams had been sitting when Sean had woken up. "She also told me about Patricia Jennings." Cathy stopped and sat perfectly still, like a cat about to pounce. "She told me that we're half-sisters. When I heard her say those words, I almost hit her. Hit my own mother! Thank God I didn't. But to this very moment, I don't know what stopped me."

"Love," Sean uttered without thinking, which had the effect of washing away the anguish soiling Cathy's face. "But you still haven't told me how it is you came to be at Merrywood Garden."

Cathy snapped out of her trance. "When Mother showed me that note you'd left, she also told me that there was something terribly wrong. And that's when she told me about Dr. Lucien."

"What about Sharon?" Sean asked, a look of confusion, mottled with apprehension, falling down over his face, trying its best to find its way into his body.

The Taking

"I don't know if I'm remembering this right or not, but Mother said something about her being"—Cathy looked at Sean with disbelief—"your 'bastard half-sister.'" Cathy gave a weary shrug of her shoulders. "Those were her exact words," she said, and returned to staring out the window. "She told me that her real name was not Sharon with an S, but Charon with a C. And that Lucien was derivative of Lucifer." Cathy looked at Sean and asked, "How could you have been so naive? You!"

Surprised at her question, and hurt, Sean shrugged his shoulder. "I don't know," he whispered.

"She also said that the only way you would not die would be if you 'truly didn't believe.' And if you were able to 'free yourself of the rage that had ruled your life for so long,' whatever that means." Shutting her eyes, Cathy rested her head on the back of the chair. "I'm dead tired. So tired I can hardly keep my eyes open. I haven't slept in three days. Can this wait until tomorrow?" she asked in a frail, plaintive voice, sounding totally unlike herself. Then, dragging herself out of the chair, Cathy started for the door. "Sean, I'm going—"

"Wait," Sean asked. Cathy kept walking. "Come here," he said, gingerly patting the bed with his hand when Cathy looked back over her shoulder to see what he wanted. "Turn the light out and come lie down and get some sleep. It's a good two-hour drive back to Red Hook." Without arguing, Cathy hit the switch by the door and walked back, sitting down, then tipping over onto her side. Within seconds, she was sound asleep.

Sean rolled over and onto the book Cathy had dropped beside him. Pawing at it, he was finally able to pick it up with a tender pinch of his bandaged thumb and forefinger. What's this? he thought when an oversized bookmark fell out into his lap. Repeating the maneuver that he'd just mastered, Sean grasped the square sheet of rigid paper and held it up, squinting and reading in the fading light what was written in red with what appeared to have been a quill.

Here Faith died, poisoned by this charnel air.
I ceased to follow, for the knot of doubt

Donald Beman

Was severed sharply with a cruel knife:
He circled thus, for ever tracing out
The series of the fraction left of Life;
Perpetual recurrence in the scope
Of but three terms . . . dead Faith, dead Love, dead Hope.

Life divided by that persistent six,
LXX divided by 666 = .105105105105105 . . . six, ad
infinitum

What are *you* doing with this? he wondered, brushing his band-aged hand over the all-too-familiar words, then again, as if there was something there, something to be felt, to be absorbed through the layers of gauze, through the pores in his skin, into his capillaries, his veins, and sucked back to his heart and forced into his lungs, then pumped up into his brain.

Sean turned and looked at Cathy, who was barely breathing. You've lost weight, he thought, resting his hand on her hip. But then I haven't seen you since New Year's Eve. He leaned over, kissing her tenderly on her breast. Even your breasts are smaller, he thought, and smiled. When I get out of here we're going to eat out every night for a month, he resolved. Maybe that will put some color back in your face, too.

Sliding down, Sean closed his eyes and whispered to himself under his breath, "The Roman numeral seventy is symbolic of the span of man's life here on earth as written in Genesis. Three score and ten," he muttered. Sean then repeated from memory the quotation taken from Robert Thomson's nineteenth-century narrative *The City of Dreadful Night*. He smiled and thought, six-six-six equals eighteen, one plus eight equals nine, and nine is the sum of three threes. "So goddamn obvious!" he blurted out. His eyes were now wide open. But he was blind to the soft light from the waning January moon bleeding in through the window and casting shadows onto the floor, staining everything with subtle shades of red and gray.

Each of them was a nine, he thought. And three nines make twenty-seven, the sum of which results in nine, beginning the cycle all over again. Perhaps none of them are dead! Or is it that one of them lives, the collective sum of them all? But if one lives, then they all must live. And all of those before them. An infinite number of souls taken over a thousand millennia. And if so, in whose body are they? Or is *she* in us? In me. In every man? Hiding on the other side of us, that side we fear and never want to see. Sean fought back an incredulous laugh, which started him coughing. Pain knifed into his chest, silencing him.

The bed rocking side to side stole his next thought. He lay perfectly still, holding his breath, hoping that he hadn't woken Cathy up. She rolled over, her warm and surprisingly damp body seeping through his hospital gown and pressing against his cool, dry skin. Her hand slid up his leg, hesitated, toying with him, then moved up over his stomach. He braced himself, anticipating the weight of Cathy's dream-filled gesture on the tender wounds stitched closed across his chest. But it didn't help. Tears squeezed out and rolled down his cheeks as her hand came to rest on his chest. He waited for the throbbing to stop. The sound of Cathy talking in her sleep invited him closer. He kissed the top of her head, tasting the unwashed sweat. And something else, something slightly bitter. Don't be ridiculous, he told himself, swallowing it away. He felt her hand grow tense, then jerk up. He stole another breath, waiting for her arm to settle back down. His eyes flooded closed when her hand fell onto him, over his heart. "Why?" she said in a distant voice, deep and strong and heavy with sleep.

Sean blinked his tears away, only to have them replenished when her hand balled up into a fist, raised up, then opened and fell onto his chest. Pain pounded his eyes shut. She began whispering again. Sean tipped his head to one side, listening, hoping to share in her dreams, or perhaps chase away a nightmare.

"I love you, Catherine," he whispered.

"No!" she shrieked, startling him. She then sighed with a heavy breath. "He's *mine* now."

Sean pulled back, shaking. *"Karen?"* he asked.

There was only the roar of silence as sleep suddenly began pulling him down into darkness, his body growing colder with each beat of his heart from its unwanted touch. Fighting it off,

Donald Beman

he reached over and clumsily grabbed the huge knife off the table. "Forgive me, Lord," he cried out, plunging the knife deep into Cathy's chest—again and again and again—holding onto it with both hands and refusing to let go as she thrashed and kicked about, scratching and tearing and ripping at his bandaged chest. But he held firm, his eyes shut tight, refusing to look at her.

"Oh, Sean," they sighed, a chorus of seductive voices. But before he could open his eyes, her chest split apart, filling the darkened room with a thousand angry voices, screaming and crying, shattering the windows into a million granules of crystaline glass as they burst out into the night—taking the lifeless body with them—and leaving behind a fireworks display of vaporous swirls, blood red and coal black and dead white, lighting up the moonlit sky.

Author's Note

For those who wish to learn a little more about numerology, goddess worship, ancient religions, the works of Edgar Allan Poe, the cycles of the moon, and a touch of folklore, I suggest the following for further reading; they are but a few of the many sources I used in researching *The Taking*.

Numerology, by E. T. Bell, Ph.D.; *The Mystery of Numbers*, by Anne Marie Schimmel; *City of Dreadful Night*, by James Thomson; the Bible, King James version; *The Oxford Companion to the Bible; The Oxford Classical Dictionary; The Encyclopedia of Religion; Plots and Characters in the Fiction and Poetry of Edgar Allan Poe*, by Robert L. Gale; *Moon Tables for Times Past, Present and Future*, compiled by Rolf Brahde; *New and Full Moons—1001 B.C. to A.D. 1651*, by Herman H. Goldstine; and *The Old Farmer's Almanac*, which I sometimes refer to as *my* bible, for the years 1943 through 1993.

HORROR THAT WILL HAVE YOU CHILLED TO THE BONE!

Rough Beast by Gary Goshgarian. A genocidal experiment conducted by the government goes horribly wrong, with tragic and terrifying results for the Hazzard family. Every day, their son gradually becomes more of a feral, uncontrollable, and very dangerous…thing. The government is determined to do whatever is necessary to eliminate the evidence of their dark secret and protect the town…but it is already too late. The beast is loose!

_4152-9 $4.99 US/$5.99 CAN

The Neighborhood by S.K. Epperson. Abra Ahrens's neighborhood looks like quintessential smalltown America. But it doesn't take her long to notice that beneath the Norman Rockwell exterior a hideous darkness is festering. Someone in town is decidedly *un*friendly, but she couldn't know how grotesque it really is. And the more she finds out, the more she wants to hide her welcome mat.

_4109-X $4.99 US/$5.99 CAN

Dorchester Publishing Co., Inc.
65 Commerce Road
Stamford, CT 06902

Please add $1.75 for shipping and handling for the first book and $.50 for each book thereafter. NY, NYC, PA and CT residents, please add appropriate sales tax. No cash, stamps, or C.O.D.s. All orders shipped within 6 weeks via postal service book rate. Canadian orders require $2.00 extra postage and must be paid in U.S. dollars through a U.S. banking facility.

Name _____
Address _____
City _____ State _____ Zip _____
I have enclosed $_____ in payment for the checked book(s).
Payment <u>must</u> accompany all orders. ☐ Please send a free catalog.

HOWL-O-WEEN
Gary L. Holleman

Evil lurks on Halloween night....

H ear the demons wail in the night,
O ut of terror and out of fright,
W erewolves, witch doctors, and zombies too
L urk in the dark and wait for you.
O ther scary creatures dwell
W here they can drag you off to hell.
E vil waits for black midnight
E nchanting with magic and dark voodoo,
N ow Halloween has cast its spell.

___4083-2 $4.99 US/$5.99 CAN

Dorchester Publishing Co., Inc.
65 Commerce Road
Stamford, CT 06902

Please add $1.75 for shipping and handling for the first book and
$.50 for each book thereafter. NY, NYC, PA and CT residents,
please add appropriate sales tax. No cash, stamps, or C.O.D.s. All
orders shipped within 6 weeks via postal service book rate.
Canadian orders require $2.00 extra postage and must be paid in
U.S. dollars through a U.S. banking facility.

Name_____
Address_____
City _____ State_____ Zip_____
I have enclosed $_____in payment for the checked book(s).
Payment <u>must</u> accompany all orders.☐ Please send a free catalog.